The Devil's Third

Book 3

Rebekkah Ford

Interior formatting by Tugboat Design

First Edition November 2013
Second Edition December 2015

Table of Contents

Acknowledgments

I like to thank my husband, Kevin Ford, my sister, Angel Motter, and my dad and step-mom for your support. It means a lot to me, and I love you to bits.

I want to thank my wonderful editor, Chase Nottingham. Thanks for your support and help. I appreciate it. You're awesome.

I want to give a shout-out to my cover artist, Stephanie Flint. You did a great job and a pleasure to work with. Thank you! www.sbibbphoto.com

Dedication

I dedicate this book to my fans. Thank you for your support. It means the world to me. You're awesome, and I heart you.

Chapter One

Paige

Nathan, Carrie, and Tree stood, staring at me–slack jawed. An ominous wave of energy seemed to roll into the living room, crashing through the middle of our loose circle. Something inside me buzzed, my flesh breaking out in goosebumps.

I said it again, *"Africa."*

A loud boom shook the house and rattled the windows, causing Carrie to shriek, startling me. At once, a steady flow of rain battered against the rooftop like an army of tiny feet running into battle. A deafening crack erupted above my house, flickering lights before plunging us into darkness . . . well, Carrie and Tree. Nathan and I could see in pitch black conditions–one of the many perks of being immortal.

The hair on the nape of my neck rose, and I couldn't help but laugh nervously at how like a crazy, scary movie this moment was. I thought how coincidental and creepy to have mentioned the name of the continent King Solomon's incantations were hidden in, only to have it punctuated with Mother Nature's display of power.

For thousands of years immortals, dark spirits, and a handful of humans had been searching for Solomon's ring and incantations, which together could control the dark spirits. It was believed the invocations couldn't be found without the ring first. Therefore, finding it was top priority, but now that Bael had it and was the oldest known dark spirit of them all, unrest settled in my murky world. Lucky me, I happened to be the only one who could find the incantations, thanks to my ancient bloodline of witches, and my grandmother Kora who transferred Solomon's power out of that ugly piece of jewelry into me. Trust me. It was a fugly piece of ornamental wear. I saw it when Bael showed me, and now he knows I hold the power instead of it.

"Did you do that, Paige?" Carrie asked, the whites of her eyes gleaming.

"No," I said, feeling a bit scared, thinking this might be an omen to what was to come. Nathan wrapped his arm around my shoulders, holding me close.

"Cool," Tree said. "It was like Thor just slammed his hammer down as if to say 'Hell, yeah, they're there.'"

Carrie rolled her eyes. "You're such a dork." She laced her arms around his waist and leaned against him. "But you're my dork, and I don't like this. Turn the lights on, Paige."

"I can't. The power is out." *Even if I could, I wouldn't*, I thought. Not after what happened the last time I turned them on with my mind, how sick and nauseous I'd felt. No thank you. I didn't want to experience that again. "Why don't you and Tree sit, and I'll get some candles."

"I'll get them." Nathan squeezed my shoulder and went into the kitchen. I could hear him rummaging in the drawer and thought about him living in the 1800s without electricity. I bet he felt a bit nostalgic right now. He didn't seem put out like Carrie did trying her cell phone.

"Damn it." She dumped it back in her purse and frowned at Tree. "No cell phone service."

"Good," Tree said. "At least we won't be distracted by calls while we talk about why Paige thinks Solomon's spells are in a cave in Africa." He led Carrie to the love seat, and they sat.

"My phone isn't a distraction," Carrie muttered, "and I love it."

I sat on the couch across from them while Nathan placed candles around the living room, lighting them. The orange flames flickered erratically, casting shadows on the walls. Carrie anxiously looked around, appearing on edge with the howling wind rattling the windows and the rain whipping across them. It was odd behavior for her; she'd never been afraid of the dark or storms before.

Tree placed his arms around her and kissed the top of her head. "It's okay," he whispered in her ear, then answered my questioning eyes. "Ever since she got Aosoth's memories of where a dark spirit goes when they're cast out, she's afraid of the dark and storms."

"Why storms?" Nathan asked, sitting beside me, resting his hand on my leg.

"Because they can be violent and unpredictable," Carrie answered with a shudder.

I could totally sympathize with her, remembering when Nathan, Ameerah, and I went to the negative place Anwar sent Aosoth to. I remembered not being able to stand the feeling of being heavily weighed down, and it felt like I was in a pit of thick, gooey mud. Not to mention I was uncomfortable as hell. I didn't feel any pain though, or what it was actually like for a dark spirit to experience that, but with Aosoth's memories, Carrie could.

Poor Carrie.

Then I thought of something Nathan and I should have caught when Carrie told us about having those memories. Aosoth once informed Nathan and me she had never been cast out, so how could she have those memories? Then I remembered Carrie telling us when Aosoth inhabited a Nazi, she got shot, which hurled her out of the body straight to a dark area. So that place had to have created the memory. I decided to ask Carrie to make sure. "Carrie, was Aosoth ever cast out by an immortal before, besides Anwar that is?"

Carrie shook her head. "She likes to switch bodies a lot and has been too crafty to have that happen to her. But remember, I only have some of her memories."

"How do you know it's in Africa?" Tree asked me, changing the subject.

I shrugged. "Just a feeling."

Nathan turned to me. "Can you describe the cavern?"

"I was underground," I said, looking into his deep blue eyes before shifting my gaze onto Carrie and Tree. "Alongside me was a stream. There were arched portals, columns, and pillars carved out of what looked like limestone. The ceilings were high and eroded."

Carrie gave me a doubtful look. "Are you sure it was a cave?"

"Yeah, I'm sure." I wished Carrie would trust me, and Tree looked just as skeptical. I glanced up at Nathan, and he smiled. There was no doubt in *his* face. Well, at least Nathan had faith in me. "You two don't have to believe me," I said to them, hearing the hurt in my tone. "But I know it's a cave, and it's somewhere in Africa."

Tree shifted in his seat. I could tell he knew they had hurt my feelings by the guilty way he moved and the *I'm sorry* look he threw at me. "It's not like we don't trust you, Paige," he said. "I know there are holes in the earth like what you've described, but it sounds like a place in a fantasy book where goblins live."

I made a face, appalled at his comment. "I can't believe what you just said after everything you and Carrie now know." My voice was raised in annoyance. I leaned back and yelped. My back was still sore from the bullwhip Roeick used on me. The throbbing pain had finally gone away, but the sucky part was forgetting about the wounds until something touched them.

"Are you okay?" Nathan asked.

I nodded and fixed my eyes back on Tree, my temper flaring "–Like dark spirits inhabiting soulless humans," I continued, "me being able to communicate with animals, me being able to turn the lights off and on with my mind, portals around the earth, and huge apelike creatures crossing over from their world to ours. So just because the cave sounds like something straight out of a Tolkien novel, doesn't mean it doesn't exist."

Tree raised his hands in surrender. "Whoa, I'm sorry."

"I'm sorry, too" Carrie said. "It's just sometimes hard to believe this stuff is true."

I sighed and rubbed my temples, feeling a headache coming on. "I know what you mean."

A bright flash sparked behind the curtains, followed by another loud peal of thunder. It was still pouring outside, and I could hear the rain pounding on the ground and a channel of water rushing down the street. I wondered mindlessly how long this storm would last and about the outside of Nathan's house being a muddy mess. He would have to build a walkway or something, after everything got back to normal.

I had to laugh at myself for even thinking that. What the hell was wrong with me? I would never lead a conventional life again. I'd known that when I accepted immortality, and at least I could be with Nathan, frozen at the age of seventeen, for an immeasurable length of time.

Then, of course, I thought about Brayden. How could I not? Like me, his youth would never fade on this earth–always seventeen. I wondered if he came across Cassondra yet, and if she would tell him Nathan had broken her neck. And if she did, how would Brayden react? Knowing Brayden like I did, he'd probably think she deserved it after what she pulled on me. But then again, I wasn't too sure because of her being his mentor and him buddying up with Anwar and possibly Bael, which made me sick to my stomach. I mean, how could–

"Hello. Earth to Paige," Carrie said, waving her hands in the air, snapping me out of my internal babble.

I blinked. "Huh?"

"I was wondering if you had a sudden connection to the spiritual world when you didn't say anything." She sounded amused, and when I gave her a blank look thinking *why would she think that?* Her amusement surfaced into a smile. She continued, ticking the examples she laid out on each finger. "You get premonitions you can hear. When you played a song for your dad on your whistle, you visited with him. Your grandmother Kora appeared before you, and your mom whispered to you when we were on Cannon Beach."

"What about when she saw her parents after Aosoth tried to kill her," Tree commented, and I felt Nathan flinch. I took his hand, lacing my fingers with his.

"I forgot about that," Carrie said, tapping her finger on her lips as if she were pondering those events.

I scratched my head, and Nathan sat up. He looked at Carrie, then shifted his gaze to the floor. I could hear his heart beating faster, which told me he was seriously considering this. I didn't know what to think, and as my mind quickly reviewed the examples she had presented to us, Nathan laughed, startling me.

"Of course," he said.

"What?" all three of us asked in unison.

He turned to me, grinning. "Remember when you had the nightmare about the dark spirits chasing you, and one of them kept saying, 'Vos ero pessum ire'?" I nodded, and he went on. "Then, Aosoth repeated it to you?"

"Yeah," I said apprehensively, not wanting to revisit those creepy memories and actually had done a good job forgetting about them so I could sleep at night.

"What does it mean?" Tree asked, trying to repeat it, but failing miserably.

"Wait," Nathan said, focusing his attention back to Carrie. She was staring off into space, her brown eyes wide with horror. "Carrie?" Nathan asked, his voice soft with concern. "What is it?"

Tree cupped his hands on her shoulders. "Are you okay?"

Noticing the tears brimming her eyes, I jumped up and kneeled in front of her, taking her hand. "What's wrong?"

She blinked, and a tear trailed down her cheek. She looked at Tree. "It means, you will be destroyed," she choked.

"How did you know that?" I whispered, my heart thudding in my chest. In the back of my mind, I knew the answer but needed to hear it from her own lips.

She sniffed and took a deep, shaky breath. "Sometimes Aosoth's memories come to me through dreams, and last night I had a nightmare of you stumbling through the forest while black, ghostly entities chased you." She paused, and I shivered at the memory. It was so weird she experienced the same dream. "Aosoth happened to be one of those beings, but not the one who said those words to you."

"Who said it?" Nathan asked.

"Volac," she answered.

Nathan groaned.

I glanced over my shoulder at him, and he looked worried. "But I thought Volac doesn't like Aosoth. That's what Ameerah told you, right?"

"He doesn't," Carrie said before Nathan could respond, "but she butted in anyway, wanting in on the fun of scaring you. Afterwards, when Aosoth was laughing, Volac rounded on her. He told Aosoth, unlike her, his intentions toward you were pure. "

"What the hell is that supposed to mean?" My voice raised in confusion, and I was silently grateful to Anwar–of all people–for casting Volac out so he wouldn't bother me for a while. I wondered how long it would take for Volac to regain his energy. Hopefully, a long ass time because I didn't need him on my tail.

Carrie shook her head. "I don't know, but then he told Aosoth to leave and never to show her face around him again."

I combed my fingers through my hair and leaned forward on my knees, dropping my head in my hands. I didn't understand any of this. I mean, I was dreaming, so how could dark spirits enter my dream? The whole idea of it made me never want to sleep again. I almost felt like I was trapped in a *Nightmare on Elm Street* movie. This was so not good.

"Why didn't you tell me this?" Tree asked. "And do you know Latin now?"

Carrie turned to him apologetically. "I'm sorry. I was planning to this morning but couldn't stomach it. I wanted to forget about it for a while. And no, I don't know Latin well enough to speak it fluently. I can comprehend it when I have one of Aosoth's memories and Latin is being used, so I'm starting to understand it more."

I sat next to Nathan and shook my head. "I don't get any of this."

"I think I do," Nathan said, and we all stared at him. "I think when we sleep, our spirits sometimes go to a different plane of existence . . . to the spiritual world, where our deceased loved ones can sometimes visit with us while we're in slumber. So I'm sure dark spirits can reach us there as well."

"I don't think I'm ever going to sleep again," I mumbled, not liking his theory, even though it made sense.

"If what you're saying is true," Carrie said, "then why haven't the dark spirits pestered Paige every time she falls asleep?"

Nathan thought about it for a minute. "Maybe because her spirit hasn't traveled to that plane of existence since then."

I frowned. "I think you're grasping at straws."

"I'm with Paige on that one," Tree said.

Carrie made an agreement sound. "Yeah. Me, too."

"It's a theory explaining things until a better one comes along." Nathan shrugged. "Paige was sick when it happened, so maybe being ill had something to do with it. If you think about it, when a human is being occupied becomes sick, the entity vacates the vessel. So the night Paige wasn't feeling well, her spirit left her body."

"But if that's true," Carrie argued, "how come malevolent beings don't take advantage of every sick person when they fall asleep? And when Paige was in a comatose state, they didn't take advantage of her then."

"You have a good point, Carrie," I said, feeling better about the situation. I mean, seriously, if they could, they'd totally ambush my dreams. They'd also do the same to other people, especially since they despised humans.

"There's a connection there somewhere because it did happen," Nathan mused. "Maybe Paige does have a connection to the spiritual world, which would stand to reason why it happened to her."

Carrie sounded exasperated. "Yeah, but, *again*, if what you're saying is true . . . how come it only happened to her that one night? It doesn't make sense."

My head was whirling.

"I don't know." Nathan threw his hands in the air. "But I don't want it to happen to her again because there's nothing I can do about it!"

"Hey," Tree said, and when we looked at him, he flashed us his famous goofy grin, drawing a smile out of me. "This is going nowhere, and since we can't do any research on the caves in Africa, let's talk about Paige having a connection to the spiritual world 'cause I think Carrie was on to something."

Nathan inhaled through his nose and exhaled through his mouth, making a loud whooshing noise. "Good idea," he admitted.

I thought so, too, though it made me a bit uneasy until Tree's next suggestion, which made me nervous as hell.

"I think with the present circumstances"–Tree swept his hand in the air, gesturing around the room at the candles–"Paige should try conjuring her grandmother to see if we can get any answers out of her."

To my horror, Carrie squealed with delight, and Nathan nodded in agreement.

Chapter Two

Paige

Opened-mouth, I looked at Tree. "Are you serious?" I couldn't believe that not only was he suggesting I should try to conjure my dead grandmother, but both Carrie and Nathan had sided with him. When he grinned and nodded, I turned to Nathan. "Why are you agreeing to this?"

"Oh, come on, Paige," Carrie said, picking a candle up from the end table. "It'll be fun."

"I'm agreeing," Nathan said, "because I'm curious about it."

"My grandmother," I replied, narrowing my eyes on Tree, "appeared before Nathan and me on her own accord. I had nothing to do with it . . . Where you going, Carrie?"

"I'm going to get some salt to keep the dark spirits away," she said over her shoulder, heading toward the kitchen.

"It's not necessary here," Nathan told her. She stopped and looked at him, raising the candlestick level with her face. The flame flickered wildly, and her features seemed to twist in an eerie fashion. I knew it was an illusion, but it still bothered me. "With Zeruel around, we're safe from the intrusion of malevolent entities."

Carrie gestured to the window. "But it's raining, and I didn't see him earlier."

"Just because it's raining and you didn't see him, doesn't mean he's not here," I said with a sigh, my heart pounding against my chest. I had no idea how I was going to do this, and I tried to recall shows and movies I'd watched that had characters summoning spirits. But was it real or just made-up Hollywood crap? Of course, the writers had to have done research on those scenes in order to make them seem realistic. So there had to be an element of truth to it, right?

Carrie sat beside Tree, perched on the couch. "How does she do it?"

"You can get your whistle and play a song for your grandmother," Tree suggested. "If we're going by your actions connected to the spiritual world, that's what you were doing when you saw your father and heard your mother."

"But then you guys won't be able to experience it," I pointed out and at the same time thought about what Tree just said.

That was totally true. The last two times I'd played my whistle with my father and mother in mind, I'd experienced their presence. But why? I then thought about all the other times I'd played it, trying to recall how I felt. My eyebrows pulled together as I considered long and hard about it, but nothing unusual came to mind. All I could remember was feeling happy and enjoying playing it.

"Why don't you concentrate on your grandmother, like you would if you were playing your whistle, because personally," Nathan said, "I think maybe that was how you did it. It had nothing to do with the whistle, although the music probably made the process a lot easier for you."

"Have you ever seen spirits before you saw your father?" Tree wanted to know.

I shook my head. "The ghostly voice was my only connection."

"I think Bael's presence is what triggered it," Nathan stated. I stared at him, shocked at how sure and confident he sounded. "Because when Bael was inhabiting Matt, his spirit over-rode Matt's humanity, which is why our ears ring whenever a dark spirit is dwelling inside a human. Their spirit is at the very surface of the human vessel. I think having direct contact for three months, like you did with Bael's spirit, might have unlocked an unknown door within you."

I thought about the out-of-body experience I had at The Lion's Den when Carrie, Matt, and I were there. We were dancing, and the next thing I knew, I was hovering way above the floor. I remembered not being scared and having this wonderful sense of release. But then I saw Matt watching my swaying body, and when he looked up at me, his eyes were glowing.

"Do you think Matt . . . or I mean Bael . . . actually saw me when I left my body at the Lion's Den?" I'd never thought about it before and wondered if dark spirits possessing humans could see ghosts lurking around. I recalled when Aosoth tried to kill me, and my spirit shot out of my body. Again, I had felt free and more alive than ever. As I relived those two wonderful moments, something in my heart ached.

"I think he did," Nathan answered, and when I looked down, remembering how freaky that moment was, he tilted my chin up so I had to look at him. His eyes were gentle on my face, sweeping away my fear. "I don't think he heard your premonition, though."

"Why?" Carrie asked.

Nathan's eyes were still on my mine, his thumb rubbing soft circles around my cheek, shooting electrical waves through me. "When they're in the human body, they're free from many restrictions placed upon them when they're in the spectral form. However, they can't involuntarily hear or see spirits around them. They have to focus their energy on it in order to achieve that." He paused long enough to whisper to me not to be afraid. When he saw the infinitesimal nod I gave–*God, I didn't want to do this*–his gaze went to Carrie and Tree. "I think Paige can be the same way."

Confusion flickered across Carrie's face. "But she's not a dark spirit possessing a human."

"But we're all spiritual beings, housed inside the human flesh," Tree said, following what Nathan was saying.

Nathan smiled. "Correct. I think Paige's spirit is closer to the surface than most. Not to mention her DNA is saturated with psychic power from her bloodline."

"But she comes from an ancient line of witches, not psychics," Carrie said, sounding frustrated now because she wasn't getting it.

I had to give Nathan credit for being patient with her, because he didn't sound the least bit annoyed when he responded. "To be a witch you have to study and practice the beliefs of one. You can't be born a witch."

I didn't know what was up with Carrie. Maybe it was that time of the month, but she was in an argumentative mood. She raised her chin as if it would validate her statement. "Well, I think since Paige has witches' blood coursing through her veins, that makes her a witch. She doesn't have to *practice*"–she made air quotes–"the beliefs of a witch in order to justify she is one. The beliefs are already ingrained in her."

"I have to disagree," Nathan said. "I think in Paige's case, her psychic ability comes before being a witch, and it would be something she'd have to choose to become."

Tree raised his eyebrows at me, a look that said, *what's with these two?* We'd never seen Nathan and Carrie go at it like this. They were totally acting like siblings. I wondered if Tree thought the same thing.

Carrie vehemently shook her head. "You're wrong."

Nathan scooted to the edge of the couch and leaned forward on his knees. "No, I'm not."

"Yes, you are," Carrie shot back. "Now, if we were talking about anyone else who didn't have a history of witches in their family tree, I'd agree with you. In order to become one, me for example, I'd have to study and practice and follow that path for me to honestly say I was a witch. Not, Paige."

"How can you think such a thing?" Nathan asked, his tone edging toward exasperation. He was losing his patience, and I seriously hoped this wasn't going to get ugly. "Paige knows very little about witchcraft and their beliefs."

Carrie folded her arms across her chest and gave him a smug look.

Uh-oh.

I knew that look and so did Tree. He glanced at me. *Here it comes,* his expression told me, and I noticed him shifting a few inches away from her. Carrie was going to light Nathan up. This was so not good.

With the smug smile still plastered on her face, she shot back, "Have you ever seen Paige barefooted outside in the woods playing her whistle and how much joy it brings her?" When he didn't respond, she continued. "Did you know she secretly desires to dance around a bonfire at night . . . naked, while playing her whistle beneath a full moon?"

"Carrie!" I gaped at her, feeling the heat in my cheeks. I couldn't believe she told him something personal I'd shared with her. That was something I wanted to keep between her and me.

She shrugged apologetically. "Sorry, Paige. I had to mention it to prove my point."

Nathan turned to me, shocked. "Is it true what she's saying?" When I nodded, he turned back to Carrie, who wasn't finished making her point.

"Did you know she talks to the moon and feels right at home in the forest?" She paused, waiting for Nathan's rebuttal, and when he didn't respond, she went on. "Of course you don't know, but you know what? *Brayden* does."

I gasped at the same time Nathan jerked his head back, as if Carrie slapped him in the face. "Carrie!" What was wrong with her? She knew how sensitive Nathan was when it came to Brayden. That was downright mean. I glanced at Nathan. His eyes were focused on his lap, his face a pinkish red color. I locked eyes with Tree, and he shook his head, frowning in disapproval.

"It's true," Carrie said, defensively. "I don't mean to hurt your feelings, Nathan, but your assumption about Paige not being born a witch is dead wrong. She's been subconsciously following their beliefs her whole frickin' life."

"You didn't have to be rude about it," I snapped, glowering at her.

Nathan sighed, his eyes flicking to her. "You're right. I stand corrected.

I didn't know those things about Paige."

Carrie sat back, grinning in triumph. "You're damn right I'm right."

None of us said anything, and an uncomfortable silence fell among us. I didn't know what Carrie's problem was, but I didn't like it and told myself if she kept it up, I'd tell her to leave. It would be a first. I mean, Carrie and I have had our fights before, but I'd never kicked her out of my house. It crushed me to even think about it.

The rain was still hammering the roof and pavement outside, and shadows from the candlelight danced across the walls. The tension in the air floated around us like thick smoke signals of a broken truce. I wished Carrie would say she was sorry, but I knew how stubborn she was—to a fault. There was no way she'd try to amend her behavior with a rueful apology when she believed strongly in the rightness of her actions. That was the thing about Carrie; she could be brutally blunt, and for the first time since Nathan had met her, he became her target.

I hated this and felt sick to my stomach. I knew there was only one way to extinguish the tension, but I really, really, didn't want to do it; however, there was no other option.

Not really knowing what I was doing but following my gut instincts while hoping I didn't make an ass out of myself, I took a deep breath. Clearing my mind of all thoughts but one—*Grandmother*, I rose to my feet and moved to the edge of the room, ignoring the weight of their eyes on me. With my feet apart, I raised my hands above my head and visualized my grandmother. I somehow knew the theatrics of my actions weren't necessary, but I went with it anyway.

I took another deep breath.

Closing my eyes, I tilted my palms and faced heavenward. In a strong, commanding voice, I said, "In love and pure light, I call forth grandmother Kora to join us in this room." To my surprise, a tingling sensation developed on my palms and at the crown of my head, moving down my arms and through my body, leaving an energizing warmth in its wake. "In love and pure light, I call forth grandmother Kora to join us in this room." I repeated in the same forceful voice.

Carrie gasped, and Tree said, "Holy shit." I opened my eyes.

In the center of the living room, a glowing basketball sized orb hovered in the air. Bright, beautiful colors were swirling inside it: violet, pink, orange, green, and blue. It was like a living lava lamp in a white round ball.

I dropped my hands and smiled, feeling an overwhelming connection to it. "Forgive me for disturbing you, Grandmother, but I need some answers." I realized then, I didn't have any questions prepared. But then one popped in my mind, something that had been troubling me for quite some time, causing a lump to form in my throat.

The orb plummeted to the floor. When it bounced up, my grandmother appeared before us in the same white cloak she'd worn last time. She looked exactly as she had then, with her long, fiery hair framing her delicate face. I could hear the sharp intake of Carrie's breath and her whispers on how beautiful my grandmother was. Then there was Tree, staring at her in awe, mouthing, "Wow." Nathan, on the other hand, rose to his feet and stood beside me, facing my grandmother. He draped his arm around my shoulders and smiled at her while giving her a slight welcoming nod. She returned his gesture, then focused her attention on me.

"There is no need to ask for forgiveness, my child," she said. The timbre of her voice was like melted chocolate in my mouth–smooth and sweet.

"Grandmother, this is Carrie and Tree." I flicked my hand at them. "They're my best friends and family."

"Yes, I've heard about you two," she said.

I wrapped an arm around Nathan's waist. "Of course you already know Nathan."

"You have?" Carrie squeaked, sounding nervous. "Anything bad?"

Grandmother chuckled and waved a hand like she was clearing the air. "No, no, child. I've heard nothing but good things about you two. In fact, it brings both Gordon and Marissa great comfort to know you're rooted in friendship and love in Paige's life."

Hearing my parents' names made the lump in my throat grow to where I wasn't sure if I'd be able to speak, but I attempted it anyway. "How are they doing?" The raspy part of my voice cracked, and I cleared my throat. Nathan gave my shoulder a comforting squeeze.

She smiled reassuringly. "They're wonderful, but they do worry about you and vow to stay in Summerland to be closer to you."

"What's Summerland?" Carrie asked.

"It's a realm closest to earth," my grandmother told her.

"What am I?" I blurted before my throat became too tight to ask the question that had been plaguing me.

She turned to me and glided across the room. The flames on the candlesticks spit and jumped as she floated past the coffee table. She stopped in front of Nathan and me, her soft emerald eyes pouring into mine. She raised a hand to my cheek, causing it to tingle.

"You, my child, are a skeleton key," she said with great reverence. *Skeleton key? What the hell is that supposed to mean?* When she saw the confusion on my face, she stepped back and went on to explain. "You can unlock the spiritual doors closest to this realm."

"How do you know?" Nathan asked.

"I'm not permitted to say." She shook her head, and a twinkle entered her eyes. "But I can tell you it came from a most reliable source. When the time is right, your question will be answered."

"How come dark spirits had entered Paige's dream?" Tree asked.

Boy, I was so glad he asked because I would have totally spaced it.

Her image flickered. She glanced down at herself, frowned, and lifted her gaze to Tree. "I don't have much more time, so I must be brief." Her eyes shifted to mine. "At night, when you sleep, the astral body withdraws from the physical. Most of the time the conscious mind shuts down, so you're unaware of what's really going on. Anyway, there are different levels to the astral plane. Close to the earth is the etheric plane, which is a dim and misty region. This dimension blends into the astral plane–Summerland. Usually, when you're sleeping, you remain at the etheric level, and there are parts of this level where the dark spirits roam. The night you encountered those entities, your spirit happened to stumble into their dark region."

Out the corner of my eye, I could see Carrie shaking and Tree curling his arms around her. The thought of dark spirits having their own realm outside of earth never occurred to me. I mean, of course I knew about Hell, but I'd never believed in the whole fire and brimstone nonsense. But now that I knew there was a Hell-like place—minus the fire and brimstone—where malevolent beings could infiltrate your dreams, if your spirit wanders into their territory, seriously made my skin crawl.

Nathan shifted his weight and ran a hand through his hair. "How can Paige prevent it from happening again?"

My grandmother's image was still fluttering, but faster now, and I could see the anxiousness and desperation on her beautiful face.

"Say a prayer of protection," she quickly said, addressing all of us. "You can create your own, but be diligent about it. As you say it, use visualization to cement it into your spiritual consciousness." She took a deep, hurried breath and turned her full attention on me. "I'm sorry Bael found out what I had done to you. I'd never meant to have put you in this compromising position."

I averted my gaze from her sad eyes as a collage of feelings whipped through me: sorrow, frustration, anger, resentment, understanding, and love. She waited for me to respond, her image flickering like a strobe light. So I looked at her and said the only thing I could, "I know."

"This is the last time we'll meet," she said, trying to hold onto her image long enough so we could still see her, bringing tears to my eyes. "I'm moving to a higher dimension where you can't reach me. But before I do, I need to ask your forgiveness."

Stunned, I blinked back the tears. For a split second I wondered if I didn't forgive her, would she stay in Summerland? Because if she did, I'd be able to see her again. But it was a selfish thought, and I wouldn't want to do that to her, regardless of me hating what she had done to me. So I looked her square in the face, managed a small smile, and said, "I forgive you."

Right when I said those three words, her face glowed with pure joy. Her happiness expanded, pouring into the room. She was now as solid as I, but beaming, overwhelming us with her joy. All four of us laughed, and she joined in.

And then she began to shimmer like glitter sparkling in the sun. I could hear Carrie stifling a sob, whispering, "Omigod." Because behind Grandmother appeared a threshold to a wide-open door. Beyond it was a meadow filled with brilliant, beautiful flowers that put the colors on earth to shame. The sky was a tranquil, lilac color. I could see shadowed figures waiting for her, and past them were gorgeous, snow-capped mountains. And in that moment, I envied her.

She turned to me, her expression filled with excitement. "I'll look after you. This isn't a goodbye because although my spirit can't manifest in your world, eventually I'll be able to learn how to communicate with you on a higher level, like your Guide."

My throat was too tight to respond, so I pointed to myself, crossed my arms over my chest, and pointed at her.

She smiled. "I love you, too."

A flash of white light sparked out of her chest, exploding her into beautiful pieces of incandescent colors, like broken stained glass. It scattered in the air, briefly illuminating the room in a rainbow of colors. In awe, we watched it come together, forming back into an orb. It flew through the doorway leading to the meadow. The door slammed shut, leaving behind an air of finality. My grandmother was gone, taking the portal with her.

Chapter Three

Nathan

In all my life—all hundred and seventy-three years of it—I'd never had a glimpse of the hereafter. Now I couldn't help but think about my family, wondering what they were doing and if any of them were still in Summerland. The thought of asking Paige to contact them crossed my mind. I peeked at her but then felt guilty for even considering it. She stood, shoulders slumped, looking sad and lost in the direction Kora had left.

Damn.

Here I was thinking of myself when Paige just lost her grandmother and will never see her again. At least in this life she wouldn't. I took her hand and led her to the couch. When we sat, I wrapped my arms around her shoulders, careful not to touch her back. She clung to me as if her life depended upon it, as if she were afraid I'd disappear as well. It broke my heart.

Carrie was leaning on her knees, sniffling in her hands, chanting in a low whisper, "It was so beautiful . . . so beautiful . . . so beautiful."

"I'll be right back," Tree said to her. He picked up a candle, curled his hand around the flame and left the room. Carrie didn't move, her face still buried in her hands. Shortly after, Tree returned with a roll of toilet paper. He tore some off and handed it to her. She took it and blew her nose. "Here." He tossed the roll to me. It arched in the dark space between us, and I snatched it midair.

"Thanks," Paige said when I handed her a wad. She wiped her nose and turned to Carrie and Tree but didn't say anything.

Carrie lifted her watery eyes to us. "I'm sorry"–for a second I thought she was apologizing to me. I raised my hand to wave it off and then realized she was talking to Paige, not me–"about your grandmother."

Paige looked down and wiped her nose again.

"That was intense," Tree said, swiping a hand across his face, releasing a slow breath. He looked at me, concern shadowing his face. "I'm guessing nobody knows Paige is a skeleton key except us, but what would happen to her if somebody finds out?"

"They won't." The words fell from my mouth in a fervent rush. Every muscle in my body tensed, and my heart raced at the thought of Paige being a perpetual target to those who'd want to either destroy her for having those abilities or seek a way to claim it for themselves by imprisoning her and doing unthinkable things. My blood boiled just thinking about it.

No. I wouldn't allow it to happen.

Sure, Paige had the power of Solomon's ring in her, but the power to control the dark spirits was impotent without the incantations. Once we found the incantations, Paige could use them to control the dark spirits and rid this world of them. However, now that Bael was aware the power of the ring resided inside her and not Solomon's ring, I was almost certain he'd want those incantations destroyed or Paige dead. If he wanted the latter, we were in deep shit.

"We need to keep this between us," I continued. "Otherwise, Paige is–"

"Done for." Paige made a horrible choking sound, slapped a hand over her mouth, and disappeared. The toilet seat banged, and in one loud strangling sound, she got sick.

In an instant, I was behind her, holding her hair back as she got sick several more times. I could hear hurried steps moving toward us, and then the power came back on. Light from the hall flooded into the dark bathroom.

"Are you okay?" Carrie asked, stepping beside Paige.

I glanced over my shoulder and saw Tree standing in the doorframe looking green. Our eyes locked. He frowned and left the room.

Paige spat in the toilet. "Uh. No. I'm not okay." When she rose, I let go of her hair and stepped back. She flushed the toilet and grabbed some mouthwash off the shelf beside the sink. After she rinsed her mouth, she sank to the floor. Pulling her knees up, she leaned her face against them and rocked. I sat beside her and pulled her into my arms. "Why me? I don't want this."

I tucked a lock of hair behind her ear. "Ignore it then." She stopped rocking and looked at me. Knowing I had her attention, I quickly went on before her mind drifted backward. "We don't know anything about it, you don't know how to use it, so we'll pretend you don't have the capability to unlock those doors."

"Good idea," Carrie said, surprising me. "Tree and I will never mention it. Right, Tree?" Her gaze swept to the open doorway.

"Right." Tree came in view, his huge shadow swallowing the tiny bathroom.

I cradled Paige's face, seeing a glimmer of hope in her dark green eyes. "See? It'll be all right, and once we take care of the current situation, we can start building a life together."

She smiled. It was weak, but I'd take it over a frown any day. I brushed my lips against hers and rose. I offered my hand. She took it, and we went back to our places in the living room. The rain quieted, drizzling at a lazy pace. Damp cool air seeped through the cracks, kicking on the heat. A rush of air blew through the heating vents. An easy conversation followed with Tree initiating it about the ethereal plane, dark spirits, and doing what Kora had told us. Paige thanked Tree for bringing it up to Kora, admitting she would have probably forgotten if it weren't for him. I could tell by the bright smile on his face Paige's *what-would-I-do-without-you*, tone flattered him. Carrie stared at her lap the whole time, her lips in a tight line. Something was going on with her, and I wasn't about to let her little pissy attitude sabotage the rest of my night. I'd be damned if I would walk on eggshells whenever she was present. "Carrie, can I talk to you in the kitchen?"

Paige raised her eyebrows at me when I stood, and I squeezed her hand before exiting the room. I could hear Carrie following behind me, her feet dragging on the floor. As soon as we entered the kitchen, I faced her. "What's going on?"

She blinked and feigned ignorance. "I don't know what you're talking about."

Now I was pissed and could feel my ears getting warm. The attitude was one thing, but to take me as a fool and lie straight to my face was another. I'd never had a problem with Carrie except for her occasionally annoying me when she acted juvenile, which I ignored, but this I could not.

I ran a hand through my hair and squinted at her. "You know exactly what I mean. Let's start with the attitude you have with me and throwing Brayden in my face. Does that jar your memory or are you going to keep pretending you have no idea what I'm talking about?"

She crossed her arms and glared. "Fine. I'm mad because you didn't call me when Paige had disappeared."

Interesting. I could understand why she'd be upset, but in my opinion she was being overly dramatic about it. She knew the situation. I'd already told her and Tree about what happened, and she'd seemed fine at the time. I thought she understood, but I guess I was wrong.

"I apologize, Carrie," I said. "I wanted to call you, but I knew Paige wouldn't have approved because she didn't want you or Tree involved in any of this."

She looked up at me with tears in her eyes. "But if you called me right away, I could have told you Paige was at Cannon Beach, and since you didn't, Paige went through all that unnecessary pain, and Bael now knows Solomon's power is inside her. So what's going to happen to her since he knows? Is he going to put a hit on her or kill her himself?"

"You think what happened to Paige is my fault." It wasn't a question, only a statement hanging in the air between us. My tone was flat, emotionless, and I felt like she just kicked me in the stomach.

Carrie jutted her chin out. "Yes, I do."

In a flash, Paige stood at my side. "How can you say that, Carrie? Nathan did the right thing. He knew I didn't want you two involved."

Carrie raised her hands in defeat. "I'm sorry. I'm just scared. Okay?" She didn't sound regretful. She sounded more irritated than anything. She turned to Tree. "Let's go. I'm tired."

"Wait." Paige snatched Carrie's arm and voiced my thoughts. "You don't sound sorry." Carrie tried to yank her arm back, but Paige was too strong. "What's your problem?"

"Let go of my arm, Paige," Carrie said, trying to break free. When Paige wouldn't let go, Carrie finally relaxed. She looked exhausted. "I'm tired, and Aosoth's memories keep haunting me, and sometimes I don't feel like myself. I'm afraid I'm becoming like her because there are times when I feel like her memories are actually mine." Her brown eyes were wide with fear, brimming with tears.

I felt like shit, remembering telling her how rarely a human possessed by a dark spirit will obtain some of its memories and either go mad or become a recluse. I should have never mentioned it to her because now the fear had rooted inside her.

Paige embraced her, but when Carrie squeezed her arms around Paige's back, Paige released a small painful cry. Carrie apologized and placed her arms around Paige's shoulders, her somber eyes meeting mine.

"I'm sorry, Nathan," she said. "I don't hate you." Her lip trembled, and she burst into tears. "I really don't blame you for what happened to Paige. I do wish you would have called me, but I understand why you didn't." She clung to Paige tighter. "I-I don't feel like myself. Wh-what if I'm going crazy?"

My heart went out to her, and I made a silent oath to save her from this madness. I had thought because she was aware of what was going on, she'd be able to distinguish her memories from Aosoth's, but I'd underestimated the human mind and the raging emotions of a teen. I could see clearly now on what her problem was. Mind, body, and spirit, weak with exhaustion, therefore allowing Aosoth's memories to pour in and mingle with her own, confusing the mind and altering her moods. Thus, the mood swings and her irrational behavior. If it continued, we'd lose Carrie.

"I can help you," I said, thinking of a good friend I hadn't spoken to or seen in over a decade. I'd have to track him down, but it wouldn't be hard to do. He owed me a favor and now was a good time to collect.

Hope flooded into her eyes. "You can?"

"Yes," I said.

"How can you help her?" Paige asked, turning to me.

"Awesome," Tree said, relief crossing his face. "Can you do it now?"

"I have to track down an old friend," I told them and quickly added when their faces fell. "It won't take me long. I have an idea where he is. I'll start on it right away tomorrow. I promise."

"Who?" Paige wanted to know. "How can he help?"

"His name is Pippins. He's eccentric, but he's skilled at the workings of the human mind and can remove Aosoth's memories through hypnosis."

Carrie's face lit up. "That would be great." She yawned and flashed me a tired smile. "Thanks, Nathan."

I gave her shoulder a squeeze in an attempt to comfort her. "I'll give you an update tomorrow, and hopefully we can do it within a couple days."

She nodded and slipped her hand in Tree's. "C'mon. I need to get some sleep."

After they left, I made Paige and me bacon, eggs, and toast while she threw a load of laundry in the washer and did some light cleaning around the house. I was going to suggest we hop on the internet and start researching the caves in Africa, but I had the feeling she didn't want to deal with it tonight, so I didn't mention it.

The past couple of days had been more difficult than usual, and I knew she needed a reprieve from it, for which I couldn't blame her. I felt the same. But despite all my efforts of ignoring the dark cloud hovering over us, I couldn't help but wonder what was going through Bael's head.

As we were eating, Paige wanted to know more about Pippins. Pip was what I called him. I told her everything I knew about him, like how he was a loner and scoffed at the idea of ridding this world of dark spirits. How he agreed we immortals needed to police them. However, if we could exterminate them, it would throw off the balance, like having no night only day. I used to love chatting with him for hours over a nice glass of fine brandy about philosophy and religion. I always thought the genius in him was what made him odd to others because his eyes and mind were wide open, whereas a lot of people sleepwalked through life.

"I didn't know you drank," Paige said while loading the dishwasher. "I mean, except for when you were going through a hard time in your life."

"I like to have a glass of good brandy or wine once in a while," I admitted. "It's the culture behind it I find alluring, I think. It reminds me of a classier time when individuals would sit and chat for hours about meaningful things to feed and grow their minds." I stopped, suddenly feeling silly for some reason, thinking maybe she had to have been in those times to understand the concept behind it. After all, she was born in the age of technology.

"I can understand that," she said, surprising me. "I wish I was born in those times. In fact,"–she leaned forward and cupped the side of her mouth with her hand, like she was going to tell me a deep, dark secret. I leaned toward her, and she whispered–"I'm secretly a Humphrey Bogart fan." When I raised my eyebrows, shocked and pleased she even watched classic movies, she continued. "I've seen all his movies, and *Casablanca* is one of my favorites."

The corner of my mouth lifted, and I peeked at her sideways. "Did you have a thing for Mr. Bogart?"

She shook her head. Her cheeks flushed, turning cherry red. "Ingrid Bergman was who I had a crush on because of her beauty. I used to wish I looked like her."

"What about Marilyn Monroe?"

"Her, too," she said, still embarrassed. "I feel bad for Marilyn, though, because she seemed so lonely and had a childlike sadness to her."

"Well," I said, sitting on the kitchen chair and pulling her onto my lap, "I love knowing this about you, and I think you're way sexier than Ingrid and Marilyn."

Paige swung an agile leg and straddled me. "Such sweet things you say," she said before planting her mouth on mine.

Her lips were hot, and I kissed her long and deep, my tongue flicking against hers. She pulled at my shirt, her short breaths coming faster now, her bright green eyes on mine. I took it off and tossed it aside. She followed suit, and I was pleased to see she wasn't wearing a bra. A deep involuntary sound vibrated in my throat, almost primal. My lips made a trail down her neck, and she leaned back on her hands, arching her back. She softly moaned when my fingers found their way down her pants. I discovered she was naked down there and made a pleasing sound against her breast. My fingers slipped inside her, and she moaned louder, rocking against my hand, driving me crazy.

I had to have her.

Now.

We stripped our pants and made passionate love with her legs bracketing my lap on the kitchen chair. It was erotic, mind blowing, and intense. All I could think about was Paige. Us. Nothing else crossed my mind. It was a wonderful release from the world oppressing us, and we took full advantage of it because deep down we didn't know when would be the next time we'd be able to do this again.

* * *

The next morning after we ate and took our showers, I made a few phone calls to track Pip. I knew he wouldn't be listed in the phone book because he valued his privacy. I thought about taking a trip to where he used to reside, which was surprisingly nearby in Washington, but I didn't want to be away from Paige for long. Pip would have to come here, since it wasn't safe for Paige to leave the house. I got a few leads and was about to act on one when my phone rang. Paige looked up from the magazine she was reading and eyed my phone next to my coffee cup.

"Maybe it's Pip," she guessed, reaching for her coffee, taking a sip.

I wasn't so sure, but then again Pip and I were good friends. And even if he didn't owe me a favor, I had no doubt he'd be there for me.

I picked up the phone half expecting to hear Pip's British accent he had managed to hang onto for more than four hundred years, but I heard Tree's tearful voice call my name instead. Paige sat up, worried eyes boring into mine. My heart did a nosedive.

"What's wrong?" I asked.

"C-Carrie," Tree choked out.

Paige jumped up, knocking the chair back. It fell with a loud bang. Her face went stark white. "What happened?" she yelled, knowing Tree could hear her.

"Sh-she was in a car accident this morning," Tree said, his voice unsteady.

"Oh, God!" Paige wailed, slapping her hands on top of her head, staring at the ceiling.

A burning pain stabbed my eyes as anger and sorrow swelled inside me. Paige had lost her mother in a car accident less than a year ago. She couldn't go through this again.

Why?

Why was this happening?

Tree took a deep breath and cleared his throat. "She's alive but in I.C.U."

A loud, spine-chilling buzzer went off, and I heard somebody yell, "Code Red!"

And then the phone line went dead.

Chapter Four

Paige

I pulled Nathan with me through the hospital lobby, through the maze of halls, dodging nurses, patients in wheelchairs, patients shuffling along, gripping their IV poles, straight to the intensive care unit. I knew this hospital well. Before my mom decided to be a traveling nurse, she used to work here with Tree's mom, Tori, a lifetime ago it seemed.

I spotted Tori right away, standing at the nurses' station, doing her charting. As if she could feel our presence, she looked up. Bags were forming under her hazel eyes, and the lines on her forehead wrinkled with worry. Wrapping a stethoscope around her neck, she greeted us with a weary smile. I wondered why she was still here. She usually worked the night shift. She must have pulled a double. That was the thing about nurses, they worked long hours and did a lot of the doctor's crap work without being acknowledged for it. I never understood why Mom and Tori wanted to become one, but I knew it took a special person to be a nurse, and they were good at it.

She embraced me, and amazingly enough it didn't hurt my back. Huh. It must have finally healed. But honestly, that was the last thing on my mind. I thought about Tree's horrible phone call and my reaction afterwards. I had grabbed my stuff and headed out the door to see Carrie. I saw the objection in Nathan's eyes, but it disappeared as quickly as it came. I knew it was his fear of me getting hurt and appreciated him keeping his trap shut about it because frankly, I wasn't in the mood for any hassles.

Tori pulled back and held me at arm's length. She placed her cold hand on my cheek, diverting my thoughts to now wondering why hospitals always chilled me so. "She's in a coma from head trauma."

"What"–I cleared my throat and swallowed the tears back– "happened?"

To my horror, her eyes filled with tears, causing my own to do the same. "I know this is hard for you," she whispered. "I-I think about your mother every day, missing her." Nathan stepped beside me and took my hand, gently squeezing it, lending me some of his strength. "Carrie was at a four-way stop sign, and when she crossed the intersection a car barreled into the tail end. Her vehicle spun and flipped. A drunk driver hit her, and he's in custody now."

With my free hand, I wiped the tears off my cheeks. "Is she going to be okay?"

"There appears to be no brain damage, but a neurosurgeon is looking at her CT results, so at this point, we really don't know much." She looked away, blinking the tears away. "Tree is beside himself with worry and won't leave her side. I've never seen him like this–distraught and lifeless."

A continuous beeping noise went off, and our gaze followed in the direction of the sound. A few doors down, above the door, a little round light blinked.

Tori released a tired sigh and frowned. "I think Mrs. Spencer wants more pain medication. I better go check her morphine drip."

When she turned away, I took her hand, halting her. "When Nathan was on the phone with Tree, we heard a code red. What happened?"

She looked at Nathan and blinked as if he'd appeared out of thin air. Realizing he'd been standing there all along, she recovered graciously from her prior obliviousness to his presence. "I'm glad you're here, Nathan. It's always nice to see you."

"Likewise," Nathan said, offering her an understanding smile.

She glanced over her shoulder at the constant beeping noise. "We had an elderly patient," she said, meeting my eyes, "go into cardiac arrest. He expired shortly after." She paused and shoved her hands into her Snoopy scrub top. "Caroline went home to get some things, and Brayden is on his way. Apparently, he was in Seattle with his girlfriend." A pang pierced my chest, and I must have had a strange look on my face because she went on. "I think her name is Cassie." *Cassondra*, I mentally corrected her, wondering how Brayden could do this to me after what she had done. "If you need anything, you know where to find me." She pointed to the powder blue door across from us. "Carrie is in there."

"Thanks," I said, watching her hurry down the hall and disappear into Mrs. Spencer's room. Half a minute later, the beeping stopped.

When we entered Carrie's room, the smell of alcohol and medicine assaulted my nostrils. I could also detect the rusty scent of blood, though I couldn't see any. A white bandage was wrapped around her head, and with a start I covered my mouth. Could her brain be bleeding, and that was the blood I smelled? Tree sat beside her with his forehead resting on the bed. I wondered if he'd fallen asleep.

Nathan pulled me into the bathroom. "What is it?" He kept his voice low so only I could hear him.

"I can smell blood. What if her brain is bleeding?" I whispered.

"Her hematoma is what you smell. It's when blood collects in the space between the skull and brain, due to head trauma."

I blanched. "That doesn't sound good."

"Would it make you feel better if I found out more details on her prognosis?"

I nodded, grateful and amazed at his knowledge on this.

He gave me a quick kiss. "I'll be back in a few minutes."

After he slipped out the door, I took a deep breath and told myself not to cry. I had to be strong for Tree. Besides, as much as I wanted to drape myself over Carrie's body and bawl for her to come back to us, I knew she wouldn't want me to.

I laid a hand on Tree's shoulder. "Tree?"

He jerked and squinted up at me, his brown eyes glazed from sleep. I suddenly felt bad for waking him. Dried tear lines stained his face. I hugged my arms around him from behind, resting my chin on his shoulder. He smelled like leather and fabric softener, reminding me of home long ago.

"How you holding up?"

He covered my locked fingers around his shoulders with his huge hand. "Not good."

My ears began to ring.

"Oh, no."

Tree heaved a heavy sigh. "Yeah, I know. What if she nev–"

"No, Tree." I dropped my arms and stood erect, my heart pounding. "There's a dark spirit nearby."

He sat up, wide eyes on my face. "Are you serious?"

I nodded right when a handsome dark-haired young male doctor waltzed in. I moved to the foot of the bed, and Tree followed me. The doctor raised his hand in a halting gesture, his blue eyes nonthreatening and glowing. I knew who it was by the vessel he chose and his mannerism.

Bael.

He took a chair and wedged it beneath the door handle.

"Hey. What the hell are you doing?" Tree asked, puffing up. He took a step forward, but I snatched his arm.

"It's Bael. There's nothing we can do."

"Bullshit!" Tree reached into his pocket, but again I stopped him.

"He's not going to hurt us." At least I hoped he wasn't going to. I took Tree's hand and squeezed it in short spurts, doing Morse Code, telling him to keep his hand in his pocket, but don't do anything unless necessary. I silently prayed he would understand and remember Morse Code from our war games we used to play. He squeezed back, saying okay. I breathed a sigh of relief. Thank God he remembered.

"I only need a moment of your time," Bael said to me. He glanced at Carrie and frowned. When he made a move toward her, Tree stepped in front of him, all six-five of him.

"Don't even think about going near her," he said, glaring at Bael, his voice dark and threatening.

Bael smirked and shrugged, unfazed. "Very well." He looked at me, the smirk melting into a friendly smile. "Nice to see you again."

I crossed my arms. "Are you going to kill me now that you know Solomon's power is inside me?" I might as well cut to the chase and voice what I'd been wondering since that night. "And did you tell anybody?" Like he would tell me the truth. But I had to ask.

"I'm not going to kill you, Paige." He touched his chest as if it crushed him I would even consider the thought. "You intrigue me too much to do such a thing. I also enjoy your company. Believe it or not." A slow enigmatic smile formed on his face. "As for anybody knowing . . . no, and I don't plan to."

I eyed him suspiciously. "Why?"

"Because it doesn't fit my agenda."

Tree made a disgusted sound. "Yeah. Right."

Bael glowered at him. "I do wish you and Carrie would keep better company," he said to me.

"What do you want?" I demanded.

"Have you found where the incantations are?" He studied me closely, probably to see if I would lie or not. I wasn't sure if he could read auras like Anwar, so I knew I had to be tricky about my answer. But I honestly didn't know where the incantations were, so it wasn't hard to answer.

"No. Not yet. And with Carrie like this, I'm not going anywhere but here and home until she gets better," I said firmly. I didn't care what anybody said–Nathan, Bael, the whole damned race. I wasn't budging on this one.

"Well," he said, sounding both amused and astonished, "we must get Carrie better then."

"What's with this *we* shit?" Tree asked.

Ignoring Tree, Bael held his attention on me. "I have a proposal for you." Before I could answer, he continued. "I'll save Carrie's life if you promise to take me with you when you discover where the incantations are and then destroy them."

"You don't know Carrie's life is in danger," I said, feeling sick to my stomach, hoping to God this was one of his ploys to get me to do what he wanted.

"Paige isn't helping you do *shit*," Tree said, jabbing the air with his finger.

Bael raised his eyebrows in mock surprise, a cocky smile crossing his face. It was the same smile he wore when he had possessed Matt. I knew that smile. Hell, I knew that look. He was telling me the truth. I could feel it in my gut. My stomach twisted, and the room spun a little. I grabbed the footboard on the hospital bed and glanced at Carrie. She didn't look good. At all. And the machine hooked up to her kept beeping, filling the short silence. I hated that disconcerting sound, and I hated how pale and lifeless she looked. But if he could save her–

Tree moved to my side and held my hand. "Don't even think about it, Paige." He pointed a harsh finger at Bael who still held the cocky smile on his face. "He's full of shit."

I looked up at Tree, my heart racing. "No, he's not." I swallowed back the bile rising in my throat and fixed my eyes on Bael. "How are you going to save her?"

"Her brain is swelling, which is causing the blood supply to it to be blocked," he told me. "The brain stem regulates the breathing. If her brain continues to swell, it'll compress its stem, and she'll die. Not to mention she has an intracerebral hematoma."

I glanced at Tree. All the color from his face had vanished. In the back of my mind I wondered what was taking Nathan so long. My stomach sank when I thought about him tracking down Carrie's doctor and getting the full details of her . . . What did he say earlier? Prognosis? Yeah, that was it. Maybe it was taking so long because her prognosis was grim and every detail had to be explained to him.

"You still haven't answered my question," I said.

Bael pulled back the sleeve of his white lab coat to look at his watch.

Glancing at me he said, "Let's just say the neurosurgeon here is involved in the dark arts and is well acquainted with me. In fact, he's conversing with Nathan as we speak, and although for confidentiality reasons, the physician is not supposed to divulge Carrie's cat scan results, he's doing so on my direct orders. However, his allotted time to distract Nathan for me is almost over, so before you reply to my request, I need to make an amendment to my proposal."

My heart thudded in my ears. I knew there were humans with a soul who partnered with dark spirits. I just never thought there would be one here and a surgeon of all people. It shattered my image of prominent, professional people having the sense not to get entangled in the dark world. One might not be able to sell his or her soul as mythology claimed, but a person could swear a blood oath instead where both parties had to fulfill their agreement or otherwise become a slave to the party owed. So I guess in a sense it was like selling your soul.

Omigod! What if Bael wanted me to do a blood oath? Feeling lightheaded, I swayed. Tree held my hand tighter to keep me steady.

"Neither one of you can mention this arrangement to anybody," he continued. "If you do"–he looked at me and pointed to Tree–"he dies." He turned a cold gaze on Tree. "If you do, your whole family dies, including offspring." His lips twisted into a devious smile. "So what's it going to be, Paige?"

I had no choice. There was no way out of it. I hated him for putting me in a position where either way, I would surely lose someone I loved. I'd finally got Nathan to realize we needed to work together as a team and not withhold secrets from each other, and now I was going to do exactly that.

"Will I have to perform a blood oath?"

He frowned and shook his head. "The blood oath won't work on you. You can thank Solomon's power for that, thus, the drastic measures I have to take to seal this deal." He paused. "Do we have a deal?" He stuck his hand out, waiting for me to shake it.

Tree pressed my palm in Morse Code, saying he'd keep his mouth shut, and I wasn't alone, he'd help me through this.

I grabbed Bael's hand and squeezed it harder than normal, yanking him toward me. "If anything happens to the people I love, I'll find those incantations on my own and make your existence a living hell."

His glowing eyes poured into mine, amused. I balled my other hand into a fist, wanting to punch him.

"I love that about you. Your fierceness," he said. I pushed him, causing him to dance backwards. He almost lost his footing but recovered and straightened his lab coat. "You don't have to worry about me keeping my word. I always do." He removed the chair from the door, cheerfully whistling to himself. Shooting a dark look over his shoulder, he flashed me a sparkling smile. My blood ran cold. "I'll be in touch." He strolled out the room with a hop in his step.

I was in Hell.

Chapter Five

Nathan

Dr. Sweeney explained Carrie's CAT scan results to me in a room much like where Carrie lay hurt, except unoccupied on a different floor.

With the help from Tree's mom, I tracked down the neurosurgeon with no problem. He'd recently finished going over Carrie's results with the radiologist and her primary care physician, when I had caught up with him halfway down the hall. I noted his slouched shoulders and his brown hair graying at the temples, though he looked no older than thirty-five. He held a manila folder close to his chest, his slender fingers splayed across the back. He was cordial when I explained who I was, but I couldn't help but notice the odd way he kept looking at me, as if he were waiting for me to sprout wings or something.

"I normally don't do this, Mr. Caswell," he whispered, his eyes darting around us, "but follow me." For a guy barely five six with short legs he moved fast, and I followed appreciating his hastiness. "It's not good," he said out the corner of his mouth. I bent my head toward him to appear like I had to strain my ears to hear when really I heard him fine. We crossed several halls to the end of a deserted one. Without hesitation, he entered a room and held the door open for me. When I stepped past him, he stuck his head out the doorway for one last sweeping look. "Carrie's physician is gathering a team as we speak to do immediate surgery on her."

I took a couple deep breaths to compensate for the sudden stillness of my heart. If Carrie died, it would completely shatter Paige. I shook my head, pushing the thought aside and listened to Dr. Sweeney lay out Carrie's results in a detailed manner. He stopped several times to look at his watch, and I felt a sting of guilt for keeping him from his duties. He still had to explain all of this to Carrie's family. Then I wondered why he seemed eager to tell me. Why would he jeopardize his job by violating the patient-doctor confidentiality law?

I noticed the beads of sweat dripping down his broad face.

What was going on?

But before I could get a word in edgewise, he continued with his assessment. I had to admit he knew what he was talking about, which gave me some comfort. He also wasn't shy to boast about him being one of the best neurosurgeons in the country, and Carrie's life rested in good hands.

He looked at his watch again. "I'm going to grab Carrie's doctor and set up a quick meeting with her parents. If all goes well, we'll start the operation within a couple hours."

"What procedure are you going to do, and how will it help her?" I asked.

"We're going to relieve the pressure in her skull by placing a ventriculostomy drain in there. Its function is to remove the cerebrospinal fluid."

"What's the recovery rate?" My eyes were wary on his face. I didn't feel comfortable with this solution, but I knew I had to trust him.

He clapped a hand on my shoulder. "Don't worry. I've done this procedure many times. It's quite simple and could actually be done at the patient's bedside." He smiled, but the corners of his mouth twitched nervously. "I'll take good care of her."

"Thanks, Doctor," I said, feeling reassured when I saw the sincerity in his eyes. I could imagine it being nerve-wracking to have people's lives depended upon you, which would explain how nervous he seemed. I followed him to the door and stopped when he turned.

"Will you please keep this between us, because what I've told you could cost me my position and possibly my career?"

"Yes, of course," I reassured him. "But may I ask why divulge information not meant for my ears?" I knew he was in a hurry, and I hated wasted more of his time, especially with Carrie's life hanging by a thread, but the question fell out of my mouth.

He released a strangled laugh. "Let's just say I had no choice and leave it at that." He shook his head in disgust and turned away from me. "I was such a *fucking* idiot," he scolded under his breath, flinging the door open. He practically ran down the hall, his white lab coat billowing behind, his heavy footfalls, echoing against the powder blue walls.

I stood, staring after him as everything clicked into place, like puzzle pieces snapping together to form a whole picture.

Son-of-a-bitch!

Bael's filthy hands were smeared all over this. But why would he–

Oh. God. Paige.

My heart jackhammered against my chest as I raced through the halls, nearly knocking a few scrub wearing people out of the way, throwing out "sorry" and "excuse me" in my haste. Instead of taking the elevator, I took the stairs two at a time. My ears rang, alerting me of a dark presence nearby. As I flew down the stairs, a dark-haired guy was about to exit when I slammed my hand against the door. "What's going on, Ayperos?" Like Bael, he was predictable in the vessels he chose. This one was a little different from the last one he possessed, by about ten years older. He looked like a young Sean Connery with long hair he had gathered in a ponytail. I stepped back when he turned and greeted me with a plastic smile.

"Nathan. Fancy seeing you here. Shouldn't you be comforting Paige and her *wretched* friend?" His condescending, carefree tone turned disdainful when he said the last part.

Tree and I were definitely on his hate list, but I didn't give a shit.

"What's going on?" I repeated.

He batted his eyelashes, his smile turning tight. "I don't know what you're talking about."

In one swift move, I had him by the throat and pinned to the door. "I may not be able to cast you out, but I can break your neck, and it might be days, weeks, maybe even months before you can possess another human." His dark eyes narrowed on my face, the iris partly glowing with annoyance. "So what's it going to be?"

"Very well," he choked. I released him and watched him rub his neck and cough. "Bael paid Paige a visit. He had a doctor distract you so he could do it. That's all I know."

"Does Bael want to kill Paige?"

He looked at me, aghast. "No. Why would he want to do such a thing? He needs her to find the incantations. Otherwise, the ring is useless. He's also quite fond of her."

The tension in my shoulders lifted. He wasn't aware of Solomon's power inside Paige, which meant Bael probably hadn't told anybody. Ayperos was his right-hand man. If he told anybody, it would have been Ayperos. But why would Bael pay Paige a visit? I didn't like this. He was cooking something up, and it had to do with Paige. I had to get to her. Now.

"Wait," Ayperos said when I pushed past him and opened the door. I stopped and threw him an impatient glare. "There are others who want to destroy Paige and willing to risk your wrath."

"Well, if Paige is so important to Bael, then why won't he stop them?" It was a smoke and mirrors question–a hidden form of manipulation designed to give me more information without him realizing it. I lifted my brows to prompt him to answer the question.

"It's not Bael's style to babysit every disgruntled spirit out there, and we don't know who they all are," he said. "But if you're worried about Paige's safety, you can hand her to us. I can assure you we'll keep her safe."

I gritted my teeth. "Not going to happen."

"You can't fight us all, Nathan," he said. "At least Bael and I want to keep Paige alive."

"Until she gives you what you want, which she's not going to do." Before he could reply, I bolted out the door, a feeling of dread consuming me.

When I entered Carrie's room, it was swelling with her family, a nurse and two men in lab coats, one of them was Dr. Sweeney. Tree stood beside Carrie's bed with his arms around his chest, his head bowed as if in prayer. My eyes frantically searched for Paige, and when I saw her walking through the wall of bodies around and near Carrie's bed, I breathed a sigh of relief.

"How are you doing?" I asked. She looked so pale and sad I couldn't help but embrace her, desperate to comfort her.

"I love you," she said, squeezing her arms tightly around my waist.

Something wasn't right. She said "I love you" in a way that spoke of longing and possible broken hearts. I heard it in her tone. "Let's go get some coffee and give Carrie's family some time alone," I whispered in her ear. I took her hand, and we left the dismal scene.

A half hour later, we were sitting on a bench outside the hospital, drinking coffee out of Styrofoam cups, watching a couple squirrels chase each other into the woods. The crisp, cool air held the smell of autumn while wafting the scent of burning leaves and pine cones around us in its feathery breeze. I breathed it in through my nose, loving this time of year.

Paige took a sip of her coffee and gazed up at the colorful trees blazing around us in rich red, gold and orange colors. She sighed. "I love this time of year." I smiled. "What are you grinning about?"

"I was thinking the same thing." I kissed her soft hand. "I love how connected we are."

She smiled in agreement, and then it faded. She took another sip and looked away. I knew she was worried about Carrie. She had told me everything the doctors had said when I wasn't in the room, including the procedure Dr. Sweeney mentioned to me. I kept my promise to him and didn't tell Paige everything he'd told me. It didn't really matter though, because he essentially gave the same information to Carrie's parents, and they'd decided to go through with the surgery today.

While Paige updated me on what I'd missed, I clamped my mouth shut to keep from hijacking the conversation by asking her about Bael. It would have been insensitive to do in a time like this where Paige's thoughts should be with Carrie and loved ones, not on insidious beings such as Bael.

So I gave her some space and support, but now as we sat, listening to the gentle rustling of the leaves, I decided to bring it up. "Did Bael visit you while I was out of the room?"

She looked at me in surprise and stared into my eyes for a long moment. "Yes," she finally said. I waited for her to continue because I could see it on her face. There was more. A lot more. But then she blinked, and her expression turned hard. She looked away.

I nudged her chin so she had to look at me. "What are you not telling me?"

"Bael wanted to know if I found out where the incantations are. When I told him no, he said he'd be in touch. I just wish he'd leave me alone," she mumbled, breaking eye contact.

I dropped my hands and sighed, wishing the same thing. The only way to get him completely out of her life would be to find the incantations and have her use them to control him. We never really talked about what she would do once we found them. Originally, we were going to find the ring and destroy it, but since the power dwelled in Paige and not the ring, that plan was shot to hell. I guessed I'd assumed she'd learn those incantations, rally up all the dark spirits and keep them on a short leash.

I suddenly realized we were going to have to engage in an in-depth conversation on the topic real soon. But in the meantime, the current situation with Carrie and what had occurred today took precedence over all things. Besides, it wasn't like we were going to find Solomon's incantations tonight.

"I ran into Ayperos," I said, deciding to deal with our present situation and to stand by my word to share all information with her—except the promise I made to the doctor.

"You did?" Her eyes were wide, and she listened intently when I told her everything. "I wonder . . ." She trailed off and rubbed her shoe against the dry grass.

Alarmed, I turned to her. "You wonder what?" I had a feeling of what her answer would be but had to hear it to be sure.

"I wonder if I should go with them and get it over with."

"No, Pa—"

She placed her fingers on my lips. "Ayperos is right, Nathan. You can't fight them all." She sounded defeated, and it scared the hell out of me.

This was unacceptable. I took her shoulders in my hands, feeling every muscle in my body tightened. I may not be able to fight all of them, but I'd be damned if I would sacrifice Paige's safety because of it.

"Listen to me," I said, my voice hard with desperation. "I may not be able to fight every single one of them, but if we're cautious and use our wits, we can find the incantations and end this." She didn't look convinced, so I continued. "Paige, please don't give into them. Instead, believe in *us,* and know we'll get through this."

She laid a hand over my racing heart and with some hesitation, met my gaze. "I believe in us," she said, and though I felt relieved to hear her say those four words, the dreadful feeling I had earlier reemerged.

Paige's pocket vibrated. She pulled out her cell phone and read the message. It was Tree telling her they were getting ready for Carrie's procedure, and the doctor said it wouldn't take long to do. Paige texted him back telling him we'd be right there.

"Carrie is going to be upset," she said as we entered the hospital lobby. "The doctor has to shave a small section of her head to do the procedure, and she's not going to be happy about it." She tried to smile but couldn't and bit her bottom lip instead.

"Paige!" a familiar voice called when we turned down a hall leading to the waiting room.

We stopped and watched Brayden hurry toward us. His face was red and blotchy, worry shadowing it. Paige released my hand and stepped into Brayden's outstretched arms. I stood there while they hugged, wondering if I should give them a moment to console each other about Carrie's misfortunate circumstances. When I turned to leave, I caught Brayden's eyes looking up from Paige's shoulder with a gloating expression on his face. I knew then he decided to stick to his previous threat:

"Paige and I were destined to be together. She may not realize it, or maybe she doesn't want to admit it to herself, but one day she will, and when she does, she'll be in my arms instead of yours," he had said, adding, *"I'm going to do what I can to get her to realize it."*

I had hoped he'd changed his mind in trying to manipulate Paige's feelings for him to gain her favor but apparently not. His gloves were on, so I mentally reached for mine. Drawing myself up, I squared my shoulders. If Paige wanted to be with him, I'd step aside. However, I wouldn't allow Brayden to toy with her emotions to get want he wanted. His deplorable behavior disgusted me, using this fragile time to try and benefit from it. His moral compass seemed to me to be cracked beyond repair.

"Where's your girlfriend Cassie?" I asked, knowing Cassondra wouldn't dare set foot in this town after I had snapped her neck. Maybe one day she'd have the nerve to face me, but not now, not after what she'd done.

Paige released Brayden and shoved him back. I couldn't help but smirk at the stunned look on his face. I knew it was juvenile for me to take pleasure in it. But I also knew if I were to tell Paige about Brayden's devious plan, it would be another added problem to her list of things to worry about. I wouldn't do that to her and would deal with Brayden's self-centered, tenacious behavior starting right now.

Chapter Six

Paige

"I can't believe you're hanging around her after what she'd done to me," I said to Brayden, shoving him in the chest. He stumbled backwards, tripping over his feet. He latched onto an empty meal cart standing beside the wall, trying to steady himself, not realizing it had wheels. His feet flew out from under him, and his butt smacked the linoleum floor, the cart toppling with a loud bang. Nathan howled with laughter. I bent over, clutching my stomach, busting a gut.

Brayden and I had been BFFs since we were kids, and we dated on a steady basis the first two years of high school. I was totally crushed when he moved to California, and I didn't really get over it until I met Nathan six months ago. I remember when I first saw him, something fluttered in my chest, and we instantly connected. I never had taken much stock in the whole soulmate thing, and I still remained skeptical about it; however, I couldn't deny the magnetic energy between us. I didn't fall instantly in love with him, and it wasn't sexual energy either, although he was frickin' hot.

Anyway, when my mom died, Brayden went to the funeral, and when he discovered my relationship with Nathan, it pissed him off. I later tried to explain to him I wasn't infatuated with Nathan, that we had a deep bond. Brayden wouldn't listen, though, because he believed we were meant for each other. Then to my complete surprise, he was marked for immortality as well, which cemented his belief we were destined to be as one because how weird was that, right? Two people who grew up together being marked for immortality.

But still, I told Brayden I belonged with Nathan and not him. Brayden of course wouldn't accept it and still believed one day we'd be a couple again.

So now I was annoyed because if he cared so damn much about me, why in the hell was he canoodling with Cassondra in Seattle? Brayden knew she had set Nathan and me up so I would see her kiss Nathan and believe he was cheating on me. She even fed half-truths to Brayden about her and Nathan's relationship back in the 1800s, just so he would tell me, and I'd believe her whole charade. Yet Brayden still remained her friend? I felt betrayed by it and deeply hurt. Laughing at him felt good, though, because it took away the sting.

"You didn't have to do that." Brayden pushed himself off the floor and righted the cart.

"I guess I don't know my own strength." I shrugged and walked past him.

"Cassie is my mentor, and she's truly sorry for what she did to you," Brayden said.

Biting my lip, I kept walking. *So he calls her Cassie now. How cozy.* That would explain Tree's mom calling her that.

I wanted to lash out at him right then, so he knew exactly how I felt, and he could see my disappointment in him. It seemed like when he became immortal, not only did he lose his humanity but his sense of reasoning as well. I didn't understand or like this side of him, which was the same side that became friends with Anwar and possibly Bael and Ayperos.

What was wrong with him?

The waiting room swelled with Carrie's relatives. I didn't realize how many she had until now. Like me, she was an only child, but she possessed lots of cousins to make up for no sibling. I'd always envied Carrie for her tight-knit family and now getting a good look at how much they loved her, a part of me wanted to weep. I recognized the feeling all too well. Carrie's good fortune in the kinfolk department made me feel sorry for myself.

But when Carrie's six-year-old cousin Molly came running to me with her arms spread wide and a grin on her red lips, the feeling subsided. She jumped up like she always did when she saw me. I lifted her, liking that my immortal strength made it easy. She giggled and wrapped her legs tightly around my waist. "I missed you," she said, looping her arms around my shoulders. She smelled like cherries.

"I missed you, too, my little monkey girl." I tickled her sides, causing her to squirm and laugh. I peeled a lock of her dark hair off her cheek and tucked it behind her ear. "Why is your cheek sticky?"

She bounced in my arms. "Sucker." She stuck her tongue out, and it was a bright crimson color. "Is it red?" she asked, trying to look at it, her brown eyes going cross-eyed.

"Yeah, it is." I used my omigod–how–cool tone of voice. Out the corner of my eye, I could see Nathan smiling at us. "I have a secret to tell you," I said and grinned when her eyes widened. I cupped my hand around her ear and whispered, "I have a boyfriend."

A small squeal escaped her lips, and she turned her head, her nose almost touching mine. I could see the sprinkle of freckles across it, just like Carrie had. "You do?" she whispered in awe.

I nodded and placed my mouth next to her ear. She was totally eating this up, and I could hear Nathan softly laughing. "I really love him, too."

Molly pressed her lips against my own ear. "Are you going to marry him?" Her hot breath tickled my ear, making me jerk my head back and giggle.

I didn't want to answer her because honestly with the way things were going, my future with Nathan looked grim. My heart twisted at the very thought, and I mentally shook myself, shutting off those painful emotions.

"Do you want to meet him?" I asked, dodging her question.

She grinned and nodded.

Nathan stepped beside me, and I introduced them. He offered his hand to Molly. "Please to meet you," he said when she stuck her tiny hand in his.

"You, too." Molly shook it like a pro and blurted, "Can I be in your wedding?"

"Well, um . . ." I looked away.

"Molly." Carrie's aunt broke free from the circle of family conversing with one another, saving me from that awkward moment. "Hi, Paige," she said, flashing me an exhausted smile.

I set Molly on her feet and pushed my hair back. "Hi, Carly." I opened my mouth to introduce her to Nathan, but she took Molly's hand and told her they had to go run some errands.

"Nice to see you again, Paige," Carly said over her shoulder, rushing out the room, pulling Molly along who obviously didn't want to leave.

I blew a kiss to my monkey girl who kept looking back at me with longing in her eyes. She rewarded me with the same gesture, warming my heart.

"Cute kid," Nathan said.

"She is," I agreed. "Carrie and I used to babysit her." I scanned the room for Tree, wondering how he was holding up. "I don't see Tree here."

"He's talking to his mom at the nurses' station," Brayden said behind me. "They're done with the procedure, so the doctor should be explaining the details of her recovery to Carrie's parents in a minute."

"Wow. You're Mr. Informative," I said, facing him. I bounced on my tiptoes when I thought I spotted a familiar person enter the waiting room, craning my neck so I could see over Brayden's shoulder. "Max is here," I announced, gesturing for him to join us.

Max and I have known each other since second grade. I've always thought he was cute with his short black spiky hair, blue eyes, and adorable dimples. This past summer though, he had totally grown into a hot, cute guy. I think his confidence in knowing he wanted to be a chef and what he wanted out of life added to his hotness. I totally envied him for it and the simple life he had.

When he waved to me, a stab of guilt pierced through me. Less than a week ago, Roeick kidnapped me outside Max's dad's restaurant. He knocked me out, and Max caught him in the act. Max attacked him, but since Roeick was a dark spirit possessing a human, and dark spirits added strength to the human they occupied, Max didn't have a fighting chance. Roeick knocked him out as well.

When Max came to, he became frantic, but thankfully Tree and Carrie took care of the situation. At Nathan's suggestion, they told him I'd discovered my father had been murdered, and the guy who kidnapped me had something to do with it. They also told him Nathan found me, beat the crap out of the guy, called the cops, and I was okay.

But now as I watched him coming toward me, I felt bad for not calling him to see how he was doing and to thank him for trying to save me from my captor.

"I'm going to thank Max for what he did the other night," I told Nathan before breaking away from him.

I crossed the room and pulled Max aside. I noticed the dark circles under his eyes, which made me feel even worse. I could sense Nathan and Brayden staring at me. I opened my mouth to thank Max, but he spoke first. "How are you?" He looked equal parts worried and curious.

"I'm fine, thanks," I said with a reassuring smile, but he didn't look convinced. "I've been meaning to thank you for trying to protect me and to apologize for you getting hurt."

"You don't need to apologize," he said. "It wasn't your fault."

"Yeah, but I shouldn't have brought my problems to your doorstep," I said miserably, dropping my gaze to my feet, feeling like crap because truthfully, I did.

"Hey." He rubbed my arm, causing me to lift my eyes to his. "It wasn't your fault," he repeated forcefully, as if he were drilling it into my head.

I didn't say anything, just stared. A small part of me wondered what it would have been like to have dated him. I had no idea he always had a thing for me until the other night. Too bad his shyness had prevented him from asking me out, but then again, if things had worked with him, I wouldn't be with Nathan.

Carrie's dad burst through the door with Tree behind him. "Okay everybody, this is what's going on." I think we all stopped breathing because the room suddenly became silent. My heart even paused. I shot a worried glance at Nathan, our eyes connecting above a sea of heads. He looked concerned, which made me more nervous. Tree beelined his way to me, maneuvering his way through the crowd. He took my hand and squeezed it in Morse Code, telling me so far she's okay. The tightness in my chest loosened a bit while I waited for Carrie's dad to give us the news. He cleared his throat. "The procedure went well," he continued. "However, to protect Carrie's brain from further stress, they induced her into a coma."

"What!" I shouted. Everybody turned and stared at me, at the same time Tree squeezed my hand, telling me to calm down. I ignored him and the hundreds of eyes glued to me. All I could think about was Carrie being stuck in Aosoth's memories and not being able to wake up. I shook when the thought of her never being conscious again consumed me. "You got to get them to wake her."

"I know you're worried. We all are," Carrie's dad said, sounding hoarse. "But being in this coma will relieve the pressure in her cranium and reduce the swelling, allowing her brain to heal. Once she shows improvement, they'll gradually wean her off the barbiturates and out of the coma."

"But how will they know when her brain is healed?" a male voice asked from the group.

"They're going to do an EEG every day. It measures the electrical activity in her brain. They'll also run other tests," Carrie's dad told him.

My body continued to shake after everybody dispersed, but not only from fear, but anger as well. I wondered if Bael had any idea this would happen, and I had the sudden urge to find him. I squeezed Tree's hand, telling him just that. He responded with Bael probably didn't realize the extent of her injuries and knew I wouldn't be looking for the incantations until Carrie was okay. He released my hand when Nathan headed our way.

"I'll catch ya later, Paige," Max said in a low voice next to my ear when he walked past me.

"Okay." I watched him join Brayden, talking to Carrie's uncle as a wave of anxiety pounded through me.

I needed to talk to Nathan about finding a way to help Carrie while she remained in a coma. But I couldn't do it with Brayden's bionic ears around, and since nobody but immediate family could visit Carrie right now, there was no sense in staying.

"I need to get out of here," I said and looked up at Tree. "Do you want to come with us?"

He frowned. "I would, but they're letting me sit by Carrie in a little while. So I'm going to stick around." He swallowed hard, holding back tears.

"Let me know if you find out anything," I said, hugging his waist.

He embraced me. "I will, and you do the same." He pulled back to look at me. The crease between his brown eyes crinkled. I slowly nodded as a silent understanding came between us. Tree and I were in this together, and it was up to us to keep our bargain with Bael. He looked at Nathan. "Take care of my little fairy friend."

Nathan reached for my hand. I took it, and he pulled me to him. "Sure thing."

* * *

"I want to go to your house and do a rite of consciousness inside the circle," I told Nathan when he slid behind the wheel of his pickup. The sun was setting, and wispy clouds were swimming across the salmon colored sky, like a sea monster snaking its way through an ocean of pink lemonade. I sniffed the air and got a strong whiff of leather and rain. The smell of leather immediately whisked me back to my father's jacket.

I loved that aroma, even though it always caused my heart to ache.

"I don't think it's a good idea," Nathan said.

Of course he wouldn't. But I wasn't backing down on this. I had to find out if Carrie was okay, and although I wasn't sure if the rite of consciousness would work, it was worth a try. Besides, Nathan had seven grimoires, and maybe one of them might have some information that would be helpful to me.

"I know you don't," I answered. "But I'm afraid Carrie might be stuck in one of Aosoth's memories, and if I can help her, I'm going to." I could hear the stubborn determination in my voice. I sat up straight and turned to him, my chin raised.

He closed his eyes, shook his head and groaned.

"Look," I told him, "whether you like it or not, I'm going to do this, with or without your help. It's your choice." I wondered what I'd do if he refused to help me. I wouldn't be able to use the hidden room in his house with the pentagram on the floor or his grimoires. I'd have to perform it all on my own, starting from scratch. But I didn't care. All that mattered was making sure Carrie was okay, and I'd jeopardize my safety for that. Nathan knew this because he knew me well and groaned again.

He opened his eyes and the corner of his mouth curled. "God, you're stubborn." He ran a hand through his hair and sighed. "All right." He pulled out of the crowded parking lot and headed to his house.

Chapter Seven

Paige

I sat on the brown couch, watching Nathan pull a grimoire from the cherry wood bookshelf. We were at his house in a hidden room within a hidden room.

On the way here, I'd talked Nathan into stopping at a sandwich shop for subs to take back with us. Every muscle in his body turned to steel as we waited for our sandwiches to be made. I saw why when I noticed the girl assembling them had the same dime size mark on her neck as Carrie. It was a three-dimensional spiral, forming a conch shell–a self-protection mark a mortal received after an immortal cast a dark spirit out. It locked her body from ever having further spiritual possession again.

It surprised me to see somebody who didn't look a day older than fifteen bear that mark. Maybe that's why Nathan was on edge because of her youth, and she wasn't soulless. If I concentrated really hard I could hear her soul's low vibrations. It had a gentle yet chaotic sound, like waves lapping against a harbor wall. It made me sad to know she had a good heart yet issues hampered her life which probably drove her to dabble in the dark arts. But then again, it could have been something else. I didn't know, but whatever it was, I hoped she would work through it and be okay.

Now, as I finished my veggie sub, I shoved all thoughts of the young girl aside and focused on the task at hand. Nathan owned seven grimoires he'd collected over the years and knew what each one entailed. The one he chose for me was the only one he thought would be the most helpful in Carrie's situation.

"There's a section in here," he said, fanning the pages to find it, "on dream walking."

"What's dream walking?"

"Here it is." He caught the page with his fingers and sat beside me, placing the book in my lap. "It's when you enter somebody's dream and interact with the person."

I tucked a lock of hair behind my ear and looked at the open pages. They were yellowed from age, and the elegant penmanship looked ancient, scripted with a quill rather than a fountain or ballpoint pen. On the bottom of the page was a carefully hand-drawn picture of a man lying on a bed of straw.

My eyes skimmed the text, hungry for an easy way to accomplish this. Unfortunately, it wasn't what I had hoped for. Of course not. Everything in my life had to be complicated. The text was informative but detailed. In order to dream walk, you had to practice lucid dreaming so you'd be aware you were dreaming. It could take months, possibly years to master, the author stated, but it could be done.

Great. This was going to be much more difficult than I thought. There had to be another way. There just had to be.

I continued to read the grimoire as my mind wheeled through alternatives. Nathan had said Pippins was skilled at the workings of the human mind. I wondered if there was a way he could still help us. "Have you followed up on that lead about Pippins' whereabouts?" I asked.

Nathan pulled his phone out of his pants pocket and rose. "No, but . . ." He trailed off. Caught by his abrupt silence, I looked at him. He stared at his phone with a blank expression on his face. "Damn."

"What?" That didn't sound good.

He sighed. "I was hoping he still resided in Washington."

"And?" I prompted when he fell silent, his eyes drifting to his phone again.

He frowned. "He's in England."

I had the sudden urge to scream but balled my hands into fists instead, willing myself not to. All I could think about was why couldn't we get a frickin' break? Pippins was our only hope to wipe Aosoth's memories from Carrie's mind. I knew he couldn't help us while she was in a coma, but still. Unless–

"Do you think Pippins could tell us what to do over the phone?"

Nathan thumbed through his messages. He paused on one. "How could I have missed these last two?" he mumbled to himself. "I had the phone in my pocket the whole time. You'd think I would have felt or heard it vibrating."

"Who are they from?" My stomach clenched. *Please don't be more bad news.* He smiled, and my heart skipped.

"They're from Pip. He wants me to get online so we can video chat." Nathan moved to his desk and opened his laptop.

"Are you serious?" I'd never chatted by video before and had no idea Nathan knew how.

"Have you ever done this?" I set the grimoire aside to watch him, thinking maybe Pippins could help us after all. Things were definitely looking up now, and I could feel the excitement bubbling inside me.

"Plenty of times," Nathan answered, flashing me a heart stopping smile. "I'm surprised Pip even owns a computer since he's an old school type of guy." He sat and clicked on his Skype account. I watched as he entered Pippins into his contact list.

"Is his real name Pippins?"

Nathan shook his head and laughed. "No. It's his middle name. His birth name is actually Cornelius." He glanced at me, his dark blue eyes twinkling. "But don't ever call him that. He loathes his name."

I smiled, feeling in good spirits. "You should ask him if he needs T.P. for his bunghole."

Nathan stared at me, completely clueless.

"Omigod. Haven't you ever watched *Beavis and Butt-Head*?"

The corner of his mouth lifted, and he shook his head.

I rolled my eyes. "Never mind," I said when he turned his attention back to the computer.

He entered Pippins' information and then just like that, Pippins popped onscreen.

"Nathan," he said. "How the bloody hell are you, old chap?" Pippins looked like he could be in his mid-twenties. His dishwater blond hair disheveled, framing a scholarly type of face. I imagined if he were still mortal, he'd be wearing wire spectacles.

"Hello, Pip. I'm sorry to cut to the chase, but I need your help," Nathan said.

"Of course, dear boy, but may I ask who this little bird is behind you?"

Little bird?

"Oh, excuse me. This is Paige, my girlfriend." Nathan reached around and pulled me onto his lap. I'd never heard him call me his girlfriend before, but I liked it. A lot.

"Hi, Pippins," I said with a little wave.

"Hiya there, Paige." He smiled and winked. "Now, what can I help you two with?"

"My best friend has some horrible memories that need to be wiped out, but the thing is she's in a coma."

"Oh, my." The corner of Pippins' mouth pulled down.

"I'm afraid she's trapped in those memories," I continued. "Can you tell me what to do so I can help her? I read about dream walking. Is it possible for me to do it?" I realized I was rambling, but my sudden anxiety overwhelmed me. I had to know if Carrie was okay and help her if I could. Right now that was the most important thing to me. Screw the incantations. They could wait, whereas Carrie couldn't. For all I knew she could be stuck in Hell.

Pippins wiped a hand across his face and ran his fingers through his hair. "The human mind is tricky and complex." He sighed. "But it is possible to enter other people's dreams. However, it takes considerable discipline and practice to accomplish."

"But I don't have time," I said, hearing the panic in my voice.

"Okay, love. I need to know more about you and what you're capable of."

Nathan and I both told him everything we could about me. Of course we didn't tell him about Solomon's power residing inside me or that I could communicate with animals or about the incantations. We did tell him about me performing the rite of consciousness but were vague with the details. When we mentioned it, Pip's doubtful mood shifted to a perky one. A hopeful excitement surged through me, causing my heart to race.

"Crikey, Paige, I think you can bloody hell sort it," he said. "The rite of consciousness is your ticket in."

"Are you serious?" I almost couldn't believe it. Finally, we got a break.

I thought it would be complicated, and we were going to have to take notes or have him stay online and guide me through it, but I was wrong. Pippins told me all I had to do was think about Carrie as I executed the rite of consciousness. Also, I had to be in a place where there were no disturbances and orchestrate it within a sacred circle with four candles representing the four corners. It was for protection, he told us, in case I encountered some *dodgy* spirits.

"How do you know Carrie is in the spiritual realm?" I asked, thinking about what my grandmother had told me, my blood running cold.

What if Carrie's astral body had withdrawn from her physical one? What if she was trapped on the etheric level in the dark region where the dark spirits roamed? This could be worse than I thought.

"Of course she's in the spiritual realm, love." He said it as if I should have known that, like, duh, bacon comes from pigs. I knew he wasn't being rude because he sounded more surprised than sarcastic. "And since her conscious mind is shut down, you can assist her into eradicating those awful memories."

"But how? I don't understand." The panic rose in my voice again. Nathan wrapped his arms around me. "How could she have had nightmares from those memories yet be in the spiritual realm? I didn't think our spirits disconnected from our bodies every night."

He held up his hand. "We go through five cycles a night. During REM there is a high level of brain activity. This stage is associated with dreaming. The thalamus and the cerebral cortex are responsible for most thought processes."

I squirmed against Nathan, feeling anxious and restless. I hope Pippins wasn't going to seriously lecture us on the mechanics of the brain and why we sleep. I didn't give a flying flip about it. I just needed a clear, short answer, so I could get on with this. Thank God Nathan was on the same page as me.

"You sleep so your body can repair and go through detoxify–"

"Pip," Nathan said. "I don't mean to be rude, but isn't there an easier way to answer Paige's question without getting into a detailed, scientific explanation?"

I noticed Pippins' cheeks coloring. "Right," he said. "My apologies." He touched his fist to his mouth and cleared his throat. "Simply put, you experience both while you're asleep but not simultaneously."

"Okay, but what happens if Carrie isn't in the spiritual realm?" *If I can even get there*, I thought.

I'd only done the rite of consciousness twice. The first time I failed, and the second time I somehow ended up observing a secret meeting the dark spirits were having, which might had been a fluke. But then I remembered my grandmother telling me I had the ability to unlock the door to the spiritual realms connected to this one. So maybe I could pull it off.

He leaned forward and narrowed his eyes. "You call to her and her spirit will respond. Once she does, it'll be up to you to guide her through the process of plucking those unwanted memories." He went on to explain the steps, warning me of potential danger of unforeseen events that might occur. But despite his caveat, he seemed rather optimistic about it, stating since Carrie would be interacting with me on a subconscious level instead of a conscious one, it would make it a lot easier to tap into those memories.

After Nathan and I thanked him and said our goodbyes, promising to pay him a visit when we were in England and to let him know how things went, Nathan started gathering candles. I rolled the rug over to the couch, unveiling a black pentagram painted on the concrete floor. There were cool markings inside the points of the star that looked like ancient Rune symbols.

Nathan placed the four candles where they were supposed to be around the circle. The green one representing earth, he placed on the north side of the circle. The yellow one standing for air went on the east. The red one depicting fire went on the south, and the blue candle symbolizing water went on the west. He then filled a small copper bowl with salt.

"You're going to have to incorporate the rite of consciousness ritual with invoking this pentagram," Nathan told me, pulling his Athame from a wooden trunk that looked like it belonged on a pirate's ship. The artificial light in the room glanced off the silver blade when he handed it to me. My fingers tingled as soon as the knife touched it. "I have some of the incense you made out of sandalwood, cypress, and pine resin. You'll need to burn them to increase your psychic powers." He dug into the trunk and pulled out a small wooden box. "Here are the incense and matches." He set them outside the circle and closed the trunk.

Looking at all this stuff made my stomach churn. I had no idea how to conduct this ritual, and as I watched Nathan fluttering around, knowing the exact procedure, my confidence dwindled.

"How am I going to know what to do?" I asked, rubbing my thumb over the smooth black handle of the Athame.

Nathan handed me a black book with a pentagram etched into the cover. "This *Book of Shadows* shows you how."

I set the Athame on the couch and flipped open the book. Sure enough, the instructions were there. I read through them a few times while Nathan finished his sandwich. I realized we were lacking some things mentioned in this book and how methodical it was going to be to cast a circle. I wondered if there was a quicker way, so I asked Nathan.

"Considering your abilities and circumstances, I think there is." He finished his Coke and placed the paper cup in the plastic bag our subs came in. "But you need to follow your instincts and perform this ritual by what feels right to you."

Great. Just what I want to hear.

He pulled me into his arms. I sighed against his chest, curling my arms around his waist. But then I pulled back when I realized he hadn't mentioned taking part in any of this. I thought at least he'd help me with casting a circle. "Wait a minute. Aren't you going to help?" I didn't like the idea of me going through this on my own. I mean, what if I totally screwed up? Maybe I should have taken notes when Pip verbally illustrated the tasks to follow in order to help Carrie. No. Nathan was my safety blanket, and I needed him here.

He gently pushed my hair off my shoulder, then cupped my face in his strong hands. "This is something you need to experience on your own. Your love for Carrie, and the bond you share is what will bring you strength and will aid you on this journey."

"But–" I wanted to say there had to be a way, but he placed his finger on my lips.

"I'm not going to abandon you." It was a fierce promise that made my stomach flip. "I'm going to leave you in here to cast the circle and do your magic. In the meantime, I'm going to fall asleep on a mat outside this room."

I gave him a funny look. How could he sleep at a time like this? Why would he?

"This room is soundproof, so feel free to be as loud as you want. I won't hear a thing." Still cradling my face, he softly kissed my lips. "I'm going to sleep because if you need help, all you'll have to do is think about me, and I'll be there."

"How do you know if it'll work?" I asked, hearing the doubt in my voice.

"To be honest, I don't," he admitted. "But with you being a skeleton key, I'm betting on you."

"And if it doesn't?"

"Here's the thing, Paige," he said. "I'm giving you two hours. If you're not awake by then, I'm waking you up. I'm going to call Tree to inform him about what's going down. I'll tell him to call me at a certain time to make sure I don't sleep over our allotted timeframe." I must have had a scared, nervous look on my face because his arms went back around me. "I wish I could be there with you, and it kills me I can't. Just remember though, love is the most powerful thing in the universe. It's why you're here . . . I believe in you."

It was funny. Not ha, ha, funny, but weirdly funny. A few weeks ago, I'd longed to hear those words from Nathan, but now I wished he were back to the way he used to be—at least at this moment. His belief in me meant a lot, but honestly, I wasn't sure if I believed in myself enough to take this leap. However, I had no choice because Carrie might be suffering right now, and I'd be damned if I was going to chicken out. Besides, what was the worst that could happen?

Um, well, I didn't really know and that was the root of the problem right there. I didn't know.

Silently, I instructed myself not to think or dwell on it and began a mantra, telling myself I could do this.

I had to believe it.

I had to believe in myself because I might be Carrie's only hope.

Chapter Eight

Paige

After Nathan gave me a passionate kiss that made me weak in the knees and then left the room, I sat on the couch and went back over the instructions in the *Book of Shadows*. I didn't really have to because when I looked at it earlier, my immortal mind had already absorbed all the information I needed. But I did it anyway—for comfort I think. Or maybe I was stalling. Taking a deep breath, I set the book down. Nathan had given me only two hours to do this, so I'd better get on it.

I stepped into the circle and immediately felt a change in temperature. It was much warmer inside this barrier, and I felt at peace, like I had the last time I sat inside it.

Weird, but cool.

I lit the candles, welcoming each element as I did so. After I dipped the point of the Athame into the bowl of salt, I raised it in front of me and said, "Let all malignity and hindrance be cast aside, and let all good enter herein. I bless thee that thou aides me, in the names of Cernunos and Aradia." Pointing the tip of the knife down, from north back to north, I went around the perimeter. "I conjure thee oh circle of power that thou be a place of love and truth, a shield against wickedness and evil, and a boundary between the world of men and the realms of the mighty ones. I bless thee and consecrate thee in the names of Cernunos and Aradia."

I set the Athame down, lit the incense sticks that were in an ornately carved holder and waved it in the air, the thick smell of sandalwood engulfing me. Afterwards, I picked up the shiny copper bowl, pinched the granules between my forefinger and thumb and then scattered salt from east back to east again. When I finished, I faced that direction with the Athame back in my hand and raised it. Making a sign of a star in the air before me, I said in a commanding voice, "Ye Lords of the Watchtowers of the east. Ye Lords of air. I do summon, stir, and call ye up to guard my circle." Turning to the south, then west, I did the same routine as the first, except I used the element representing each one: fire for south and water for west. When I reached north, again I made the sign of the star before me and said, "Ye Lords of the Watchtowers of the north. Ye Lords of earth. Boreas, thou Guardian of the northern portals. Thou powerful God. I summon, stir, and call ye up to guard my circle. So mote it be." I kissed the tip of the knife before placing it beside the incense on the eastern part of the circle.

The candles flickered and danced around in their short crystal containers as if a draft sailed through them. The hair on my arms rose when I noticed the incense smoke twisting and whipping around the edges of the barrier. Taking another deep breath, I sat in the middle, lotus style and closed my eyes, concentrating on turning the lights off. Half a minute later, an instant buzz of energy swirled through me when the shadow behind my eyelids grew darker. I knew then the lights went out, and the high I was feeling came from its energy that transferred into me.

Crap.

Maybe I shouldn't have done that because I might be too wired to go into a meditative state.

Sighing, I lifted my hair off my shoulders. I had to at least try and subdue this wiry energy because I didn't have much time. I switched positions, deciding to lie on my back and took deep, cleansing breaths. In through the nose. Out the mouth. Eyes closed. In through the nose. Out the mouth.

Slow.

Calm.

Breaths.

One by one, I concentrated on relaxing each part of my limbs while slowly breathing. The incense entombed my body in its thick, heady aroma, lending assistance in the unseen layer of transcendence.

As each muscle relaxed, the energy inside me became docile, cuing me to focus on Carrie and nothing else.

My mind flipped through memories of her like flash cards, daring to be recognized and answered by Carrie herself. It called to her, and at the same time I realized I could no longer feel my body. I sat up and looked around. The circle around the pentagram was glowing a beautiful lavender color.

Huh.

The candles were still flickering, the incense still burning. I rose, thinking, okay cool, some magic was going on here. Awesome. At least I'd accomplished casting a circle and providing protection from outside malevolent forces. But now what? Then, something at the edge of my vision caught my attention. I turned, my gaze moving to the figure on the floor.

Holy crap!

The figure was me!

What the hell?

As soon as the realization came that I was out of my body and in the spiritual realm, I immediately thought of Carrie, knowing I had to reach her before my two hours were up.

The walls began to spin, briefly showing different landscapes: a meadow like the one I'd seen before my grandmother left me, a village nestled among emerald green hills, houses with thatched roofs, horses running wild in a vast prairie shimmering in gold, a coliseum much like the one in Rome but new and constructed out of white marble.

"Carrie!" I yelled when the scenery wouldn't stop. "Where are you?"

The spinning reversed, then accelerated at a rapid pace. Globs of gray and black colors and an occasional bolt of lightning whipped around me. Finally, it stopped, and my stomach lurched at the dismal scenery it now displayed.

The dark, clear sky shined and glistened, reminding me of black ice. A dirt road led to a town that appeared abandoned, and there were fires burning inside large trash cans along the side of the trail.

I closed my eyes. "Carrie," I whispered, calling up a wonderful memory from our childhood of us playing in our tree house, seeing it in my mind. A cool breeze swept across my arms, raising goosebumps. How I could feel this in my spiritual form, I didn't know. All I could figure was because I remained attached to my body, I somehow could experience it.

When I opened my eyes, I gasped. Before me stood a shabby wooden building. Orange light flickered behind the cracked, smudged windows, and I could hear somebody softly crying on the other side of a crooked plank door. My heart squeezed at the heartbreaking sound.

"Carrie?" I rushed through the door. A pungent, sour smell slapped me in the face and lodged in my throat. Covering my mouth and nose with my hand, I looked about. It was a small room crusted in dirt and garbage. The fractured windows had streaks caked with some type of black residue, and the candles standing on broken shelves flickered wildly, casting eerie, ghostly shadows. Something rolled across the room. It sounded like glass. It knocked against my foot. I looked down, baffled. It was a clear, amber bottle.

The crying that was coming from the back room turned to whimpering. I hurried down the short hall, my feet crunching broken glass. Along the walls hung grimy fluted glass containers housing lit candles. The flames blinked at me compulsively, shedding a tunnel of pale light.

"Carrie?"

I entered a room, immediately taken aback. It looked exactly like Carrie's bedroom, except for the round, wooden medieval looking type doors. There must have been at least a dozen of them looming around the walls, daring to be opened.

Then I saw her.

She was in a fetal position in the center of her bed, still whimpering with her arms around her head.

I went to her and gently shook her arm. "Carrie. It's Paige."

"Paige?" She looked up, tears streaming down her face. I thought I was going to bawl right there but was able to swallow back the sorrow. "Omigod! Are you really here?" She sat up and threw her arms around me. "It is you." She shook from the sobs wracking her body.

"Shhhh. It's okay. I'm here to help you." I rocked her, holding her tight.

She released me and clutched her head with both hands, a painful expression held on her face. "But how?" she managed to say.

"The rite of consciousness and casting a circle, but I don't–" I paused, watching her closely. "What's wrong?"

Her face twisted in agony. "My head hurts really bad," she moaned. "And I don't understand where I am or what's going on. Is this a nightmare I'm stuck in?"

I quickly explained what happened, including the details of the procedure the doctor performed and being induced into a coma. We were both shivering, so I pulled her brown and pink butterfly comforter over us. To my surprise, she didn't freak out about her situation. In fact, she admitted to hearing people talking around her but thought she imagined it. She sounded relieved when she told me now she understood she wasn't going nuts.

But then she slung her arms around her head again and cried out in pain. She rested her forehead on the bed and whimpered. I'd never felt so helpless in my entire life. I curled my body over Carrie's, like a soldier shielding a friend from incoming fire.

My mind searched for solutions. Pippins and I hadn't conceived the possibility Carrie would be in too much pain for me to eradicate Aosoth's memories through hypnotic suggestion. So now what was I supposed to do? I had no idea where we were, why Carrie was here, or how much time I had left. All I knew was I had to do something to try to free Carrie from this self-induced hellhole.

Wait a minute.

Self-induced?

Was she creating this experience for some reason? But why would she do that?

I sat up. "Carrie, what were–"

"I can't take this anymore, Paige. I need to get out of here for a while." Carrie hopped off the bed and headed toward one of the wooden doors across the room. She was crying in a way that told me it wasn't out of pain but fear and dread.

I grabbed her arm. "What's behind these doors?"

She looked at me, her face wet with tears. "Aosoth's memories."

Chapter Nine

Paige

At first I couldn't believe those doors led to Aosoth's memories. I mean, how could it be? But then again, glancing around the exact replica of Carrie's bedroom, minus the imposing doors, I guess it could be possible. Regardless, though, I had to express my doubts. "Are you serious?" I eyed Carrie incredulously.

Carrie nodded and turned to the one in front of us. She tried to pull away from me, anxious to reach it.

I tightened my grip on her arm. "Why are you doing this?"

She continued to jerk her arm back, panic filling her voice. "I have to, Paige. It's the only way to stop my head from hurting, and I feel like the walls are pressing in on me. I–I can't breathe." She gasped for air, making sharp sucking noises.

I yanked her to me and took hold of her arms. She curled forward, still gasping.

"Stop it." I pulled her up and held her face in my hands. Despite the chill in the air, her forehead glistened with sweat. "I need to figure out a way to get rid of Aosoth's memories, and you freaking out is not helping the situation." I hated seeing her like this, but truthfully, she was annoying me. I didn't know how much time I had left, and with her spazzing out, I couldn't think straight. The thought I had a minute ago escaped me, and Carrie's behavior was totally stressing me out.

"Please," she begged. "Just for a few minutes." She dropped to her knees and held her head in her hands, crying and hyperventilating.

I sighed, and my breath materialized in a cloud of vapor from the sudden drop in temperature. A distant roaring filled the room, and the trinkets on Carrie's shelves rattled. The rumbling was quickly gaining speed. Pictures flapped against the wall, the trinkets crashing to the floor. The room began to shake, swaying me. Carrie hopped to her feet and grabbed my hand. I was too stunned to resist.

"What's happening?" I asked above the harsh screeching of metal grinding against metal. Her hand felt like an ice cube.

"I think it's a train," she called, wrenching a door open. "But I've never stuck around to find out."

I was still staring off into her room, transfixed on the icicles hanging from the ceiling like a mouth full of pointy sharp teeth ready to chomp, when she pulled me through the door. The icy veil instantly lifted from my body. The familiarity of the warm, dry air brought me back to my senses.

"Oh, no. We got to get out of here." Carrie wheeled around, bumping into me just as I turned to look at our surroundings. She clamped her hands on my shoulders, twisting me the other way, but I broke free and stepped around her.

We were in a concrete warehouse with exposed wooden beams. Two orange tripods stood opposite each other across the room, the bulbs incased in a round, metal half-domed shell, shining bright light about.

But in that moment, those things were irrelevant, along with the forklift next to a stack of wooden boards and the white plastic buckets lined against the far wall. What caught my immediate attention was the young man standing on a scaffold.

"Daddy," I said in a childlike voice.

He looked like he did in the pictures I had: tousled auburn hair and a lean athletic built. He was looking up, and to my surprise, a cigarette dangled out the corner of his mouth, a thin wisp of smoke snaking in the air from its ashen tip. I wondered if Mom ever knew he smoked or if he'd kept it from her.

"C'mon, Paige," Carrie said, her hand encircling my wrist.

For a second, I couldn't understand why Carrie was being so pushy, but then the shock of seeing my father receded, only to bring a tidal wave of gut-wrenching realization. I doubled over, clutching my stomach, remembering these were the last moments of his life, right before Aosoth killed him.

"Daddy!" I yelled. "You need to leave!" My words fell on deaf ears. I blinked away the tears blurring my vision and saw a teenage girl with short, dark choppy hair stepping out of the shadows behind us.

"He can't hear you." Carrie pulled me through the door as I kept screaming for my father to look out. She slammed it shut, and we were back in her room. Bright lights were rapidly flashing like a strobe, making our movements appear slow and distorted.

"Stop!" I yelled, wanting to go through the door I just came from, but the roaring was so loud now Carrie couldn't hear me. I tried pulling her in that direction but became suddenly exhausted and too weak to break her grip.

The floor began teeter tottering, and I stumbled behind Carrie as she pulled me through another door.

"You're rotten to the core," a haggard-looking woman said. The permanent frown lines that etched her pallid face deepened. Her black hair was pulled into a tight bun, and her dark skirt swallowed her feet, brushing the floor.

Like a vulture leaning over its prey, she was bent above a child who sat in a corner of what appeared to be a garden tool shed. The little girl hugged her knees to her chest, her blue eyes peeking out of a mass of bushy, dirty blonde hair. Thin rays of light streamed through the cracks of the wooden shed, casting soft light around them. The little girl's long white skirt was splattered with mud, her black boots caked in it.

"I am not, Auntie," the girl mumbled into her knees.

Her aunt leaned farther, hands on her hips. "What did you say?"

I looked at Carrie. She was staring at this hideous woman, a glaze of fearful intimidation plastered on her face. I took her hand and squeezed it, getting prepared to drag her back through the door, but then the girl spoke, and I hesitated.

"I am not!" she said, jumping to her feet, her small hands balled into fists.

The woman snatched the girl from beneath her armpit, her nails digging into flesh. She shook her and peered into her face. "How dare you speak to me in that manner!" She raised her hand and drove it down across the child's round cheek.

Carrie's head jerked to the side at the same time the girl's did, and a whimpering sound came out of both of them. A bright red handprint rose against Carrie's cheek, just like the little girl's. I realized then I had to get Carrie out of there and headed toward the door with her in tow.

"You're a rotten, wicked child, spawn from the Devil himself, Elizabeth. The moment you came out of my sister's loins and killed her, I knew then what a vile creature you were." She pushed the girl down, and Carrie fell backward, pulling me with her. I tripped and landed beside her on my hands and knees.

Pushing myself from the floor and wiping off mulch, I removed Carrie's hand from her face and pulled her up. A dark shadow caught my eyes. It slithered across the floor toward the girl whose face was buried in her hands. My heart pounded in response to the dark energy stewing in the air, and I raced to the door before it consumed Carrie as I knew it would Aosoth who was once that small girl.

When we stepped back into Carrie's room, I was relieved to find it in perfect order and silent, though a chill still hung in the air. I sat a dazed Carrie on her bed and examined her cheek. It looked fine. There wasn't a red mark. I held her chin gently and fixed my eyes on hers. She stared blankly past me.

Why was she acting this way?

What was wrong with her?

"Carrie." She didn't move or glance away. I waved a hand in front of her face. Nothing. "Carrie," I said louder, snapping my fingers next to her ear. She blinked and looked at me.

Thank God.

But then confusion clouded her eyes. She jerked away and lifted her legs on the bed, crawling crab-like across it.

"Carrie?"

"Who are you?" she demanded, sliding off the mattress.

"It's Paige."

"I don't know you. Get away from me."

"Huh?" What the hell was going on? Then something clicked inside my head, but before I could fully process the situation, I blurted Aosoth's birth name. "Elizabeth."

Carrie had a pewter candlestick raised above her head, poised to throw at me. She lowered it when I said that name.

"How do you know my name?"

Thinking on my feet, I said, "My mother was the midwife who delivered you. She told me what a beautiful baby you were, so I thought I'd meet you in person." I gave her a pleasant smile, hoping she'd fall for it, while the other part of my brain tried to figure out how to wipe Aosoth's memories from Carrie's mind. I almost felt like calling out Nathan's name to see if it would bring him here. I could use his help; however, using him as a crutch didn't appeal to me even in this precarious situation. I had to find a way to help Carrie on my own and stop relying on Nathan all the time.

"Oh," she said, her eyes filling with tears. "Did your mother ever mention I killed my own mother?"

"It wasn't your fault," I gently said. "A lot of women die giving birth. It's a risk they're willing to take in order to have children."

For a second, her hard expression broke into a heart shattering, wanting-to-truly-believe-me kind of look. But then Carrie violently shook her head, her shoulder length hair whipping her face. Dark, snakelike shadows slithered up the wall behind her onto the ceiling, dangling from it. A deep, guttural growl that sounded more beastly than human reverberated in her chest, sending chills across my body. When she raised her hands above her head, her fingers stretching for the creepy shadows, I threw myself across the bed and knocked her away. She stumbled a couple steps back, then charged at me, the brown pigment in her eyes gone colorless.

"I'll kill you, too," she said, growling. In a quick gesture, she skirted the bedframe, coming toward me. I tried to dodge her, but she was too fast. It was like she was the one with the immortal powers, and I became the helpless mortal here. "You deserve it for feeding me filthy lies."

"Please. Carrie . . . I mean, Elizabeth. I wouldn't lie to you," I said when she shoved me against the door I came in.

I slid to the floor, feeling the same earlier exhaustion. I tried kicking her feet out from under her, but my legs were too weak. She grabbed a fistful of my hair and yanked me up, bringing tears to my eyes. Pinning me to the door, her hands encircled my neck, choking me. Her top lip curled, baring her teeth, and her colorless eyes held a lunatic's smile. The room swam across my vision where every few seconds blackness obstructed my sight. I thought this was it. I failed Carrie, and she may be lost to us forever because of my ineptness.

But then between flashes, I saw a tall man with a gnome-like face. He had a snow-white beard that went down into a point touching his brown robe. At first, I thought I was seeing things, but the image remained. He held a flaming torch, and when my gaze met his, a word picture popped in my mind. I then knew who he was and what to do.

A jolt of energy sparked through me, and I managed to swing my arms up and down on Carrie's, forcing them from my neck. I darted to her right and caught the flaming torch Boreas tossed to me, his image vanishing when he released it. I swung the torch wide, the flame striking Carrie's chest. Screeching, she jumped back. I paused, waiting for her to advance on me, but she shook her head instead, blinking, the brown returning to her eyes. The tightness around her mouth loosened. The maliciousness carved into her features cracked like pottery being heated too fast, causing it to shatter.

"Paige?" Carrie said in a small voice. "How did we get back here?" Her eyebrows knitted. "I don't remember . . . " She trailed off.

"It doesn't matter." I moved to the first door leading to Aosoth's memories, setting it on fire with the torch. In a whoosh, the orange flames shot up, engulfing it. I moved to the next door and did the same.

Carrie ran to me. "What are you doing?"

"I'm getting rid of Aosoth's memories from your mind." I continued the process, eager to burn every last flippin' one. My heart pounded from the adrenaline rushing through my system. I didn't know how much time I had left, so I moved as fast as I could, ignoring the black smoke clouding the air.

"How do you know it's going to work?" Carrie asked between coughs.

I lit the last one and snatched her arm. "Trust me. It will."

Carrie covered her mouth and went into a coughing fit. I glanced at her and saw panic in her watery eyes. She stared at the half circle of fire that reminded me of an angry frown. The smoke stirred around us, thick and heavy. Waves of smothering heat stretched across the room like groping fingers reaching for whatever it could possess.

"C'mon," I said, leading her to the door I'd entered through. She stumbled behind me, then dropped to the floor, halting me.

"I-I can't go any farther." She covered her mouth and coughed violently.

"Yes, you can," I said through gritted teeth, yanking her arm up with my free hand. "This is *your* mind. You don't have to be feeling this way. Why do you think I'm not hacking up a lung? Damn it, Carrie. Help me." She was dead weight, and her lack of effort to rise to her feet made it impossible to pull her up. I longed for my immortal strength.

"I'm tired, and my head is killing me again," she complained, trying not to gag. "Just leave me here." She lifted the collar of her T-shirt over her mouth and lay down.

I couldn't believe it. Did she really think I'd leave her here? Didn't she realize if I did, she'd never recover from her accident?

"You've got to be kidding me." I let out a disgusted laugh. When she didn't respond or move, I kicked her foot and grabbed her ankle. "Fine. I'll drag your ass out, then."

"Stop it, Paige." She tried to kick me. Reflexively, I brought the torch down on her kicking foot. "Ow." She drew it back and at the same time I dropped her other foot and opened the door. She scrambled backward, but I caught her ankle and dragged her out the room. She reached for the frame, but the door slammed shut before she could touch it. I stepped over her and lit the portal like the other ones. When I turned around, Carrie was on her feet. She took my hand, and we half ran out the building. "Burn it!" she yelled.

I threw the torch inside the structure, and we rushed to the road, watching it go up in flames. Carrie jumped up and down, clapping, making gleeful sounds. She threw her arms around my shoulders. "It worked. Thank you so much, Paige."

I hugged her back, laughing from relief, knowing she'd be okay. But then a disturbing thought entered my mind.

What would happen to her now?

I released her and stepped back. I didn't want Carrie to linger in this dreary, depressing place. If the stupid doctors hadn't induced her coma, I bet she'd be able to wake up this minute. Deep down, though, I knew they had done the right thing because her brain needed to heal from the trauma it sustained. However, I still didn't feel comfortable with her staying here.

I looked up at the sparks of burning wood hurling through the air, raining down, leaving tracers in the black sky. The blazing building crackled and popped as it collapsed, making a pit of fire. Instinctively, we moved to the other side of the road, leaving a huge gap between us and the pyre. I wondered if there was anything I could do to make sure Carrie would be okay until the time came when she could wake up. I also wondered where we were.

Crap.

What if this place resided next to where the dark spirits lingered? If that was true, Carrie needed to stay here in one of the other buildings because if she were to wander off, she might stumble into their territory.

"Carrie, we need to—"

"Paige, look." She pointed to the end of the street where two figures emerged from a wall of fog that wasn't there a minute ago. At first, their images were fuzzy, but I could tell they were holding hands. I looped my arm through Carrie's, determined not to let go unless it was in her best interest. "Omigod. It's your parents," Carrie gasped at the same time a weird, choking sound escaped my lips when their figures became clearer to us. "What are they doing here?"

The overwhelming joy I felt in that moment rendered me speechless. My body jerked forward, wanting to run to them, until a frightening thought exploded in my mind, overshadowing the rest. I tightened my hold on Carrie.

She looked at me, confused. "What's wrong? Why aren't you going to them?"

I straightened my back, hoping to God Nathan doesn't wake me up yet. "Because they might want to take you with them, which means you're going to die in the coma."

Chapter Ten

Nathan

I bolted upright when I heard the loud ringing next to my head. My mind snapped to attention, swiping the normal bleariness aside like a hand waving away a swarm of pesky gnats.

"Hello." Despite the rush of adrenaline, my voice sounded groggy.

"Nathan, it's time to get up," Tree said. I caught the nervous hitch in his tone, and my heart hammered against my chest. "Is Paige awake?"

My eyes strayed to the closed door leading to the room she was in. Running a hand through my hair, I stood and moved toward it. "No, she's not. Is everything okay? How's Carrie?"

"Carrie is fine now." Tree paused and took a deep, unsteady breath. "But she wasn't a half hour ago. We-we . . . I think we almost lost her."

"But she's better, right?" I had to know for certain Carrie was okay to set my mind at ease because it may mean Paige was able to reach her. One could only hope.

"Uh-huh. Yeah. She's stable now and seems to be resting peacefully."

I paused outside the door, intending to end this conversation before I headed in. Feeling a wave of relief, I released the air hovering in my lungs. "Good to hear." I took some deep breaths to calm my heartrate, trying not to entertain dreadful thoughts about what I might discover behind this closed door. Paige and Carrie were both fine, I silently told myself. There was no need to create problems where none may exist.

"It is," he agreed. "But do me a favor and call me after you wake Paige up and find out what happened."

"I will."

After we said a goodbye, I pocketed my cell and entered the room. The smell of incense hung thick in the air, and the flickering candles spit inside their crystal holders, reminding me of the sound of a hissing cat. The hair on the back of my neck rose from the powerful energy floating in the room.

My gaze fell on Paige lying on her back in the center of the circle, glowing a brilliant lilac color. My stomach dropped at how pale and still she appeared. I focused on her heart and breathing. They were both slow and steady. A good sign. Apparently she wasn't in any stress at the moment.

Making a snap decision, I decided to give her a few more moments and stood watching, thinking of Sleeping Beauty–still and beautiful under the witch's spell.

I remembered the first time she'd caught my eyes. I had tracked Bael to Astoria and was observing him from afar when I originally saw him with Paige. I was standing on a balcony to one of the buildings downtown watching Bael–Matt actually–and Carrie hanging around the courthouse square. It was a normal gray and cloudy day, and there was a biting chill to the January air. They were playing hacky sack when Paige emerged from her black Morris Mini and wandered to them.

My breath had caught in my throat when my eyes fell upon her. Never in my life had someone drawn such a reaction from me. All my attention narrowed on her–nothing else existed.

"What is wrong with you?" I had murmured to myself, unfamiliar with the feelings exploding through my body and mind. I tried to look away but couldn't, not understanding why I suddenly felt protective of her and compelled to be in her company. "This is madness." Little did I know at the time she had captured my heart.

For weeks I tried to deny my feelings, telling myself I was bewitched by her beauty and nothing more. I refused to discover where she lived or anything about her family, yet I still kept an eye on her. I became keenly aware how every time I saw her, she inflicted the same reaction out of me as the first time. And when I wasn't watching her, I thought about her. Feeling like a roguish, filthy stalker, I began questioning my sanity.

But then I noticed Bael showing a great interest in Paige, and all my energy became focused on his attentions, all other concerns long forgotten. After a while, when I knew Paige was safe, I tracked down other dark spirits and forced answers from them.

"There's a powerful light inside her some of us can see, and we don't know why," one of them told me before I cast him out of a young man who looked like he belonged in a science lab instead of squatting in an abandoned house preparing to shoot up.

After several more dark spirits mirrored the first one's response, I became nervous and insanely uncomfortable with Paige being around Matt.

Then the night at The Lion's Den happened. I was on the platform watching Paige dancing to techno music. I had leaned forward on the black railing, watching her hips shake in time to the beat, her pleated skirt on her black mini dress sensually slapping her thighs. I couldn't help but imagine my hands on them. And when she raised her arms above her head, revealing a perfect hourglass figure, a fierce desire to have her sprang forth. It was like molten liquid surging through my veins, desires raging in me like an untamed beast. I knew my eyes were bright with desire and kept the hood of my jacket up to conceal my face.

But then I noticed Matt's intense attention on Paige, taking a step closer to her, and I immediately bristled. He leaned forward and then looked up, his eyes glowing.

Oh, shit.

Bael was up to something, and Paige wasn't safe. I had to intervene regardless of the consequences.

Nobody was watching, so I jumped off the platform, over the railing, onto the floor, and ran toward Paige, my heart racing. When I found her passed out on the floor, it took all my self- control not to rip Matt's throat out.

That night completely changed my world in ways I could never have imagined, and now as I stared at Paige's resting body, I became overwhelmed by the endless fountain of love pouring through me for her. I never knew one could feel so much love for another before she had entered my life.

In reflection, I stared at my boots, and when I glanced up, Paige was levitating a foot above the floor, then dropped. I rushed at her, but when my foot touched the circle, the toes of my boot pressed against a hard surface. It was like hitting a brick wall. I was being denied access.

I couldn't believe I hadn't considered the possibility this might happen. Of course the only way I'd be able to enter the circle was if she were to cut an opening for me.

Damn it.

Horrible choking noises sounded from her, sending me into a panic. Her body remained still—arms slack, next to her side, as she continued to choke.

I tried once again to breach the barrier, but the invisible wall wouldn't relent. In frustration, I punched the air, only to have my fist thrown backward. "Paige," I called, hoping it would wake her. Thankfully, she stopped making those horrible strangling sounds, but nothing else changed. "Wake up, Paige!" I yelled.

Nothing.

I could feel the heat in my ears.

I was such an idiot not to think about this. There had to be a way to reach her.

The grimoires.

I made a move toward the bookshelves when a fierce wind blew through the room, skirting the edge of the circle, the candles and incense undisturbed.

I made an attempt to move forward, but stumbled backward from a wall of wind pushing against my chest, pinning me to the door. I could feel a charge of electricity in the air, the tips of my hair sizzling when a thick smell of burning wood blew through me. The wind shifted from clockwise to counter clockwise, the air turning damp and humid. The smell of rain filled my nostrils. I looked up to find the ceiling replaced by gray, heavy moving clouds. Red and blue lightning bolts, continually sparked through them.

Never in my life had I ever experienced such magical wonder. I'd heard of it through ancient tales, but this type of magic died out long ago. When the clouds parted revealing a bright, blue sunny sky, I smelled fresh cut grass and realized this had to be elemental magic. Stunned, I watched in awe until I saw a tall being flickering across the room toward me. At first, I couldn't distinguish whether it was male or female and kept my eyes trained on it.

The warmth of the sunlight felt wonderful on my face and a sense of peace and well-being flowed through me.

The image became solid, his brown eyes meeting mine. I blinked, surprised by the kindness and wealth of knowledge radiating in his eyes. His face reminded me of a goblin with a snow-white pointy beard. He raised his hand, and the bell sleeves from his brown robe fell back, revealing an elongated, wrinkled hand. Still staring at me, he balled his hand into a fist, placed it over his heart, and bowed his head. Without thinking, I returned the gesture, wondering why he honored me with such respect. Instantaneously, I received the answer and knew who he was. I smiled and nodded.

A picture of him tossing a flaming torch to Paige flashed in my mind. I blinked and jerked my head back as more images kept coming. Telepathically, Boreas told me Paige was all right, and she would come back on her own. There was no need to wake her. She was safe. Let her be. Her journey wasn't over yet.

I frowned, not understanding why she wouldn't be done. She accomplished what she had set out to do. Aosoth's memories were erased from Carrie's mind, so what was the delay? Boreas pointed to the walls and vanished. The walls spun. Different types of scenery blurred into one another as if it were fast forwarding from the beginning of time until now. Abruptly the panoramas stopped, and my heart caught in my throat when I saw Paige holding Carrie's arm while Paige's parents approached them.

She felt *so* close.

I stuck my hand out, reaching for her, but it didn't penetrate the scene. I tried walking into it, and oddly enough, I remained in the same spot.

Shifting my gaze back to Paige, I helplessly looked on. Fear slithered into my stomach when I realized what was happening and couldn't stop it.

Chapter Eleven

Paige

"Hello, Paige," Dad said, his green eyes bright and happy.

"You did a wonderful thing here." Mom's eyes shifted to Carrie, then back to me. She sounded proud.

"It's so good to see you two," I said, my voice thick with the tears I tried to hold back. I'd missed my parents more than I could ever say, and to see them now–holding hands–reminded me of a life I could have had if my dad hadn't died when I was four. I bit my lip and held onto Carrie, fighting the urge to release her so I could hug them. But I was determined not to let her go and would fight for her life if my parents were here to help Carrie crossover.

"Hi, Mr. and Mrs. Reed," Carrie said, scooting closer to me so our hips touched.

My dad's gaze moved to my arm tightly looped around Carrie's, then to our faces. His expression remained soft and easygoing. Carrie and I shared a look, not understanding why both my parents seemed so carefree. Considering the current situation, it didn't make sense. Mom must have seen the confusion on our faces because she spoke.

"There's no need to worry, Paige. Carrie's corporal body is going to be fine." When she took a step forward, Carrie and I moved backward in unison. Mom stopped, her shiny brown eyes filled with understanding and love. "Girls, Gordon and I are not here to cause you any grief."

"Your mother is right," Dad said, stepping beside Mom. "We're here to take Carrie to a place where she can rest and recover peacefully from her unfortunate accident."

"I'm not going to die?" Carrie asked, unsure.

"No, darling," Mom said. "You're going to be fine."

Carrie slapped a hand over her heart. "Thank God." She turned to me and smiled. "It's going to be okay. Now you can go back and tell Tree and find those incantations." But then she frowned. "Wait a minute. I don't want you looking for them without me. What if you need my help?"

My mind whirled with everything that happened since I arrived here.

"Paige!"

Huh?

It sounded like Nathan calling my name from behind. I glanced over my shoulder and saw nothing but a deserted town with fire still burning in large metal trash cans along the dirt road. There was an empty lot where the building I'd burned down used to be. The ground was black and smoldering, wisps of smoke rising. I looked at Carrie, my mind finally catching up to what she just said. "I'll be okay," I answered before I could process all the information connected to her question, like making a deal with Bael so she could live.

Crap.

I almost totally forgot about my pact with him and since I couldn't tell anybody about it, I kept my mouth shut.

Carrie eyed me suspiciously, not buying it. "I think I rather help Paige," she declared. "But thanks for coming. It was nice seeing you." There was a finality in her tone, and she made a move to steer me away from my parents.

My dad's voice halted us. "You don't have a choice. Your human body needs more time to heal."

"He's right," I said. "Remember what I told you about the doctor inducing a coma so your brain and body can heal?"

Carrie sighed, not hiding her annoyance. "Yeah, but there's got to be way I can still help."

I shrugged. "Knowing you're going to recover from your injuries and come back to us is a tremendous help." She made a face. I released her arm and playfully shoved it. "I'm serious. Now that I'm sure you're okay, I'll be able to find those damn . . ." I paused and sheepishly glanced at my parents. They had amused looks on their faces. "I mean, *stupid* incantations and destroy them."

"You're going to destroy them?" Dad sounded surprised.

"Why on earth would you do that, honey?" Mom was equally surprised.

Oh, man. How I wished they knew everything that was going on in my world. You'd think once you passed on from your earthly life to the spiritual one, you'd be all-knowing and aware. But no, it didn't work that way. I wondered why, and just like that, I turned the tables on them, bypassing their question. "How come you two didn't already know what I planned on doing?" A fuzzy thought surfaced in my mind about somebody telling me it didn't work that way. Was it grandmother Kora who told me? "You knew about Carrie, so why aren't you aware of everything happening in my life?"

"We don't watch you twenty-four/seven," Dad simply stated.

"We knew about Carrie because we felt the distress you were in," Mom added.

"How does that work?" I asked, intrigued. I never really given it much thought, but how did people in the spiritual realm know when their loved ones on earth were hurting? Like Dad just said, they didn't watch us 24/7, which made sense. I mean, really. They had a life, too.

"We're connected, sweetheart." A warm smile lit Mom's face. She was so pretty. She always had been, but her sadness from the loss of my dad had dulled her looks when she was on earth. But now, here and happy with him, her beauty was vibrant and alive. Deeply touched by how happy she was, knowing how much heartache she endured, I swallowed against the lump forming in my throat. "When something is bothering you," Mom continued, "your father and I can sense it. Sometimes, though, it takes a while to pick up on it."

"Why?" I wondered.

"We have no idea," Dad answered.

"Where are you taking me?" Carrie asked.

"It's a realm where spirits go to get rehabilitated," Dad told her. "Some spirits are taken there to be cleansed, to sleep, reawakened, and be counseled."

Carrie snorted. "I don't need to be *cleansed* or *counseled*." She was clearly insulted, and I stifled a giggle.

"Of course you don't," Mom said. "But spirits also go there to rest and recharge themselves."

"Can I come?" After the words flew out of my mouth, I could have sworn I heard Nathan calling my name again. I glanced over my shoulder, not surprised he wasn't there. Then a thought occurred to me. He might be trying to wake me. I ignored the thought and turned back to my parents, a thrill running through me.

Wide-eyed, Carrie looked at me. "Great idea." She fixed her gaze on my parents. "Can she come with us?"

Mom shared an apprehensive look with my dad.

"I'm not sure, Gordon. What do you think?"

Dad looked at me and shook his head. "You need to go back."

"How come? Why can't I go with you and leave when Carrie recuperates?" I didn't see any harm in it. I mean, what was the big deal anyway? It wasn't like I'd be stuck there. And yeah, Nathan was probably waiting for me, but he could wait a little bit longer. It wasn't like the world would end without me.

Carrie looped her arm back around mine, silently protesting against my dad's decision. The corners of his mouth twitched into a slow smile. Mom crossed her arms and playfully rolled her eyes, half-smiling. "You girls are something else," she said, trying not to laugh. "But you need to listen to your father and go back. I'm sure Nathan is waiting for you and might be beside himself with worry."

My heart squeezed with guilt when she mentioned Nathan. Now that I thought about it, it was selfish of me to make Nathan wait and cause him to worry. Carrie was probably thinking similar thoughts because she untangled her arm from mine and nodded to what Mom said.

"I think your mom is right. You need to return to Nathan now." She pulled me into a hug. "Thank you so much for helping me." I could hear the tears in her voice. I embraced her tighter. "I'm sorry for being a pain-in-the-ass."

"It's okay," the raspy part of my voice cracked. I closed my eyes, willing myself to get a hold on my emotions and felt two warm bodies close in on us. I opened my arms to my parents enfolding theirs around Carrie and me.

"We'll take good care of her," Mom whispered in my ear. "I promise."

Carrie thoughtfully stepped out of our group hug, so the three musketeers (as I always imagined us to be) could say a goodbye.

Goodbye.

I clung to them, not wanting to leave.

Screw the dark spirits. Humans have been dealing with them since like forever. They got along fine without me. Why should I give up my family for them? Was it too much to ask to take a much needed break for myself and spend some time with my parents? I mean, I was already here. It wouldn't be much different from living in a different state than your parents back on earth and taking time off to go visit them, right?

But then a little annoying voice in my head said one name, jolting me out of my mental tangent–*Nathan.*

"I don't want to go back," I said. "I miss and love you two so much."

Dad brushed a lock of hair from my face. "We know, Peanut." When he said my nickname, a short sob escaped my lips, surprising me because I thought I had my emotions under control. He used to call me that when I was a child, and it made my heart ache even more. "But you have a gift and mustn't waste it. It would be tragic for you to ignore it and–"

"Yeah. Yeah. I've been told," I said in frustration, swiping my hand across my cheeks. I was so frickin' tired of hearing the same thing over and over again. "I understand and will keep my promise to you and Mom. *I'll do the best I can do to make things right.*" I sounded like a moody teenager, but I didn't care and released a dramatic sigh for good measure.

Dad chuckled and ruffled up my hair. I suddenly realized this was probably how my life would have been like if he were around when I was growing up.

Wow.

So that was what it felt like to have a father figure in your life. I didn't know whether to cry because there was so much I'd missed or laugh because that simple gesture of messing my hair made me feel like his little girl again. I felt kind of giddy and silly.

I gave all three of them one last hug. Mom took Carrie's and Dad's hand. I watched with envy as they walked in the direction they came from, desperately longing to go with them, wondering when it would be my time to get what I wanted instead of pushing my wants aside so I could do the right thing.

Would I ever be able to live the life I desired with Nathan? The way things were going, it looked downright bleak. I would have to betray Nathan in order to fulfill my agreement with Bael, and Nathan may never forgive me for it. So ironically enough, I may end up where I'd been before Nathan entered my life–alone and with the belief of never having a partner for the rest of my days.

I pushed that miserable thought aside and watched a wall of fog appear in front of my parents and Carrie. A door made out of the same substance swung open. A soft melody reached my ears–part instrumental and part humming. It sounded like a peaceful lullaby. Carrie glanced at me and winked. I waved, resisting the urge to run to her.

The doorway widened, giving me a glimpse of a vast meadow surrounded by a circle of enormous mountains. The mountains were covered in lush, thick emerald grass and tall trees. And the waterfalls cascading down them had prisms of colors dancing along the front. Without pause, they stepped through the door, and as soon as their feet crossed the threshold, a white light sparked, illuminating the entire opening. In a flash, it disappeared, and I stood staring at the vacant road, feeling an unbearable emptiness in my chest.

Turning on my heel, I ran to the nearest empty building, burying my sorrow, visualizing my body lying in the circle instead.

When I entered a two-story wooden building that reminded me of a western salon in a Clint Eastwood movie, I must have missed a gaping hole in front of the entrance, because I dropped into it, freefalling into darkness. A scream bellowed out of me as I flailed my arms in the cold rushing air, groping for something to hold onto. I must have passed out because that was the last thing I could remember.

Chapter Twelve

Paige

My body jerked. The sudden jolt and heavy pressure on my chest had me gasping. I sat up, hearing Nathan anxiously calling my name. Placing a hand over my heart, curling my shoulders forward, I gulped in large quantities of air. Warm air, I noticed, tasting like sandalwood.

Gross.

The thick smell of incense engulfed me, which explained why I could taste it. Disoriented, I kept my eyes closed and concentrated on my breathing, trying to ignore the thumping sound of a racing heart not too far from where I sat. Nathan said my name again. Could this be a dream?

"Paige, can you hear me?"

I heard somebody moving in front of me, but I refused to open my eyes, afraid this might be a dream. Hugging my stomach, I rocked back and forth, humming the lullaby I'd heard before Carrie crossed over.

"Paige. Baby. It's Nathan. Can't you hear me?" Panic and frustration oozed from Nathan's voice, but my concern to put him at ease placed secondary to the soothing feeling the melody I hummed gave me. Besides, I was probably imagining it.

My thoughts were swimming in an eternal ocean of the never-ending story of my life. I could see the ocean–dark blue like Nathan's eyes.

I continued to hum and rock, feeling all floaty, riding on a gentle wave of scattered images. Bit by bit, my thoughts began to form like tiles from a Scrabble game. Words followed, congealing into sentences. It was all coming back to me, every minute detail like individual dust particles hovering before my eyes.

My body became still.

"Paige?"

This can't be a dream, I thought, my mind now sharp and alert. I must have brought my spirit back when I fell into the dark hole. Despite the warm air, I shivered from that memory and at the same time decided to risk opening my eyes to see if I was right.

I smiled when I saw Nathan kneeling before me. The circle was still glowing a brilliant lilac color like it had been earlier.

Nathan hung his head and sighed. When he peeked at me he smiled, relief visible in his eyes. Something in my chest fluttered.

"Are you okay?" he asked in a low and husky tone.

I nodded, my eyes fixed on his. I pushed myself to my knees and crawled to him, but when I leaned forward to kiss him, my forehead touched an invisible barrier.

What the hell?

I lifted my hand and placed my palm on it.

Solid.

I gave Nathan a quizzical look. How was I going to get out of this one? And I had to pee.

"You have to perform the closing ritual," he said.

"Does this normally happen?" I made a sweeping motion with my hand, indicating the glowing circle.

The corner of his mouth lifted. God, he was cute. "No. It's all you." He rose to his feet, picked up the *Book of Shadows* off the couch and moved in front of the incense. "Did you read the instructions on how to carry out the closing ritual?" He opened the book and flipped through the pages.

"No." I pushed my hair off my shoulders and stood. Man, I had to pee. "Now what am I going to do?" I felt a slight irritation toward Nathan. Why hadn't he told me I had to enact a closing ritual? He must have spaced it, I rationalized. With everything going on, that was understandable. The irritation left me as quickly as it came. I raked my fingers through my hair while I waited for his reply.

"Here it is." He placed his thumb in the crease of the book to keep the pages in place. "I'm going to tell you how, and you can recite the closing rites after me." He looked up from the book, and I nodded in response, thankful he'd come up with a plan. "Raise the Athame and face east," he instructed me. I did what he said. "Now repeat after me." He held the book up, leveled with his face. "Ye Lords of the Watchtowers of the east . . . " He paused so I could repeat it, which I did. "Ye Lords of air, I thank you for attending my rites. Ere ye depart to your pleasant and lovely realms, I bid you hail and farewell." He paused, and I repeated it. "Now, draw the banishing pentagram in the air with the tip of the Athame, like this." With his free hand, he motioned from bottom left, then up and to the bottom right, like he was drawing a star. I mimicked him as he did it. He smiled in approval. "Lick your forefinger and thumb and snuff out the east candle," he told me. I did and turned my body to the south like he did.

We repeated the same rites for south, west, and north, the only difference was saying the element they represented, like south for fire, west for water, and north for earth.

As I was closing the ritual, thanking and saying farewell to the Lords of the elements, I swear I could feel the energy leaving the room, and oddly enough, I felt a quiet sadness.

When I turned to the north and thanked and bid a farewell to Boreas, my eyes welled with tears. I couldn't understand why I'd get so emotional. It was silly. But nevertheless, I did. Nathan's eyes flicked up at me from the book. Feeling stupid, I turned to wipe the tears away. I could hear him entering the circle, the warmth of his body closing in on my back like the sun breaking through the clouds, offering its heat to the world. Strong arms wrapped around me from behind. I pressed my back against his chest, welcoming his comfort with a contented sigh.

"Are you okay?" he asked in a low whisper next to my ear, resting his chin on my shoulder.

"I'm perfect now," I breathed.

"I was worried about you," he confessed. "But then Boreas paid me a visit and–"

I twisted around in his arms. "You saw Boreas?" I didn't hide my surprise.

Why had Boreas paid Nathan a visit? For that matter, why did he help me? Not that I was complaining. In fact, I thought it was one of the coolest things ever. I mean, Boreas was the guardian of the northern portal, and to concern himself with us had to mean something, right? Not to mention, I felt a connection with him, like we were comrades or something.

Crazy, I know.

But I couldn't help the way I felt or wonder if Nathan sensed the same thing.

Nathan's fingers slowly trailed down my face to the back of my neck, his eyes following its movement on my skin. My stomach fluttered continuously at his delicate touch, and my breath caught in my throat. His thumbs brushed against my jawline as he cradled my face and peered into my eyes. "Yes, I saw Boreas. He was kind enough to let me know you were all right and showed me what you did to get rid of Carrie's memories."

I gasped. "Are you serious? Did you actually see what happened?"

"I did. Boreas showed me telepathically you holding a torch and burning doors."

"That's right," I confirmed, shifting my weight. "Those doors led to Aosoth's memories. We went through a couple of them. Did you see us?" The memory of my dad standing on the scaffold popped into my head, and I abruptly cut it off, replacing it with the memory of Boreas helping me.

"No. I didn't. I didn't see anything before you had the torch." Nathan tilted his head to the side and had a funny look on his face. "What's wrong? Why are you so antsy?"

"I have to pee," I said. "Is there a bathroom down here?" I hopped from one foot to the next to emphasize how badly I had to go.

He laughed. "Out this room to the right. There's a little alcove at the end where the bathroom is."

"I'll be right back," I said, rushing out the door.

The small bathroom reminded me of a tiny walk-in closet with only a toilet and sink. After I washed my hands and dried them on a burgundy hand towel hanging beside the pedestal sink, I sneaked a peek at myself in the oval mirror above it. My dark green eyes had a look in them I'd never seen before. Perplexed, I blinked and leaned forward, trying to decipher my image. My pupils held a knowing spark with a depth to them that had secrets tucked between the crevices.

I closed them and thumped my forehead with my fingertips. I hated keeping secrets from Nathan. I just hoped I could keep up the facade of him and me going after the incantations. I had no choice though. I had to try. Carrie was going to be okay now, and I had to make sure it stayed that way, and Tree would be safe as well. At least Tree was in on the deal, and as much as I hated him being involved in Bael's sinister plot, I had to admit I was glad I wasn't completely alone in this.

When I returned to the hidden room, everything was put back in place. The smell of incense lingered, an afterthought of the magic I'd stumbled across and roused by forces still elementary to me, forces dormant for centuries until tonight. I didn't know what that meant. Had I caused a shift in the universe? I shivered from the sudden chill I felt at the possibility of unknowingly opening a door that might create havoc in this world.

Nathan was on the phone, his back turned to me. I could hear Tree's voice. It sounded both tired and relieved when he asked Nathan if he was sure Aosoth's memories were gone from Carrie's mind. I smiled when a flashback came to me of when we were kids, pinky swearing to reassure the skeptical one about the issue at hand.

"Absolutely," Nathan replied. "Here's Paige. She'll fill you in on the rest." He crossed the room and handed me his cell. I said a silent prayer Tree wouldn't say anything to tip Nathan off about our bargain with Bael.

I took the phone and sat on the couch while I filled Tree in on everything. Nathan sat beside me, listening. A few times my eyes flicked to Nathan, catching a smorgasbord of emotions crossing his face like surprise, anger, sympathy, awe. I was glad he was hearing this because now I wouldn't have to repeat what had happened. Kill two birds with one stone, Mom used to say.

A painful ache tugged at the edges of my heart. I missed my mom and dad. I closed my eyes, willing my mind to focus on what Tree was saying, instead of giving in to an internal pity party I was about to have. I had no time for it, and feeling sorry for myself would get me nowhere. Believe me, I'd felt sorry for myself many times, and nothing good ever came out of it.

"I pinky swear," I told Tree, applying the memory I just had to ease his worries. He laughed. "My parents promised to take good care of her," I added and then finished with details of what I saw and heard before they crossed over to the next realm.

"So the music was a lullaby?" Tree asked, fascinated.

"I think so," I answered. "It was the most beautiful melodies I had ever heard, and I could have easily drifted off into it."

"Amazing."

"It was. It sounded like this." Closing my eyes, I wheeled my mind back to the memory of when I heard the music and hummed it. I didn't think I did it any justice, but when I finished, I heard a sharp intake of breath from Tree.

"Th-that was extraordinary," he stammered, his voice sounding rough.

I opened my eyes. Nathan's gaze was downcast. He must have felt me staring at him because he peeked at me from beneath his long lashes. He looked sad and . . . guilty?

I chatted with Tree for a few more minutes, watching Nathan pacing the room, running his hands through his hair. I knew something was bothering him and ended the conversation with Tree.

"What's wrong?" I stood and handed Nathan the phone.

"I saw the whole thing," he said and continued when he noticed the baffled look on my face. "You and Carrie with your parents." He pointed to the wall, and I knew right away what he was talking about. I gave him a look that said he didn't need to explain to me about how he saw it, since he now knew it had happened to me as well. "And I'm so sorry."

"For what?" I didn't understand why he'd apologize. He didn't do anything wrong. But it was clear by the heartbreaking look on his face, he felt a deep regret for something.

He ran a hand through his hair again and sighed. "I know how much you miss your parents, and you wanted to leave with them. I also realize the hard life you've led since I turned you immortal."

"Yeah, but it's not your fault. I chose it. If I hadn't, I'd be dead right now, and we wouldn't be together. Not to mention Carrie would still have Aosoth's memories," I pointed out.

He held my eyes with his, and in all honesty said, "I would have still turned you immortal that day you bled to death."

I stared at him.

"I'm a selfish bastard," he admitted with a shrug. "There's no way I could ever sit back and watch you die. I love you too much." He cupped his hands on my shoulders, his gaze locked onto mine. "I feel bad you can't be with your parents and your life has been a constant struggle since the day you were marked for immortality. However, I'll never regret loving you too much and keeping you here. I just wish there wasn't all this strife in your life, and I feel partly to blame for it."

"Don't criticize yourself," I said. "I don't blame you for anything."

"You miss them," he whispered, his eyes glassy with emotion. "I saw the heartache in your face and heard it in your voice when you asked if you could go with them." With his thumb, he wiped a stray tear off my cheek. "It crushes me, and I can't do anything about it."

I swallowed hard and gathered my thoughts as if they were poker chips, and I had to weigh how much I was willing to put out on the table to play out the hand I was dealt.

Sure, I could be with my parents right now if the circumstances were different, but I had made my choice for reasons that far outweighed my desire to hang with Mom and Dad. And if I were being totally honest with myself, it would get old after a while latching onto them. Then what would I do? Mom and Dad had their own life to live, just like I had mine.

No. It was much better this way. I had made the right decision.

I stepped back and turned away from Nathan, clasping my hands on top of my head.

"Paige?" His voice broke. He was worried, probably thinking I blamed him for everything. But that wasn't the case.

"Give me a minute," I said, finally stumbling onto the root of my problem.

Of course. My problem wasn't that I yearned to be dead to this world so I could live in the next life with Mom and Dad. My issue was wanting to have them here in this life with me. And every time I saw them, I wanted to capture what could have been so the hole inside me would no longer exist.

I dropped my hands and faced Nathan. "I figured out my problem, and it has nothing to do with what you did or didn't do." I took his hand. "C'mon. Let's go to bed, and I'll explain it to you then."

I longed to be under the covers, all warm and snuggly in his arms. I wasn't particularly tired, but we had made a silent ritual months ago of crawling into bed and talking for sometimes hours before we fell asleep and now seemed as good as a time as any to do that.

Nathan gave me a ghost of a smile, looking totally bummed. I squeezed his hand and led him up the stairs, too happy with myself to give into the feeling of doom twisting in my gut.

Chapter Thirteen

Nathan

The day after she rescued Carrie, Paige persuaded me to stay home with her and do absolutely nothing. When she suggested it while we were eating breakfast, adding with a tired smile she was exhausted, I didn't have the heart to disagree. She did look spent, which led me to believe her energy had been drained by last night's journey. Besides, she looked adorable in her Hello Kitty pajama bottoms with her long hair pulled into a messy bun. There was no way I could say no.

I stayed in my gray sweats and black T-shirt while we lounged around watching daytime TV, being complete couch potatoes. I hadn't realized how much garbage aired on TV during the day until I flipped channels. There was a reality show about rich housewives getting into cat fights over the dumbest shit, each one of them undeniably plastic. Plastic looks, plastic personality, plastic heart–plastic, plastic, plastic. Then there were the less than meaningful talk shows, serving no purpose but to perpetuate more trash into the minds of humans. I was relieved Paige wasn't into that sort of rubbish, so we watched sitcoms for a while instead.

As we zoned out on an episode of Seinfeld, my mind drifted to last night when Paige led me upstairs. "You're blameless in me not being with my parents," she told me.

I followed her into the bathroom, and we brushed our teeth together. I shook my head. I turned her immortal, and I ultimately separated her from her parents. I truly felt sorry for it and hoped she didn't resent me, but I couldn't be sorry for turning her immortal.

Her dark green eyes flashed up at me in the mirror, the light catching a glint of protest in them. Her lips were lined with white, foamy toothpaste. She frowned before she spat into the ceramic sink.

"Stop feeling guilty. This has nothing to do with you." She sat on the wooden toilet seat, watching me rinse. The potent antiseptic smell of mouthwash wafted into my nostrils. It had a strong, minty taste. I threw her a doubtful look while swishing the germ killing liquid. "Listen to me," she said. "I finally realized tonight my parents have their own existence. They have their own path to follow."

I still wasn't convinced. I'd seen the expression on her face when her family told her she couldn't go with them, and in essence, I was the one to blame for the heart-wrenching feeling of rejection I'd seen. The very thought of it raised a lump in my throat.

But after we settled ourselves in bed under the soft flannel sheets, Paige relentlessly made it clear to me it had nothing to do with me turning her immortal. It had to do with her insatiable desire to have her mother and father in her life, but she knew now, even if she were dead, it wouldn't be the same as having them here in this world. Now that she realized it, she had to accept the fact she'd never have them in this life like Carrie and Tree had theirs.

Once she explained it to me, I understood where she was coming from, and frankly, it was one less worry on my mind. But now, as I sat with Paige curled in a blanket, pressed against my side, the dreaded feeling at the hospital slithered through my stomach. I wondered if I was being paranoid.

Paige looked at me. "What's wrong?"

My eyes flicked to hers. "Nothing. Why?"

She rocked against me and smirked. "Bull crap. You're such a liar. I can tell something is bugging you because you keep shifting in your seat, which by the way is getting annoying."

I laughed. I loved how candid she could be with me and the cute little smirk on her face. "Oh, really?"

She nodded.

"Well, excuse me, madam," I said in a British accent, "for repeatedly upsetting the position of your bum. For you have a smashing bum that I—"

Paige smacked my arm and giggled.

The corner of my mouth tilted, my eyes narrowing. I imagined holding her down, tickling her until she pleaded for me to stop. She squeaked, and like a jack-in-the-box, she jumped up, a tracer darting across the room. My body jerked forward to follow her, but then her phone vibrated on the coffee table. I bent to look at it when a gust of warm air brushed my face. I looked up, and Paige stood in the same spot as before, except now she held her phone in her hand.

I smiled. "You're getting good with your speed."

She returned my smile. "Thanks. It's Tree," she said before answering it. She moved to the spiral staircase and sat on one of the steps. "Hey, Tree. What's up?"

I turned the TV off and kicked my socked feet up on the coffee table. I could hear the dinging sound of rain hitting the copper rain gutters and the dried leaves rustling around the house. I closed my eyes, listening to Tree talk to Paige.

"Yeah, I'll ask him," Paige said.

"Tell him I'm not in the mood for training tonight," I told her before she even asked. I opened my eyes and looked at her. "Sorry. I didn't mean to eavesdrop. Tell him I'll do it tomorrow, though."

She relayed the message, then asked about Carrie.

"She's sleeping like a baby, thanks to you," Tree said. He sounded happy and deeply grateful for Paige's help.

I tried not to listen to their conversation, but I guess my curiosity overrode my blocking abilities. I could turn the television back on; it would be the polite thing to do. I grabbed the remote and channel surfed.

I could still hear what they were saying and paid them more attention than the History Channel I settled on.

But then I sat up, my full attention focused on the TV. It was a documentary on King Solomon and his signet ring. Paige moved to my side, staring at it while listening to Tree tell her how Carrie's vital signs have been perfect and her recovery was meeting the doctor's expectations. A few minutes later, we both realized we'd seen this show before. She rose and drifted to the picture of us on the fireplace mantel. It was in a square, silver frame. Anwar had taken the photo on the island last summer. It was a romantic caption of Paige and me kissing beneath a waterfall. Later on, we made love beneath it. I halted all thoughts connected to the memory of our passionate night. Now wasn't the time to awaken the physical desires I had for her, so I returned my attention to the show. Then a thought occurred to me, and I turned to Paige. Something in my glance must have alarmed her because she told Tree to hang on and held my gaze. "Do you mind inviting Tree here so he can draw a picture of the cave in your vision?" I knew Tree to be a talented artist. He once showed me his sketch book full of cyperpunk pictures he had drawn, and they were quite remarkable. "Unless, you're not up to it," I added, hoping she was, but I decided to push the issue anyway, because it had to be dealt with. Ignoring it wouldn't make it go away, and I'd point that out to Paige if I had to.

She stared at me for a long moment, biting her bottom lip. Her eyes held a bothersome somberness I didn't like. I opened my mouth to tell her to forget the whole thing, going back on what I had resolved to do, but then she raised the phone to her ear and invited Tree over, turning away from me.

* * *

A while later, there was a knock at the door. Tree came in carrying two large pizza boxes with his sketch book and supplies on top. I welcomed the sight with a grin. My appetite was raging, not to mention my eagerness to visually see this cave Paige had talked about. All three of us headed to the kitchen. Tree placed the food on the counter. I got us some plates while Paige filled the glasses with ice and pop.

"If you don't mind," Tree said, holding a piece of pizza in his hand, a string of melted cheese hanging off the edges, "I want to eat first before I start sketching." He lifted the slice above his mouth and lowered the dangling cheese into his mouth.

"No problem," I replied, taking a wedge myself and biting into it. The spicy, sweet tomato sauce, exploded delightfully in my mouth, along with the gooey mozzarella and pepperoni. This was an excellent idea.

"Have you heard from Brayden?" Paige asked Tree.

"Yes, I have." He took a drink, his ice cubes clinking against the glass. "He wants me to try to iron things out with you for him. He told me to tell you he'd choose you over Cassondra any day."

Paige made a sound of annoyance and rolled her eyes. "He doesn't get it, does he?"

"I'm not finished yet," Tree said, catching our full attention. "He's been hanging around Cassondra because she's close to Anwar. Not to mention she's a sex machine and Brayden can–"

"Stop!" Paige covered her ears to demonstrate her request. "I don't want to hear about Brayden's sex life."

I looked away, stung by her comment. Why would she care? But deep down I knew. She still had feelings for him, and it bothered the shit out of me.

Tree laughed and held a hand up. "Okay. Okay. I'll spare you the details on the steamy part of his life."

"Good," Paige said, taking a slice of pizza out of the box and playfully bumping her hip against his thigh. "Otherwise,"–she flashed me a devious smile and winked–"I'll go into explicit detail about *my* own sex life."

I laughed, knowing how horrified Tree would be to hear it. He thought of Paige as a sister and didn't even want to think about her being less than virtuous. I laughed even harder when I saw the horror on his face.

He shook his head as if he were rolling marbles around in it. "No. Paige. Please don't."

She snickered. "Relax. I'm messing with you."

His forehead wrinkled, and he frowned. "Don't do that." He took another piece of pizza.

Jesus Christ, the boy can eat. This had to be his fifth one already.

"Anyway," Tree continued, "Brayden told me he thinks Anwar is having a change of heart toward Bael."

"Why?" I asked.

"Because Anwar has a sneaky suspicion Bael is hiding information from him. At least, it's what Cassondra told him." Tree washed and dried his hands before sitting at the table.

"Interesting," I said more to myself than them.

"It is," Paige admitted.

I looked at Tree, flipping through his sketch book for a blank page. He plucked a graphite pencil from a white tin box.

"Did Brayden tell you anything else?" I asked.

"Nothing important or stuff you already know, like his determination to steal Paige's heart from you."

Instantly, my temper sparked; heat rose to my ears. Paige must have noticed because she cleared her throat to divert my attention from the angry thoughts taking form. I took a deep drink of my Coke, focusing on the dark, syrupy taste. The ice cubes knocked against my front teeth, and the fizzy, coldness slid down my throat. I drank the whole thing and released a loud, drawn out burp. "Excuse me." I pounded a fist against my chest and released a smaller version of the prior one. "Excuse me again."

"Damn. Those were some good ones." Tree laughed. "I'm impressed."

"Do you feel better now?" Paige asked, laughing as well. She looked happy, which lightened my mood even more.

"Why, yes, I do," I said.

Tree held the tip of his pencil above a blank page and turned to Paige. "Now describe into detail the vision you saw the other day."

An hour later, we were looking at Paige's vision in total awe. I was completely taken aback by Tree's talent. He'd managed to achieve every fine detail Paige described to him from the depth of the cave to the chamber of columns made out of limestone to the arched portals and the subterranean stream of water.

"Wow. This is amazing," Paige gushed. "I think you should park your wrenches and be an artist instead."

"Paige is right," I said. "You definitely have a gift."

A shy smile broke across Tree's face, but his brown eyes were beaming. "Thanks, guys." He paused to take in his work. "Do you think this cave actually exist?"

"Yeah, I do," Paige answered, staring at the picture in front of him.

I thought so, too, and felt a spike of adrenaline. I recognized it as excitement. We were one step closer to finding those incantations, and I wondered if we pushed a little harder where it would lead us.

I glanced at the clock on the microwave. 9:42. My gaze shifted to the coffee pot. I wasn't ready to quit for the night and looked at Tree. "Do you have to work tomorrow?"

He blinked, a bit startled by my abrupt question. "No . . . well, I should go in for a little while because my dad has been covering for me so I could stay by Carrie's side. Why?"

"I thought maybe I could make a pot of coffee, and we can do some research on this for a while. I figure you can stay the night, and tomorrow we can do some more training."

"Sounds good to me." Tree reached into his army green cargo pants and pulled out his phone. "I'm going to call my folks so they don't worry." He rose to his feet and went into the living room.

As Tree was talking to his dad, my phone vibrated on the kitchen counter. Paige and I exchanged looks, both of us knowing not many people had my cell phone number, which meant more than likely, this wouldn't be a pleasurable call. I hated assuming the worse, but according to the sinking feeling I had in my stomach, this wouldn't be good.

I picked it up. When I saw the number, I sighed and stared at the ceiling.

"Who is it?" Paige wanted to know, moving to my side, sounding anxious.

"Anwar." I pressed the talk button. "What is it, Anwar?" I asked, my voice filled with disgust.

"I need to talk to you, Nathaniel." His phone crackled. Long distance, I gathered.

"I think I'm through talking with you."

My thoughts shifted on that moment when I had caught Roeick maliciously bullwhipping Paige's bare back, and Anwar taking part in her suffering. A blaze of anger whipped through me. My body tensed; heat rose up the back of my neck.

"It's about Ms. Paige." He sounded worried, but I wasn't falling for his tricks anymore. As far as I was concern, he could piss up a rope.

"Said the spider to the fly," I retorted in a deep, careful voice.

"Nathaniel, please. I think Bael is pla—"

In a fit of impulsive rage, I threw the phone across the room. It struck the wall and shattered, exploding tiny pieces, raining down in the kitchen, scattering like bits of shrapnel.

The good thing was Tree happened to be in the other room talking to his parents, and Paige was standing next to me. The bad part was I didn't know for sure if Anwar was lying through his teeth or not, but at this moment, I didn't give a shit.

Chapter Fourteen

Paige

Nathan startled me when he threw his phone across the room. It starburst against the wall, spewing debris everywhere. I turned and covered my face with an arm, but there was no need. Nathan stepped in front of me, using his body as a shield to deflect whatever came flying my way. Scattered sounds of plastic raining on the wooden floors and countertops filled the room.

"What the . . ." Tree said, running into the kitchen. He took a couple steps back when he saw what used to be Nathan's phone, now in tiny pieces all over the room. Wide-eyed, he looked at Nathan. "What did I miss?"

"Anwar," is all Nathan said. He turned to me. "Are you okay?" His voice was low, rough with anger.

I nodded, still shocked at his abrupt behavior. I hadn't realized until now, the magnitude of anger he harbored for Anwar. He downright loathed him. That was the thing about Nathan though, if you screwed him over, he was done. He'd keep you at arm's length with a distrustful eye planted on you, or he'd completely shut you out of his life. It made me wonder how he would act toward me after I betrayed him.

"Why don't you and Tree hang out in the living room while I clean up this mess?" Nathan asked.

"I can help you," I offered.

"I need a few minutes alone, if you two don't mind?" Nathan's gaze swept from me to Tree.

Tree held his hands up. "No problem. I totally understand."

I grabbed Tree's sketch book and followed him into the living room. He turned and gave me a that-was-intense look. I jerked my chin to the loft, signaling we should go up there. He understood right away, and we climbed the spiral staircase in silence. When we reached the top, I thought it would be a good idea to start talking so Nathan wouldn't get suspicious.

"There's a laptop up here we can use to see if there are any caves in Africa that might remotely resemble the one I saw." I set Tree's sketch book on the wooden trunk used as a coffee table and crossed the room to Nathan's mahogany desk. I snatched the laptop, placed it beside the sketch book, and sat down.

"I don't know," Tree doubtfully said. "I still find it kind of hard to believe a cave like this"—he flipped open his sketch book to the drawing of the cave, and jabbed his finger on it—"does exist."

"Well, I think it—"

"*The innocent locked in grief from the illusion before the eyes. An unlikely pair reunites in treachery and affection.*"

My whole body became rigid, and my blood turned to ice, raising goosebumps on my arms. I couldn't move nor remove my gaze off the steel lock on the trunk.

"What's wrong?" Tree asked.

The cushion beside me shifted against my thigh, and I felt a wall of body heat down the left side of my body. My preternatural hearing picked up the acceleration of Tree's heart, and Nathan's shifting feet, lightly scuffing the wooden floor in the kitchen, then pausing. He must have heard Tree's question and the worry in his voice. A draft of warm air stirred the hair around my face, and a large image disrupted my view of the lock. Two hands reached out, cupping my cheeks in them, gently tilting my head up. I blinked a couple times to refocus, feeling a crushing grief I hadn't experienced since my mom died.

"Baby, what is it?" Nathan softly asked. He wiped the tears off my cheeks with his thumbs.

"She had another premonition, huh?" Tree guessed.

The premonition kept replaying in my head, and I couldn't shake off this gut-wrenching belief someone close to me was going to die. I opened my mouth to tell Tree yes, but the words from the premonition fell from my lips instead, my voice grim. Tree inhaled a sharp breath that plucked on my nerves like a guitar string being tuned. Nathan leaned forward, resting his forehead on mine and sighed. "This isn't good," he murmured.

"What do you think it means?" Tree asked, sounding nervous.

"I'm not sure," I replied. "But I have a horrible feeling someone is going to die." I wasn't going to mention it because I could be totally wrong, but Tree needed to know since he was in on this pact with Bael.

"Just because it said 'locked in grief' doesn't mean someone must die," Nathan pointed out, trying to soothe the uneasiness out of me. "Maybe it's a dark spirit locked in grief, and the illusion of the eye is the human vessel." He paused to look at both me and Tree. "Do you follow me?"

I nodded, and Tree's worried expression relaxed as he quickly latched onto Nathan's idea, gladly pushing aside my unfavorable answer for Nathan's Mickey Mouse version. But deep down, he had to know it wasn't that simple. And if he didn't, well then I was going to burst his bubble with my next comment. "I think you're wrong, though," I said to Nathan. "It's too easy a solution for it to be that."

Tree made a vibrating sound with his lips in an obvious objection. When I looked at him, he gestured toward Nathan. "Nathan is totally right," he said. "It makes perfect sense."

"Yeah, it does," I admitted. "But that's not what the premonition is talking about."

"How do you know?" Tree demanded a little too harshly.

His heart was racing, and it became clear to me this situation was getting to him. I needed to find a way to get through to him that it was imperative to keep clearheaded and to look at all facts, not just the ones we'd prefer.

I took Nathan's hand. "I need some time alone with Tree."

He glanced at Tree and back at me. "I'll call Pip from the room downstairs."

"Oh. Right." I slapped the palm of my hand on my forehead. We were supposed to call Pip to let him know how things went with Carrie. "I can't believe we forgot to call him."

Tree gave us a weird look. "Who's Pip?"

"He's the friend Nathan told us about the night before Carrie's accident." Tree had a blank look on his face, so I continued. "The one who can erase Aosoth's memories from Carrie's mind." My words came out slow in a don't-you-remember kind of way. A spark of understanding entered his eyes.

He slapped his knee. "I got it . . . Jeez, sometimes I can be such a space cadet."

Nathan kissed my hand, bringing my attention back to him. "Come get me when you're finished."

He didn't seem at all bothered or suspicious by my request, which made me realize he trusted me–explicitly. I felt a pang of guilt as I watched him leave the room, hating Bael for putting me in this position. After I heard Nathan enter the room beneath the kitchen, I turned my full attention on Tree. "You need to get it together," I said in a high whisper. Even though Nathan was in the sound proof room, I still didn't want to take any chances.

"What are you talking about?" Tree looked at me like he didn't have a clue.

"Just because you didn't like the answer I gave earlier doesn't mean it's not the right one," I said.

He made a face, which annoyed me. "What the hell are you talking about?"

"Hel-lo! The premonition I just had." *Where's his head tonight?*

In a fit of frustration, he jumped to his feet, towering over me. "Like I was supposed to know what you were talking about, Paige. I can't read your *fucking* mind!"

My mouth dropped in surprise. Like Nathan, Tree rarely used the eff word, unless he was downright pissed or joking around. I knew then something was deeply disturbing him, and I was determined to draw it out of him so we could confront it and move on. We didn't have the time or luxury to make mistakes or give ourselves a false sense of security. Tree needed to accept that, and if I had to drill it in his head for him to do so, I would.

"I know you can't." I kept the tone of my voice even, hoping it would siphon some of his frustration out. "I'm sorry if I wasn't being clear, but we need to face the fact that part of my premonition means someone is going to get hurt and possibly die. We have to fig–"

"I can't lose Carrie," Tree blurted, moving about the room like a restless bear in a cage. "After you became immortal, Carrie and I were eager to help you because we thought we could handle the possibility of losing one another if it came down to it. And I know you've warned me about it . . . Paige"–he faced me. With wide, tearful eyes, he thumped his fingers against his chest–"I can't lose Carrie. I can't." He hung his head and shook it. Tears rolled down his face, breaking my heart, causing my own eyes to well.

I hopped up and took his hand, towing him back to the couch. When we sat, I wrapped my arms around him. He was shaking.

"Carrie is going to be fine," I reassured, trying to keep my voice steady, but he must have heard the sadness in it because he pulled back to look at me.

He frowned. "I'm sorry. I didn't mean to make you cry." He wiped his face off with the palm of his hand.

"Don't worry about it," I said. He looked down, as if in shame, so I continued. "I know how you feel, so don't be embarrassed by it. I mean, I'm scared to death something is going to happen to either one of you. I understand and accept I'm going to outlive you two, but I don't know what I'd do if one of you died young, especially by the hands of a dark spirit. You and Carrie are the only family I have."

Tree lifted his eyes to mine. "I never really thought about that . . . us being your only family now."

"It's true," I said. "That's why I want to keep you out of danger." I gripped his arm, and he started at the intensity of it. "We have to get through this *together*. Do you understand? I can't have you falling apart on me. I understand your fear of losing Carrie, but she'll be okay. I need you, though, to be clearheaded through this sticky situation we're in with Bael."

"I know. I'm sorry for losing it."

"Don't be." I took a deep, unsteady breath and dropped my voice to a bare whisper again. "Nobody can know about our bargain with Bael." I pointed to the floor. "Nathan, especially, can't know about it. Therefore, when the time comes, I'm going to need your help to make him believe I don't want anything to do with him." I could feel my eyes stinging and mentally hardened myself. Instantly, my vision cleared.

"You don't have to–"

"Yeah. I do," I said. "Otherwise, Nathan will do everything in his power to find me, and he can't get in the middle of this. You'll have to get him to believe . . . " My voice cracked. I took a deep breath and cleared my throat. I attempted to turn off all heartbreaking emotions concerning Nathan again. A hardness grew inside me. It rose from the pit of my stomach to my face. "You'll have to get him to believe I don't want to be with him anymore." There I said it. Then a thought came to me on what I could do that would leave no doubt in Nathan's mind I didn't want nothing to do with him.

"He's not going to fall for it," Tree said, unconvinced.

"After I'm done doing my part, he will," I stated, hearing the determination in my voice.

He rolled his eyes. "Yeah. Right. You're a terrible liar, and your face will totally give you away."

"I know. That's why I'm going to handle it in a different way. Just be ready to do your part when he confronts you."

Tree leaned forward, his expression poised for some juicy information, as if I were going to tell him aliens did exist, and the government was covering it up. I laughed. It was short and humorless, but it cracked a silly look on his face, and his forehead wrinkled.

"It's better I don't tell you, so your reaction will be genuine when Nathan confides in you about it," I reasoned.

Tree sat back and draped his arm off the couch. "What a gyp." He looked away, acting all disgusted.

I shoved his knee a couple times until he looked at me. He gave me the stink eye, and I narrowed my gaze in return. He didn't waver–just kept staring. I continued to do the same but then pretended to pick my nose, flinging an imaginary booger at him. His gaze shifted to the peaked ceiling. Dramatically, he made a repulsive sound, wiping an imaginary booger off his face.

"You got me," is all he said. Then he became serious, and our short playful mood was over. "Don't worry about me. Okay? I promise you I'll do my part. But we need to start getting busy on finding those incantations, so we can be done with this."

"Carrie is going to be okay," I reassured him again, squeezing his knee. "If I know two things about Bael, it's he likes Carrie and keeps his word. As long as I keep my end of the deal, he'll keep his. So Carrie will stay alive and so will you." I noticed the sadness in his eyes when I mentioned Carrie. "All right?"

"Yeah. I hear ya. I'm fine." He scooted to the edge of the couch and picked up Nathan's laptop. "Now, let's see if we can find any information on that cave."

I rose from the couch and headed toward the stairs. "I'll go get Nathan."

"Hey, Paige."

I half turned, alarmed at the somberness in his voice. Could he still be upset about Carrie?

"I'm sorry about Nathan. I know how much he means to you." He took a deep breath and continued. "I feel like shit for you giving him up to keep me alive."

"It's not your fault," I said, "and who knows? Maybe when this is all over, Nathan will understand why I did what I did." I turned on my heel and descended the stairs, wondering if in the end, Nathan would ever trust me again.

Chapter Fifteen

Nathan

When Paige came downstairs to let me know she finished talking with Tree, I'd just got off the phone with Pip. It was perfect timing, although he wanted to visit with Paige. She intrigued him with her abilities, and knowing Pip, he'd want her to give him a detailed explanation of her journey, merely to quench his curiosities and feed his scientific mind. But he'd have to wait for another time, possibly when we were able to call on him in England. Right now we needed to funnel our energy into finding those incantations before things got ugly with Bael.

I noticed the sullen expression on Paige's face when she entered the room. Our eyes met, but then she glanced away as if she couldn't bear the sight of me, yet she leaned toward me like she wanted to be in my arms. Dread stirred in my gut again. "What's wrong?" I asked, trying to beat off the sickening feeling I might be losing her. Paige and I were good, I told myself. I knew she was in love with me. It was ridiculous to speculate otherwise. So I chalked it up to insecurity and left it alone.

She shifted her gaze to me and bit her lip, attempting to compose herself. I could see the emotional distress in her eyes. "Tree is still afraid he's going to lose Carrie and is having a hard time," she said, the raspy part of her voice cracking. "I've never seen him upset like this before."

Now her mood made sense, and I was secretly relieved it had nothing to do with us. I've had over a century of keeping my emotions in check when I wanted to, hidden from those who'd use them as tools for their own gain. So I made sure not to display the relief I felt, because I didn't want to appear insensitive to what Tree was going through. "Is there anything I can do?"

She ran her fingers through her hair. The dark red color caught the light just so, to where it shined like glossy paint on a hot rod. I had a quick mental visual of it hanging around my face, being surrounded by the smell of peaches and desire. I averted my eyes before racier thoughts took hold.

"He's okay now," she answered. "I think it would do him some good if you did some training with him. It would make him feel more confident and distract his mind for a while by focusing on that instead."

"You're right," I agreed and laced my arms around her when she stepped into them. She hugged me tighter than normal and felt cold. "Are you all right?" Her head moved up and down on my chest.

"I'm okay." Her voice sounded distant, but then it shifted into a perkier tone. "I made coffee for us, and Tree is looking online to see if there are any caves in Africa resembling the one I saw."

"Good. We should get busy, then. But we still need to talk about your premonition," I said, pulling back so I could look at her. "Don't you think?"

"I know what it means, Nathan," she said, her tone exasperated. "At least, I think I do."

"What?"

She yawned, stepped away from me, and headed up the stairs. "It means someone is going to die, and Bael and Aosoth are going to be teaming up again."

Taken aback by her revelation, I followed without saying a word, wondering if she was right. I wasn't sure because Bael had betrayed Aosoth, and it didn't make sense she would hook up with him again. Not to mention it would take her a while to regain her energy after what I done to her. But still, I grew curious to know why Paige would think so since she was getting better at interpreting her premonitions. "Why do think Bael and Aosoth are working together again?" I asked as I poured coffee into three mugs.

"Think about it," she said, getting the milk from the refrigerator. "An unlikely pair reunites in treachery and affection. Bael doesn't like Aosoth, but Aosoth has the hots for him."

"He betrayed her," I countered.

She shrugged. "So? She's in love with him; thus it doesn't matter."

"He *betrayed* her," I repeated firmly, "so it has to matter."

She looked away, carefully handling two full coffee mugs in her hands. She walked out of the kitchen, leaving me standing there, staring after her, wondering if I said something wrong.

* * *

The next day, in my makeshift gym below my kitchen, I trained Tree more on hand to hand combat, how to think strategically out of tight situations and knife throwing, at which Tree excelled.

In close quarters fighting, I taught him not only to use his fists but the heels and edges of his hands, even fingers were also viable weapons against the enemy. Wrists and forearms made important defensive tools, and the elbows delivered deadly blunt force trauma, as did driving in forcefully with his shoulders. Afterwards, we went down to his hips, legs, knees, and feet used as bludgeons. Then I instructed the target areas to immediately cripple his opponents: temples, ears, eyes, nose, jaw, neck, and its Adam's apple and cervical vertebrae. We went over how to stand properly to balance his body while executing unarmed battle techniques and follow up with blocking and counter punching.

"Show him the hand knife," Paige said, straddling the balancing beam, swinging her feet back and forth. Despite us not finding anything about the cave, she looked like she was enjoying herself.

"What's the hand knife?" Tree wondered.

"It's the cutting edge of your hand I taught earlier." I lifted my hand with the fingers together, facing the meaty side, below the pinky, toward him. I thrust it forward and stopped when my hand reached his neck. He jerked his head back in response, his eyes wide.

"Cool," he said, impressed.

"Now, I'm going to throw a punch at you," I told him, "and I want you to show me what you'd do."

"Okay." Tree positioned his body in a fighting stance, getting into an offensive position.

"That's good, Tree," Paige said, lending her encouragement.

I threw a punch at Tree. He stepped forward, raised his left arm and deflected it with his forearm.

"Excellent," I said, pleased he seemed to have a knack for this stuff. "Now, let's practice the turning throw."

I stepped closer to Tree in a threatening manner. He grabbed my right wrist with his left hand and stepped forward with his right foot. Placing it outside my right foot, he pivoted on his back heel. He then hooked my right arm with his, and pinched his arm between my biceps and forearm. Pulling my wrist downward, he pivoted to the left, rotating it outward, throwing me off balance.

I fell to the floor.

"Yay!" Paige clapped. She swung her legs around and hopped off the balancing beam. Taking my hand, she pulled me up.

"Very good," I said to him.

"Yeah," Tree said, grinning. "I think all those Power Ranger moves I done as a kid"–he twirled around and threw kicks in the air– "are resurfacing."

Paige laughed. "You're such a dork. What Nathan is teaching you has nothing to do with Power Ranger moves."

Tree rolled his eyes, looking indignant. "You have a short memory. They totally did blocking moves and elbow strikes."

"It's not that I have a short memory," Paige said, making a face. "I just never watched the show because of how lame it was."

"Well, then, you shouldn't be opening your mouth about stuff you don't even know about," Tree responded defensively.

"Whatever," Paige sighed.

I was beginning to feel like the only adult in the room and found myself making allowances for it. Maybe it had to do with the stress of everything going on causing them to behave in this manner toward each other. It was almost comical, though, and reminded me of when my older brother Jeremiah and I used to bicker back and forth like this.

"Maybe you two need a break from each other," I suggested, using the same line as my other brother Thomas used on Jeremiah and me.

Paige and Tree exchanged looks. Paige stuck her tongue out. He laughed and pulled her into a headlock, rubbing his knuckles on top of her head.

"We're fine," Tree said, releasing Paige before she had the opportunity to take him down.

Then, to my surprise, Paige kicked his feet out from under him. He toppled to the mat, his back smacking hard. A lungful of air escaped his lips, making a low hissing sound.

"Yeah, we're just fine." Paige laughed, offering her hand to Tree. He took it, unfazed by her quick retaliation, aside from the fact he was covertly trying to catch his breath. I pretended not to notice. "I think I should quiz you on your Latin," she told him.

Dark spirits were notorious for speaking in Latin, so I had given Carrie and Tree a CD player with a CD to listen to while they were asleep. The disk had several learning modules: how to understand Latin, how to think your way out of a tight situation, and about combat fighting. Secret agents in the military used this same concept for learning different languages, because your subconscious mind absorbed information while you slept. This method had been proven to be effective, and by what I had seen today, Tree was benefitting from it.

"What an excellent idea," I said, curious to see how well he'd do on his Latin.

"Fine by me," Tree said, shrugging.

"I take it you've been listening to the lessons?" I asked.

"Yup," he replied. "Well, except for when I was with Carrie and last night."

Paige headed for the stairs. "C'mon. We'll do this in the living room where we can be more comfortable."

Paige was right. The fluorescent lights were bright and made it a bit warm in here. The air was also stuffy and reeked of sweat. I could see a shower in my near future.

* * *

"I think Tree did a really good job today," Paige said, hopping on the computer for more research on the caves in Africa. She sat cross-legged on the couch in the living room with the laptop propped on a pillow on her knees.

I didn't know what had gotten into her while I was taking my shower. Maybe it had to do with Tree doing so well today, but it seemed like a fire had been lit underneath her. I on the other hand, wasn't feeling it and began having doubts about the cave being in Africa.

"Yes, he did," I answered, not really paying attention to her screen. Instead, I settled in next to her and closed my eyes, listening to the slow drumming of her heartbeat.

I must have fallen asleep because the next thing I knew, a sharp gasp startled me. For a second, I didn't know the day or time. But when I looked at Paige sitting beside me, computer in her lap, I quickly got my bearings. She had an expression on her face of shock and excitement, causing my heart to lurch.

"What is it?" Bleary-eyed, I squinted at the screen and saw a picture of a cave resembling the one in her vision. I sat up, alert now. "My God. You found it. But where?"

She gave me a smug look. "In Ethiopia." She handed me my MacBook. "It's called the Sof Omar cave. It has forty-two entrances; however, only four are useful for access."

"Interesting," I said, scrolling down to look at each photo, my heart racing.

"Yeah. Check this out," she said. "There were some archaeological investigations in the area, and in 1971, a geologist discovered new passages into the cave. Then in 1972, a British expedition arrived in Ethiopia where they explored and surveyed the cave. They also discovered more new entryways."

I stared at her in disbelief. "Do you think?"

She bounced in her seat, tucking her legs beneath her. "I think they were looking for something, possibly Solomon's ring or the incantations." I could hear the thrill in her voice.

I laughed. I couldn't help it. The knot in my chest began to unwind because, realistically, if we hopped on a plane to Ethiopia in a couple days and found those incantations, all of this strife in our lives would end.

But then I stopped laughing when a disturbing thought popped inside my head, throwing a sabot into the works of my plan. "Do you know if the local people who live there go inside the cave?"

"Probably," Paige said. "I mean, I read they revered it as a shrine, and the cave has been an object of prayer and sacrifice." She paused, staring at me, and her face fell. "Oh. I see what you're getting at. We may have a problem gaining the access we need to the cave."

I ran a hand through my hair and rubbed the back of my neck, feeling the same knot in my chest recoiling. There had to be a way around it; we just had to figure out how. If only Anwar and I were on good terms–

I shut out the thought. No way in hell could I ever trust Anwar again, and the phone call he made to me last night was probably another ploy to get me away from Paige. I had made up my mind then not to play into his theatrics concerning Paige. "Let me see what I can do to get us in there," I finally said, running a mental list of all the people I knew who might be able to pull some strings without me telling them why.

Paige stood and stretched. "Okay. I think we should go back to my house and figure it out there." A sheepish look entered her face that I found absolutely adorable. "I really miss my bed," she admitted.

"What? My bed isn't good enough for you?" I joked.

"It's too soft. I like it firm and hard." Her cheeks turned beet red.

I was trying to keep a straight face, but my eyebrows raised in question, and I could feel my lips twitching. "You do, huh?"

"That's not what I meant," she said, laughing.

"Uh-huh. Sure you did," I teased. "I know how you like it." I rose from the couch and chased her into the bedroom, and all was forgotten for a while.

Chapter Sixteen

Paige

Nathan didn't have a clue about what was really going down, although I was almost sure he felt–*something*.

How could he not? I wasn't good at hiding my emotions, and since I've become immortal, they'd been heightened exponentially. I was able to harden them, like I had done earlier, but obviously I needed more practice because a few had slipped to the surface after I spoke to Tree. So I was almost positive Nathan picked up on those feelings, because he'd asked me what was wrong. I knew then he sensed something, so I thought of a quick answer before he realized it had to do with us. It was a good thing I could use Tree as my scapegoat, and I told myself I wasn't completely lying to Nathan because it did break my heart about Tree being so upset.

"Are you ready to go?" Nathan asked, snapping me from my guilt-ridden thoughts.

I stood in the middle of the living room looking around, taking mental pictures of the stone fireplace, the wooden railings bordering the loft with its perfect scroll design, and the books adorning the back wall behind it. My heart squeezed as a sadness washed over me that this would probably be the last time I'd ever be in this house again.

"Paige?"

Out the corner of my eye I could see Nathan watching me with his head tilted to the side, his concern evident. I didn't move. Instead, I looked up at the high-peaked ceiling with the wooden beams. I knew I should have responded right away, but I wanted to savor this moment and lock it inside me so I could revisit it in my mind in the future. My eyes drifted toward the kitchen. I had the sudden urge to go in there and stare at its U-shaped construction of wood, like everything else in this wonderful rustic A-frame house.

"What are you looking at?"

I could hear his feet shifting against the rug next to the front door. I noted his heart pounding a little faster, too. He was getting anxious, and that sudden realization prompted me to throw a quick and believable answer at him before I blew my cover.

"I was wondering if we should clean your house before we head over to mine." I scrunched up my face. "I can see grit on the mantle, and those railings can use some Old English. There's also a film of dust on your TV." I pointed to the flat screen.

He let out a short laugh. "We're on the verge of finding the incantations, and there are dark spirits who want to get their hands on you, and you're worried about my house being too dirty?"

"Well," I said, mentally patting myself on the back because once again I had distracted him from the truth, "grimy houses bother me."

"The dirt is not going anywhere. We can clean when we get back from Africa."

He turned off the lights, a nonverbal signal telling me it was time to go. My eyes swept the house one last time, and I followed him out the door into the night.

The yellow crescent moon shone bright against the black sky, and the crisp air brushed against my face. The crickets chorused around us, chirping as if their life depended upon on it.

Abruptly they stopped and so did Nathan.

We were between the cab and bed of his pickup, and he placed his hand on my chest. An eerie earsplitting shrieking sound ripped through the night, growing in volume as it rushed toward us. My eyes were trained on the black forest ahead of us, and two glowing orbs peered between the black trunks. I gasped, and Nathan pressed my back against his truck, shielding my body with his.

Something large and fast bounded across the clearing, snapping logs in its path, grunting each time its feet hit the earth. I sneaked a peek beneath Nathan's arm and saw a beast that could only be described as half man, half gorilla.

Nathan flew to the side, and the beast slammed his hand above my shoulder almost tipping the pickup over. His black eyes were inches from mine. I stood frozen in shock and fear. His gorilla-like face was a leathery black, and his upper lip curled, revealing long, sharp, pointy teeth. His breath smelled like burnt flesh, causing me to recoil and turn away.

"I have a message to pass along," his deep, gravelly voice said. "Accept the offer or suffer the consequen–" The half-breed stopped short when a feral, growling noise broke from behind him. White, powerful hands, gripped the nape of his neck and lower back, lifting him off the ground.

"You keep away from her!" Nathan hurtled him across the clearing, and the creature smashed into the ground, rolling a couple times before jumping to his feet. Nathan charged forward, a blurry streak peaking at an incredible height, cannon balling down where the creature stood. Before Nathan landed, the gorilla humanoid disappeared into the trees. "Get in the truck and lock the doors," Nathan hollered before he vanished.

"Nathan!" I screamed. Instinctively, I wanted to run after them, but I wasn't sure if this thing was more powerful than I, and something in Nathan's voice told me I'd be better off in the pickup.

I stood listening and jumped when a suffering wail broke through the silence. Shaking, I hopped in the vehicle and locked the doors. I pressed my hands against the cold window. A trumpeting high shrill of undeniable agony twisted at my heart, and I hoped beyond hope it wasn't Nathan making that sound. The window fogged over from my erratic breaths, and I swiped a shaky hand across it.

I stared at the trees across the clearing where they both disappeared and heard a whining sound surround me. I held my breath, and a whimper escaped my lips. I pinched them together, forcing myself to be quiet.

I turned back to the window, debating on what to do, and at the same time wondered what the hell that thing was. Then I remembered what Carrie told us from one of Aosoth's memories about a being such as this. Bigfoot is what Tree called it. A creature that could enter our world through a portal–

Omigod. Had I opened a dimensional doorway when I did the ritual to reach Carrie?

Nathan stepped out of the forest. I flung the door open and ran to him. A trail of dried blood stained his cheeks, and he no longer had his shirt on. Deep, red claw marks ran across his bare, muscular chest and arms, streaked with caked blood.

"Are you okay?" I stopped him and touched his face. Part of the blood crumbled beneath my fingertips. He pulled my hand away and held it. A disturbing look hovered in his eyes that made my stomach churn.

"I'm fine," he said.

"Is he dead?"

He nodded. "C'mon. I'd feel better if we were at your house."

He seemed anxious to get out of here and a little high-strung. He wasn't saying anything, though, but I think I knew why. He needed some time to ponder. I decided to give him some space and kept quiet until we were almost to my house, and I couldn't stand the silence any longer. "What do you think?"

A black Tahoe drove past us. The headlights flashed across the windshield, briefly illuminating inside the cab of Nathan's pickup. Nathan gripped the steering wheel, his eyebrows pulling together in a deep frown. He didn't answer right away, so I stared out the window at the trees along the shoulder of the road, wondering if there were any more of those beings lurking beyond them.

"I think Aosoth summoned him," Nathan finally said.

I stared at him open-mouthed. "Why would you think that?"

"Dark spirits are attuned to the energies in this world when they're not in the flesh, so they would know when a portal is on the verge of activating. I think Aosoth has always been intrigued by those creatures. The reason I think so is what Carrie told us about Aosoth dwelling in the Nazi and watching a Yeti crossing from their world to ours. Not to mention what he said to you."

"But she shot him," I said, recalling the story of Aosoth being part of the Nazi Occult Bureau and had set out to murder one of those beasts so they could do medical experiments on it. "Besides, remember what Bael told Carrie about most of the portals being closed because the earth is too congested with people and infrastructure. Unless I opened it when I did the ritual to contact Carrie."

Nathan pulled into the driveway and killed the engine. Clouds obscured the moon, shadowing us in pitch darkness. It was a good thing we could see in the dark. Otherwise, I'd be uncomfortable sitting in Nathan's pickup like this.

"I don't think you opened any doors," he said. "And Bael is right about the other portals. I also think it's very rare these creatures can cross from their world to ours. But . . . "

I turned to him, expectantly. "But what?"

"But I don't *know*," he said, frustrated. "I don't know if Aosoth had anything to do with this, but it seems like something she'd cook up. However, why would that monster even listen to her or anybody for that matter?" He dropped his head in his hands and massaged his temples.

"Do you think there are any more out there?" I peered out the window, scanning the forest around my house for any movement. I didn't see nor hear anything out of the ordinary, just some squirrels making low clicking sounds at regular intervals.

"I'm not sure," Nathan answered. "I don't think so. I feel safer with you here for the time being though. I think Zeruel would keep them away, if there are more of them, that is."

Without waiting for my reply, he stepped out into the night. I followed, looking about for Zeruel. I didn't see him, but knew that didn't mean he wasn't around. We entered my house and checked everything to make sure nothing was disturbed. It all looked fine, just as we left it. Nathan flopped on the couch, looking exhausted. I eyed the dried blood on his cheeks, chest, and arms. The claw marks had almost vanished. I could smell the blood if I focused on it, though. The scent was different from ours–rank and fishy. My gag reflexes twitched in protest against the awful odor. I kept my distance, and sat on the recliner across from him.

"How did you kill it?" I asked, trying to distract my mind.

"I ripped his head off," he said in a matter-of-fact tone of voice. "And Carrie was right. Their bones do disintegrate when they die."

That was a mental visual I didn't expect to be laid on me. Gross.

"Why didn't you let me help you?"

He released a heavy sigh and ran a hand through his hair. "Because you're still a fledgling to the immortal world, and he was stronger than you." He looked at his arms and chest. His muscles flexed and rippled with the infinitesimal movements he made. "I better go take a shower."

"Okay," I said, staring at my lap as he left the room. His depressing mood made me feel even worse for what I was about to do to him.

But I had no choice. Bael was a powerful entity who had a lot of followers. I knew if I were to breach my agreement with him and tell Nathan, Bael or one of his lackeys would kill Tree. I wasn't about to allow it to happen.

When Nathan had taken a shower earlier, I'd received a text message from Bael. He wanted to know if I'd made any progress, and I told him no, which was the truth. I wasn't sure if he believed me; however, he requested my presence tonight for a private discussion with him. He had given me his cell number and instructed me to call him when I was able to slip by Nathan without him noticing.

"*I'll get a hold of u later 2 night*," I told him, my fingers flying across the cell phone's keypad.

"*Good girl,*" he texted back.

"*How did u get my cell?*"

"Anwar."

A cold feeling settled into the pit of my stomach when I read that one word. I shoved my cell in my pocket, not bothering to reply.

Then I wondered why Anwar hadn't tried calling me like he had Nathan. I guess he wasn't as concerned about me as he claimed last night with Nathan.

Now, I could hear Nathan closing the bathroom door. I hopped up and got a piece of paper and pen out of the kitchen drawer. I leaned into the granite counter and wrote a quick note to him, biting my trembling lip as I did so. I paused and closed my eyes, once again mentally hardening myself. I wished I knew how to keep the wall in place so it wouldn't falter. I supposed in time I'd be able to completely shut off the emotions I didn't want to feel for as long as I wanted. But for now, I'd have to keep practicing and try to be patient. I opened my eyes and continued writing. After I was done, I folded it, wrote Nathan's name and hid it underneath the microwave.

Nathan had just turned the shower on. I could hear the water spraying against the ceramic tub. I zipped upstairs and in a blur, I grabbed some clothes to change into tonight and a pair of sneakers. With my arms full, I paused in the middle of my room to listen. The faucet knob squeaked from Nathan turning it.

Crap.

Why in the hell did he take fast showers? You'd think he'd want to linger in there for a while to relax.

Without further hesitation, I took off down the stairs, straight to the bathroom. I closed the door and turned the faucet on, just in case he was listening. Carefully, I slid my clothes and shoes beneath a bunch of towels in the linen closet. I adjusted the towels so even if he were to come in and get one, he wouldn't notice my stuff. Turning the faucet off, I made a mental note to bring some money, a credit card, and my passport with me tonight.

I came out of the bathroom just as Nathan descended the stairs. We ran into each other in the hallway. The next thing I knew, he had me in his arms. He smelled like soap and his black hoodie like Downy.

"I'm sorry about my cruddy mood earlier," he said. He pulled back to look at me, his expression apologetic. "I didn't mean to make this situation worse for you. The last thing you need is more gloom and doom."

I hugged him tighter, loving the feel of his strong arms around my body. Something inside me wavered—the wall maybe. So I tried not to think about this being my last time in them by replacing the heartbreaking thought with me keeping Tree alive by complying with Bael's demands. I felt like a martyr, giving up the love of my life for the well-being of my best friend—me suffering in exchange for his life. But I didn't see myself as a martyr or would I ever act like one either. "I understand. There's no need for apologies," I answered.

"It just bothers me," he admitted. "I think I'm more upset at myself than anything else, because I never really did any research on those creatures."

"Well, you had other things to deal with." I pulled out of his embrace and went into the kitchen. "More important things," I added. "It's not like Bigfoot crosses over to our world every day. It's probably one in so many decades, and I bet you money that most of the Yeti sightings are false." I turned off the kitchen light and headed to the living room to do the same thing.

"I don't know," he responded. "I agree with you about them coming to our realm within so many decades. However, those who have crossed to our realm might have found a way to coexist among us without being caught, only seen." Nathan stopped. He had a weird look on his face. "Bedtime?"

I yawned and stretched my back. "Yeah. I'm tired. What about you?"

"Actually, I am pretty beat," he said.

I took his hand and led him to my bedroom, swallowing against the tightness in my throat, shutting those weepy emotions off. In my mind, I was saying goodbye to him, but in my heart I was loving him even more.

Chapter Seventeen

Paige

I lay beside Nathan, listening to his shallow breathing. I glanced at the green numbers on my alarm clock.

11:42.

I knew I should be going, but I watched Nathan sleep for a few more minutes. I hovered my hand above his face, wanting to touch it, then pulled away. His breathing shifted into a deeper, hollow sound. He was in full-out sleep mode. Now would be the time to leave.

Silently, I slipped out of the covers, careful not to jostle the bed, still watching him. He didn't stir. I crept out of the room, hesitating in the doorway. For a long moment, I stared at him. He looked at peace, as if he'd been unscathed by the world.

"I'll love you forever," I said below a whisper. I blew a kiss and walked away.

After I had my clothes, shoes, and coat on, I retrieved the note from beneath the microwave and placed it on the kitchen table. I took all the things I'd need: cash, credit card, driver's license, and passport out of my purse and stuck them in my pockets, along with my cell phone. I made a point to wear black cargo pants, knowing I would need the extra pockets for my belongings. Zipping up my Army surplus jacket, I took a deep breath and told myself I could do this. I was Paige Reed, fighter against evil. In the end, if my body ever did expire, I'd be going from this plane to the next on my own, like all souls who chose to do so. I wouldn't be able to take Nathan with me even if I wanted. It was a solo journey where I'd be accountable for all my actions, so I needed to make them count and face the fact the footprints in the sand were mine. Nobody could carry me. I had to do it by myself to further my own evolution.

When I stepped out into the night, the brisk autumn air stung my cheeks. I longed to be back in bed with Nathan, to be in his arms. And now it would never happen again. Clutching my stomach, I took another deep breath. I could do this, I told myself. Something rubbed my leg. I glanced down and saw Zeruel. I lifted him into my arms, his thoughts instantly consuming mine like a broken dam flooding into an empty town.

"It's not safe out there. You need to go back inside."

I wanted to tell him I had no choice, but then I'd be breaking my deal with Bael. So I had to do something I really didn't want to do—lie. I hated to fib to Zeruel, and in my heart I cursed Bael for it. I then wondered if Zeruel could hear my silent thoughts.

"Zeruel, can you hear my personal thoughts?"

"No. Nobody can breach your privacy. Not even I can. However, I can see your aura."

I blanched. I knew then he was on to me, and this was his way of telling me.

I didn't respond. Instead, I held him closer for comfort.

"Fair warning, my friend. I've encountered Aosoth lurking about in these woods while you were away."

My stomach dropped, and my heart thudded in my ears.

Why in the hell would Aosoth be hanging around my house? After what Nathan had done to her, you'd think she'd leave me alone.

"Did she see you?"

"No. I hid in a clump of bushes, stifling the light so she wouldn't flee from it."

"What about Roeick? Did you see him?"

"No, only Aosoth."

"Do you know anything else that might help me?"

"Only she still has her sights on you, and like Bael, Ayperos loathes her."

I thought about the recent premonition I had and wondered if I'd misinterpreted it. Maybe Bael and Aosoth aren't going to reunite after all. But if that were the case, then what an unlikely pair reunites in treachery and affection?

A crow cawed in a nearby tree, jarring me out of my introspection. I had to get a move on before my plan imploded. But I had a question I couldn't ignore and leave without asking Zeruel.

"What about Anwar?"

"As you already know, Anwar's loyalties lie solely on himself. His heart is good; however, he's misguided by a weariness some immortals become afflicted with through the changes of time. His spirit is now hovering in a gray area between light and dark."

The crow cawed again, as if punctuating Zeruel's caveat, like he heard and understood the mental broadcast, sending chills up my spine. I also felt a deep sadness for Anwar, because despite his underhandedness and withholding information about my father, I'd hate for him to turn dark.

"Paige." It was Nathan's sleepy voice.

"Crap!"

I hugged Zeruel and set him down. Without a second thought, I took off down the desolate street. The cool air made my eyes water and nipped at my nose. My hair flew back, lifting off my shoulders as if I were in a wind tunnel. I could feel the weight of my cell phone bouncing against my thigh in my pocket, reminding me to contact Bael.

There was a convenience store on the other side of town where I knew it would be safe to stop. When I reached an intersection, I made a sharp left and ran along dimly lit streets, desperately trying not to think about Nathan. But despite my efforts, thoughts of him traipsed through my mind: What was he doing right now? Did he read my letter yet? What was he thinking?

My heart shuddered, releasing an agonizing ache that almost caused me to stop and double over into myself. I shook my head instead, refusing to give into those feelings. I then wondered if Nathan would believe what I had written and if Tree would be able to convince him we were through.

In the distance, dogs were barking, rattling their chains in a nearby neighborhood.

I made a turn onto a historic neighborhood where antique wrought iron street lamps lined the road, like guardians in front of tidy Victorian homes. Those houses reminded me of the one where Roeick had held me captive until Nathan came to my rescue.

But Nathan wouldn't be coming this time. I was on my own. What would befall me from here on out, I'd have to deal with by myself. A familiar feeling of loneliness fluttered across my chest, a *too* familiar one. It mercilessly kicked me back to before I met Nathan.

The convenience store was up ahead. Its bright lights illuminated the dark streets surrounding it, a beacon guiding people to safety. I stopped to evaluate the area.

A semi-truck was parked in front of a gas pump where a shaggy dark-haired guy with dirty jeans and a potbelly stood fueling it. He looked bored. A mother and a small child gripping a candy bar in his pudgy little hand, stepped out of the store. I wondered mindlessly why a child would be up this late, let alone about to eat a candy bar.

Everything seemed normal, so I stepped inside and bought a small cup of coffee and a peanut butter cookie. In the back were small tables where people could sit and eat. Pulling out my phone, I sat at the red table and texted Bael. To my surprise, he answered right away. I told him I knew where the incantations were and left it at that.

I took a sip of my coffee, and my cell vibrated. Ignoring it, I took my time drinking the rest of the warm, creamy java while eating my soft cookie. A few people came in the store, but none of them wandered to the back, which was fine by me. I didn't feel like being bothered or stared at. The cash register dinged several times, ringing up the customers. I listened to the cashier tell them to have a good night, and I imagined what it would be like to have a simple life. In my heart I knew we all had our secret demons to slay, and nothing was as it seemed. My phone vibrated on the table again. I reached for it, then stopped myself.

Bael could wait.

I wasn't his damn lackey.

I ate the last piece of my cookie and thought about Tree, wondering what he would tell Nathan about me. And then a thought occurred to me. What about Brayden? I hadn't thought about that. When Brayden found out I'd broken it off with Nathan and bailed, I was sure he'd pull his resources together and find me.

Crap.

I wanted him to stay out of this. The last thing I needed was to worry about Brayden. I picked up my phone to text Tree, and when my eyes fell on the texted message I stopped breathing.

Nathan.

I held my stomach, feeling winded.

Where r u? I luv u. We need 2 talk. Pls. I'm sorry.

He left a voice message, but I couldn't bring myself to listen to it. I bit my lip. I thought my letter would have halted him from trying to reach me. My only hope was Tree. My phone buzzed in my hand.

Bael.

Time 2 meet at Cannon Beach.

On my way.

After I answered Bael, I threw my trash away and went into the restroom, locking the door. I called Tree.

"Hello," he said in a groggy voice.

"Tree. It's Paige."

"Paige?" He sounded alert now. "What's wrong?"

"I don't have much time to talk. I'm on my way to meet Bael, and I–"

"I don't know about this. I have a bad feeling."

"Listen. It doesn't matter. If I don't do this, Bael will have you killed."

"But–"

"But nothing. I need you to do your part. Nathan has already discovered I'm gone. I left a note, and he's looking for me. I'm sure he's going to contact you soon. Also, don't tell Brayden I broke it off with Nathan. Do what you can to keep it from him."

"I will."

"I have to go."

"Be careful."

"You, too. I'll see you when I get back."

"Okay."

I pocketed my phone, did my business in the restroom and left the convenience store without a second glance. When I reached the cover of darkness, away from the glaring lights of the store, I ran all the way to Cannon Beach. I could feel the difference in temperature as I neared the ocean. The cool, salty air filled my nostrils. I wondered if Nathan would be here, knowing whenever I missed my parents, this was where I came to feel closer to them.

My heart pounded.

But when I slowed to a brisk walk toward a cluster of boulders next to a massive craggy rock, I didn't sense Nathan's presence. I took a deep, shaky breath, not sure if I was relieved or not.

I imagined Nathan enfolding me in his arms and whisking me away from all this strife. I shook my head to dislodge the thought of him and me being together. Eventually Nathan would give up on us, especially when he realized I betrayed him. So it did me no good to wish for something unattainable. I had to forget about him and what we once had. This was my life now.

I stopped and stared at the ocean, watching the waves crashing against rocks. The surf roared and slapped the shore. The silvery moon was like a bright light on the sea, spotlighting the ripples of whitecaps.

Then my ears rang.

I hugged myself and scanned the beach for Bael. I saw movement behind trees on a hilltop to my right. A figure emerged. I didn't move and was sure it was Bael as he approached me. He had a penchant for tall, dark, and handsome vessels with light blue eyes.

"I knew you'd pull through," he said, looking pleased.

"Why is that?"

"Because you'd do anything for the people you love." He grimaced. "Even for that wretched friend of yours–*Tree*. You even terminated your relationship with Nathan, which in my opinion was a wise decision. Nathan is too much of an altar boy and smothers the reality of this world with unrealistic values."

"How do you know I ended my relationship with him?"

He smirked. "Did you?"

I didn't answer.

"I thought so," he said, still smirking. He flipped his hand out, palm skywards. "Give me your phone."

"Why?" I shoved my hand in my pocket, brushing my fingers against the tiny buttons on the keypad. "I'm not going to contact anybody and jeopardize my deal with you."

"I know you won't. However, it can be used to track you, and although I detest acknowledging this fact, I must admit that Nathan is the best tracker of them all."

"When Nathan discovers what I'd done, he'll want nothing to do with me," I told him, knowing how bad I'd hurt him.

"It doesn't matter. I take all precautions in everything I do. Now give it to me."

"Fine. If you want it so badly"–I threw it in the ocean–"go get it." I glared.

He laughed. "You have a fire in you I find quite charming. Kora had it as well, but I have to say, yours is much more potent and alluring."

I knew he and my grandmother Kora once had a thing for each other, and my father was a product of it. But I didn't know the story behind it. I still couldn't fathom why she would date a dark spirit, but at least Bael's darkness hadn't transferred into her womb. Dark spirits were dark because they chose to be. They weren't born that way. "Whatever," I said.

"I have to say I was quite surprised when I discovered Solomon's power resides in you instead of the ring," he told me. "Kora was a clever little witch. I do miss her."

"Do you know Aosoth killed her?" I spat.

Something flashed in his eyes. Disdain? "Yes. I'm quite aware she caused Kora's demise."

"Yet, you didn't do anything about it," I said in disgust. "You used my grandmother and didn't give a crap about her." I didn't know how our conversation took this track, but I was too curious enough about his relationship with my grandmother to let it go. Besides, a tiny piece of me was hoping if I stalled, maybe Nathan would find me.

"Your accusation regarding my lack of affection toward Kora is false," he snapped.

I stared at him, unflinching. I waited for him to continue, my eyes darting around me, silently praying to find Nathan heading our way. Of course he wasn't here, and I reminded myself to stop wishing for him.

Bael straightened his shoulders and wiped his hand down his gray wool sweater. His voice dropped to a high whisper, his tone drenched in hatred. "I will take care of Aosoth when the time is right. My actions may not suit your principles, but I assure you in the end it'll be justifiable."

"Well, then, let's get on with it," I said, wanting this whole nightmare to stop, realizing nobody would come to my rescue, and his principles were why I ended up in this horrible position.

"Follow me." He brushed past, and I fell in step with him.

We were heading toward the public parking area, and I refused to speak to him. When we reached a black Tahoe with tinted windows, my stomach churned. I glanced over my shoulder, wondering if I'd ever see Cannon Beach again. Silently I said goodbye and opened the passenger door, not realizing somebody was in the backseat until now.

Chapter Eighteen

Nathan

I read the letter.
Five times.

The *letter*.

Paige was gone.

Snatching it from the kitchen table, once more I unfolded the pink stationary with a faded whimsical fairy in the center and examined the familiar slants and strokes only she could make. It was real–not fake like I'd wanted to believe.

Nathan,

This relationship isn't working for me anymore. To be honest, I do blame you for me not being with my parents. Yeah, I had agreed to immortality, but I think it was because you pressured me into it.

Remember the night I told you I wanted to become immortal? It was after the horrible nightmare I had. You were so upset because you thought you almost lost me to a cardiac arrest. Well, I felt bad for you and guilty you were feeling that way. So of course I'd agree to becoming immortal. But lately, I've realized you were actually manipulating me into it. You were toying with my emotions for your own gain. I think Brayden was right. You were using my vulnerability to get what you wanted.

Everything about you and our relationship is now clear to me. I have to say, though, I was totally in love with you, but now I know it was all about you from the start. I'm crushed.

I don't want to see you again. Ever. So please remove your things from my house and never come back.

Paige.

I crumbled it into a ball and threw it across the room. Running a hand through my hair, I paced. I could feel the life inside me shriveling like a neglected plant starved of nourishment and warmth.

Paige was my sunshine in this dark world.

My everything.

But I had to admit to myself, subconsciously I'd known beforehand something wasn't right. I had felt it in my gut when we were at the hospital, but I thought it was just Paige being worried about Carrie. And then the same gut-wrenching feeling came to me at my house. More than once. Why hadn't I listened to those internal warnings and confronted Paige about it?

Why?

I already tried texting her and left several messages. I needed to talk to her, to let her know I'd never manipulate her.

I sat on the couch and held my head in my hands.

How could Paige possibly believe what she accused me of? Unless she was right. Did I manipulate her into accepting immortality? Was I more of a selfish bastard than I thought?

Oh, God.

I did tell her I would have still turned her immortal when she was dying because I loved her too much to allow her life to end. So of course she would have taken it as me only thinking of myself.

Okay, she was right on that account; however, there was no way in hell I'd ever toy with her emotions or manipulate her into doing what I wanted. I thought she knew me better. Her well-being and happiness were always my top priority, above anything else, including me.

My hand slipped off my face. I stared at it for a long moment. The lines in my palm glistened in the dull light from the tears I hadn't realize I was shedding. I wiped it on my knee and leaned back with the heel of my palms pressed against my eyelids.

Paige.

How could this be happening? How could one day Paige decide not to be in love with me? It didn't make sense. We had a rare and uncanny connection. The magnetic energy between us was undeniable.

I. Didn't. Get. It.

The house was quiet, as if holding its breath. The world outside was teeming with life, but where I sat these walls were like the sideboards of a coffin, entombing me in darkness and finality, sucking me into a chasm of despair and heartache.

My chest felt empty.

Our relationship couldn't be over. Not like this. Where the hell did she go? *Jesus Christ*, she wasn't safe out there on her own.

Then a thought occurred to me. I dropped my hands, my ears burning.

Brayden!

That son-of-a-bitch had to be behind this. He'd made it clear to me he'd do what he must to win Paige's affections. I bet he was the one who used Paige's vulnerability to twist our relationship to his favor. Their history together was his ammunition to use to his advantage.

My blood boiled.

I snatched my phone off the coffee table and called Tree. Jumping to my feet, I glanced at the clock on the wall. It was 2:30, but I didn't give a damn. I needed Brayden's number, and Tree was going to give it to me. I swear to God, if Brayden was behind this and something happened to Paige, I'd–

"Hello."

"Paige is gone," I said.

"I know."

Tree's answer threw me, and he sounded awake, but I detected a sadness in his tone, sending my heart racing.

"What do you know?" I held onto the kitchen counter for support, bracing myself for news I hadn't anticipated.

"She called me earlier," Tree said.

"How long ago?"

"An hour."

Silence again.

"*And?*"

"I'm sorry, Nathan, but she doesn't want anything to do with you. She told me she needed to get away from everything, but she'd stay in touch."

His voice didn't sound right, and although my stomach fell out from under me, I couldn't bring myself to believe his admission.

"Where did she go?" I persisted. There was something about me nobody knew. I could tell when somebody was lying, thanks to over a century of interrogating dark spirits before casting them out. Tree's next answer would verify my assumption.

"She didn't say," he replied.

"Why didn't you talk her out of it? Aren't you concerned the dark spirits might kidnap her like Roeick did? Do you really want such a thing on your conscience?" I knew I was being harsh, but I'd do whatever it took to find Paige.

"No," Tree's voice cracked. He cleared his throat. "Listen. I'm tired–"

"What's Brayden's number?"

"She's not with Brayden."

"How do you know?"

"She told me not to tell Brayden about her breaking up with you because she didn't want him to find her." His voice was unsteady, and a brutal fear slammed into me.

I could tell Tree was telling me the truth, which meant I was wrong about Brayden's involvement. But something wasn't right. There was no way Paige would end our relationship like this, and I knew Tree was lying to me about her whereabouts. He knew, but for some reason, he refused to tell me.

"Where is she, Tree?" My voice was low, dangerous.

"I have no idea."

I pushed myself off the counter and moved about the room. "Don't insult my intelligence. You and I both know you're lying to me."

"I have no idea what you're talking about," Tree said, sounding mechanical. "I'm sorry. You need to let Paige go."

"No." I said through clenched teeth, my temper flaring. "You listen to me. You know where she is, but for some *fucking* reason you won't tell me." I paused to calm myself. My mind spun with rage and frustration. A tourniquet of panic tightened my muscles. I took a couple deep breaths to reorient my brain.

Tree was only being loyal, like my father who kept my immortality a secret when the rest of our family thought I was dead. There had to be a damn good reason for Tree to withhold vital information from me, knowing how fragile a position Paige was in.

"Nathan. I'm sorry, man. I know–"

"Listen. Just give me Brayden's number, and I'll leave you alone," I told him.

Without further objections, he rattled off Brayden's number. I called Brayden right away. He didn't answer, and the mailbox was full. Gritting my teeth, I texted him.

Where is she?

I waited with my breath caught in my throat for his reply. And then my phone jingled, alerting me I had a text message. When I read the two words Brayden sent, I had to restrain myself from smashing my phone because I didn't have another spare. I glanced at Brayden's message again and roared.

I win.

Chapter Nineteen

Paige

A hand reached between the driver's and passenger's seats. I jerked away and screeched, standing halfway out of the vehicle with one foot on the floorboard and the other on the pavement. Bael took the phone offered to him and threw it on the ground.

"It's okay, Paige," an all-too-familiar voice said.

"Brayden?" I peeked around the seat and squealed. "Omigod." I hopped in and grabbed his hand, an onslaught of tears clouding my vision.

"I'm here. Everything is all right," he said.

"But you shouldn't be here," I choked, even though I was secretly relieved he was.

His fingers flitted to my cheek, and he gently brushed at the tears. I sucked in a sob, comforted by his touch and feeling guilty that I wanted to latch onto him like a spider monkey, to be in the safety of his arms.

"Yes, I should," he said. "My place is by your side."

"No. Don't you see you're a pawn in Bael's twisted plan?"

Bael glanced at me, his eyes glowing. "Brayden is here on his own accord. I'm simply allowing it because he shares in my ideals and to give you some solace."

"Don't do me any favors, and I'm sure you have *other* reasons," I said.

"My, my. What would they be?" His tone was mocking. I balled my hand into a fist, fighting the urge to punch him.

"Don't worry, Paige," Brayden said. "I'm not an idiot. I know what I'm doing."

"I don't think you do." I shook my head, wondering if Bael told him about Solomon's power residing in me instead of the ring, and that he wanted me to destroy the incantations. I opened my mouth to ask him but decided on another question instead. If Brayden knew, he would have mentioned it already. "Did you know Bael gave me an ultimatum? If I don't help him find the incantations, he'll have Tree killed?"

"Yes," Brayden admitted, "and that's one of the reasons why I'm here, to make sure you'll be okay, so you can find the incantations and spare Tree's life."

"How can you even be around him knowing he's willing to kill Tree?" I didn't try to hide the disgust in my voice.

"I know it–" Brayden started to say, but Bael cut him off.

"Where are the incantations? Are they in Ethiopia?"

I let go of Brayden's hand and turned to Bael in surprise. "How did you know?"

He smiled. "For centuries I've had a feeling they were there. You see, there's a tale of King Solomon and the Queen of Sheba. Her kingdom is believed to have been in Ethiopia. They fell in love and procreated. Their son's name was Meneliki, and he became the first emperor of Ethiopia."

"Why hadn't you ever followed through on this assumption?" I was dumbfounded he had all this knowledge, yet he disregarded it.

"He needed the ring to find the incantations," Brayden replied, "and a person worthy enough to break through the barriers Solomon placed around them."

I snorted. "I'm not a *worthy* person."

"On the contrary," Bael said, looking at me. "Your youth and humbleness blinds you of how significant you are to all of us."

I rolled my eyes. "Whatever."

"It's true," Brayden said. "I always knew you were special."

I made a disagreeing sound, thinking I was far from those things because right now Nathan was in pain because of me, and there was an internal battle I was fighting at the moment.

I wanted to be in the backseat with Brayden, in his embrace to ease the fear swelling in my chest. Brayden reminded me of home and eating an ice cream cone on a hot sunny day. He was the laughter echoing through the woods when Carrie chased after him and fell into a mud puddle. He was the past I longed for, but Nathan was the future I wanted.

"Where in Ethiopia are the incantations?" Bael wanted to know, snapping me out of my thoughts.

"They're somewhere in the Sof Omar cave in Bale." I glanced out the window and realized we were on Route 30, driving toward Portland. "Where are we going?" My heart raced.

"You and Brayden are going to be my guests for a few days while I get my affairs in order." He paused as if considering something. "After our deal is fulfilled, you can go on your merry way." He smirked. "However, I have no doubt our paths will cross again, and I may require your assistance in other matters."

Will this ever end?

I didn't like the hidden meaning behind those words or his self-assured tone. I knew then if he remained in this world, I'd be forced once again to do what he pleased. He was the puppet master, and I was his puppet. I hugged myself and stared out the window into the night. The headlights cast a bluish tint on the road ahead. The darkness seemed to press against the cold glass, and there was no escaping it.

I turned to him, boiling mad as the thought of being at his mercy kept wheeling in my mind. "I'm not your marionette," I said, and before I could stop myself, I continued. "I will destroy you before that could ever happen." I blinked, surprised at my brazenness at threatening an ancient spirit.

"You are a pistol." He stared at me, not minding the road, his eyes glowing once again, his expression turning dark. "But you need to hold your tongue and show some respect. Just be–"

I burst into laughter. I didn't know if it was out of nerves or his obnoxious behavior, but I couldn't quit. I glanced at him, and he glowered at me. I laughed harder. My sides began to ache. I curled an arm around my stomach, trying to catch my breath. I could hear Brayden snickering behind me.

"Silence!" Bael shouted.

Startled, we stopped.

"You infantile immortals have no idea who I am or what I'm capable of," Bael spat.

"Yeah, we do," Brayden said, trying to sound serious. "You're the great and powerful Oz. I mean Bael."

"No," I said between giggles. "He's actually Jesus Christ, and he got so pissed at God for bringing him here to sacrifice and suffer for a bunch of worthless humans that he went rogue. I mean, he does have a messiah complex and thinks he can walk on water."

Brayden roared with laughter.

"Jesus Christ never existed, you imbeciles," Bael said, annoyed.

"So?" I shrugged. "That's soooo not the point. The point is you *think* you're 'all that'"–I did air quotes–"but really you're not because if you were, you wouldn't need me."

"I had enough of your lack of respect." Abruptly, he pulled to the shoulder of the highway, took the keys out of the ignition and stepped out.

I turned to Brayden. "What's he doing?" I clutched his arm when his door opened. "No!" I screamed when Bael snatched Brayden's other arm.

"Get off me." Brayden hollered, kicking him.

"Leave him alone." Awkwardly, I climbed to the backseat and laced my arms and legs around Brayden's torso, yanking him back.

But Bael was stronger. He grabbed Brayden's ankles and dragged us out. My back smacked into the asphalt. I yelped in pain, and my grip loosened. Brayden was now out of my reach. He jumped up. In a flash he shoved Bael's chest, and he flew past the sparse trees lining the road into a vacant field.

"Brayden, no. He'll hurt you." I scrambled to my feet, wincing from the road rash. I rushed to his side. I could hear his heart thumping and his quick breaths.

"C'mon"–he took my hand–"let's get out of here."

"Are you insane?" I watched Bael push himself off the ground. "If I leave with you, he'll kill Tree."

"Tree will eventually die anyway," Brayden said, "but you and I will live on. Do you really want Bael to continue to have a hold on you by threatening Tree's life?"

I released my hand from his grip and stared at him in disbelief, stunned he would casually disregard Tree's life. "How can you be so . . ." I lost the word, but then it came to me. "Callous?" Bael was walking toward us. "Tree is our best friend."

"You know Tree means a lot to me," he said. "But you mean a hell of a lot more."

"I'm not leaving," I crossed my arms. "Besides, I thought you were pro Bael."

"I believe in his vision of reshaping this world in how it's supposed to be. To go back to the old ways. I don't, though, like the stranglehold he has on your life. And I won't stand aside and watch him make your life miserable until Tree or Carrie dies of old age or whatever." He pointed a finger in Bael's direction, jabbing the air, and yelled, "It's not happening!"

Bael's arrogant laughter echoed across the field.

Impulsively, I threw my arms around Brayden. Standing on my tiptoes, I whispered into his ear. "Listen to me. Solomon's power is inside me, not the ring." I felt him jerk in surprise, and I tightened my arms. "Bael knows this and wants me to destroy the incantations, but if I'm quick about it, I might be able to use them on him. Now, act like we're saying goodbye, and don't breathe a word of this to anybody."

"I don't want you to go. Not without me," Brayden said, playing along.

"You lost that privilege when you disrespected me." Bael halted in front of us.

Brayden wheeled on him. I darted between them and quickly decided to take Bael's side, not only to appease him, but to hopefully blind him to the fact I would consider controlling him. I wasn't sure if it would work but hoped Brayden would catch on.

"Back off," I said. "I'm going with Bael, and you should accept the fact he doesn't want you coming with us."

"Like hell I will." Brayden glared at Bael. "He's lucky I didn't snap his neck."

"I'm not a fool, Paige," Bael said. "I know you crave Brayden's presence, yet for some reason you're suddenly willing to release him from our company. Why the change of heart?"

My stomach dropped.

He *knew*.

My mind went blank. I could feel the blood draining from my face, and my mouth went dry.

"You're naive to think I haven't considered you defying me once the incantations are discovered."

The world seemed to cave in on me. I staggered into Brayden. He locked his arms around my shoulders so I wouldn't crumble to the ground. It was useless to try to defeat Bael. He was too wise and always one step ahead.

"I'm going to be candid," he continued. "I wasn't expecting anything less from you considering your stubbornness and youth tends to be your downfall. Those months of me impersonating Matt were quite useful. And although you have qualities I admire, and I do enjoy your company . . . when you're being reasonable that is, I won't think twice to wipe the people you love from this earth if you were to attempt to harm me. You see, I already have reinforcements in place to ensure my safety and to carry out my orders."

In the distance, I could hear several vehicles heading our way. I turned to look. Headlights pierced the night. They must have been doing at least a hundred miles per hour because in no time the beams were spotlighting us, causing me to shield my eyes, while a high-pitched ringing sounded in my ears.

"Get in the car," Bael barked, reaching for me, but Brayden backed away, pulling me with him. "If you want to come, get her in the car now," he said to Brayden, suddenly filled with an anxious energy that caused my stomach to sink.

As Bael opened the door behind the passenger seat, Brayden swung us around. We hurried inside. White brightness flooded through the windows, and tires squealed on the asphalt. A glossy black extended cab pickup parked sideways in front of us.

Nathan?

I leaned forward, digging my nails into the leather seats, peering through the glass.

Please be Nathan.

My heart thudded at the anticipation it could be him.

"Paige," Brayden said behind me.

I didn't respond or move. I kept my eyes trained ahead of me. But when several people exited the pickup, none of them Nathan, I released the air from my lungs and hung my head. I was pathetic. Why couldn't I stick to the agreement I'd made with myself? Nathan wasn't coming to my rescue, and being with him wasn't part of my life now. Dealing with Bael was.

"We're in deep shit."

I turned at Brayden's troubled voice. "Wh-what?" He gestured to the three vehicles boxing us in. I hadn't realized it until now, but Bael remained outside, standing beside the driver's door. "Crap. Who are they?" I glanced around, counting ten people moving toward Bael. None of them I recognized.

"I don't know." Brayden glanced out the window toward the sparse trees and open field. "I think we can make a run for it."

"Volac," Bael said.

I gasped, knowing Volac was an ancient dark spirit who wanted me dead so Bael couldn't go through with his plans. Anwar had cast Volac out not too long ago, and I couldn't fathom how Volac regained his energy so quickly. It usually took weeks, if not longer, for that to happen.

"Fuck," Brayden mumbled. "This must be Volac's group." He snatched my hand and popped the door open.

But when we stepped out, we were confronted with a wall of bodies, halting us in our tracks. Three pairs of eyes were glowing at us, a beam of light swiped across the other two pair, and their arms were linked together, forming a powerful barrier we couldn't breach.

We were so screwed.

Chapter Twenty

Nathan

I went home as she requested. Out of her–
Life.

Jesus Christ, I can't even stomach the thought.

I didn't bother turning on the lights when I opened the door. The overnight bag was slung over my shoulder, and I froze with the handle still in my grasp. The moonlight spilled onto the wooden floor, illuminating the dust motes floating above the dull surface. A cold darkness seeped into my pores. My heart jackhammered against my rib cage, thudding in my ears like a war drum reaching its peak before sending an army off to battle. My breath caught in my throat, the air curdling in my lungs, robbing me of oxygen. I could hardly breathe.

In the far distance an elk bugled as if to punctuate the overwhelming loneliness crashing upon me. My grip tightened on the handle and at the same time my shoulders rolled forward. The strap slid down my arm, releasing the bag. It hit the floor with a heavy thunk. I stumbled forward, but then managed to steady myself.

Brayden's text kept flashing through my mind:

I Win. I Win. I Win.

Paige wasn't a possession. He damned well knew it, and I knew his "*I win*" statement wasn't spawned from such mentality. Sure, Brayden was determined to gain Paige's affections, so they would overshadow what she felt for me, but had he actually succeeded?

My throat constricted, and the room spun. I swung the door closed. It slammed, and I staggered sideways. My shoe caught my bag, and I lurched forward. With my arms splayed in front of me, I braced myself before my face smashed the floor. I rolled onto my back and lay there trying to catch my breath. It sounded ragged and broken, a manifestation of how I felt inside.

In the far dark corners of my mind, an old comfort presented itself, as if to say *"Hello, remember me? I comforted you once before, made you numb to where you felt nothing. I can do it again, and this time especially warrants my assistance."*

I rested an arm over my eyes and groaned, involuntarily swallowing, remembering the smooth amber liquid sliding down my throat, leaving a trail of warmth in its wake, soothing my body and senses, paralyzing them. I also remembered the time where I drank myself into a stupor and would wander into a brothel in a drunken daze, only to find the next morning, I could barely recall what actually took place the night before. Of course Cassondra, who worked there by choice not by necessity, couldn't keep her legs closed whenever I was around—

Wait a minute.

I backtracked those thoughts. She couldn't keep her legs closed, period. She latched onto me when I'd stumbled through their door, swinging a bottle of whiskey by its neck at my side. My white button-up shirt wrinkled and half untucked from my rumpled brown trousers.

But I didn't want to think about that. Besides, I couldn't remember much anyway. Those pockets of time in my life were foggy, until I'd decided drowning my sorrow wasn't a way to live. I had to admit, though, it did take the edge off for a while and had given me a reprieve from my grief over outliving my family, which sure was nice.

With the thought, the voice raised its ugly little head once more. *"So how about it? You deserve to feel nothing for a while. To feel detached, yet relaxed. You know Anwar always keeps bottles of brandy and whiskey in your house."*

In my mind's eye, I could see Anwar getting a brandy glass from the oak china cabinet and opening the cupboard beneath it where he stored his liquor. He'd pour it, his huge hand warming the delicate glass. Slowly he'd swirl the caramel color around, some of the liquid sticking to the sides, and he'd gingerly hold it to his lips, his nostrils widening as he sniffed it and finally he'd take a sip. The very act of drinking a fine spirit was a ritual Anwar held in high regard, something I learned to emulate throughout the years of spending nights playing chess with him.

My mouth watered, and I found my reservations not to give into it faltering. One lousy night of complete and utter drunkenness to take away this unbearable ache in my heart wouldn't hurt.

Just one.

"Then you could forget about her."

My hand flew to my chest when a jolt of fear stabbed my heart. I bolted up and sat motionless for a long moment.

Something wasn't right. Fear and panic surged through me. I tried to decipher if those feelings were self-induced or coming from an outside source. Closing my eyes, I took slow deep breaths while trying to swipe aside the web of thoughts entangling me moments ago.

"We're so screwed," I heard Paige say.

Her words were so clear in my head, as if she said it right beside me. I didn't know how I heard her, but I did. There was no doubt in my mind, and I knew in that instant those feelings of fear and panic raging through me were hers.

I leaped to my feet, ready to walk through the pit of hell and do battle with whatever it was threatening her. Whether she chose to be with Brayden or not was irrelevant. Even if she never wanted to see me again, it didn't matter. My feelings for Paige hadn't changed, and there was still something not right with how she ended our relationship.

I zipped to the door, then stopped cold in my tracks. I had no idea where she was, so where would I go? Running a hand through my hair, an annoyed sigh escaped my lips.

I paced.

Now what the hell was I going to do? Son-of-a—

My mind stilled, and the mental chatter retracted, an army of thoughts abandoning their posts. All but one—a straggler. It was a solution. A very slim one, and I doubted it would work, but right now I had no other leads. Within seconds, I was in my pickup, fishtailing down the dirt path through the woods, white knuckling the steering wheel, gritting my teeth. I stopped and shifted into reverse. Slinging an arm over the backseat, I peered out the back window and slammed my foot on the gas, the tires blowing clouds of dirt in the air. I spun the pickup in front of my house and hopped out. I could run faster to my destination than driving there. So I sped through the dark forest, hoping this one unlikely person would be able to help me.

* * *

"Nathan?" Tree's mother stood behind the nurses' station looking a bit taken aback from my sudden presence. "What are you doing here at this hour?" Tori must have seen something disturbing in my face because an anxiousness entered her eyes. She stepped around the counter. "Is Jack okay?" Her eyes filled with tears.

"Tree . . . um, Jack is fine," I told her. "I need to see Carrie, though." My voice was deep and rough with emotion.

She reached in the front pocket of her white scrub top and extracted a Kleenex. She dabbed at the corner of her eyes and frowned. "It's too early for visiting hours."

I was afraid she'd cite policy, but I wouldn't give up so easily. I stared at her, silently pleading with my eyes to make this one exception.

She blinked and looked away, wiping her nose with the Kleenex. "If you're worried about Carrie, she's doing quite well," she said, balling up the tissue and dropping it in the trash can next to the counter.

"That's wonderful, but I still would like to see her," I replied, still staring at her.

She lifted her gaze to mine. Her forehead wrinkled. "Does Jack know you're here? They're in love, you know."

I couldn't believe what she was implying. I shook my head and let out a humorless laugh. I ran a hand through my hair, and it took every ounce of what willpower I could muster not to blow up. My ears were burning.

She raised her hands, the skepticism vanishing from her face. "Okay. Okay. I can see your feelings for Carrie are strictly friendship and nothing more. But I had to be sure because Paige isn't with you, so I assumed–"

I squinted at her. "I'm still in love with Paige," my voice cracked. I cleared my throat. "But I must see Carrie . . . for Paige."

An older woman with jet black air in a tight bun wheeled a large gray plastic cart with cleaning supplies down the hall. She wore dark green scrubs, and the artificial light reflected the silver strands threaded through her hair.

Tori glanced at her. She opened her mouth to ask another question, but she must have seen the impatience tightening the muscles in my face because she sighed instead. "Very well," she finally said. "Try to be quick about it."

"Thank you." I dashed in the room without giving her a second look.

The room was dark, except for a small lighted lamp on a table in the far corner. Machines surrounded Carrie's hospital bed. Thin white plastic tubes were strung over the metal rail, disappearing beneath the covers where Carrie lay. A constant beeping pulsed between us, and although the air held a floral scent from all the blossoms crowding the other tables, my nostrils burned from the lingering antiseptic smell. I dragged a blue vinyl chair next to Carrie.

"Carrie," I said in a low voice, sitting in the chair and scooting it closer to her. "It's Nathan." My hand snaked beneath the thin white blankets. I held her limp hand and lightly squeezed it. "I'm sorry to bother you, but it's important." I paused and studied her for a few moments, hoping to see any hint of recognition on her face: a twitch on the lips, eye movement, anything. I got nothing, only solid stone; a mummified version of her. I continued, silently begging for some spiritual help. "I know you can hear me. I know you're in there somewhere." I paused again. No response. I rested my head on the edge of the mattress. Hope was slipping through my fingers. I knew it would be a matter of time before Tori would barge in to ask me to leave. The morning crew would be arriving soon.

Taking a deep breath, I thought I'd give it one more shot. I lifted my head and gave Carrie's hand another soft squeeze. "Paige is in serious danger, Carrie, and you're my only hope." Her fingers wiggled. I sat up, the sound of my heart pulsing in my ears. I leaned forward, my lips next to her ear. "Without your help, Paige might die." I knew it was extreme, but I was desperate, and in a sense it could be true.

Carrie's eyelids fluttered open. "Paige," she whispered and at the same time I breathed a sigh of relief.

"Yes," I whispered. "She's in serious trouble, and you're the only one who can help me save her."

Her eyes shifted to mine. I could tell she was in between worlds by the faraway look in them. "Paige," she repeated as if she were calling from another land.

"If you know anything, please tell me. Paige's life is depending upon it," I said.

She closed her eyes. My heart stopped. What if I'd lost the connection with her? But then her chest rose, and she released a slow, steady breath. She opened her eyes, and the cloudiness in them vanished.

"Bael forced Paige and Tree into a deal with him," she said in a clear high whisper.

I jerked my head back and gaped at her. "What?"

"I was unconscious, but I heard everything. He told her he'd save my life if she promised to take him to the incantations and destroy them. He warned her if she told anybody about their agreement, he'd have Tree killed. He also threatened Tree that he'd wipe out his whole family if he were to squeal about this arrangement."

I stared at her, my vision out of focused. Everything started to make sense. Paige's behavior and the note she had written. All of it was completely out of character for her, but she had no choice. She ended our relationship to save her two best friends.

"She still loves me," I said to myself.

Carrie looked at me in confusion. "Of course she does. She's crazy in love with you." She closed her eyes and hummed the same lullaby Paige hummed when she got back from helping her.

I knew she was drifting from me, and I suddenly became panic-stricken. She couldn't leave just yet. I still needed answers. And now that I knew Paige made a bargain with Bael, I had no doubt in my mind she was with him right at this moment. Where Brayden came to play in all of it, I didn't know.

"Carrie, where's Paige?" I heard the desperation in my voice. "I need to find her." I squeezed her hand, but it was dead weight. She stopped humming. "Carrie?" I shook her arm.

No response.

I stared hard at her, mentally willing her to come back to me, to answer my one last question.

Only this one question.

Please.

But she had returned to the place Paige told me about. I released her hand and stood, pushing the chair back. I leaned next to her ear and whispered, "Thanks, Carrie, for telling me what you could. Sleep well, and I'll figure out a way to bring Paige back to us."

I stepped away from the bed and locked my hands behind my head. Now what was I going to do? If I were to confront Tree about what Carrie told me, it might put him in a compromising position. I wouldn't do such a thing to him or risk the lives of his family.

"She's crazy in love with you." Carrie's words repeated in my head.

I closed my eyes and rubbed my temples. What Paige had done was the ultimate selfless act, something I myself could have never done if it involved losing her to save another life. But Paige was an anomaly set apart from anyone I had ever known. I could feel a dampness around my eyes and ran my fingers across them.

"I'll find you. Even if I have to scour the earth and torture every dark

spirit who crosses me. I. Will. Find. You."

My ears rang, and my muscles instantly tensed. I could hear Tori arguing with someone, saying it was too early for visitors. Another female voice responded. Her words were clipped and downright rude. "Back off, lady, I'll be gone in a minute."

In a flash, I grabbed the door handle, prepared to subdue the situation by whatever means to protect Tori and Carrie. The door slammed into my chest, knocking me backwards. Reflexively, I snatched the arm and pushed the woman against the wall, my hand around her neck.

"Excuse me. You're not supposed to be here," Tori said outside the room, her raised voice pissed. "I'll call security."

The door closed in her face, but she swung it open and entered. She gasped. "Nathan. What on earth are you doing?"

I released my grip. The female coughed and rubbed her neck. A yellow beam of light swiped across her green eyes. "He's protecting Carrie from me," she said, fixing her gaze on Tori.

"What?" Tori shrieked.

"I'm in love with Carrie," the female dark spirit continued. "I've been obsessed with her."

Tori gaped at her, dumbfounded.

The female smirked, enjoying herself. "Yeah, that's right. But no worries. Carrie doesn't swing that way, and I just came here to say goodbye."

Tori blinked at her, then looked at me for confirmation. I nodded and could hear the air escaping her lips, and her heartrate slowing down. Her shoulders relaxed and the fine lines at the corner of her eyes and around her mouth sagged from exhaustion. "You two need to leave," she said, sounding spent. She step aside and pointed her finger out the door. The female left the room, the smirk still on her face. When I made a move to follow, Tori took my arm, halting me. "I don't know what's really going on," she said, "but I appreciate you looking out for Carrie."

"Paige and the people she loves matters to me," I said, mentally excluding Brayden from my statement.

She released my arm, a tired smile forming on her lips. "Yes, I know that now."

"Get some rest," I said before stepping out of the room.

I headed through the maze of halls, having no idea where the female dark spirit went, knowing damn well who it was. I took the elevator down to the main floor while trying to formulate a plan. When I reached the lobby, my ears rang. She was sitting in one of the chairs with a leg draped over the wooden arm, looking bored.

"Ameerah, what the hell are you up to?" I asked, cautiously.

She swung her leg and stood, swiping a piece of dark hair out of her face. "I'm here to help you."

I crossed my arms. "Why?" The last time she had helped me, I was ambushed by a group of dark spirits, so my trust level with her remained on shaky ground.

She rolled her eyes. "I told you that night I wasn't aware I was being followed," she said, sensing my apprehension. "Besides, what other options do you have?"

She had a point.

She headed toward the automatic sliding glass doors. "C'mon. We have work to do." She paused when she realized I wasn't following her, the doors sliding back and forth in front of her, making a hissing sound. She glanced over her shoulder. "Your lack of trust in me may be the cause of Paige's demise."

I flinched and then followed her out into the predawn world, not thrilled with having to resort to a dark spirit's help.

Chapter Twenty-One

Paige

Brayden took my wrist and pulled me to his side. His hand slid into mine. He squeezed it in spurts, sending Morse code, like we used to do when we were kids playing war against another group. Despite the unfortunate circumstances we were under, it touched me Brayden remembered this tactic we'd used long ago to our advantage, and I couldn't help but smile. He told me to keep a clear head and not to provoke them.

I looked up at the five men standing shoulder to shoulder in front of us. The two on each end looked like they were in a biker gang. They were both stocky. The one to my left had shoulder- length brown bushy hair and a wild look in his blue eyes. He sneered at me, revealing a gold tooth and rubbed his chin with his meaty hand. I noticed tattoos covering his arm. He narrowed his eyes, giving me an icy stare. I pressed my side against Brayden's and glanced away. I squeezed his hand several times, telling him I'd stay calm, but I didn't like this one bit.

"I'll make a deal with you, Bael," Volac said behind me, on the other side of the Tahoe. "You give me the ring, and I'll let Paige go."

I drew myself up and squared my shoulders, refusing to be intimidated by the men who stood before me. The guy in front looked like Billy Idol, with his pale hair short and spiky, and a sharp-studded dog collar around his neck. His gaze latched onto mine. His brown eyes were glowing. I acted like I hadn't noticed and took in the other two guys. One was big and black with a buzz cut, and the other was normal in height and had a mop of dark blond hair. They were both muscular and wore blue jeans and black T-shirts.

Bael laughed, an amused, cocky sound. "Now why would I surrender the ring to you . . . or anyone for that matter?"

"Because you know I'll destroy it," Volac countered. "I also know Paige is an enigma you're dying to figure out. However, if I were to destroy her, the mystery of her would never be solved. It would haunt you for the rest of your existence."

"You think you have it all figured out, don't you?" Bael said, his tone edging toward threatening.

Brayden and I shared a look that could clearly be read as, uh-oh this situation could quickly become volatile at any moment. The guys in front of us seemed unfazed, except for the Billy Idol wannabe; he immediately spoke up in Volac's defense.

"Bloody hell, he has it figured out, ya wanker," he said to Bael, surprising me with his British accent.

"You're not helping, Felix," Volac said. "So I advise you to shut that hole in your face."

Felix glared at a spot above my head and cracked his knuckles. I thought about jumping up in the air and taking off into the prairie behind them, but they were too close to Brayden and me and could easily snatch our arms, preventing us from doing so. Besides, I wasn't in a position to do it. I had to think of Tree.

"I know you value your autonomy," Bael said to Volac. "I give you my word. I will not intrude on your way of life. I'll even go as far as to perform a blood oath if you so desire."

"A tempting proposal," Volac said, "and a week ago I would have accepted. However, I must decline your offer because it's not about me anymore. There are others like myself who refuse to have the yoke of tyranny around their necks."

An idea came to me, and before I could stop and think about it, the words were already flowing from my mouth. "I agree with Volac," I said. Brayden turned to me with a what-are-you-doing expression. I smirked, knowing he would know what it meant: *play along with me.* He squeezed my hand, telling me okay.

"What?" Bael said, sounding displeased.

I raised my voice. "I *said*, I agree with Volac, because how would you like it if somebody had the power to control you? You wouldn't, would you?"

"I'm starting to like this girl," the blond guy whispered to the biker next to him.

"You know," Brayden interjected. "I think Paige has a point. I do agree with you, Bael, on bringing back the old ways, but you have no right to control other people's lives. You're not God, and even God gives people the freewill to do what they want."

Bael laughed. It was dark and menacing. When he spoke, the loathing he felt dripped from each word. "The people in this world are unruly. They lack structure and discipline. They are a cancer which keeps spreading and feeding off the natural resources without giving something back in exchange or replenishing it. You cut down a tree . . . you plant another one in its stead.

"The God you speak of, *Brayden,*" he went on in a haughty voice, "doesn't care. I had questioned his authority one too many times and was cast to earth with words as sweet as honey, promising me this would be my eternal domain. I could roam freely between this world and my own spiritual realm. But I later discovered thy enemy was not one but many." I glanced at Brayden, wondering if he was able to follow what Bael was babbling about. My plan to get Bael to speak freely worked, but I wasn't following what he was saying. Brayden shook his head and shrugged. "There's not one but many gods, all part of one godhead."

"I don't understand," I said without thinking. Brayden elbowed me in the side and shot me a look to be quiet. I think he was afraid of me distracting Bael's train of thought that he wouldn't finish divulging what could be useful to us if we live through this mess. I bit my lip and released his hand so I could wipe my sweaty palms off on my jeans.

"As for controlling the dark spirits," he continued, totally ignoring my comment. I could hear him moving around in a circle. His movements were slow and casual. "I plan to control the ones who are no better than the humans."

I think I knew what Bael was doing by telling Volac this because he already knew his opportunity to control the dark spirits had vanished when he discovered Solomon's power was in me and not the ring. Of course he didn't want Volac to discover that, so he was playing him.

"I'm not concern with the spirits who do horrific things to humans or take delight in scaring them. In fact, I encourage such behavior and will eventually lead an army of them, like I'd done in World War II, only I won't segregate a certain group like I had done with the Jews."

My throat tightened, and my stomach clenched into a knot. I couldn't believe what I just heard. I knew the dark spirits created horrific acts against humanity, but I'd never given thought to Bael being the one who orchestrated such acts. I don't know why, but his admission to it wheeled me into a thick cloud of heartache, despair, and nausea. "What?" I squeaked and then went into a coughing fit. I bent over and held my stomach. "Why? You—you lost the war," I choked. "What was the p-purpose?"

Brayden draped his arm around my back. "It's okay, Paige," he said in a low voice next to my ear. "Calm down. Now is not the time to fall apart."

I knew he was right, but a vision of naked bodies piled on top of each other in a ditch hovered in my mind. I remembered watching Nazi week on the History Channel, trying to understand how humans could turn into monsters and how someone like Hitler could gain so much power and control over a nation.

My throat and eyes burned from my harsh coughing. Brayden gathered my hair and held it away from my face, reminding me of when Nathan had done the same thing.

Nathan.

My heart ached, and I hugged my arms tighter around my stomach. I wanted desperately to be in Nathan's embrace, away from all of this, in the comforts of my home.

Nathan.

"Why?" Bael echoed. "Because there was a purpose behind it, which included losing the war."

Between my coughs I became mildly aware of feet shifting uneasily in front of me, but they remained where they were. I dropped to the ground, not caring if I lived or died. I'd lost Nathan over this, and even if I did destroy the incantations, Bael could still gather another army of dark spirits and do a mass genocide on the human race. And where had the immortals been when War World II happened? Why didn't they stop it? Unless, there were not enough of them. I once asked Nathan how many were there in this world, and he didn't know. I was starting to realize we were sadly outnumbered—there were way more dark spirits than immortals. I was an idiot to think I could make a difference, and that I could help make this world a better place by protecting humanity from the darkness encroaching upon them. The hope I once had dimmed inside me. I pulled my knees to my chest and wrapped my arms around them.

Brayden kneeled next to me and leaned his head to mine. Softly, he started a song he used to sing to me when we were kids, when I was feeling alone and missing my dad. "This little light of mine, I'm going to let it shine. This little light of mine, I'm going to let it shine."

"I don't mean to step on your toes, Bael," Volac said, clearing his throat. "I'm also well aware you're more powerful than I."

"Let it shine, let it shine, let it shine."

"But I have to be frank with you. If you don't give me the ring, I will not only kill Paige, but you'll also have a war on your hands."

Brayden placed his arm around my shoulders and continued singing. "Hide it under a bushel? No. I'm going to let it shine. Hide it under a bushel? No. I'm going to let it shine."

I scooted closer to Brayden and leaned into him. One of the guys in front of us was humming the song. It sounded like it came from the biker guy with the tattoos.

"Let it shine, let it shine, let it shine."

"You're treading in dangerous waters by threatening me," Bael arrogantly said, unfazed by Volac's warning.

"Don't let Satan blow it out. I'm gonna let it shine. Don't let Satan blow it out. I'm gonna let it shine."

"Randall!" Volac shouted, causing me to look up. "Stop humming that ridiculous song."

"Sorry. It's a catchy tune," the biker with the tattoo arm said. Red-faced, he looked down and kept quiet.

I took a deep breath, and Brayden pulled me to my feet. He slung his arm around my shoulders again, keeping me close. The hopelessness I felt a few minutes ago still lingered inside me, but that song did spark a strength I forgot I had. Brayden remembered, though. He knew it was tucked away in a part of my soul like an inspirational quote written in a journal you had long forgotten about, only to discover it on the day you needed to read it the most. A familiar feeling toward Brayden reawakened inside me, causing my stomach to dip, and thoughts of our mortal life together and all the things we have done and been through, flooded my mind. Brayden reminded me of home, of fun and easy times. I longed for them, where the only problems I had to deal with were my premonitions and home life. Was it possible we were meant to be together? But then a vision of me lying in Nathan's arms popped in my head. A terrible ache gnawed at me heart.

"I realize the consequences of my actions toward you, Bael," Volac said. "I'm also not deluded enough to think I can overthrow you. However, I'd give you a good fight, and I believe we'd end up sparring for a very long time, possibly for centuries." He paused, and the air seemed to grow thicker around us. Nobody made a sound. Dead silence, as if the earth and every living creature on it were frozen in the moment. "I'm not your enemy," Volac finally said. "I don't care if you bring back the old ways or gather another legion. I just want my freedom and so do others like myself. I know you're a man of your word, but my mind cannot be eased unless you give me the ring, and I destroy it."

"I have to admit," Bael said, gauging each word carefully, "your boldness is a trait I admire. How do you propose to destroy the ring? Kora couldn't do it. What makes you think you can?"

"I can't," Volac admitted. "But I've found an alternative to suit this unfortunate situation quite well."

I glanced at the guys in front of me. They were all staring above my head, their expressions not at all surprised at Volac's statement. It became obvious he had filled them in on his plan. I was curious to find out and found myself holding my breath, afraid I might miss what Volac had to say.

"Do tell," Bael said.

"Have you heard of space burial?" Volac asked.

"Yes, I have."

Space Burial? I wondered what that was. It sounded like something straight out of a sci-fi movie.

"May 22, 2012," Volac stated, "three-hundred and eight remains were successfully launched into space, along with SpaceX's Dragon spacecraft on a Falcon 9 rocket. The next liftoff is scheduled for August 2014; however, I can get Solomon's ring rocketed into space within a week, if you relinquish his ring to me, that is."

Wow. I hadn't known humans could get their remains launched into space after they died. That was kind of cool, actually, and Volac's idea struck me as a good one.

"I'm impressed," Bael said. "But how will I know if the ring made it to space successfully?"

"You can see it for yourself if you like, or you can have Ayperos go instead."

A long, uncomfortable silence fell between them. I closed my eyes and listened to what they were doing. A heart was racing. It had to be Volac's, anticipating Bael's response to his proposal. I realized then that Volac was scared of Bael. Well, I guess I couldn't blame him. Bael was the most devious and underhanded of them all. I also knew what Bael was doing. He was completely manipulating Volac. Silently, I made a vow to myself I would pay special attention to Bael's every word and action because like I told him earlier, I was not his marionette.

"I have no ill will toward you," Volac nervously said, "But–"

"I will accept your offer," Bael abruptly said, "on the condition you accept mine as well."

"Of course."

"You and your followers leave Paige alone."

"Fair enough."

"I will have Ayperos go with you to launch the ring into space," Bael said, "and he will remain with you until it happens. He's on his way right now, so I suggest you stay put and wait for his arrival."

How weird. Bael didn't have a phone with him, nor did he know we were going to be held up by Volac's group. I wondered how he got hold of Ayperos. They were walking away from the Tahoe to the other side of the street, and I knew why. If the ring was near me, it would hum. The closer it got to me, the louder it hummed. I imagined Bael didn't want to take that chance.

"Before I give you the ring," Bael said. "I would like for you to have your men stand down and let Paige and Brayden go."

A sharp whistle pierced the night. The men stepped away from us and walked to where Bael and Volac stood. This would have been the perfect moment to take off, but I had Tree to think about. So I remained, even though Brayden gestured toward the field. I shook my head and mouthed, "Tree." He rolled his eyes and opened the door, waving for me to get in. I slid into the backseat and stared out the side window, watching Bael give a tall, broad shoulder guy the ring. The door closed behind me, and I felt Brayden's body heat against my back.

"Your stubbornness is going to get you killed or seriously hurt one day," he mumbled. "We can still make a run for it."

"I'm not leaving," I firmly said, not bothering to look at him. "If you want to go, then go."

"I'm not leaving you," he said, his voice raised, as if my comment was the most ridiculous thing he'd ever heard.

Bael shook Volac's hand, and Volac promised he would wait for Ayperos before he got rid of the ring for good.

I turned to Brayden. He was sitting there with his arms tightly across his chest, his knees apart, scowling. I pretended like his attitude didn't bother me, even though it did. I mean, come on. He was free to go about his life, where I was quickly losing hope, and the despair I felt earlier, still stuck in my chest like a glob of dried glue. But I had to at least try and defeat Bael or put him in his place. Not to mention making sure Tree and Carrie were going to be okay. I decided to overlook his little hissy fit and asked him a question instead. "Do you know how Bael got hold of Ayperos without using a cell phone?" I was still perplexed about it and thought maybe my question would ease the soupy tension in the air.

"When you join in a blood oath with a dark spirit, you two can communicate telepathically with each other," he said, sounding bored.

"Seriously?"

Brayden looked at me and nodded. "You can also listen to the other one's conversation, if the oath partner allows it."

"Why would Ayperos create a blood oath with Bael?" I wondered.

Brayden shrugged. "I don't know, but they go way back."

I opened my mouth to say something but heard Bael approaching. I sat back and wondered what was going to happen next. I had to come up with a plan, but at that moment I didn't know what. Brayden lifted his arm and placed it around my shoulders. I scooted closer to him, wanting desperately to be reassured everything would be okay and to feel the comfort of his arms around me.

"He won't be bothering you anymore," Bael said, sitting behind the wheel, glancing in the rearview at me.

I didn't say anything. I couldn't. His very presence sickened me. I caught my mind trying to revert to World War II. I wouldn't allow it. Instead, I glared at him. I had no idea what was going to happen from here. All I knew was I had to beat him at his own game, but the question was how?

Chapter Twenty-Two

Nathan

I fell in step with Ameerah. We crossed the half empty parking lot to a Jeep Grand Cherokee. Beads of early morning dew clung to the shiny black paint, making me wonder how long Ameerah had been lurking around the hospital. She pulled keys out of her pocket and pushed a button. A clicking noise resounded inside the vehicle. I quickly scanned the area for intruding eyes. A red Ford Focus pulled into a parking space, and a petite blonde emerged wearing blue scrubs. Other vehicles were filing in. The morning shift was arriving and nothing seemed out of the ordinary. Ameerah opened the door and disappeared from my sight. I followed suit, sinking into the soft leather seat. In no time, we were exiting the hospital grounds, turning off of Exchange Street toward twentieth. Trees towered above houses built in the early 1900s, shedding their crimson and gold leaves around the spacious properties. The early morning sun poked through the gray clouds, highlighting the brilliant foliage scattered on patches of bare earth.

Without taking her eyes off the road, Ameerah reached between our seats to the back, producing a pale yellow, leathery book with brass clasps holding down leather straps. She tossed it to my lap. "It's a grimoire," she said, a smirk tugging at the corner of her mouth.

I picked it up and ran my fingers over the strange cover. I found it odd there was nothing written on it. I turned it over. There were no words or pictures on the back as well. The spine was even blank. There were dark brown wrinkles, bunched on the bottom and fanning out on the top of the cover. I examined it some more and realized on close observation it resembled The Tree of Life. I pointed to the image. "Is this The Tree of–"

"Life," Ameerah said, her smirk crossing her face now. "Yes, and it's bound in human flesh."

I raised my eyebrows, knowing back in the seventeenth century there were people who practiced binding books in tanned, human skin, called anthropodermic biblipedy–an exercise I found quite gruesome. In all my travels, I'd heard stories of these books but never encountered one until now.

Ameerah reached to brush her fingertips on the spine. "I take it you don't possess one of these macabre artifacts?"

"No, but I've heard tales of them," I answered, wondering who was the poor bastard this skin belonged to.

"You do have a grimoire, right?"

"Of course. I have several." I unlatched the book and opened it. A gasp of air blew into my face, assailing my senses with a musty, sour odor. I wrinkled my nose at the foul stench, my mind pulling up an image of a putrefying, gaping wound.

"The smell will subside in a minute," Ameerah said, slowing behind a flatbed trailer piled with logs. She leaned to her left to see if she could pass him. "Dammit. I can't see around him." She released an annoyed sigh and sat back.

I focused my attention back on the grimoire, not bothering to ask her why we were on a back country road or where we were headed. I became too interested in what I held in my hands to care at the moment. The parchment paper was yellowed from age but in fine condition considering its ancient origin. Latin was the chosen language in this book of magic. Black magic to be exact. I could tell by the occult symbols displayed on almost every page I thumbed through. One of the pages had a glyph which stood for sulfur–a cross with a smaller horizontal bar above it and what looked like the number eight attached to the bottom on its side. The emblem stood for spiritually of the human soul. Below, it talked about its nature and how to merge and take control of another spirit housed in a temple made of flesh and bone. It also spoke of boundaries and invitations. One could not gain access to the dwelling of a spectral being unless permission was granted. A list followed on how to acquire such authorization and deceive *innocents* by using such measures as the talking board. I immediately thought of Bael tricking Carrie when he was possessing Matt, and they were playing with the Ouija board.

"Blind magic," Ameerah said, glancing at the page I was reading. I looked up, and she shrugged. "Compelling, actually, but not in the fictitious vampire kind of way. It's a cunning act performed by slipping through the back doors, using tools that dazzles the mind and dulls all reasoning."

"Have you done this before?" I asked.

"Every dark spirit has." Ameerah tore her eyes off mine and stared out the windshield. The road ahead branched into a fork, and the logger in front of us slowed. His left red blinker light came on, signaling he was turning left. "I'm not proud of it," she continued, "but at the time I was bitter toward humans."

"Because of what your parents did and what happened to you in the asylum, right?" I guessed.

Her eyebrows pulled together. "Yes."

I turned my attention back on the book and noticed a thin, purple ribbon poking out toward the middle. "What changed your mind?" I asked while using the side of my thumb to open the page. I was met with a hand drawn picture, similar to the one in my own grimoire, except the image was reversed. Instead of a male figure standing inside a circle, it was a hooded one.

"Nadia. One day I had decided to work at a *care facility,* as they call it nowadays. There was a young counselor, fresh out of grad school who was dabbling in the dark arts, which gave me a pass to possess her body. Nadia was one of her patients and . . ." she paused and looked at me. She nodded at my lap. "It's a deadfall."

"I've seen this before," I said, "but the figures are opposite of each other. The circle of power protects the individual from any malevolent harm."

"It does," she agreed. "However, this spell traps the entity, and the caster can force answers or harm it if he desires to do so. Sometimes even banish the spirit from earth."

Something clicked inside my brain. I looked out the window. We were on a twisty, scenic road, driving through farm and forested land. This page was marked for a reason, and the way Ameerah was looking at me with a half-smile and a devious, almost defiant look in her eyes, I knew. I knew what her plan was to find Paige. The tightness in my shoulders loosened, but there were questions I needed answered beforehand. "Where are we going?"

"To an abandoned house. We're nearly there."

"To cast this spell?"

"Yes."

"Why this house?"

"I feel safe there, and it's away from prying eyes."

I narrowed my eyes and stared at her until she looked at me. "There's more to it than what you're telling me."

She sighed. "Fine. There are strong energy sources throughout the earth. The negative areas are where darkness dwells, only released if called upon, its likeness enters the area, allowing it to leach onto the source, or to reenergize ourselves. There's also positive as well as mystical energy. The house we're going to is teeming with the latter, which will aid you in this deadfall spell."

"How do you know this?"

"Some of us can see energy. That's why we can see the light inside of Paige. I think it has to do with having physic abilities when we were human. I'm aware Anwar shares the same gift, and I'm guessing when he was mortal, he had extraordinary senses as well."

"He did," I confirmed.

"In the spiritual form, we can see energy but not in the flesh. Although, when we inhabit a human, we can feel it if we pay attention to our surroundings. I think it's the same with every sentient living being."

My pulse quickened when a thought occurred to me. "This deadfall spell," I said, pointing to the page, "can we use it to trap Bael?"

She gave me a funny look. "Bael?"

"Bael is the name of the 'old one.'" I forgot she didn't know his true identity. For some odd reason, the "old one" had kept his given name a secret, and only a few in his group had known it, but then he decided to tell Paige, and I imagined our dark world would know it soon enough.

"It's true then?" Ameerah asked, her mouth agape. I didn't need to respond. She saw the answer in my face. "Rumors started circulating within the past twenty-four hours about his name, and now you're confirming it."

Her hands began to shake. She gripped the steering wheel and fell silent, focusing her attention on the road. She turned right onto a narrow, dirt path, lined with oak trees. I looked at the side mirror and watched the prairie and distant farms fade away. I thought about conjuring a dark spirit. I had a spell for it, but nothing like what I held in my hands. I thought about trapping Bael and how advantageous it would be for all of us.

"Ameerah, can we capture Bael?" I watched her. She looked pale.

"I knew he was powerful, but I never realized who he really was," she murmured to herself. "It makes sense. The Devil's third."

"Ameerah?"

She parked on the side of the road and turned to me. "To answer your question, no, we can't trap Bael or an older dark spirit, and if we can, I don't know how. Bael has spies, and anybody who even attempts to ensnare him or his lot is punished in some form or another."

I've lived for almost two centuries, and I'd never heard of the things she was telling. I suspected these were secrets coveted by the dark spirits, and since Ameerah was breeching the laws among them, she would suffer for her betrayal. She was risking a lot for reasons unclear to me.

I held a hand up, halting anything else she had to say. I glanced at the clock on the dashboard. Almost 7 a.m. We had to get busy before Paige left the country with Bael. "We don't have much time, Ameerah. I need quick answers from you, so we can get on with what we need to do. I don't mean to be an asshole or any–"

She waved it off. "I understand. I'm throwing a lot of information at you. Go ahead and ask me."

I closed the book and latched it. "Where did you get this?"

The corners of her mouth curled into a mischievous smile. "I lifted it from Volac's lair."

"What's the Devil's third?"

"According to the rumors I've heard, it means the executive, legislative and judiciary." She must have seen the confusion on my face because she continued. "Bael's followers have been working to infiltrate the United States government, and some of them are already in, slowly spilling their agendas across the nation. Once Bael has the ring and incantations, he'll be able to control everything. He's grown impatient and is disgusted with what humans have done to this world. With Solomon's power, he can seize control over not only the U.S. government, but all governments, as well as the U.N., instead of waiting for it. The dark spirits calls this operation The Devil's Third." She shrugged. "Personally, I don't believe it. I think it means something completely different, and Bael is allowing these rumors to fly. He's planning something else . . . much darker than what is being said. At least, in my opinion he is."

Despite her doubts, what Ameerah said about the government didn't shock me. I knew dark forces were at play within those areas, and there were immortals monitoring it. They were doing what they could to prevent a series of powder kegs the dark spirits strategically placed within the system, from being ignited and bringing the world to its knees. But what did make me take a step back was they had a code name for it, and it wasn't progressing fast enough for Bael. The world had been sitting on death row far too long, and Bael wanted to execute it as soon as possible. But then again, maybe Ameerah's hunch was right, and this was a ruse to throw others off Bael's trail.

"Any more questions?" Ameerah asked, interrupting my thoughts.

"You're risking a lot to help me and Paige. Why?"

Her gaze dropped to her lap, and she knotted and unknotted her fingers. When she looked up, there were tears in her eyes. "One word. Salvation." She cleared her throat, then continued. "I've been carving out a different path for myself, hoping I can be with Nadia. I miss her . . . I'm changing my ways, Nathan, but I do want something in return."

"Of course. If you help me locate Paige, and I find her, I am in your debt."

"I believe Paige can open spiritual doors—doors I do not have access to. I want to know I'm forgiven for my sins. I want Paige to contact Nadia, and if my wrong doing is absolved, I want to crossover, so I can be with Nadia."

I ran a hand through my hair and peeked at her sideways. The sadness in her eyes betrayed the hard look in her face. I knew Paige was a skeleton key who could unlock spiritual doors connected to this realm, and for some reason, Ameerah knew it as well. I wondered if Paige's house was bugged, then quickly waved off the absurd thought. But I had to know why she thought Paige could contact Nadia. What Ameerah was asking was a tall order I wasn't sure could be served. "What makes you think Paige can do those things?"

"When we met at Gnat Creek, and Paige touched my hand before she transported us to where Aosoth was . . ." She paused, and her eyes grew wide. The tone of her voice dropped to a whisper. "I saw it."

I leaned forward, my breath caught in my throat. I could only manage to say four words, "What did you see?"

"Doorways," she said, closing her eyes. She leaned her forehead against her fingers and continued. "I saw several. I can't recall much detail because they flashed before me in a matter of seconds." She dropped her hands, and her eyes poured into mine. A beam of light flashed across them. "One was dark with flickering lights. I'm guessing it leads to our realm. But when I saw the one with dark green rolling hills covered with brilliant, colorful flowers and a lilac sky, I lost my breath. I believe it's where Nadia resides."

"What if you're wrong?"

She shook her head. "I'm not. There is no doubt in my mind Paige can help my transition. If I'm welcomed there." Her shoulders sagged, and her face fell with her last statement.

My heart went out to her. "I think," I said, covering her hand with mine, "you have to forgive yourself and do the right things. Once you do, you'll be able to move on."

A weak smile formed on her lips. "Thanks." She sat up and started the Jeep. "Now let's get down to business."

I looked at the image on the cover. The Tree of Life. An unperceptive eye would not catch the symbolism skillfully embossed on it. I thought about the meaning behind it. A tree of knowledge, connecting to all forms of life, including heaven and the underworld. It was interesting to say the least. But I couldn't deny the sick feeling I had holding it in my lap. This book was definitely dark, and I particularly didn't care for its ghoulish binding.

"What the . . .?" Ameerah said when the Jeep jerked forward. I braced my hand against the dashboard as the vehicle violently shook. "This should *not* be happening." Ameerah shifted gears. "My human bought this car two weeks ago."

Up ahead was a small one-story house with patches of white paint peeling from years of neglect. It stood in a round clearing surrounded by trees and bushes. There were shingles missing from the roof, and the covered, rickety porch appeared to be separating from the frame, slanting downward.

"Pull over next to the tree." I pointed to the shoulder of the road where a huge apple tree stood. "We can walk from here."

Ameerah parked. She turned to the backseat and grabbed a black duffel bag. "Supplies," she said when she saw the questioning look I gave her.

"I want to get this done as quickly as possible," I told her as we crossed the narrow road toward the cottage. "I don't care who we . . ." As soon as I stepped on the edge of the clearing, the book ejected from my hands. It flew across the road, arching in mid-air and then vanished.

"Evil is not welcomed here," a female voice called, echoing around us.

I looked at the house and saw a woman in a dark purple hooded cloak standing on the porch with her arm raised and a finger pointing past me. I glanced at Ameerah, wondering if she knew what was going on or who this person was.

Ameerah gasped. "It's Jade."

"Jade?"

She met my eyes in disbelief. "Haven't you heard of her?"

I shook my head, suddenly realizing for over a century I'd been too focused on being a thorn in the dark spirits' side that I'd missed out on a lot of useful and intriguing information. I then made a promise to myself I wouldn't make the same mistakes again.

"She's a legend. I didn't think she was real," Ameerah breathed.

"Who is she?" My patience was running thin. The book was now gone, which knocked me another step back. I didn't give a shit if there were campfire stories about this Jade character or if songs were written about her. All I cared about was finding Paige and if Jade would be a problem.

"She was a witch back in the 1700s and burned at the stake," Ameerah said. "When they lit the pyre at her feet, she cast her eyes to the heavens, chanting an incantation. Clouds began to form, whipping around the sky, blotting out the sun." Ameerah made a shooing gesture above her head in demonstration. "A fierce wind blew through the crowd of spectators, extinguishing the fire," she continued, getting into the story. "Her laughter echoed throughout the village, and mass hysteria ensued. The crowd dispersed, but there were a few curious souls who stayed. A hole punctured the sky above her, and a shimmering ray of light beamed down upon her, and she disappeared."

I glanced at the cottage, and Jade was no longer there. "What happened to her, and why would she be here?" I could hear the annoyance in my voice but was too perturbed about not having the book to care. I closed my eyes and rubbed my temples. "You know what? I don't give a damn. We're wasting time. All I'm concerned about is if she can help me."

"I don't know why she's here," Ameerah said. "When I checked this area yesterday, I didn't see her, but now . . ." She paused long enough for me to look at her. Her brow furrowed. "She said evil is not welcomed. I don't think I can go with you," she confessed.

Jade suddenly appeared in front of us, and though her image was transparent, from the shadowy depths of her hood, her striking green eyes jumped out, holding a life of its own—solid and alive. They settled on Ameerah. "You may enter, dear child of the fallen and misguided ones."

And then she vanished.

Ameerah looked at me. She bit her bottom lip, unsure. I shrugged and stepped inside the open space. When my foot touched the ground, a surge of warm energy engulfed me, causing the hair on my arms to rise. Blood rushed in my ears, and my heart pounded. This all happened in a matter of seconds, only to be replaced by a dose of energy I'd never felt before—a high to where I felt alert and wide awake despite my sleepless night. I turned to see if Ameerah was coming. She remained rooted in her spot, her image distorted, as if I were looking through thick, beveled glass. I glanced around the area and realized it was a perfect circle, encased inside a barrier resembling a warped lens. The trees and clouds outside it even appeared distorted.

"Extraordinary," I said, tilting my head back to a sunny, clear blue sky, feeling its warmth on my face. I looked at the house. The wood siding was no longer chipped and appeared freshly painted white, its roof in perfect order. Even the covered porch was now attached and leveled. Daisies filled flower boxes beneath the windows, adding more charm to this homey abode. The tall trees flanking the structure were in full bloom, bearing plump Gravenstein apples, appearing ripe for the picking. I glanced in Ameerah's direction and smiled. "You have to see this," I called, watching her twisted image shifting back and forth.

For a second I wondered if she would chicken out, but then her boot appeared on the dark green grass. Her hand followed, then shoulder, like she was wedging her way through a narrow doorway. Finally, she made it through and the first thing she did was laugh.

Chapter Twenty-Three

Paige

I slouched in the backseat and crossed my arms, causing Brayden to shift away from me. I stared out the window, watching the forest on the side of the road whiz by. Vibrant aspen and maple trees in a spectrum of crimson, orange, and yellow colors, were shedding their leaves. Some of the bared branches exposed pockets of dull light from the overcast sky. I didn't know the time, but it had to be early morning. The sun remained scarce, but the world around us slowly brightened into a milky, gray landscape. I closed my eyes, wishing for a cup of coffee to perk me up. I could feel the exhaustion creeping through me, something I wanted to keep at bay considering my circumstances. I sat up and opened my eyes. Yawning, I pushed the hair out of my face and blinked a couple times.

"You're welcome to take a nap if you like," Bael offered, glancing at me in the rearview mirror. "We still have over an hour before we reach our destination. We'd arrive there sooner; however, I do enjoy the scenic route much better. Besides, if you have to relieve yourself, squatting behind a bush is far superior than those vulgar public washrooms."

"How kind of you," I said sarcastically.

"My sources spilled the news to me about Nathan's merciless actions toward Aosoth and Roeick," he said, changing the subject. "They told me when he discovered what Roeick had done to you, he became . . .

what's the word humans use . . . unglued?"

I hugged myself, suddenly feeling cold. That memory was still fresh in my mind and one I didn't care to revisit, but obviously Bael wasn't going to drop it. A vision of me shirtless with my chest pressed against a stone wall and my wrist bound above my head entered my mind. I could still hear the sound of the bullwhip whooshing in the air and then smacking my flesh, paralyzing me in a void of white-hot pain.

"Yes, unglued is the term they use," he mused, answering his own question. Brayden remained quiet, sitting with his legs apart, his knee touching mine. He appeared in deep thought. His arms were crossed over his chest, his eyes hard and serious. I knew the look. He was planning something and didn't seem to hear us. "I hate to admit this," Bael went on. "I'm not one to disregard impressive behavior, even if it is coming from someone I abhor. However, Nathan is quite inventive when it comes to striking against those whom rattle his cage enough to unleash a side of him I admire. It's too bad he's easily distracted."

I took the bait. "What do you mean?" Brayden slipped his hand in mine and squeezed it in short Morse spurts.

Seatbelt.

Oh, God, what the hell was he planning on doing?

I glanced at him, and he was staring at the back of the front seat with a bored look on his face.

Why? I squeezed back.

Just do it.

"For over a century Nathan has been too focused on tracking us. It has crippled his awareness and blinded him to the great mystical chasms in this world," Bael said.

"Mystical chasms?" I echoed while slyly slipping my seatbelt on. I had no idea what he was blabbering about and would like to know, but I had a feeling it wasn't going to happen.

I was right.

Brayden scooted to the edge of the seat and leaned behind Bael, feigning interest. He rested his arm on the headrest behind Bael. "Are you talking about parallel universes?"

"Yes, along with–"

In one swift move, Brayden reached around the top of Bael's seat and twisted his neck. I heard a "pop."

"Brayden! What the hell?" I screamed, and then everything seemed to go in slow motion.

The human Bael had occupied slumped against the driver's side door– lifeless. Brayden leaned over the console and took hold of the steering wheel, but we must have been going fifty miles an hour. I looked out the windshield, thankful there were no vehicles in sight. Brayden jerked the wheel to the right. I sat back, digging my nails into the cushion, my heart thumping in my ears. I thought about my mom dying in a car accident. I was immortal, so I wouldn't die, unless I lost all my blood or head. I thought about Nathan. I had to see him and explain everything. He'd understand. I wasn't going to give up on us or on myself. I had to fight, and I'd figure out a way to protect the ones I loved and not allow Bael to corner me ever again. All those thoughts raced through my head in an instant. My quick, immortal mind, logging and etching them onto my very soul. A strength I've never experienced before rose, like a phoenix from the ashes, reborn.

The Tahoe fishtailed, then spun several times. I braced myself, unable to see what Brayden was doing. I closed my eyes, and my body jerked sideways. We hit a bump or something, causing me to bounce, but the harness held me in place, preventing me from knocking my head against the roof. I was forced to my right when I heard an "Oomph!" Everything stilled. I opened my eyes. The Tahoe was on its side, and the safety strap prevented me from falling against the door which was pressed against the ground.

"Are you okay, Brayden?" I asked, trying to push myself up enough so I could see him. I walked my hands up the seat toward my body, lifting myself.

"Other than bumping my head on the dashboard and trying to get this human off me, I'm fine. What about you?" Brayden was struggling with the dead body lying on top of him. His hands were on the human's chest. He lifted his arms, locking them in place, suspending the lifeless figure above him. The head lobbed to the side in an unnatural manner. Brayden hefted him against the dashboard and wormed his way on top.

"I'm okay," I finally answered. "I can't believe what you did, though. What about Tree?"

"Bael is a man of his word," Brayden said, unconcerned. "You did nothing wrong, so Tree is safe. I, on the other hand, will now be on his shit list. But let's talk about it later. We need to get out of here before someone discovers us."

"Okay, so what's your suggestion?" Before he could respond, I unlatched the belt and dropped against the door, smashing my shoulder. A sharp pain zapped my shoulder blade as if someone drove a nail into it. A yelp escaped my lips, and I flipped myself onto my stomach, anchoring my feet against the door.

"Are you all right?" Brayden asked, peeking through the gap between his seat and the door.

"Yeah, just crushed my shoulder. It'll be fine."

I could hear Brayden moving around, the soles of his shoes squeaking against leather. His hand flew up, gripping the headrest, and he lifted himself to where his backside pressed against the door. He looked over at me. "I want you to do the same thing. Push yourself up and lean your back against the door to where you're half standing like me."

I moved my hands like I was going to do pushups. Bending my elbows and ignoring the pain in my shoulder, I lifted myself. Again, I walked my hands on the seat toward my body, and as soon as my butt touched the door, I slowly dropped back.

"I'm going to bust the windshield with my fist, so cover your face," Brayden told me

"What about you?" I didn't want glass to get in his face either or cut himself for that matter. I knew he'd heal right away . . . hell, my shoulder was already feeling better. But he'd still feel the pain. "Isn't there a better way to do this?"

Brayden lifted his fist. "Maybe, but we don't have much time. Don't worry about me"–he pulled his arm back and met my eyes–"Look the other way and cover your face."

I did what he said and heard his fist smack the glass. A cracking sound filled the silence, followed by a tinkling noise as shards of glass scattered everywhere. One stung me in the ear. My hand flew up, touching the skin where the glass tagged me. I thought some landed in my hair as well, but I'd worry about it later. I turned and saw Brayden using the sleeve of his jacket to brush off the dashboard. Without saying a word, he climbed out the corner of the windshield. I followed suit, awkwardly scrambling between the two front seats, trying not to allow gravity throw me backward.

"C'mon, Paige. I think someone is coming," Brayden said.

I was in the front seat and braced my foot against the passenger window. Boosting myself up, I crawled out and slid off the hood into a ditch where the Tahoe lay sideways. Brayden reached down and offered his hand. I took it, and once he pulled me up to higher ground, we fled into the forest. I breathed in the smell of decaying leaves, tree bark, and earth, loving Mother Nature's aroma. As I ran, I leaped over tree stumps and an occasional log. I came across a bull elk with a six-by-six rack, lapping at some water in a creek. I stepped beside him and hurtled myself to the other side. When my feet smacked the ground, I continued to run. I knew Brayden was beside me, because I could see his image out the corner of my eye. To anybody else, though, we'd be a blur to where their minds wouldn't be able to accept the reality of it and in turn shrug it off. But since we were moving at the same speed, side by side, we could clearly see each other.

"I think it's safe to stop," Brayden said after we were probably twenty miles away from our starting point. He halted in his tracks, and I did the same. "How's your shoulder?"

I slowly rolled it forward and backward and smiled. "Perfect."

Brayden grinned. "Isn't it great being immortal?"

I nodded. "It does have its benefits."

Brayden turned in circles, surveying the area. He pointed west. "I think Astoria is that way, but we need to get to the nearest airport, which is Portland International."

I scratched the back of my head and made a face. "Are you seriously thinking we hop a plane and go to Africa?"

Brayden shrugged. "Yeah, why not?"

I gave him a doubtful look. "Do you have a passport?"

"In my back pocket."

"When did you get one?"

"After I became immortal, Cassondra insisted I get one and carry it on me at all times, like my driver's license."

"What about shots?"

"I did those as well."

"Me, too. Anwar had me get them before we went to the island, because he knew I wanted to travel and see the world. He told me more than likely his friend Shem could taxi us to wherever we wanted to go; however, there would be times when we'd have to fly commercial."

Brayden glanced over his shoulder. "I think if we run we can make it to Portland in about a half hour." He looked at me and frowned. "You look tired."

"I am," I admitted. "Aren't you?"

He rubbed his forehead and sighed. "I can use a few hours of sleep."

I looked around. We were deep in the forest, and I had no idea where we were, except between Astoria and Portland. I listened, reaching out my sense of hearing beyond the woods. I pushed the sound of a squirrel gnawing on a nut, birds scampering in a bed of dried leaves on the ground, bees buzzing around I was guessing, a hive, and other sounds of nature aside, so I could hear other rackets of life. I cocked my head to the side and continued listening. And then I heard the choppy roar of several motorcycles not too far away. I glanced at Brayden. He was listening, too. Our eyes connected, and a smile crept across his face.

"I think we should go the edge of the forest and see what's up," I suggested.

Brayden pointed at me. "Good plan."

We took off again, and shortly after we were facing a narrow, black, curving road. There was a yellow, diamond shaped deer crossing sign on the other side of the street. We had to be close to civilization. I rubbed the back of my neck and blinked several times. I could feel the heaviness in my limbs from the exhaustion pouring in them. I needed to sleep soon, otherwise I would be useless.

"I think we should follow in the direction those motorcycles went," I said, thinking it was early morning, and maybe they were heading off to get some breakfast. It was a long shot but the only thing my sluggish mind could think of at the moment.

Brayden glanced down the street where the noise of the bikes had gone. "Okay," he said, fixing his eyes on mine. I could see the smile in them and knew he was enjoying himself. He then broke away, and I followed, easily catching up with him despite my fatigue. We kept hidden behind the trees, close to the shoulder of the road. We ran for probably fifteen miles when I spotted a gas station and convenience store up ahead. Brayden looked at me and jerked his finger forward a few times, indicating to keep going. I nodded and continued to run beside him. The trees were starting to thin out, and I heard traffic up ahead. Brayden grabbed my wrist. We stopped behind a huge Douglas fir and saw at the end of the road there was a four way stop sign.

"What do you think?" Brayden asked.

I pushed my hair off my face and rubbed my eyes. "I think we should go east."

"Why east?"

"I don't know," I said with a sigh, trying not to sound grumpy. "It's a guess. Maybe because I hear more traffic in that direction."

"Let's cross the street and over to the north, so we can keep to the forests," he said.

"Okay."

Looking both ways to make sure there weren't any cars coming, we zipped across and over, behind the safety of the trees. We stopped, and to my relief, on the other side of the street stood a structure made out of logs with a red wooden sign beneath the peak of the roof that said: *Timberlake Lodge*. It looked like an A-frame house, reminding me of Nathan's home. Attached to it was an elongated building in a U-shape with dark, wooden doors lining its length. I imagined they were rooms, and I longed to be sleeping in one.

Brayden elbowed me and grinned. I returned his smile, and we jetted over there. When we stepped into the lobby, a bell dinged, and a burly looking middle-aged guy greeted us. I noticed the kindness in his brown eyes right away, and I began to relax while Brayden stepped up to the glossy, oak counter to get us a room. There was a rustic couch made out of cedar logs in front of a blazing fireplace with a matching chair beside it. I was tempted to sit, but knew if I did, I'd probably crash right there. So I waited for Brayden, enjoying the smell of pine wafting off the burning logs.

"If you two get hungry, we do have room service," the guy told Brayden. "The menus are on the bedside table."

Brayden thanked him, and with the key in his hand, we stepped outside. I followed Brayden to the end of the building. He stopped in front of room 22, stuck the key in, and opened the door. I entered first and discovered there was only one king size bed. I knew I should have said something about it–to remind him I wasn't interested in pursuing a relationship, but I was too tired to hold a lengthy conversation, and frankly I didn't care at the moment. All I wanted to do was sleep. I kicked my shoes off, crawled into bed, and I was out.

Chapter Twenty-Four

Nathan

Ameerah laughed again. "I can't believe I'm able to come inside of here." With a grin on her face, her arms opened out wide, she turned in a circle. "Do you realize what this means?" She stopped and shook my arm.

The corner of my mouth lifted. "I have a good idea."

"It means I'm not evil, and my intentions are genuine and good. Maybe," she said, "I will be forgiven for all the heinous stuff I'd done."

I squeezed her shoulder. "I think you're on the right path. Now let's see if Jade can help me find Paige." I walked toward the house with a purpose in my stride.

"Right," Ameerah said, jogging to keep up with me.

When we reach the porch, the door swung open. Layers of different incense filled my nose: sandalwood, sage, and lavender. We climbed the steps and entered the house into a small entryway. I paid no mind to the empty coat tree on the wall or the oak bench across from it. I continued moving forward, anxious to see if Jade would help us or what I needed to do to reunite with Paige. To my right, tendrils of gray smoke reached out of a spacious sitting area like tentacles from an octopus. I entered the room. It was dark, except for the dozens of lit candles, displayed on the hearth of a stone fireplace on the far wall and silver candelabras in each corner. There was no furniture except for a low table with a black, velvet cloth draped over it. On top of it was a couple more lit white tapers, a tiny brass bowl, and a book. The wood floor had a large, round blood red rug with a black pentagram on the face of it and gold thread heavily stitched in loopy designs around the edges.

"I hear you need my assistance," Jade said behind Ameerah, causing her to jump and move aside. Jade's robe swished past us. She turned and lowered her hood. Her skin was black as tar, and when her striking green eyes met mine, I couldn't help but think how attractive she was.

"May I inquire where you received word?" I asked.

"Carrie," she replied, smoothing out her shoulder length hair.

I jerked my head back and blinked "Carrie?"

"A short while ago you spoke with her, yes?"

"Yeah, I—"

"Carrie and Paige's friendship and love is boundless. After you spoke with her, a part of her spirit reached out to me—the part that is a witch as well."

"Carrie is a witch?" Ameerah asked, sounding as surprised as I felt.

"In a previous life she was, yes." Jade nodded. "If she were to tap into that part of herself in this life, Carrie has the potential to become a remarkable witch. Bael knows this and aims to have both Carrie and Paige by his side."

"Does Carrie know this about herself?" Ameerah asked.

"She does now," Jade answered. "Her spirit is receiving instructions as we speak, on how to get reacquainted with that side of herself when she awakes from her coma."

"I was here yesterday because I knew a positive, mystical energy dwells here and thought it would be the perfect place to help Nathan find Paige. But I didn't see or sense you around," Ameerah said to Jade, sounding perplexed.

"At the time of your arrival," Jade said, "Carrie hadn't beckoned me, but once she did, the ley lines in this area jumped to life, creating a barrier you and Nathan encountered between your world and this one.

For thousands of years, ancient civilizations knew how to do this, so they could perform ceremonial magic. However, the know how has been lost throughout the ages, and earth's energy or ley lines, has been stifled. Fortunately, the circumstances at hand due to the realm in which Carrie's spirit lays, allowed me to be here with you now."

"So can you help Nathan, then?" Ameerah asked.

"Yes, but we must be swift about it. The channel of energy flowing in this area can only stay fluid for so long." Jade motioned us farther into the room. "We need to do a location spell to find Paige," she said to me. "Do you have anything of Paige's on your person?"

I reached in my back pocket, producing a crumbled piece of paper. "I have the letter she wrote me before she left." I handed it to Jade.

"Excellent." Jade went to the altar and placed the letter on it, smoothing it out. "It's brimming with her energy." She placed her palm on it and bowed her head, slouching her shoulders forward. Her voice sounded distant, almost haunting. "Sadness. Determination. Purpose. Doubt you would ever forgive her betrayal." She turned and looked at me. "Those were her feelings as she wrote this."

I ran a hand through my hair. "I never once thought she betrayed me."

"Nevertheless," Jade replied, "those thoughts and feelings were raging inside her." She lifted the cloth hanging over the altar and opened a drawer. She pulled out a rolled piece of paper and closed the drawer. While she picked up Paige's letter, she gathered a couple brass bowls and sat on her knees on the rug. She placed the bowls in front of her and unrolled the paper below them on the floor—a map. She motioned for me and Ameerah to kneel next to her. "Do you mind if I burn this letter?" she asked me, holding it up when my knee touched beside her leg.

"No. You're welcomed to do whatever is necessary for us to find Paige," I said.

She snatched my hand and squeezed it. Her skin felt cold, and my immediate reaction was to pull away, but I didn't. She closed her eyes, clutching the letter. I glanced at Ameerah, sitting on the other side of

Jade. Our eyes connected, and Ameerah shrugged. But then her gaze dropped to Jade's hand holding mine, at the same time I felt a warmth in my palm against Jade's. There was an orange glow between the small gaps in our grip. The note in her other hand, radiated the same color. I stared at it, mesmerized, like a child watching a magic show.

"The connection you have with Paige is phenomenal. Your spirits have known each other for many lives," she said in a distant voice.

I sat up, intrigued, remembering Anwar mentioning something along those same lines when he first met Paige. It made sense to me, though. For almost two hundred years, I'd never encountered such feelings for another until I laid eyes upon Paige.

"You're linked to her, and recently you've been picking up her feelings." She opened her eyes and looked at me.

I nodded. "Correct. Last night I suddenly felt fear and panic and heard Paige say, 'We're so screwed.'"

"I'm going to cast a location spell," Jade told me. "Afterwards, I'll project another one to allow your spirit to reach out to Paige." She released me and swung her other hand, holding the letter in front of her. It was glowing a deep orange color. Her lips moved slowly at first and then rapidly as she repeatedly recited an incantation in Latin. Wisps of smoke lifted off the edges of the paper. She dropped it in the bowl. A small flame ignited. She dipped the tip of her fingers in the other bowl and flicked the liquid into the fire as she continued to chant in Latin. There was a loud "pop" and the flame went out. She picked up the dish and dumped the ashes on the map.

Ameerah and I leaned forward and watched in amazement as the ashes gathered and formed a perfectly straight line. It slithered across the paper until the tip of it touched a small town, which was only thirty miles away from where we were at.

"Clatskanie," Ameerah said. She grinned at me. "Paige isn't too far from here."

The tightness in my shoulders lifted, and I blew out a sign of relief. At least she was still in the country and better yet, nearby in the same state. But then my body tensed when the thought of her being in trouble, possibly held captive, entered my mind. I had to know where in this town she was and if she was okay.

"Where, though?" I blurted. "She can be anywhere."

"Well, at least we know which town," Ameerah said, sounding hopeful.

"Nathan," Jade said, capturing my attention. "I need you to lie in the center of this pentagram. Fallen One"–she glanced at Amerrah who furrowed her eyebrows–"I need for you to step off the rug. I will do the same."

I had no idea what she was planning, only trusting it would aid me in locating Paige. So without question, I lay on my back in the center of the rug after she removed the items out of the way.

"I want you to close your eyes and visualize Paige." Jade's voice was soft, soothing. I hadn't realized until now how tired I was. My thoughts were drifting, and my mind went into a cycle of jabbering nonsense. I halted it and refocused on Paige. "Good." Jade sounded pleased, as if aware of my minor slip. "I want you to reach out to Paige. Call to her."

I visualized being with Paige. I could see her clearly in my mind. Her round face, dark green eyes, and dark red hair straight down her back. Her smile–sweet, yet alluring at times. The way she felt in my arms. How she smelled. The sound of her light, raspy voice which could be sultry when she felt amorous–

A warm hand touched my forehead. Under her breath, Jade chanted in Latin. I continued my vision of Paige and found myself standing in a gray, misty field with nothing but endless space–a void of some kind. I cupped my hands around my mouth and yelled for Paige. My voice echoed around me as if I were standing in a canyon bowl surrounded by rocky cliffs instead of a vast, endless clearing. Something at the edge of my vision moved. I turned my head and saw dark shadows swirling around the ground. I stepped back. My first thought was they were dark entities about to rise against me, and I positioned myself in a fighting stance. But then I looked skyward and relaxed. Clouds were whipping around a dull round ball of light.

"Paige!" I yelled once again, keeping my eyes riveted above, testing a theory: every time I called her name, something in this realm shifted. Sure enough, the clouds parted, and the orb expanded. A golden ray of light beamed down about two hundred yards in front of me. I stepped back and watched in anticipation, hoping something good would come out of this. A facet of brilliant colors–blue, green, orange, lavender, pink and so forth–rained down inside of it. It reminded me of when Paige, Ameerah, and I were in the Sahara Desert, and I saw what Paige's soul looked like.

My heart raced.

I was confident those radiant hues were parts of her soul.

"Paige!" I hollered again.

In an instant, a bright, white sunburst flashed and expanded outward. The light didn't hurt my eyes, so I continued to stare at it. But then the ray vanished, and the gunmetal gray sky was now vacant. My heart leaped in my chest when my gaze connected with Paige, standing where the beam was a second ago, looking confused.

"Nathan?" She sounded unsure, and when I smiled, a warily look entered her face. She glanced away. "This is a dream. This isn't real," she whispered to herself.

"This is real," I said, crossing the distance between us, capturing her full attention. "It's magic."

"Magic?"

I cupped her face in my hands and softly kissed her. She sighed against my lips. "We don't have much time," I told her, using every ounce of restraint I had not to continue our kiss. "I know you're in Clatskanie, but where?"

"I'm at Timberlake Lodge," she said. "Brayden broke the neck of a human Bael was possessing, and we escaped."

"Brayden is with you?"

She nodded and straightened her back. Her eyes poured into mine, filled with honesty and a strength I'd never seen in her before. The corner of my mouth lifted. "I didn't betray you. I was forced to write the Dear John letter to you and bail. I had no–"

I placed a finger on her lips. "No need to explain. I already know."

Perplexed, she blinked. "How?"

"I went to the hospital and paid Carrie a visit. I was able to rouse her enough to tell me what Bael had said to you and Tree," I explained.

"How did Carrie . . ." Paige trailed off. Her gaze wandered past me, staring at nothing in particular. "Oh. I know." She looked at me and smiled. "She heard us when she was in the coma. They say when people are in comatose states, they can hear everything around them."

"Correct," I said, sharing her smile.

She threw her arms around me. "I'm so glad you know and forgive me."

I embraced her. God, she felt good. "There's nothing to forgive."

"So how were you able to contact me? Did Pip help you?" She dropped her arms and pulled back, though, I kept my arms around her.

I shook my head. "No. It's a long story, and we don't have much time."

Paige cast fervent glances around us. "Do you know where we are?"

"We're on one of the sub-planes, but I'm not sure which one. Does it really matter?" I gave her a half-smile and ran my fingers down her spine, causing her to shiver.

She grinned and shook her head. "No." She looked at my shoulder and frowned. "You're starting to fade."

I glanced down. My shoulder was transparent, which told me soon the connection would be broken. "Listen," I said. "Stay where you are. As soon as I wake up, Ameerah and I will go there. I'll–"

"Ameerah is with you? How is she?"

"Yes, and she's well. She's helping me."

"I like Ameerah, but can we trust her?" An anxiousness entered her voice.

"I believe so. But anyway," I said in a rush, noticing my arm disappearing. "Don't go anywhere. Stay put." I paused. "What room are you in?"

"Twenty-two, at the very end," she told me. "On the south side," she added.

"All right. I'll see you soon." I leaned to kiss her, but then everything went black.

Chapter Twenty-Five

Paige

Nathan's lips brushed against mine, and then he disappeared, leaving me kissing air in this dreary realm. I threw my hands up and sighed. I finally got to see my boyfriend, and he vanishes. Not by choice I realized. A gleeful smile broke across my face. He forgave me, and he found a way to reach me. A warmth filled my chest, and I swooned a little. No wonder Bael didn't want Nathan involved. My guy was resourceful and a damn good tracker. Bael probably knew once I discovered where the incantations were, Nathan and I would be unstoppable.

He was right.

Since Nathan now knew where I was, I had no doubt in my mind we would hop on a plane to Africa and end this once and for all. And if anything got in our way, I'd fight. I wasn't too concerned with Bael because I didn't breach our agreement. Nathan had discovered the truth on his own, which freed me from Bael *and* his demands.

I couldn't stop smiling, feeling a lightness in my body I haven't experienced in a long time. Ever since Nathan and I met, something always tried to come between us.

Not anymore.

The strength I felt in the Tahoe after Brayden snapped the human's neck grew as the self-doubts I once had were quickly replaced with a fierce determination to never again allow others to use my fear to enslave or manipulate me. Bael knew my friends were my Achilles heel, and he used them as bargaining chips to get me to do his bidding. Without fear, he had no power over me. So I would figure out a way to protect the ones I loved, but for now I needed to wake myself up. Using the same tactic I'd used when I brought Nathan, Ameerah, and myself back from spying on Aosoth, I closed my eyes and visualized the hotel room my sleeping body rested in. I could see the bureau made of oak logs and the mirror attached to it framed from long, thick sticks. The red plaid curtains were drawn, and the king sized bed with a headboard matching the bureau looked inviting. I could feel myself crawling on top of the firm mattress and burrowing myself beneath the flannel sheets, soft and comfy. I took a deep breath and then released a satisfying sigh.

I was now in suspended animation within a shadow box with tinted glass and nothing but black space beyond. I couldn't feel my body until my stomach suddenly lurched, causing my limbs to jerk–waking me. My eyes flew open. Something heavy pressed against my side. My gaze fell on an arm wrapped around me . . . Brayden's.

I lay there for a few minutes, gathering my thoughts. Was my encounter with Nathan real? What a silly question. Of course it was. Somehow we were able to connect and meet in another realm. I wondered if it was the same place deceased loved ones went to visit the living in their dreams. It seemed unlikely, though, because of the drab environment. But then again, I could be wrong. I recalled what Nathan had said when I asked him where we were.

Does it really matter?

I stifled a giggle. Hell, no, it didn't matter. Nathan now knew the truth, and all I had to do was stay put until his arrival. Excitement bubbled inside me. I couldn't wait to see him and decided then I wouldn't destroy the incantations. Instead, I'd use them to rid this world of the dark spirits. Originally, I thought it would be playing God and upsetting the balance of things if I were to have such control. I knew Pip felt the same way. However, a girl could change her mind, right? And the ones like Ameerah, I'd leave alone. I wondered how it would work. Could I use the incantations on individual entities, or was it for all of them? Bael had assured Volac he wouldn't control him, so maybe I'd get to choose whom to use it on. But how would Bael know? He probably made it up in an attempt to manipulate Volac. Honestly, though, right in this present moment, I didn't really care. I'd worry about it later. I was too happy to fret about the stupid incantations and what to do with them.

An uncomfortable feeling in my bladder alerted me to its fullness. I slowly lifted Brayden's arm off me, careful not to disturb him, and rolled off the bed. He grunted, scratched his nose, and flipped to his other side. I tiptoed to the bathroom and softly closed the door. It clicked when it latched shut, and I released the knob. The room displayed a cute, rustic theme I liked. The brown shower curtain had a wilderness scene with a black bear and her three cubs trailing behind. There was even a matching rug to go along with it. Adorable. A few minutes later I was pleased to see a toothbrush wrapped in plastic and a small tube of Crest. While I brushed, I thought about Nathan. My stomach did a silly flip, and my white, foamy lips turned up into a goofy grin.

"Paige, are you okay?" Brayden asked on the other side of the door.

I titled my chin up, careful not to drip toothpaste on me. "I'm fine," my garbled voice answered.

"What?"

I spat in the sink and tried again. "I'm brushing my teeth. I'm okay."

"Do you want something to eat? We can order room service. I found a menu on the nightstand."

"Yeah, sure," I said, feeling a hollow ache in my stomach, I hadn't realized was there. It growled, confirming my hunger. I opened the door and walked out, wondering for the first time how to tell Brayden about my change in plans. He sat perched on the edge of the bed, reading the menu. "Brayden–"

"I think I want the BLT with fries and a Mountain Dew. What about you?" He looked at me, waiting for my response.

A bacon sandwich actually sounded good. "I'll have the same, except

I want–"

"Coffee," he said, smiling, "with cream of course." He knew me so well. I couldn't help but smile back.

"You got it."

He picked up the phone and pushed a clear, protruding button above the other ones. While he ordered, a thought occurred to me. I could call Nathan. But then I remembered he had smashed his phone against the wall, and I didn't know the number to his spare cell. The momentary rush I felt subsided. I'd have to hang tight here until he arrived. In the meantime, I needed to deal with Brayden. I straightened my back and squared my shoulders.

"It'll be ready in twenty minutes," he told me after he hung the phone up. He narrowed his eyes and tilted his chin down. "What's wrong?"

"Nothing is wrong," I said, pushing my hair off my shoulders. "In fact, I'm feeling optimistic right now."

"So am I." He patted the space beside him. I didn't accept the invitation. He frowned. "Okay, what am I missing?"

"Nathan is on his way here," I said.

Brayden's eyebrows furrowed, deepening the crease between them. "What do you mean?" he asked, his tone full of caution.

I took a deep breath and told him everything. After I finished, he looked at me like I lost my mind. I knew he and Nathan didn't care for each other, but Brayden would have to get over it. I loved Brayden and never wanted to hurt him; however, my heart belonged to Nathan and once again, Brayden would have to accept it.

There was a knock at the door. I jumped, and my heart pounded against my chest. Could it be Nathan? Not likely. It was too soon, I told myself when I reached the door. Brayden stood next to my elbow when I opened it. An attractive girl around our age with shoulder length dark hair stood behind a small stainless steel cart. On top of it were two plates with BLTs and a generous portion of what looked like homemade fries. In the center stood a tall, icy glass of Mountain Dew and a steaming cup of coffee. I noticed different types of creamers grouped together on the right of my drink, along with several packets of ketchup and Ranch dressing.

"Your order," the girl simply said, her brown eyes roaming Brayden's body. The corner of her mouth tugged upward when they rested on his face. "Would you like anything else? I'd be happy to get it for you," she said only to him, completely ignoring me. She lowered her eyelids and bit her bottom lip when Brayden offered her a teasing smile.

Oh, he was good.

Even I couldn't help but stare at how he used his daring, handsome looks to his advantage. He handed her a fifty dollar bill and told her to keep the change. I took the handle of the cart and wheeled it in. I turned, right when she accepted the money and looked up at him from beneath her lashes. She seemed reluctant to leave, and when Brayden thanked her and stepped away from the door, her cheeks flushed. She blinked and told him again if he needed anything else, she'd be happy to assist him.

Yeah, I bet.

"She seemed nice," Brayden said after he closed the door, "and pretty," he added.

I didn't answer right away, instead I added some cream to my coffee. I could feel his eyes on my back. Something pinched inside my chest. Jealousy? I ignored it and moved our stuff off the cart onto a small, round table in the corner of the room. I sat and took a sip from the Styrofoam cup, eyeing him over the rim. "She is," I agreed, knowing he was trying to see how I'd react to him admiring another female. I refused to play his little game, though, and kept drinking my coffee.

Brayden pulled the chair across from me out and plopped down with a sigh. "I don't want to date her." He sounded exhausted, like he'd been repeatedly kicked in the stomach, but he continued to persist anyway. "I only want you." He took a deep drink of his Mountain Dew when I didn't respond. The ice clinked against the glass when he set it down. "How can I get you to realize we belong together?" He picked up his sandwich and took a huge bite. He watched me while he chewed, waiting for my response.

"I love you, Brayden. I always will," I told him, dipping a couple fries into ketchup. "But like I told you before, Nathan and I are together. I'm in love with him."

His gaze fell to his lap, and he slowly shook his head. When he spoke, I could hear the hurt in his voice. "Like I told *you* before, he's not from the same era as us. His mind is programmed differently than ours because he grew up in a different time. He's too overprotective, and I think he hinders you." He looked up, and his eyes locked onto mine. Through tight lips he said, "I don't like it."

I shrugged. "Yeah, he has his flaws, but so do I." I took a bite of my BLT, loving the taste of the peppered bacon combined with the fresh tomato and mayo.

"How can you be so nonchalant about it?" Brayden asked, his voice raising, outraged.

"Because Nathan wants to be equals now. Once upon a time ago I told him I refused to be in a one-sided relationship. I won't do it, and he knows it. End of story."

Brayden didn't comment. Instead, we sat in silence while we ate. Normally it would have been awkward, but we were comfortable enough with each other not have it be so. I also knew he was collecting his thoughts. Maybe gathering more ammunition for his argument. I could see his point, but it wasn't going to change how I felt about Nathan or the connection I shared with him.

"I don't want him here," Brayden finally said, rising from the table.

"Too bad," I retorted defensively. I took the last swig of my coffee and stood. "Nathan and Ameerah should be here anytime now. You need to deal with it or leave." I hated telling him the last part. I didn't want him to go, but then again, I didn't want him to be an ass either.

"You're choosing Nathan over me?" The hurt was back in his voice and guilt stabbed my chest. "After everything we've been through together . . . our history . . ."

"I don't want to," I admitted. "However, this is my life–"

Brayden held up a hand, palm facing me. "Stop. I don't want to hear it." He turned his back on me. His shoulders slouched forward. I lifted my hand, edging it toward his arm, then dropped it. No. My sympathy would only encourage him to pursue his feelings for me. He turned and faced me. A deep sadness echoed from the depths of his green eyes, until a sudden willful determination glossed over them. "You can't deny we make a great team. We always have, and I know you love me. I also know if you were completely honest with yourself and gave into those feelings, you'd find you were still in love with me."

I didn't respond. I knew if I'd never met Nathan, Brayden and I would most likely be together. But then again, I wasn't the same girl as I was a month ago. I was changing. I could feel it—the strength, sense of empowerment, and duty.

"I want you and me to find the incantations," he said point blank. "We need Anwar to help us," he threw in. My mouth dropped, and he continued before I could find words to comment on his admission. "Anwar's friend Shem can fly us to Africa, and Anwar is from there, so he can be our escort."

"Are you kidding me?" was all I could say. I knew he and Anwar were friends for some strange reason, and I had an idea why. Anwar was Team Brayden and thought Nathan should be tracking instead of spending his time with me. Anwar had made that clear to Nathan the night Roeick kidnapped me. But I thought or hoped Brayden would come to his senses and decide to keep his distance from Anwar. Apparently not yet.

"Hear me out," he said. "Bael was playing dumb in the Tahoe earlier when he mentioned Aosoth. I know because Anwar told me all about it. Bael actually found Aosoth and Roeick after Nathan imprisoned them in the old Victorian house where you were held captive."

"How did Bael know where they were?" I asked, not surprised at his deception.

"I don't know. Maybe he tracked her by her cell phone."

I cocked my head to the side and chewed on my bottom lip. "He did make me get rid of my cell because he said Nathan could use it to track us."

"I had to give up mine as well . . ." Brayden paused. He stared past me like he was contemplating something, then his gaze shifted back to me, and he continued. "Anyway, Anwar told me Bael lured a soulless female and male to where Aosoth and Roeick were, probably so their spirits could jump in the bodies, vacating the ones they were trapped in."

I looked away and fixed my eyes on the unkempt bed, but not really seeing it. The premonition I had raced through my mind. I hadn't thought about it in a while, but now that I did, and what Brayden said, caused a chill to run up my spine.

Brayden touched my arm. When I looked at him, concern marred his features. "What is it?"

"I was thinking about what you said and a premonition of mine."

"What was it about?"

I recounted its ominous words, "The innocent locked in grief from the illusion before the eyes. An unlikely pair reunites in treachery and affection."

Brayden rubbed his forehead and sighed. "You're thinking the unlikely pair is Aosoth and Bael?"

I nodded. "It has to be."

"Or," Brayden piped, "it could mean Ameerah and Volac. She used to be a part of his group, ya know?"

I gave him a funny look. "I don't think so because Volac had his men capture Ameerah that night at Gnat Creek."

"It could have been a ruse."

I shook my head. "Not likely."

"Did you know Roeick and Volac were related when they were human?"

Wide-eyed, I gaped at him. "No, I didn't." I realized then Brayden knew more than I thought. "How do you know this?"

"Roeick is Volac's descendant. However, since Roeick is infatuated with Aosoth, and Volac can't stand her, the kinsmen are not on speaking terms."

"But how–"

"Anwar told me." He paused, and a thoughtful look entered his face.

"The things I know are due to Anwar and Cassondra. Knowledge is power, and I plan to be one of the most powerful immortals out there. I think together, you and I could reign our world."

All the air escaped my lungs. The room was silent except for the clicking noise the heaters were making, announcing the steady flow of heat about to escape. I couldn't believe what he said. The wall I had mentally erected to seal off my weak "human" emotions, wavered. My eyes stung, and I blinked. My throat constricted, and I swallowed several times, refusing to cry. Those were bogus emotions, attached to a mortal girl who still thrived inside me, longing for those simpler times. I silently told her to get a grip. Brayden had changed and so have I. Sure our humanity was still linked to us, and where I had chosen strength over my weakness, Brayden was intoxicating himself with fantastical power. The notion he or we could dominate our new world by using both our strengths, thus becoming almighty, was in the same vein as Bael's ultimate goal—to rule this world.

"Are you okay?" Brayden asked. "You look paler than normal."

Ya think?

I cleared my throat and decided to say it like it was. "You're no better than Bael, and I can't believe what just came out of your mouth. You've changed, and I think you should leave." I turned away, and he grabbed my arm, spinning me around.

"Wait a minute," he said and let go of my arm when I tried yanking it away. "I'm still the same Brayden you were in love with two years ago. However, the cards we were dealt have changed. Just because I'm holding a different set, doesn't mean who I truly am has changed. I'm playing a better hand now."

"But you're willing to ante up who or whatever you have to in hope you'll win the game. I mean, earlier you were willing to sacrifice Tree in order to free me from being Bael's puppet."

"I already told you why," he said, exasperated. "Tree is like a brother—"

"Yeah, sure." I could feel the heat in my face and knew it was red. "I would never," I said through gritted teeth, "dodge a bullet, knowing it would strike someone I loved instead."

"What if Bael made you choose between Nathan and Tree?" Brayden demanded. "Who would you choose?"

I threw my hands up and laughed, though nothing was funny. "He already did, and I chose Tree."

"Oh, I forgot."

"You don't get it," I told him, heading toward the door. "And I don't want anything to do with Anwar or ruling our world. If that's your thing, fine. I don't want anything to do with you then, and I want you to leave."

In a flash, Brayden stood by my side. "I love you. I think you have extraordinary gifts you haven't even tapped yet. Anwar and I can help you."

"I don't want your help."

"Paige, please. Don't you love me?"

I took a deep breath and slowly released it. "I will always love the Brayden I grew up with and dated, but the person you are now . . . I don't trust."

"I'm still the same person. If you can stop being stubborn long enough to see things through my eyes, you'll understand where I'm coming from."

Brayden's relentlessness exhausted me, and I was through with this conversation. I placed my hand on the doorknob. "You must go now. When you come to your senses, look me up. But until then, I don't want to see you." Despite what was going on, a terrible ache went through my heart, and unfortunately it manifested in my voice when I said those last five words.

"You don't mean it," he softly said. "I know you better than anybody. Yes, you want me to leave, but the part you've been denying since I've been back . . . the part that still loves me . . . is crushed to send me off on my merry way."

He was right, but I wasn't about to admit it. "Just go."

He lifted his hand and trailed the length of my cheek with his finger.

I closed my eyes, remembering his all too familiar touch. The girl I once was longed for those days when we were carefree and mortal. But those days no longer existed, and now I had my new life with Nathan. I was no longer blind. I now knew what was going on beneath our noses, whereas most humans were under the spell of smoke and mirrors. They had no idea immortals existed and dark spirits walked among them in soulless humans. I opened my eyes. Brayden was looking at me, his features set in a loving, yet determined manner.

He nodded. "I'll leave, but know this: I'll never give up on us, and I'll always keep an eye on you. One day you'll realize we were meant to be together, and I'll be there in the shadows waiting for you." He planted a soft kiss on my forehead and left.

Chapter Twenty-Six

Nathan

I sat up and rubbed my eyes.

"What happened?" Ameerah wanted to know, sounding anxious. "Did you find her? What did she say?" She was on her knees beside the edge of the rug next to my side. She placed her hands on the floor and leaned forward, closer to me.

The candles flickered around the room, creating shadows on the walls, pulling my attention away from Ameerah. I watched in fascination as they took the shape of people. Ameerah followed my gaze, and her lips parted in wonderment when the silhouettes linked hands and began to dance. My eyes followed them as they glided along the walls, circling us. Their feet and legs were moving rapidly while the upper part of their bodies remained stationary. I realized then, they were performing some kind of Irish dance.

"I must be on my way," Jade said behind me, rising to her feet. She nodded to the entertaining group. "They're letting me know the channel of energy, which opened this doorway into your world, is ebbing. They're trying to keep it ajar long enough for me to say my farewell to you." She smiled fondly at them.

I extended my hand toward her. "I cannot thank you enough for your help. I am in your debt."

She took my hand and shook it. The corner of her eyes crinkled when her smile deepened. "My assistance requires no payment. It was my pleasure."

Ameerah scrambled to her feet. "Wait." She moved to us. I stepped back so she could have Jade's full attention. The room filled with soft, lyrical whispers. I tilted my head to the side, trying to decipher what the dancing figures were saying, but even my immortal ears couldn't make out their words. All I could gather was chorus chanting. "Do you know if I'm forgiven, and have you seen Nadia?"

Jade placed her hand on Ameerah's shoulder. It sagged beneath her touch. "You must do what's right and forgive yourself, Fallen One. There is no harsher judgment than self-judgment. Your thoughts and actions and the true nature of your heart"–she touched the center of Ameerah's forehead–"which is actually the 'third eye' but in a human is felt here"– she pressed her palm on Ameerah's chest– "will determine what plane of existence you will dwell in once you abandon this realm."

Ameerah swallowed hard and rapidly blinked back the welling tears. "Nadia?"

The corners of Jade's mouth turned down. "I do not know of her. If it's your quest to rejoin her, you're now on the right path to do so." She turned to me. "My time here has come to an end, but before I leave, I must relay a message to you to give to Paige."

"What is it?" I asked, my pulse thumping against my skin as a sudden fear of bad news assailed me.

"In the future, her guide Moradin will be taking her on a journey."

"Where?" I wasn't sure if this was good or bad because the tone of her voice reflected no opinion either way, like someone saying the grass needed to be mowed.

The figures on the wall halted, but the rhythmic chanting continued. Two of them unlinked their hands and moved aside, creating a gap.

"Heaven is what humans call it," she answered, turning away to join what I presumed were her friends. "I don't care for the word because of the narrow views attached to it and false conjectures. It's not one place.

The enormity of realms spirits camp cannot be measured. Just know that Moradin will be taking Paige to some of them, and she will be safe."

"Why?" Ameerah choked out in desperation when Jade stepped into the open space on the wall between the two silhouettes.

The right half of Jade's body disappeared. She glanced over her visible shoulder and gave a heartfelt smile that reached her lime green eyes. "So Paige will get a better understanding of herself and how things work. She'll be going through an orientation. It's already been decided among her council." She turned and stepped the rest of the way into the wall.

The chanting stopped, and the figures unlaced their fingers with one another. I bowed to them, and to my surprise, they did the same. Then they dispersed, greeting Jade's shadow with hugs and handshakes.

A blinding, white light flashed through the window as if a nuclear bomb went off. Instinctively, I raised my hand, shielding my eyes, closing them. A buzzing noise filled my ears, but then vanished, along with the brightness against my eyelids. I dropped my hand and looked about. The room was bare, the wood floor worn and covered with a thin layer of dirt. Black residues coated the stone fireplace. The corners of the hearth were crumbling. The only sign of Jade's visit was the lingering smell of incense.

"You never answered my question," Ameerah said in a flat voice.

I turned. She was standing where we last saw Jade, with her arms across her chest. Something inside my brain jolted, and my focus was now on Paige–sharp and unyielding. "I found her," I replied. "We were on a gloomy sub-plane. I told her I knew why she left me, and she told me where she was."

"Where is she?"

"She's at Timberlake Lodge with Brayden."

Ameerah groaned. "I think I'll stay behind."

"I won't allow him to cast you out," I told her, remembering when we were at Gnat Creek, and Brayden had her by the neck, poised to drive her out of the human she dwelled in.

"Yeah, I know," she said, shrugging. "But I didn't intend to go with you anyway. I figure I can meet up with you and Paige after she destroys the incantations. She can then contact Nadia and if I'm forgiven, help me crossover where Nadia is."

"I can't promise you Paige can do such things," I said.

She waved a hand in the air, unconcerned. "Paige can do it. I'm not worry about it. But in the meantime, you're welcome to borrow the Jeep. I just need a ride to where this human I'm occupying lives. I'll give you my cell phone number. You can call me when Paige is ready to help me."

"I appreciate it and accept your offer," I answered, heading out. Ameerah followed, and when we reached the Jeep, she tossed me the keys and got in the passenger side. After I put the seat back and slid behind the wheel, I noticed her holding the grimoire in her lap. "I thought Jade destroyed it."

"Me, too," Ameerah said, shoving it in her bag. "I'm glad she didn't." She paused. "Do you want it? Since I plan on blowing this popsicle stand, I won't be needing it."

"Where do you want me to drop you off?" I asked, making a U-turn. She told me, and then I answered her. "Why don't you hold onto it in case I'll need your help. You can give it to me when Paige and I meet up with you."

She reached in her bag and pulled out a pen and a small notebook. She opened it and wrote something. "Good idea," she said, ripping a piece of paper out. She folded it, and handed it to me. "Here's my cell phone number."

Keeping my eyes on the road and trying not to speed, which was difficult, I stuck it in my front pocket. "Thanks." I sat straight and gripped the steering wheel tighter. I felt like I had an itch inside me I couldn't scratch. All I could think about was getting to Paige and the possibility of her not being there.

What then?

What would I do?

"You and Paige know where the incantations are, don't you?" Ameerah asked, jolting me out of my worrisome thoughts.

I glanced at her. Her eyebrows were raised in an expectant manner. "We do, and don't take this the wrong way, but I prefer not to tell you."

She shrugged like it was no big deal, but I could see the hurt in her eyes before she looked away. "I understand. I knew Paige was in trouble when I heard the rumor saying the 'old one' was also known as Bael and that he gave her an ultimatum."

"He did," I confirmed. "Tree was there, and Bael threatened him as well."

She sat up and turned toward me. "Really? I didn't hear that. What happened?"

I told her the details, and before I knew it, I was on Lewis and Clark road. I pulled onto a long driveway in front of a two-story garage, built out of the same wood siding as the ranch style house tucked behind it. Tall trees surrounded the spacious property, and in the distance, a dog was barking. Ameerah yanked her bag out of the backseat and said she'll be waiting for my call. I thanked her for her help, and then I was off, squealing the tires as I turned northeast toward Youngs River Road.

The ride there was uneventful, except for my reeling thoughts on what I would encounter when I saw Paige and how we were going to get inside the Sof Omar cave. Then I thought about Pip. He would know people who could pull some strings, so I called him.

"Nathan, how the bloody hell are you?" he asked.

"I need your help again," I answered before outlining my current situation to him, careful not to give too much away. I told him Paige and I needed complete access to the Sof Omar cave in Ethiopia. We didn't want any trouble, and the villagers or anybody for that matter needed to know the cave and surrounding area was off limits. I didn't tell him we thought Solomon's incantations were in there, and he didn't ask. He told me he'd see what he could do and would get back to me.

When I pulled into Timberlake Lodge, I parked and dashed to room 22. When I lifted my hand to knock, the door flew open.

"Nathan." Paige leaped into my arms, locking her hands around my neck. "I'm so happy to see you," she said as I walked her backward into the room, closing the door behind us.

I pulled back and brushed the hair away from her face, slowly trailing my fingers down her cheek. "Thank God," I whispered and kissed her. But then I stopped. My eyes darted to the untidy bed, and I smelled a spicy, musky scent lingering in the air–Brayden's.

"What's wrong?" She followed my line of vision to the bed. "We didn't do anything," she quickly said. "When I fell asleep, Brayden crawled in beside me." She nudged my chin so I had to look at her. "I told him I was in love with you and made him leave."

"What did–"

Her lips were hot against mine, breaking my train of thought. Her hand moved to the back of my head, pulling it to her. She parted her mouth, freeing her tongue, kissing me deeper. I groaned when she bit my bottom lip, my concerns of our precarious situation gone. Something hot and primordial pushed against the walls of my stomach, demanding to be appeased. Huffing in my mouth, she grabbed a fistful of my T-shirt, tugging us closer.

I wanted her.

I'd *always* wanted her.

She reached behind her and yanked the brown bedspread off the bed to the floor and pulled me down with her. I braced myself above her, but then she flipped me over on my back. The gesture was quick and aggressive. She had a little smirk on her face, and her eyes were bright with desire. This behavior was new to me, but I liked it. Paige was finding the strength within her I always knew she had–a confidence in her immortality and self.

I kicked off my shoes as she fumbled with the buttons on my pants. Lifting my hips, she pulled my jeans and boxers off. I sat up and removed my shirt while she stripped in front of me. I marveled at her beautiful body, a perfect hourglass. She sat on my lap and wrapped her legs around my back. I lifted the hair off her shoulders and trailed soft kisses down her neck. Arching her back, she moaned when my lips found her breast, and my fingers touched the delicate folds between her legs. They plunged through the slick barrier, causing her to rock back and forth. Her moans grew louder, her breaths short and thick. My chest rose and fell in time with my own rapid breaths. The heat beneath my skin caused it to prickle, energy begging to be released. As if she knew, Paige took me inside her. In those moments, nothing existed or matter but her and me.

Afterwards, we made our way to the shower. In the back of my mind, I was aware we were being careless with our time, but I promised myself we'd get back on track once we got dressed. There was so much Paige and I needed to talk about; however, I pushed those thoughts aside and made love to her again.

* * *

While Paige and I told each other everything that had happened from the time we were in the hospital visiting Carrie to now, I ordered myself a bacon cheeseburger, fries, and a Coke. Paige of course ordered another cup of coffee. She was stunned when I filled her in on what Jade had shared with me about Carrie, and she couldn't stop grinning. "Do you realize what this means?" she asked, her voice raised in excitement. Before I could answer, she continued. "Carrie will be able to protect herself from the dark spirits."

A smile broke across my face. She had a valid point. Once Carrie opened her superconscious mind and reacquainted herself with the magical part of her soul, she'd be able to hold her own. Paige was beyond thrilled, and her joy was contagious. We chatted about her and Carrie learning spells together and how much could be gained from it. We went through scenarios on how maybe a weakness Paige might have may be Carrie's strength and vice versa.

"This is wonderful," I said, sharing in Paige's enthusiasm. "Carrie is definitely going to be an asset to us."

"Yeah, I know," Paige replied, beaming. "This is the best news I've heard in a long time."

"Oh, speaking of—" I opened my mouth to relay the message to

Paige about Moradin, when a heavy knock resounded from the door. I crossed the room and peeked through the crack of the plaid curtain. An attractive dark-haired girl stood outside holding a tray with my order on it. "Food," I said to Paige, flashing her a crooked smile over my shoulder.

She rose from the chair and smoothed her hair. "Good. I can use some coffee right now."

When I opened the door, the brunette asked if she could come in to collect the cart. I noticed her looking past me, searching for something. I moved aside, and when she stepped forward, Paige wheeled the cart to her and took the tray. The girl glanced at it with disinterest. She didn't budge when the handle on the metal cart touched her arm. She was still looking for something.

"Where's the other guy?" she finally asked Paige.

Paige was setting my food on the table. Her back was to us, and her shoulders stiffened. She pivoted and narrowed her eyes. "He's gone . . . why?"

The girl's face fell, and she tilted her head to the side. Her dark hair shifted behind her shoulder, and my mouth parted in surprise. She had the mark on her neck. The one a mortal with a soul received when an immortal cast a dark spirit out. It protected the human from ever being possessed again.

"Are you involved in the dark arts?" Paige asked, pointing to the girl's neck.

The server's eyes flicked to Paige. They were hard and cold. I thought for sure she was going to snap at Paige, but she shrugged instead. In one split second her whole demeanor changed from looking like she wanted to rip Paige's head off to sheer boredom. She took the handle of the cart and wheeled it backward. "He's hot, and I wanted to know where he went. Sue me," she said, moving past our door. The wheels clicked on the concrete, upsetting the dishes, the rattling noise echoing in my ears.

Paige slammed the door. "She's rude, and what's with the mark? Do you think she's still involved in black magic?"

My stomach twisted as an unsettling feeling took residency. "I don't know," I said, running a hand through my hair, sighing. "But I think we should lea–"

The door flung open. Instinctively, my arm swung back, pushing Paige behind me. Brayden dashed in. His cheeks were flushed, and he had a wild anxiousness in his eyes. His fierce energy latched onto me, leaching the blood from my face. I dropped my arm, and Paige took one step ahead of me.

"What is it? What's wrong?" she asked. Her heart was racing. Or was it mine? Maybe it was Brayden's–or all three of us. Regardless, I had a cacophony of erratic drumming in my ears.

"I'm sorry what I said about Tree," Brayden whispered to Paige. I had no idea what he was talking about, and my gaze kept darting back and forth between them. "I didn't mean it." His eyes were wide on her face, brimming with tears and fear.

In a flash, Paige shoved him against the door and got in his face. "Don't you *even* say it!" her voice cracked. I moved beside her. She glanced at me. Something broke inside of her. I could see it in her eyes.

"He's not dead," Brayden said. "Yet."

A sharp choking sound came out of Paige, but she quickly recovered. She pinned Brayden's shoulder to the wall. "You asshole. Why didn't you say that in the first place?"

"What do you mean 'yet'?" I asked.

Brayden leaned to the side and skirted Paige. Rubbing his shoulder, he said, "Aosoth and Roeick has him. They're going to kill him if you don't meet them within an hour."

Chapter Twenty-Seven

Paige

I ground my teeth. Not only because Brayden scared the crap out of me and instantly shattered the barrier I erected in front of my brittle emotions, but Aosoth and Roeick threatened my friends. Aosoth killed my grandmother Kora and my father. She destroyed my family.

My hands balled into a fist, and I could feel the heat rising to my face. I made a vow right then to find a way to eliminate her. But my fear for Tree's life was fraying the edges of my hate and anger toward Aosoth. I honestly didn't know what I'd do if something were to happen to Tree. I halted all thoughts linked to the very idea of it and jumped into action.

"Where are they?" Nathan asked as I grabbed my jacket and shrugged into it.

"They're twelve miles from here deep in the forest east of U.S. 30," Brayden answered.

"How do you know this?" I asked.

"Anwar," he responded without apology.

Nathan and I shared a look. We didn't trust Anwar, and more than likely this was another one of his twisted games of chess—to move us where he wanted to further his goal in the end. I found myself hesitant on what to do. I mean, I knew I had to rescue Tree, if Tree were really apprehended, that is. But either way, we had to find out, and charging into the lion's den–

Lion's den.

An image of me, Tree, and Carrie dancing at *The Lion's Den* popped in my head. A fierce ache trembled through my heart. I mentally shook the memory away and glared at Brayden. "How does Anwar know, and how can you trust him after everything he's done to me and Nathan?"

Brayden pulled a cell phone out of his pocket and looked at it like some do when people try to hold conversations with them, and they text instead, which I found annoying and downright rude.

"Where did you get that?" I asked in an accusing tone, knowing full well Bael had made Brayden get rid of his.

"We're wasting time," Brayden said, now gracing us with his attention. He sighed. "I bought this an hour ago and called Anwar. I know you two don't trust him, but what choice do you have? Aosoth more than likely has Tree. I've been trying to call him, and I keep getting his voice mail. I even called his mom, and she hasn't seen him since early this morning. So it's quite possible Anwar *is* telling the truth. He sent me the coordinates to where they are."

Nathan eyed Brayden distrustfully. "Why won't Anwar save Tree, then, and get rid of Aosoth and Roeick?"

"Because he's in Africa waiting for Paige. His friend Shem is on standby at the airport, waiting to take us to Africa."

"If Anwar thinks–" Nathan began, his ears turning bright red, but Brayden cut him off.

"Look. I know Anwar fucked you two over, but he had his reasons, just like now."

"I don't want nothing to do with him," I said. "The last time I saw him at my house, he displayed some weird behavior. Something isn't right with him. Not to mention all the underhanded stuff with Nathan and me."

"He performed a blood oath with Bael, which explains the bizarre behavior. It wasn't Anwar's; it was Bael's," Brayden told us.

"Are you kidding me?" Nathan ran a hand through his hair and shook his head. "I guess it doesn't surprise me considering what he told me at Gnat Creek."

The room shifted out of place for a second. I couldn't believe Anwar would do such a thing. I took a deep breath and got a grasp on myself. The thought of Tree being in danger trumped everything else. I'd deal with the other stuff later.

"You know what?" I asked, then answered my own question. "I really don't care right now. All I care about is saving Tree, so let's go."

"We'll have to run," Brayden said. "Follow me." He paused and glanced over his shoulder. "When we get there, get ready to fight."

* * *

Brayden led us through miles of deep, misty forest. The rich, earthy smells enveloped me like a comforting blanket. Occasionally, we stopped when we came to a break in the trees where a two-lane road meandered through the woods, its black asphalt pitted and cracked from age and neglect. We paused behind trunks, while Brayden checked directions on his cell to make sure we were headed the right way. Once we knew the road was clear of traffic, we darted across, back into the shadow of the trees.

Brayden stayed in front of me, and Nathan brought up the rear. The forest grew foggier as we ran through terrain covered in ferns and other damp vegetation. When our feet would disturb a random puddle, the splashing sounds of water echoed in my ears. Trees covered in crusty, brown bark pressed next to each other, while others covered in moss bowed backward, some twisted in unnatural angles.

The pines gradually grew wider apart. A few yards away, the ground sloped downward and then up, creating a blind spot. We stopped when we reached the edge of the ravine. Below was a creek with a fine mist rising over it. I could see the earth tone colors of rocks through the clear, rushing water and small whitecaps.

"We're supposed to meet Aosoth on the other side," Brayden said in a low voice so only we could hear him. He rubbed his forehead and frowned. "I have an unsettling feeling this is a trap of some sort."

"So do I," I whispered, the hair on the back of my neck prickling.

Nathan tilted his chin to the right, and his eyebrows pulled together in concentration. "It is. If you listen closely, you can hear heavy movements surrounding the area."

I listened, reaching with my keen sense of hearing, blocking the natural sounds of nature. He was right. My ears picked up feet shifting against the dirt and dried leaves, hearts beating. One particular pulse was racing, and a soft moan overlapped the pounding noise.

Tree?

It had to be him.

Brayden's eyes shifted to mine.

He heard it, too.

I mouthed the word "Tree," and he nodded.

"I think we should split up," Nathan suggested. "To throw them off guard. We're fast enough to where they won't be able to see us."

Nathan's idea made sense, and I was about to say so when Brayden piped in. "I think you should cover the north side," he said to Nathan. "I'll take the south, and Paige should walk in alone."

Nathan's jaw clenched, and his face hardened. "Absolutely not."

"I can take care of myself," I told Nathan, annoyed.

Brayden raised his eyebrows and gave me a look. "Now do you understand what I was talking about?"

He didn't have to elaborate on his statement. We both knew what he meant: Nathan was from a different era, he didn't understand our ways; therefore, he hindered me, and of course, Brayden and I made a better team. Nathan must have caught on to Brayden's silent message, because he quickly changed his mind.

"Right," he said to me, "Sorry . . . I know you can."

"Thank you," I said. "So . . . you two take your positions, and I'll walk straight in. If you run into any interference or can sneak up on the enemy, take them down. If they strike at me, you can counterattack them. It would be best if you took a covered and concealed route around the point of entry." I paused when I noticed Nathan gaping at me. I glanced at Brayden, and he was grinning.

"Just like old times, except this is real instead of imaginary," he said. "God, I miss those days."

I didn't realize until Brayden pointed it out that I had unknowingly slipped into what we as kids used to call "combat mode." I guess playing war games outside when we were young had benefitted us in the long run, since it all came back to me as if it were second nature.

"Anyway," I continued, "you two go first. I doubt they'll assault me on first sight, but if they do, I'll be ready." I shrugged. "Who knows? You might be able to secure the area before it happens."

"All right," Nathan said. "I'll take the north and west side. Brayden can take the south and east side. I think we're each quick enough to handle both."

"Sounds good to me," Brayden replied, moving back a few yards from the ravine.

Nathan took my hand and squeezed it. "Be careful."

"You, too," I answered. "I'll give you both a few minutes before I make my move."

Nathan took a couple steps back and jumped to the other side, disappearing from sight. Brayden followed. They were both gone, and it felt strange standing by myself. I thought about Tree, and a jolt of adrenaline slammed through me. My sharp immortal mind shifted on the task at hand, all other thoughts gone. My focus turned extreme as if I were hardwired for this very mission.

I listened.

I heard scuffling going on to the north–feet scratching the dirt. I was positive Nathan and Brayden were going to have to kill those soulless humans. I myself might have to, as well. I didn't care for the idea but knew we had no other choice. Tree was my top priority, and if I had to end lives in order to save his, I would.

I jumped across the ravine and paused. The soupy fog made visibility poor, something I hadn't anticipated. I squinted because even my impeccable immortal eyesight couldn't see through this. In the distance, I could barely make out a figure. It looked like it was on its knees in an execution style position with hands raised level with shoulders. Cautiously, I closed the distance, aware there was no other person in view. As I neared the figure, I blinked a couple times in confusion. This couldn't be Tree. This guy didn't have a Mohawk. He was bald. For a second, I wondered if this was Roeick and some twisted game he and Aosoth were playing. But then again, my ears would be ringing and they weren't. The dark spirits must be at a safe distance so I couldn't detect them. I hurried my pace and gasped when a few yards away, I saw it was Tree. They had shaved his Mohawk. He had black duct tape over his mouth, and half his face was black and blue.

Then everything happened in slow motion. Tree's wide eyes were on mine. The urgent look he threw me gave me pause. I froze in my tracks, trying to understand his message. He violently shook his head and a muffled, broken sound came out. In that instant, I heard a *bang* and something whizzed exactly fourteen and a quarter feet in front of me, straight at Tree. In horror, I watched it strike his chest, and my best friend fell backward.

Chapter Twenty-Eight

Paige

"Noooo!" I somehow managed to scream over the lump in my throat. My vision clouded, and my body jerked forward to go to Tree. My ears rang and a dark, menacing laugh echoed around me. From all sides, people emerged—about a dozen. One of them had an AR-15 in his hands. The human must have been in his mid-twenties with long blond hair tied back into a ponytail. His leather jacket sported metal studs down the sleeves. He was about three hundred yards from where I stood. He raised the rifle, pointing it at me. Nathan suddenly appeared behind him. He twisted the guy's head and chin, reminding me of the same thing he'd done to Cassondra. The guy dropped to the ground. Nathan picked up the gun and aimed it behind me. I whirled when I heard another bang and saw blood spray out of a chest of a dark-haired guy who was obviously coming at me. He fell backward, and then I heard another round go off. Out the corner of my eye, I saw another blonde, this one female, dropped, the front of her white parka a dark crimson.

My eyes scanned the area. Brayden was fighting a dark skinned guy, and in one swift move, he drove the heel of his palm up the base of his opponent's nose. The world seemed to spin, filled with sounds of struggle, shrieking, gunfire, and the smell of gunpowder and blood. In those short moments, I remained rooted, but when my gaze fell on Tree's still body, I snapped into action.

An attacker with short, red spiky hair, ran toward Tree. In a flash, I stepped between him and my friend. I kneed Red in the groin, and when he bent forward, I grabbed a fistful of his hair, my hand poised to do what Brayden did. It would be an easy kill; however, I made a last minute decision. No. I wanted this dark spirit to suffer. No easy way out. I kicked his feet out from under him. He fell to the ground, and I straddled him. His right hand swung up to punch me in the face. I grabbed it before it made contact. Fingers pinched the back of my neck, then dropped when I bent back his wrist, snapping it. He yelped. I snatched his free arm and broke that wrist as well and was rewarded when he howled in pain. The palm of my hand smacked his forehead. He tried desperately to buck me off, his brown eyes wide with fear, but I was too strong. I heard another round go off and ignored it. In my most powerful voice, I said an incantation in Latin. He screeched and thrashed beneath me, but I continued without pause. Like the last time I'd cast out a dark spirit, I felt it shoot out of the human through the feet. In that brief instant, I became cold and sweaty as a haunting jolt went through my heart.

"Paige, behind you!" Brayden shouted.

My eyes tracked Brayden's voice. He was in the middle of tossing a body aside. I turned when a Goth chick with black hair cut in a bob style lunged at me. I rolled to my side onto my feet. She dove forward with her hands out to break her fall. I kicked her in the chest, and she landed on her back. Her lips curled over her teeth, a deep growl reverberating from her heaving chest. I was on her in a second. She caught me off guard when something sharp sliced across my forearm through my jacket. I cried out and jerked my arm away. She had a pocket knife. She raised it, aiming for my chest. I grabbed her hand when her other hand clawed at my face. I swiped it away while I bent her thumb back, snapping the bones. She hissed and snarled, dropping the knife. Without thought, I picked up the knife and slit her throat, releasing a torrent of thick blood.

I flung the blade aside and hopped off her.

The fog had lifted enough to see bodies scattered. It was over, though the smell of gunpowder and blood still lingered.

"Are you okay?" Nathan's anxious voice asked behind me. I felt his hand on my shoulder, and he turned me around. "Why are you cradling your arm?"

At first, I couldn't process his words. He could have been talking in a foreign language. All I could think about was, I killed a human, something I'd never done before–

I. Paige Reed. Killed. A. Human.

I didn't know how I felt about it. My heart pounded in my ears, and the adrenaline in my system made its presence known through my short quick breaths. I closed my eyes.

I killed a human.

I didn't break her neck, making it a clean kill. No, I slit her throat.

Was I turning into a monster?

"Paige?" Nathan said. "What you did was necessary. I'm guessing she cut your arm." His thumb moved in cycles on my shoulder blade. "Your reaction was natural, not heinous."

I understood his words this time and opened my eyes right when Brayden called out my name. He was by Tree, kneeling beside him and–

Tree was sitting up.

I zipped to him, tears streaming down my face. In that moment I came to the realization that yeah, I killed a human–a soulless human. But what I did was in the heat of battle. It wasn't as if I enjoyed it. Besides, soulless people weren't an asset to society; they were abusers, thieves, rapist, and so forth. And honestly, I'd do it again if a dark spirit in possession threatened me or the people I loved.

Tree rubbed his chest and had a dazed look in his eyes. Brayden reached across Tree's face and ripped the duct tape off. Tree's hands flew to his lips, massaging the side of his mouth. He moved his jaw around and looked at me. I flung my arms around him, feeling something hard beneath his Sex Pistol's sweatshirt. I released my arms and sat back on my heels, poking his chest. He lifted the end of his shirt, revealing a bullet proof vest.

"Son of a bitch!" Brayden said. "Those motherfuckers planned this all out."

My hand flitted to the black and blue bruises on the right side of Tree's face. He flinched away and held a hand up.

"Sorry," I said.

He cleared his throat and swallowed. "I'm sure it looks worse than what it feels."

"What happened?" Nathan asked, kneeling beside me.

"Wait." I said, my eyes surveying the area. "Where's Aosoth and Roeick?"

"I didn't see them," Brayden answered. He looked at Nathan. "Did you?"

"No." Nathan shook his head. "Unless they were one of the people I shot."

"They were here," Tree confirmed, "but they left as soon as the fighting began. They planned it all out like Brayden said." His hand went up to his head. He ran it over the top, feeling smooth skin and grimaced. The muscles in his jaw tightened. "They had to mess with my hair for no reason except to be assholes."

"Why would the other dark spirits fight us when they knew Aosoth and Roeick would bail on them?" I asked.

"Because they're Aosoth's followers, and they're a bunch of nitwits," Tree answered. "They think by getting in her good graces, Bael will admire their loyalty and except them into his group. To them, it would be a great honor to serve Bael."

"Dumbasses," Brayden mumbled.

"How did they capture you?" Nathan asked.

Tree's expression shifted into disgust. The very movement of his face muscles made him winced. His hand lifted to his right cheekbone where an angry purple welt bulged. With his fingertips, he carefully touched it, then dropped his hand. "It was my own damn fault," he began. "I had a feeling I was being followed, but I wasn't sure. I thought maybe I was only being paranoid. This morning when I went to my dad's shop to grab a couple tools, I took the trash out to the alley. As I was dumping it in the metal bin, they jumped me. I managed to fight them off and used the knife you gave me. But then more of them appeared. I was outnumbered eight to one. One of them said to make sure I stayed alive. I'm guessing it was Aosoth, if she was in a male body, so maybe it was Roeick. I don't know." He paused and drew small circles in the dirt. He had a distant look on his face as if his mind were a million miles away.

"Then what happened," I pressed.

His eyebrows knitted. "I used pepper spray on a few of them, but then . . ." He gingerly touched the back of his head. "Everything went black."

Tree went on and told us the next thing he knew, he was covered in a wool blanket you'd find in an Army surplus store, with duct tape over his mouth, riding in the back of an old panel van. He had pretended to still be unconscious and eavesdropped on the flowing conversations around him. Roeick was driving with Aosoth in the passenger seat. There were other people riding with them. Aosoth instructed them to put up a good fight but not to harm Tree too badly. She and Roeick would escape while the others were fighting, and if they did a fine job, Aosoth would make sure Bael would know about their loyalty. She gushed how Bael begged for her forgiveness after he saved her from a long, tortuous human death, and the dark spirits hung onto her every word. He even gave her Solomon's ring to win back her trust. She was giddy when she told them Bael wanted her and Roeick to meet him in Africa.

As Tree was talking, I couldn't help think what a stupid idiot Aosoth was. Her stupidity never ceased to amaze me. The ring Beal had given her was fake. He'd made a ton of identical rings to Solomon's. I wondered, though, why would Bael want her in Africa? He loathed her like Volac did. What were Bael's intentions behind it?

"At gun point, they forced me to my knees here in the woods," Tree continued, pulling me from my thoughts, "and after they yanked my jacket and sweatshirt off, they strapped a bullet proof vest on me with a breast plate under it and told me to fall backward when they shot me. If I didn't comply, they'd shoot me in the head."

At first I didn't think it made sense what he said. How could he still be alive? But then I remembered from the TV show Cops, an AR-15 held a .223 round. If you were to shoot someone with a bullet proof vest from three hundred yards away, the bullet wouldn't penetrate it if there was a ceramic breast plate beneath it.

"When did they shave your Mohawk?" Brayden asked.

Tree's hand went back to his head. He rubbed it and frowned. "They must have done it while I was knocked out."

"Why would they put a military grade bullet proof vest on you and shoot you in front of me?" I wondered out loud. "I'm thrilled they spared your life, but why?"

"Aosoth did it to let you know she can," Nathan said.

I could feel the heat creeping up the back of my neck as thoughts of Aosoth killing off my family spilled into my head. Now she was messing with my friends. This stunt she pulled today was her way of reminding me of how she destroyed my life. Hot blood filled my cheeks, stinging them. In that moment, I promised myself I would find a way to wipe her from this earth. A spell or something.

"Don't worry, Paige," Brayden said in a calm and even voice. "We'll find a way to get rid of Aosoth for good. But in the meantime, we need to get to Africa, so you can find Solomon's incantations."

Nathan stiffened beside me, and I couldn't really blame him. I wasn't sure if Brayden was trustworthy or if he was just making poor choices in the company he chose to associate himself with. Maybe in his heart, he thought he was doing the right thing. I didn't know. However, what he said earlier about being one of the most powerful immortals on earth didn't sit well with me. "We're not going anywhere with you," I told Brayden. "I explained to you earlier I didn't want to see you again until you came to your senses."

Brayden rubbed the corner of his brow and sighed. "I understand, but you need my help because of my connections. If it weren't for me talking to Anwar earlier, you wouldn't have known Tree was in trouble, and he would probably be dead now."

I flinched, hating to even entertain the idea of Tree no longer being with us. I glanced at him. He looked pale; however, several emotions were pooling in his brown eyes.

I knew the look.

He had a gift for reading people and figuring things out and was now in observation mode. So instead of answering Brayden, I asked Tree what he thought we should do. Amazingly, Nathan kept quiet through this. Maybe because he was trying to decide what the best recourse we should take, but I did notice him focusing his attention on Tree when I asked him that question.

"I don't know what Brayden said to you," Tree told me, "to cause you to shut him out of your life, but I know this . . . he would never intentionally put you in harm's way. His choice in friends is a bit questionable; however, he does have a point." My eyes drifted to Brayden. A triumphant smile crossed his face, and he nodded to Tree in appreciation. "He has connections," Tree went on, "and can get inside information you can use."

"But the information can most likely be false," Nathan pointed out.

"True," Tree mused. "But you walk into the snake pit knowing you can get bit, arming yourself with that possibility." He shrugged. "If that makes sense? It sounded better in my head."

"I get what you're saying," I said.

Nathan ran a hand through his hair and sighed. "So do I."

"I think if Brayden can help you reach your goal faster, you should accept his offer," Tree said. "I believe in my heart he wouldn't put you in danger."

"I know," I said. "But he's friends with Anwar who did a blood oath with Bael. So basically he's friends with Bael, too . . . what if unintentionally Brayden leads us into a trap?"

"Hel-lo." Brayden piped in. "I snapped Bael's neck. I think I ended the friendliness between him and me to save you."

"True," I said, acknowledging his statement.

"Look," Brayden said. "Shem is on standby right now. He can fly us to Africa tonight. If we were to take a commercial flight, it might take days to get there. I checked all the airline schedules earlier. The soonest flight to Africa is tomorrow night." He paused and looked at Tree. "I know you might not go for this, but I think Tree should come with us. Do you still have your passport?"

Tree went to Germany a couple summers ago to visit his relatives, so I knew he had a passport, but I didn't like the idea of him getting further involved in this mess. Silently, I hoped Tree would decline. To my dismay, he jumped on it.

"I do," he answered.

"What about Carrie?" I asked, hoping her situation would deter him from joining us. "And your parents," I pointed out. "Don't you have to help your dad in his garage?"

"Carrie is doing well," Tree answered. "Yeah, I'd hate to leave her, but I think she'd want me to go. As for my folks, they've been wanting me to take a break to clear my head. I'll tell them I need to get away for a while. They'll understand."

I groaned. "I really wish you'd stay here."

"I know you do," Tree replied. "But I feel like I need to go. I don't know why, but I do."

I sighed. "Fine then. We'll leave tonight."

"I really don't like this arrangement," Nathan said, groaning.

"Of course you don't," Brayden scoffed. "But admit it. You need my help."

Nathan jumped to his feet and Brayden did the same. "If anything goes wrong and something happens to Paige or Tree, I'm holding you personally responsible and will make your life a living hell."

I rose. "If something does happen. It may not be Brayden's fault," I countered, not realizing until the last minute, I was jumping to his defense.

Brayden winked at me. He faced Nathan and gave him a smug look.

Great. I just defended my ex-boyfriend against my current one, and the ex was gloating. Lovely.

Nathan froze. Speechless. But then he spoke, his words cold and razor sharp. "If you lead us into a trap, and I discover you had any knowledge of it, I'll be your worst nightmare."

"And so will I," I interjected, because honestly, I'd never be able to trust Brayden again.

Nathan slung his arm over my shoulders, and I wrapped mine around his waist.

Brayden glowered at us. "You don't have to worry about me betraying Paige. I'd never do such a thing," he said.

Tree carefully took his sweatshirt off, groaning as he did so. I made a move to help but stopped when he held his hand up. "I'm okay," he said. "I need to get past the pain." He placed a hand on his side and took in a few slow breaths, like he was mentally preparing himself for an unwelcome task he was forced to do. He then ripped the vest and breast plate from his body and tossed them aside. Slowly he slipped his shirt and jacket back on and stood. "I should go to my house and grab my stuff before my folks get home."

Nathan picked up the vest and breast plate. "Where's the van?"

Tree glanced around us, taking in all the scattered dead bodies, some in unnatural positions like broken dolls. "Aosoth and Roeick took it when they escaped."

"I'll get Ameerah's Jeep," Nathan offered. "It shouldn't take me too long, since I know where I'm going now." He pointed to the east. "U.S. 30 is that way. I'm guessing it's a mile from here. Meet me there in the cover of the trees."

An image of some hikers finding this mess entered my mind. "What should we do about the rifle and bodies?"

"Leave it as it is," Nathan answered. "Immortals don't have fingerprints, so the authorities will think it was a drug deal gone wrong or something along those lines."

"Really?" I didn't know that. I raised my fingertips and made an annoyed sound when I saw the skin on them were line free. "I can't believe I never noticed this before." I felt like such an idiot.

"Don't feel bad, Paige," Brayden said. "I didn't know either until recently when Anwar told me." He shrugged. "Besides, we still have the lines on our palms, so why would we even check out fingertips?"

I looked at my palm, knowing what some of the lines meant. The life line descended down past my wrists. The heart line below my pinky, curved up, stopping between my first and middle finger. Interesting. I wondered what a palm reader would tell me, not knowing I was immortal.

"I'll dispose of the vest and breast plate." Nathan walked over to me and brushed his lips against mine. Out the corner of my eyes, I saw Brayden turn his back. My heart fluttered from Nathan's kiss, and at the same time my stomach twisted, knowing Brayden was in love with me, and here I stood locking lips with someone else. I didn't want to hurt him; however, by the same token, if he wanted us to stick together, he'd have to get used to Nathan and me being together. "I'll see you in an hour or less."

"Okay," I said, frowning, hating to see him go.

He turned on his heel and vanished.

Chapter Twenty-Nine

Nathan

I ran through the woods, anxious to return to Paige. I stopped a few times to check if the roads were clear of traffic and to bury the body armor. As I ran, a million thoughts raced through my head.

Anwar had completed a blood oath with Bael, and if Anwar ever went against their pact, he would surely become Bael's sock-puppet for God knows how long. I couldn't understand how Anwar could do such a foolish thing. Was it required of him in order for Bael to share Solomon's power? But Bael wanted Paige to destroy the incantations. I then realized this dark ritual had taken place long before Bael knew Solomon's power resided in Paige.

Laughter parted my lips. Not because I took delight in Anwar's unfortunate circumstances, but because of its irony. Anwar had certainly backed himself in a corner this time. A part of me wanted to feel sorry for him. I didn't. His betrayal still festered inside me, and I would never trust him again.

The thought of Brayden popped in my head as I bounded over several fallen trees. His proposal left a bad taste in my mouth. He knew his idea was the best one we had, and he did make some valid points. We could reach Africa faster with Shem piloting us, and I never had a problem with him. In fact, I kind of liked the eccentric old man. Unfortunately, though, we were going to have to deal with Anwar, Bael, Aosoth and Roeick. I didn't know how it would work out and couldn't understand why Bael made amends with Aosoth. According to Paige, he detested her. His motives made no sense. It all seemed fishy to me. Bael had something up his sleeve, and it made me nervous as hell.

When I reached the Jeep, nothing appeared out of the ordinary. A couple with two young boys was crossing the parking lot with hands full of luggage. I could hear the bustling of traffic uptown and smell the glorious scent of steaks and burgers being grilled nearby. The ache in my hollow stomach reminded me I'd never had the opportunity to eat my burger. My eyes darted over the roofs of several vehicles in front of me to the room Paige had occupied. I wondered if my food still sat on the table where I left it. My hunger fueled an almost irresistible urge to go see. But I shook it off and hopped in the Jeep instead. There were more important things to address than my raging appetite.

I exited the premises, thinking this time tomorrow, we should be in Africa. Anwar was already there, and to my dismay, I'd have to face him. I clenched my teeth and glared out the windshield. Pulling my phone from my pocket, I made a snap decision to call him. I hated prolonging the inevitable. I'd much rather get past what needed to be said now than later. Besides, once we arrived there, I didn't want to waste our time over brawling words and bellicose feelings. He already knew how I felt, and I'd keep him at arm's length.

I stopped at a red light behind a black and gray Dodge Ram. I noticed Pip had texted me. He said his sources were unable to lock down the Sof Omar cave from the public. There were forty-two entrances; however, four were generally used. He apologized for his inability to assist me, but recommended venturing through the cave during the night.

My thumbs flew over the tiny keypad, the corner of my mouth lifting at his clever idea. I thanked him for his help, told him his idea was brilliant, and I'd keep in touch. The traffic steadily moved at a slower pace than what I wanted. I placed my cell on the passenger seat and pondered Pip's suggestion.

It could work, if we completed our task by sunrise. My hope slipped when reality sunk in. The Sof Omar Cave was one of the largest in the world. Unless luck was on our side, it would take us more than one night to locate Solomon's incantations. Then I thought of Anwar. He had connections rooted in Africa. He most likely already had this problem solved. I sighed and snatched my phone off the seat. I punched in Anwar's number and listened to it ring.

"Nathaniel," he answered after the third ring, and every muscle in my body contracted at the sound of his rich, African voice. "What a pleasure to hear from you."

"I'm sure," I said, my tone dripping with sarcasm. "Whom am I talking to? Anwar or Bael or both?"

"So you know about the blood oath." It was more of a statement than a question, his voice pitching in false surprise. He already knew.

"Stop with the games, Anwar, and answer the damn question."

"Bael is too busy communicating with Ayperos at the moment. My connection with him is broken, which gives me a short amount of time to speak freely with you."

"More lies?" I hissed.

"No, Nathaniel. Truths," he paused, and then he spoke fast. "I do not blame your animosity toward me. I am also aware I will never be able to regain your trust. Just know my actions were led by what I felt was right. I still stand by Bael's vision for dis world, but I will admit, I had made some foolhardy mistakes. Dis blood oath is one of them. I would have never agreed to it if I'd known Solomon's power dwelled in Paige. We had agreed beforehand the oath would be severed after we split the magic between us and had Solomon's spells in our possession. But now dat will not happen."

"Your greed sure bit you in the ass," I said.

"Not greed, Nathaniel. Not from my perspective. But I will break free from Bael and finally be at peace."

"Good luck with that." I knew once you were bound to a dark spirit, you couldn't be released from it unless the entity agreed to it. Basically,

Anwar sold his soul to the devil. The devil may also be tied to the individual, but he had nothing to lose but time. Eventually, the other party would foul something up, and the unfortunate individual would have to be Bael's slave for as long as he wanted him to. I wondered if similar circumstances had sealed Aypero's fate.

"I have some journals and books in a safety deposit box at a bank in Switzerland. I have not touched them since I carried out the ritual with Bael. The key, along with which bank, is at my house in Washington. I want you to have it. It's . . . Bael."

"Bael?"

"Yes, Nathan, you are now speaking with Bael. I have taken full control over the conversation now. How delightful to be able to chat with you by the way," a deep voice said in false charm. "Is Paige with you?"

"No, but she will be," I said, my words clipped.

"Wonderful. So we shall see you soon?"

"If you're lucky," I growled. I was now driving down a two lane road with forest on both sides. A couple squirrels darted in front. I slowed, allowing them to cross safely. I watched the pair reach the other side, hop on a large oak and chase each other up it.

"Now, don't be difficult," Bael answered. "I tried not to get you involved, but Brayden took the liberty upon himself to interfere with my plans. However, I think the boy did me favor after all. This new one is working out much better if I do say so myself."

"Why did you save Aosoth and involved her in this?" I demanded, knowing Paige would want me to ask.

He snorted. "I have my own personal reasons. It's no concern of yours."

"Wrong answer. She ruined Paige's family, encouraged Roeick to . . ." I clenched my jaw and continued through tight lips. "She encouraged Roeick to *beat* Paige, and she had her gang jump Tree. I think it is *my* concern."

"I heard what happened to Jack. I can't say I feel bad about it. If it makes you feel better, his life was spared because of the agreement I made with Paige. Otherwise, he would be a rotting corpse right now." He sighed, an irritable sound. "Such an unfortunate bargain I made with unforeseen events I hadn't anticipated due to your resourcefulness. Your very presence on this earth vexes me to no end. Jack is another one. You both remind me of my brothers."

"Hah! You just made my day," I said. "But listen, I hate to cut this fabulous conversation short. However, I'm almost at my destination, so do enlighten me on the details of this quest." I paused, and my voice dropped to a low, warning tone. "Oh, and don't think for one second I'll be taking orders from you. I'm not one of your lap puppies like Ayperos and Anwar."

"I do enjoy our chats," Bael sneered. "To answer your questions, Shem will fill you in on the details. You will meet us at the entrance of the cave called Ayiew Maco. It's near the village of Sof Omar."

"How do you propose we keep bystanders away?"

"It's already been taken care of."

One less thing I had to worry about. Good. Out of curiosity, I had the urge to ask him how, but decided against it. I'm sure he had his minions pull some strings or possess some soulless people who had the power to keep the public at bay. "We should be there in a couple days, but I'll have Brayden keep in touch with Anwar, so you'll know our exact arrival."

"Splendid. Give Paige my regards and remind her the bargain we made is still in effect until she destroys the incantations."

I gnashed my teeth and ended the connection, knowing it was going to take everything in my power not to snap his neck. For a fleeting moment, I admired Brayden for doing that. But I had no choice. I couldn't do it. Paige had to stick to their agreement, which entailed her taking Bael along so he could watch while she destroyed the incantations. I'd have to remind Brayden, in case he decided to do the same thing again.

My phone vibrated in my hand. "Yes," I answered, recognizing Anwar's number.

"One more thing," Bael said. "Pass a message along to Brayden for me. I will pardon his act of violence toward me this one time. If he does it again, I will kill his mother."

The line clicked, leaving nothing but dead silence.

Chapter Thirty

Paige

Nathan arrived a little over an hour ago. We all piled into the Jeep and headed to Tree's house. Nathan filled us in on his conversation with Bael. When he told Brayden about Bael's menacing message, Brayden blanched and fell into a deep silence. It occurred to me then that he'd never considered his mother's safety and now would have to think things through more thoroughly than act on emotional whims. I knew his mother meant the world to him, and Bael's threat was a game changer for him.

When Nathan parked in front of Tree's ranch style house, we waited while he gathered the things he needed. Thick clouds hung low in the afternoon sky, darkening the gray world around us. The black, skeletal trees in the front yard, evoked an ominous feeling in my gut. Maybe because of the way some of its branches curled downward like arms getting ready to spring forward and snatch me away. For some reason, it reminded me of the dark spirits and how wicked they could be.

I pushed the sleeve of my jacket up and looked at my forearm where the knife had sliced it. The three inch wound had sealed. Skin puckered around the raised pinkish line. It didn't hurt, and although I already knew immortals healed rather quickly, it still amazed me to see it.

Nathan cradled my arm in his hand and turned it to get a better look.

He gently ran his thumb across it. "Looks good," he said. "The skin will thin out in a few days, and the scar will be gone." He lowered his mouth and placed a tender kiss on it. The feel of his soft lips on my skin raised goosebumps. He lifted his eyes to mine, the corner of his mouth tilting into a crooked smile. My breath caught in my throat, and the energy between us sparked. His eyes were brightening, and I imagined mine were as well. But then, Brayden coughed and bumped my seat from behind, dispelling the mood.

"Sorry," he said when I leaned around the seat to see what he was doing. "I was stretching and accidently kicked your seat."

Nathan took his cell phone out of his pocket and thumbed the keypad.

"Who are you calling?" I asked.

"Shem." He lifted the phone to his ear. "I want to tell him we'll be on our way shortly."

"I already texted him," Brayden said. "But whatever."

I peeked around the seat. "What did you tell him?"

"The same thing Nathan is right now," he answered as Nathan spoke to Shem.

I didn't reply and turned forward in my seat, listening to Nathan talk to Shem about the details of our flight, getting to Ethiopia, and renting a car to drive to the Sof Omar caves. It all sounded exhausting, and I personally couldn't wait for it to be over. I wasn't even sure how I would find the incantations. I knew they were in the cave but where? Doubt seeped into my thoughts. What if I couldn't find them? What if I was wrong all along? I glanced out the window and saw Tree exiting his house. He had on a black slouchy beanie hat that covered his bald head. I grimaced at the horrible bruises on his face, but it didn't seem to bother him, or he was pretending like it didn't. He walked in long, quick strides across his yard. His eyes locked onto mine. They were hard with determination, silently saying, *Let's end this.*

* * *

On the way to Portland, we went through the drive-thru at Arby's and while we ate, we talked about what we were going to do once we arrived in Africa. We agreed to sleep on the flight, so when we landed at Bole International Airport in Addis Ababa, we wouldn't be tired and could get straight to the task at hand. Shem's jet would have to stop and refuel in Portugal. Once we arrived in Ethiopia, one of Shem's friends would drive us to the Sof Omar caves. Nathan advised us it would be an eight hour drive.

Lovely.

This whole trip seemed endless. It felt like a dream, as if I were outside myself, watching this whole thing take place.

"Who is Shem?" Tree wanted to know. "You guys never clarified to me or Carrie who he is, except that he's Anwar's weird friend."

Brayden and I snickered. "Eccentric," I corrected him.

"Bizarre," Brayden said.

The corner of Nathan's mouth tilted up. He lifted his eyes to the rearview mirror to address Tree. "Picture the Mad Hatter with loads of money, extremely intelligent with a two hundred plus IQ."

"Is he immortal?" Tree asked.

"No," Nathan answered, then went on to tell him that Shem's father Eli was. He accepted immortality when Shem was fourteen. He played the same card Nathan had done when he turned immortal–faked his own death. Eli kept his distance, watching Shem from afar. But the strain of not being with Shem's mother and seeing her visit his grave every day, grieving over him, became too much for him to bear. He consulted Anwar on the matter, deciding shortly after to make himself known to his beloved wife in secret.

One night, when Shem was staying at a friend's house, Eli knocked on the backdoor in the cover of the shadows, so the neighbors wouldn't see him. Shem's mom, Lucille, answered it, threw her arms around Eli and burst into tears, repeatedly saying, "My heart kept telling me you weren't dead, but my mind warred against it, saying I was foolish to believe such nonsense." Eli explained everything to her, and they agreed not to tell Shem about it until he was much older. So for years, Eli and Lucille met in secret. But then she got breast cancer. She fought the disease for as long as she could, even gave up both breasts, but in the end she lost the battle. Eli was devastated. By then, Shem was at MIT. He had skipped several grades and at this time was the head of his class at the prestigious Cambridge school.

"Wow. He is a brainiac," Tree said, impressed.

Nathan nodded. "He's created some high tech inventions the government bought. But to make a long story short, Eli finally confronted Shem and told him everything. Afterwards, he took his life to be with Lucille, willing all his precious antiques and art to Shem."

Tree leaned between the console next to Nathan and me. "How did Shem respond to Eli's confession?"

"He already knew," I told him and continued when he gaped at me. "Shem had noticed the change in his mom's mood after Eli came back into her life, like she stopped visiting his grave. So being a technological genius, he rigged their kitchen with a hidden camera. He told me he felt dirty doing it, but like you, he's very intuitive and knew something was amiss. That's how he discovered the truth."

"Why wouldn't he say anything?" Tree asked. "Wasn't he pissed?"

Nathan shook his head. "No. He loved his mom too much and didn't want to ruin her happiness. He never told a soul, which impressed Anwar enough to enfold Shem into his life."

Tree's eyebrow furrowed. "How did he become friends with Anwar?"

"Easy," I said. "Anwar approached him and the rest is history."

Tree sat back. "Impressive."

We all kept to our thoughts for a while, the sounds of traffic becoming more prevalent the closer we got to Portland. We were hitting rush hour when we reached the city, people getting off work, anxious to get home. Horns blared around us, tires screeching, and obscenities were being yelled out open windows. It reminded me of how much I disliked the metropolitan areas.

When we drove into the airport parking lot, everything turned into a blur until we were settled in Shem's jet. Maybe because the atmosphere around me swarmed with hurried steps, the air charged with frenzy energy. A large group of Japanese teenagers exiting their gates walked by us, their faces alit with smiles, their eyes wide with excitement. With his hand in mine, Nathan pulled me closer to his side. I glanced over my shoulder, admiring the outfits the Japanese girls were wearing. They were cross between Goth and retro wear. The next thing I knew, we were stepping outside and climbing the ladder to Shem's Bombardier. The gray sky above us began to turn a pinkish, red color. Evening time.

"Welcome," Shem said, greeting us with a warm smile. He clapped a hand on Nathan's shoulder. "Good to see you."

Nathan returned his smile. "Likewise."

Shem's thin, long arms, wrapped me in a bear hug. "How are ya?" He pulled back and tilted his chin down, his brown eyes searching my face.

My lips twitched into a wary grin. "I'm fine. Thanks for your help. I appreciate it."

He winked. "My pleasure." He turned to Brayden and Tree, who were standing a few feet away, silently watching us. "Brayden," he said, offering his hand. "How goes it?"

Brayden shook it. "It's going."

Shem laughed. "Well, you four have quite a task ahead of you." His gaze shifted to Tree.

I stepped beside Tree and hooked arms with him. "Shem, this is Jack, but we call him Tree. He's my best friend and family."

Shem placed a hand on Tree's shoulder. "Well, then, you're now family to me, too. Nice to meet you."

"The feeling is mutual," Tree answered. "I've heard wonderful things about you."

Shem's eyebrows raised, reaching the hairline of his brown, disheveled hair. He laughed. "Really? Well, Nathan is quite the storyteller. I'm sure he was kind enough to embellish in all the right places." He winked at Nathan.

Nathan held his hands up in defense. "All true. I didn't exaggerate one bit."

"He didn't," I confirmed.

"You two do wonders for my ego," Shem teased. "The next time I experience self-doubt, I'll be sure to ring you up." He tucked half of his button-up, blue checkered shirt into his khakis, leaving the other half hanging out. I noticed he was wearing sandals. Jerusalem cruisers is what I called them. "Why don't you make yourself at home while I sit with my pilot Franco who should be contacting ground control any minute now. The fridge and cupboards are stocked with food. There are also blankets and pillows in the compartment above the seats."

I remembered Franco. He was a good looking middle-aged Italian guy with olive skin and dark wavy hair. Reserved and shy. He kept to himself, a man of few words. So his lack of presence didn't surprise me at all.

Tree ran his hand over the white leather seat. "Wow. This is nice," he said after Shem left the room. "Check out the computer screen on the back of the seat in front of it."

"You can watch movies," Nathan told him. "The earphones are in the pocket below." He pointed to the pouch beneath it.

"The seat folds up and forward so you can recline the one behind it and sleep," I added.

Tree reached to the compartment above the armrest and pulled down a blanket and pillow. "Awesome. I'm taking this seat."

"Are you guys hungry or thirsty?" Brayden asked toward the front of the plane.

I really wanted some coffee, but I knew I should try and sleep. We had a lot of hours ahead of us, and I was hoping I could sleep through most of them. "I'll take a bottled water. What does he have for a snack?"

"What do you want?"

"I don't know. Pick something out for me." I knew Brayden's choice wouldn't disappointment me, and I was right. As Nathan and Tree went to see what was available, Brayden walked toward me with a grab bag of Chex Mix. "Thank you," I said when he handed it to me along with a bottled water. "Good choice."

"I would have made you some coffee, but I figured you'd want to try and sleep most of the flight to Portugal."

He knew me so well. I wondered if Nathan would have done the same thing. I stopped the thought right there because it wasn't fair to Nathan. Sure, Brayden knew me in some ways better than Nathan, but on the flip side, there were things Nathan knew about me that Brayden didn't. But still, I couldn't stop the tugging at the edge of my heart when memories of Brayden and me flashed through my mind of a time much simpler and pure.

I shifted my feet and gave him a weak smile. "You're right."

"You're in my way, dude," Tree said behind Brayden, carrying a bag of pork rinds and a bottle of Mountain Dew.

Brayden stepped aside, and I made a face at Tree. "You're eating pig skin?"

Tree grinned. "Yup, and it's gooood."

"Where do you want to sit?" Nathan asked me, causing Brayden to once again move out of the way. He glared at Nathan and moved to a window seat behind Tree.

"Here is fine." I sat in the aisle seat in the row across from Tree, moving my legs to the side so Nathan could get by. I had to admit the seats were comfortable.

"Okay, kiddies," Shem said over the loud speaker. "Put your seatbelts on. We got clearance to take off." He paused. "Excuse me. Tree, put your seatbelt on."

The plane jerked forward as it eased out onto the runway. The wheels rumbled, and I heard Tree mumbling he hated this part. The rumbling stopped as the nose of the plane lifted. It banked and turned to the east, and then the aircraft climbed. We were now airborne, and Shem announced we were rising to an altitude of thirty thousand feet.

Nathan tore his bag of Cheetos open, and I followed suit with my Chex Mix. I knew I would have to try and sleep soon, but I wasn't sure if I could. Now that we were on our way, my stomach was in a knot.

This was for real.

I mean, I knew it was, but now that we were heading to Africa, those doubts I had resurfaced. Earlier I had thought of using the incantations instead of destroying them, but now I wasn't so sure. I probably wouldn't know how to use them anyway. Unless, since I had the power of the ring inside me, I would automatically know. If that were the case, I wondered how it would work and if Bael could stop me. I was sure he had considered that possibility, so he probably had a backup plan. I shivered. The consequences would be too great, and Bael wouldn't think twice about ending Tree's life. I had no choice but to destroy the incantations, if I could find them that is.

"What are you thinking?" Nathan asked, leaning toward me. Tree and Brayden were having a discussion about superheroes of all things. I was sure Tree was as nervous as me, and this was his way of getting his mind off it.

I leaned to the side and softly kissed Nathan's lips, tasting Cheetos. "Mmmm, cheesy," I said when I pulled back. His hand cupped the back of my head and moved it forward. His lips touched mine again. He parted them, his tongue flicking against mine. A soft moan vibrated my throat. I wrapped my arms around his shoulders, wishing I could climb inside him and escape from it all. Nathan broke our kiss and rested his forehead against mine. My attention diverted to Tree. He was happy Shem had the movie *Iron Man* and told Brayden he was going to watch it before dozing off. I refocused my attention on Nathan, his warm breath on my mouth.

"It'll be okay," he said in a low, husky voice. "We'll get through this."

He knew. He knew I was worried. I bit my lip and nodded, my limbs suddenly feeling heavy from the exhaustion of the day. My mind, though, was alert, spinning with thoughts that bled into each other—mind chatter that would not be quiet. Nathan kissed my forehead, and I told him we should watch a movie. I glanced at Tree. He had the earphones on, already settled in with a blanket draped over him, watching his movie. My gaze shifted to Brayden, moving to the aisle.

"Do you want me to grab you a blanket and pillow," he asked me. "I was just getting mine, so it wouldn't be any trouble."

I gave him a half-smile. "Yes, please." He reached above me, the hem of his black T-shirt rising, revealing his hip bone and taut stomach. For some reason, I had the urge to run my finger across it but glanced away instead. "Can you get Nathan a blanket and pillow as well?"

Brayden grunted and tossed the items to Nathan, his eyes never leaving mine, saying, *I'm being nice for you.*

"Thanks," Nathan said in a flat tone after the pillow hit him in the face and fell into his lap.

Brayden smirked and handed my stuff to me. I thanked him and was surprised when he leaned over and kissed my cheek. "Sleep well," he whispered. He kissed it again before turning away to settle himself in for the duration of the trip.

That was unexpected, and I didn't really know how to react. I mean, Brayden reminded me of home, and the familiarity of his presence did bring some comfort to me. However, I hadn't forgotten about the things he told me in the hotel room and that he thought Anwar walked on water. No matter how much I cared for Brayden, I had to remind myself of his misguided ways.

"What movie would you like to watch?" Nathan asked. I turned to him and caught him looking at Brayden with disapproval, but his eyes softened when they rested on my face.

I chose *The Goonies* since it was filmed in Astoria, and I really liked the movie. But I must have fallen asleep at the beginning of it because the last thing I could remember was Chunk spraying whipped cream in his mouth.

Chapter Thirty-One

Nathan

All four of us slept most of the way to Portugal, which made time fly by. We made ourselves presentable before leaving the plane and roaming the airport to stretch our legs while it refueled. We had an hour to kill, and I knew Paige would love some coffee.

"I think we should stick together," Paige said, latching onto Tree's wrist, pulling him next to her. "There might be dark spirits around."

"Even so, there are too many people for them to cause any shit." Brayden was on the other side of Tree, watching an Indian couple walk by. They were wheeling their luggage behind, talking in Hindi. The female had a bright red dot in the center of her forehead close to the eyebrows. A bindi is what they called it. It had several meanings, one of them was to protect the person from demons or bad luck.

I squeezed Paige's hand. "I don't think you'll have to worry about it. I'm sure Bael called his hounds from Hell off for the time being."

Paige straightened her back and raised her chin. "It didn't stop Aosoth, though. I don't want to take any chances."

"Don't worry, Paige," Tree said. "I'll stick with you throughout this trip. You and I are in this together. Remember?"

Paige leaned her head against his arm. "Yeah, we are. Thanks."

"This airport is so white and sterile looking compared to Portland's,"

Brayden said to no one in particular. "At least at the food court there's a splash of color here and there."

He was right. Straight ahead was a bright, turquoise sign that said *My Bistro*. Against the white wall, the color jumped right at you. There was a large picture–hung between two metal stands–of a coffee cup on a saucer filled with a frothy cappuccino. A delightful expression shown on Paige's face when she spotted it. She hurried her steps, pulling both Tree and me with her.

After we ordered and paid, we sat at one of the square, stainless steel café tables in the eating area, waiting for our food.

"Omigod. This cappuccino is awesome." Paige took another sip and closed her eyes. "Mmmmmm. I'm in coffee heaven." She looked at me, a mischievous grin forming on her face. "I think I might order another one before we go."

Brayden laughed. "Have you forgotten what an overdose of caffeine does to you?" He raised an eyebrow, smiling at Paige.

Jealousy swept through me. Brayden and Paige had years of fond memories together, which would forever connect them. Memories and inside jokes I was clueless on and when brought up, made me feel awkward. I wasn't used to those types of feelings. I knew what they were. Insecurities. It didn't bode well with me, and I shifted in my seat, dropping my eyes to my coffee cup. In truth, I became more annoyed with myself than the present company. Since I'd been with Paige, she stirred emotions in me I could only describe as foreign, and the others were long forgotten *human* feelings abandoned after I became immortal. However, I wouldn't trade it or her for the world.

"No," Paige answered him, sliding her hand on my knee beneath the table, causing me to look up and see her smiling face.

Tree nudged my arm with his elbow. "She gets hyper and doesn't shut up," he told me.

"She gets silly," Brayden added.

"I recall you mentioning this before," I said to him, remembering it clearly. It was at Paige's mom's funeral before Paige passed out. Reminding them would be in poor taste, so I kept my mouth shut, but the memory of it caused me to narrow my eyes, and my lips formed a tight line.

Brayden's cheeks bloomed red. He caught his infraction. Harmless on his part; however, it shifted the lighthearted mood around our table to a quiet, dismal one. Both Paige and Tree were quick enough to have caught it as well.

Our food was brought to us, and Paige ordered another cappuccino to go. Tree smiled and shook his head at her, brightening the melancholy mood. "I take it you decided to be our source of entertainment for a while?"

"We have an eight hour flight ahead of us," Brayden said to her. "This should be interesting. I think I'll enjoy watching you spazzing out."

Paige flicked a hand in the air, waving off their remarks. "I'm immortal now. I don't think I'll get jacked up on caffeine like I did once upon a time ago."

She was wrong.

Thirty minutes into our flight to Ethiopia, Paige was talking a million miles an hour. She couldn't sit still. She moved from seat to seat, talking to Brayden, then to Tree. She told Tree what Jade said to me about Carrie. I didn't mind her telling him, but I didn't particularly care for Brayden knowing about it when right now his motives seemed questionable. Nevertheless, he'd find out sooner or later, so I kept quiet except for when Tree pelted me with questions about it. Of course, he was stunned by this information and told us as soon as Paige finds and destroys the incantations, he wanted to go straight home to Carrie. I assured him Paige and I would head back to Astoria with him.

We had eight hours ahead of us and the first five went by rather quickly due to the conversations initiated by Paige in her hyper state. Brayden shared some information that threw me back a couple paces. The reason Anwar performed a blood oath with Bael was he grew tired of this world and being immortal. He wasn't happy with the changes and thought if he could be a part of Bael's revolution to change back to the old ways, bring earth to its ultimate glory, Anwar would find peace and joy again. But since it was no longer going to happen, Anwar was stuck in a binding agreement he now regretted. I knew the last part from the conversation I had with him, but I wasn't aware of his unhappiness. In my mind, though, his actions toward Paige and I were inexcusable. As heartless as it may seem, I had no sympathy for him. Period.

Paige bit her lip, worry etching her features. "Do you think Anwar would take his own life?"

I shook my head. "No. His spirit is still bound to Bael unless Bael voids the pact between them."

"So Anwar is totally screwed now," Tree said.

"Pretty much," I answered. What Anwar told me earlier had me puzzled, though. Why would he tell me where his journals were, and he wanted me to have them? I hadn't really thought about it, but now it seemed he was planning on leaving. It didn't make sense, and for some strange reason an unexpected wave of deep sadness went through me. I turned in my seat and stared out the window into the star-filled night. If I were being honest with myself, a part of me still cared for Anwar.

The Anwar I used to know.

I thought about families I knew back in the Civil War. Good families with strong bonds ripped in two when one brother decided to fight for the south and the other fought for the north. I had watched in the shadows as it all played out. The war spilled into loving households and into their hearts, pitting brother against brother, father against son. And now, this war against good and evil had essentially done the same thing to Anwar and me.

With a heavy heart, I closed my eyes, tuning out the other conversations. Visions of smoky fields and the sound of gunfire encompassed my mind. Young men screaming in agony, writhing on the ground, their chests soaked in blood, some with limbs missing. Bayonets fixed, hand-to-hand combat, no mercy. A bloodbath.

I must have fallen asleep because I awoke with a jolt, my forehead damp with sweat. The loud speaker blared our landing in Abbis Ababa. Shem ended his announcement with the current time of 9:12 in the morning in the capital city of Ethiopia.

Vivid dreams of war still swam in my head, and the smell of gunpowder lingered in my nostrils. A warm hand touched my arm. Bleary eyed, I turned, meeting Paige's nervous expression.

"Are you okay?" She removed her hand from my arm and placed it on my cheek. "You don't look so good."

"I'm fine," I said, not wanting her to worry.

"I can't believe we're in Africa." Tree rose from his seat and stretched. "This is wild."

"Are you sure?" Paige asked me, her eyes never leaving my face. "You look pale."

"Maybe he needs to eat," Brayden said from behind us, a hint of sarcasm in his voice.

Ignoring his comment, I covered Paige's hand with mine. "Yes, I'm sure." I leaned next to her ear and whispered, "I was having disturbing dreams about the war is all." I pulled back and continued in my normal tone. "I am hungry."

"I think we all are," Paige said, following my lead. She stood and smoothed her clothes. She offered me her hand, and I took it, allowing her to pull me to my feet.

Brayden was leaning against the edge of a seat, texting. "I'm telling Anwar we just arrived. He wants us to hurry. I told him we're hungry and . . ." He looked at us and held a hand up. "Wait. He's answering me . . . He said to grab some food from Shem's supply and head to the Sof Omar caves now."

"Anwar is not our boss," Paige said, annoyed. "Tell him he has no right to tell us what to do."

I agreed with her. Who was Anwar to demand our immediate presence? If he for one second thought we were going to take orders from him, he had a rude awakening ahead of him.

"It's not Anwar who said it," Brayden told us, reading the text. "It was Bael."

Paige shrugged. "So. He's not our boss either. He can piss off." She moved toward Brayden and held her hand out. "Give me your phone."

A delightful expression crossed Brayden's face, giving me the impression he enjoyed Paige's spunk. He handed her his cell and stood beside her while she texted Bael.

"What are saying to him?" Tree asked.

Brayden laughed and looked at Tree. "She's actually telling him to piss off."

Tree raised his eyebrows, his eyes widening. "Paige, do you think you should be provoking him?"

"He expects it," she offhandedly said, "and likes it . . ." She looked up. "My feistiness," she added. But then she frowned when she read his response.

"What's wrong?" I asked.

She sighed. "He can only keep the locals at bay for so long, so we have to get there as soon as possible. He spun some tale of a group of scientific researchers, which is us, doing some top secret . . . whatever . . . whatever. So the cave is off limits. I just told him we'll be on our way within an hour." She handed Brayden his phone back.

"I spoke to Anwar," Shem said, exiting the cockpit. "There's a driver by the name of David waiting for you right now. I'll grab some chow for on the way there, while you freshen up."

"You're not going?" Paige asked, her tone pitched in surprise.

"No, darling." Shem knelt in front of a shiny, wood paneled wall with a flat screen TV mounted to it, facing a small white leather couch. He opened a drawer and pulled out what looked like a duffel bag. "Franco and I will wait here for you." He rose and shook the nylon, black bag. It transformed into a perfect square. He moved to the refrigerator and removed ice packs from the freezer, placing them in the cooler.

"Oh," Paige said, disappointment shadowing her face.

"It makes sense," I said. "He'll have his jet ready for us so we can leave right away. Not to mention, he'd be safer here."

"True, but I enjoy his company, and I trust him. We don't know anything about this David guy who will be driving us."

I rubbed her shoulder. "I'm sure David is a fine gentleman and will get us to our destination safely."

While Brayden and Tree were getting ready, we chatted with Shem, patiently waiting for our turn to use the spacious restroom. I had to hand it to him, he spared no expense when he bought this Bombardier Global 8000 jet. The luxuries were unbelievable and much welcomed. Shem was always thinking ahead. For example, he bought disposal toothbrushes, knowing he'd be flying us to Africa. He was a thoughtful person, and I told myself I'd find a way to show my appreciation for his loyalty and generosity when we returned to Astoria.

* * *

After we went through the airport, following the same routine as everyone else, Shem led us outdoors to the parking area. It was pouring rain. A channel of water ran the length of the sidewalk. We paused beneath the awning while he called David to tell him we were here. There were groups of taxi drivers in orange and blue vehicles lining the street. People were coming and going in all directions.

"I can't believe it's raining," Tree said. "In Ethiopia. I was expecting it to be hot and miserable."

"Me, too," Paige said, looking about. "This doesn't even look like we landed in Africa."

She was right. In all my travels, Africa was one place I'd never been to. The scenery was ordinary. There were islands in the middle of the road with grass and trees, beyond them was the parking lot. In the distance were more trees and mountains. I imagined, though, once we were on our way through the countryside, the landscape would change dramatically.

"It's cooler here," Shem said, "because this city sits on a plateau. The daily temperature rarely exceeds sixty-eight degrees. We're also in the heavy rain season."

"It figures," Brayden replied. "The rain seems to follows us."

A blue and white minibus pulled in front of us and parked. An African man emerged from the driver's side. Shem greeted him with a hearty handshake, and after a few pleasantries between the two, he introduced us to David. Right away I liked the gentleness in his face and kind smile. He said he would take us to and from the Sof Omar Caves. While we were exploring, he'd wait for us in Dinsho. David gestured toward the cooler I was carrying. "Please, let me take dat for you. I will put it in the back where you will be sitting."

I slipped the strap off my shoulder and handed it to him. "Thank you. You're more than welcome to eat with us," I offered. "We have plenty of food to go around."

He nodded and turned to place it in the backseat. Afterwards, he shook Shem's hand again and squeezed his shoulder. "Farewell, good friend. Do not worry," he said. "I will take good care of them."

"I have no doubt about your ability to follow through. Thank you, and I will see you again soon," Shem said.

We said our goodbyes to Shem, and then we were off to the Sof Omar Caves with high hopes of finding the incantations so Paige could destroy them.

Chapter Thirty-Two

Paige

My stomach was in a knot, and my nerves were on edge. I couldn't believe we were finally in Africa, now driving to the cave I saw in a vision. I twisted and untwisted my fingers in my lap, half listening to the guys talking to David about Ethiopia and how he grew up and how he knew Shem and Anwar. He openly answered their questions, throwing in jokes here and there. His unexpected humor and lightheartedness dispelled some of the anxiety in the air. I couldn't help but like him.

When we drove through the city of Addis, the traffic was heavy, and although we had our windows up, I could smell exhaust fumes choking the air. We drove by tall buildings looming over small hole-in-the wall shops with people standing beneath the awnings, chatting. We passed a small shopping mall where three African woman wearing long skirts and head scarves entered the building to escape the rain. One of them had what looked like a wicker basket hanging from her back. Not too far from there was a squat building with a pointed red rooftop. I wondered what was inside, but I didn't feel like asking David. He seemed too busy telling Tree Addis Ababa meant "new flower" in Amharic, and the trees on the wide avenues were called "jacarandas." A few miles away stood an open-air market. David said it was one of the largest in Africa, known as the "Mercato." I would have loved to check it out, but of course that wasn't going to happen.

As the guys continued to chat, I zoned out, not wanting to think about what lay ahead of us, because when I did, my stomach would roll with nausea. I stared out the window, enjoying the changing landscapes. It went from a rainy bustling city to dry, lowland plains with what looked like scrub brush dotting the open land and distant mountains as the backdrop. Rugged land stretched for miles, some with herds of livestock roaming. At times the dirt road we traveled became rocky and uneven in spots, bouncing us off our seats. Sometimes we'd pass broken vehicles along the road and natives walking beside pack mules loaded with cargo.

Hours later we drove by distant clay and stone huts with smoking fire pits a few yards from them. Men, women, and children were milling about. I leaned closer to the window, the tip of my nose touching the glass. With my keen eyesight, I could make out what looked like tan straws protruding from the males' chins and round, black disks, hanging from their earlobes. The indigenous people seemed content by the way they carried on, laughing and horsing around with the children, paying no attention to the blue and white minibus driving by.

We stopped a few times in small towns to use the restroom. Outwardly, they were shabby looking, constructed of wood, reminding me of a salon straight out of the old west. But indoors, they had clean, pleasant atmospheres. It felt good to move around, get the blood flowing back in my legs. However, I noticed the heaviness in my limbs and exhaustion setting in.

"Are you okay?" Nathan asked as we piled back in the bus.

I shifted in my seat, leaning my shoulder against the door panel. I looked at him and blinked. "I'm tired."

Brayden poked his head around the front seat. The whites of his eyes were tinged in red, bags were forming beneath them. "You're jet lagged. We all are."

"We can stop at Lake Ziway," David suggested, "and get a room for the night."

His idea appealed to me, but I shook my head instead. "No. We need to get there as soon as possible. We'll be okay." Really, I just wanted to get this done. The sooner it was over, the better.

Brayden rubbed his brow and closed his eyes. "You're right." He turned back in his seat. "I'll text Anwar to let him know what's going on."

I leaned over Nathan to see what Tree was doing. He'd been quiet since we boarded the bus. The side of his head rested against the window, his eyes closed, faced slacked in sleep. I yawned and glanced out the window.

We were on a road which seemed to be levitating above a huge body of water. David mentioned it was Lake Beseka. On the shore were yellow-bellied storks and great white pelicans. David pointed toward the bushland and told us it was inhabited by baboons. Nathan slipped his arm around my shoulders, and I rested against his chest, imagining walking in the jungles of Africa unafraid. I closed my eyes envisioning coming across a gorilla and befriending him through my ability to communicate with animals by touch. The corners of my mouth twitched into a small smile. My head shifted downward as Nathan's shallow breaths slowly moved it up and down, lolling me to sleep. The last thing I could remember was Brayden's open-mouthed snores that sounded like a cross between Darth Vader breathing through his mask and a cat hacking up a hairball.

* * *

Something moist and soft touched my cheek. I stirred in my seat and winced at the sharp pain in my neck. It felt like somebody shot an arrow through it. Slapping a hand over it, I sat up and opened my eyes. The evening sun slanted through the windows, creating a ray of pale light in front of me. I could see the dust motes swirling around inside it. I rubbed sleep from my eyes.

"Hello, beautiful," Nathan said in a low voice, his fingers brushing the hair out of my face. "We're here."

Here?

At first my foggy brain couldn't register what Nathan was talking about until Tree leaned over Nathan's lap. "Are you ready for this?" he asked me.

Then the connection was made.

Omigod.

We. Were. Here.

We were near the Sof Omar Caves, where Solomon stashed his incantations. I was the only one who could find them. But could I? What if I couldn't? What would happen then? Doubt pinched my brain, keeping all other thoughts at bay. If I couldn't locate Solomon's spells, and the vision I had of the cave turned out to be bogus, what would I do? But then something much more powerful punched a hole through my incredulous musing.

Hate.

Aosoth and Rocick were here with Bael and Anwar. I dreaded seeing that bitch. I wanted to end her.

My hands balled into fists.

Tree's eyebrow furrowed. He glanced down and back at me. "What's wrong? You look pissed."

Brayden was on the phone with Anwar or Bael. I didn't know. But he was talking to someone, announcing our arrival. David was outside having a conversation with several people. My ears automatically honed in on what they were saying. They were residents of this tiny village we were in and seemed friendly. They welcomed us, ensuring the caves were at our disposal alone. We had two days to do our "research." He apologized for the lack of time given to us. However, his village and the towns outside it would suffer a monetary loss because it was a huge tourist attraction.

Nathan rested his hand on my arm, drawing my attention back. I glanced at Tree who had a quizzical look on his face, like he was waiting for me to answer him. My hands ached, and I noticed they were still tightly balled. I opened them, allowing the blood to rush back. I then remembered Tree's question. "Sorry," I said. "I got distracted. I was thinking about Aosoth."

Understanding entered Tree's face. "Ah, no need to explain." He reached in the back and grabbed some sandwiches and water bottles out of the cooler. He handed me egg salad on wheat and some water. "Here," he said, smiling. "Get some nourishment in you before you kick her ass."

I laughed. "I don't want to merely kick her ass. I want to annihilate her." I bit into my sandwich, tearing a chunk of it off with my teeth to emphasize my statement. "After I find those damn incantations and destroy them, she'll be next in line," I declared.

"I'll help you," Nathan said. "The grimoire I was telling you about might have a spell in there we can use to wipe her from this earth for good."

I turned to him and grinned. "What a great idea." The very thought of it gave me a rush of hope and excitement. I knew Ameerah would allow us to borrow the book. Hell, she couldn't stand Aosoth either.

"What grimoire?" Tree wanted to know.

Brayden said goodbye to Anwar and peeked around his seat. "What are you guys talking about?"

"The grimoire is bounded in human skin," I told them, making a face.

Tree shifted to the edge of his seat so he could see me. "Are you serious?"

Taking a drink of my water, I nodded. Out the corner of my eye I could see Brayden staring at me, waiting for me to elaborate some more.

"It's dark magic," Nathan said, his words slow and cautious.

He didn't want Brayden to know more than what was said. I knew he didn't trust him, which I couldn't blame him there, so I changed the subject.

"What did Anwar say?" I asked Brayden.

His eyes darted from Nathan to mine, the curiosity in them still present. "He's heading here right now to lead us to the cave."

"Speak of the devil," I said when I glanced out the window and saw

Anwar walking toward David and the natives around him. "That didn't take him long."

"He shouldn't be using his preternatural speed in front of these humans," Nathan commented under his breath.

Brayden cracked open his door. "He's not. He was already heading this way when we were talking on the phone." He stepped out of the minibus and we followed.

* * *

Nathan and I didn't say much to Anwar on the way to the cave entrance. I made sure Tree was by my side, prepared to protect him if need be. I didn't trust Roeick, and I sure as hell didn't trust Aosoth. I dreaded sharing air space with her and still had no idea why Bael would even allow her in our company. It didn't make sense. But whatever. It had to be another one of his games, because why would he give her a fake ring, the exact replica of Solomon's and lead her to believe it was the real deal? She was so stupid. I snickered and shook my head.

Nathan squeezed my hand. "What are you giggling about?"

"I'll tell ya later," I said, catching Tree looking at me, his brows raised in question.

The village was perched on the cliffs above the Weib River. We trailed behind Anwar and Brayden who were talking about this part of Africa revolving around spirit worship and cults. I walked in silence, listening to Anwar's deep, rich voice talking to Brayden. He went on to tell him people from all over believed the most powerful supernatural beings had attached themselves to the ancient trees and boulders that surrounded us on the dirt path we were following. When it forked in three different directions, we took a right, which led us to a ledge. Cut out of the rich soil were steps made out of stone. We descended the hill into a canyon. A pebble beach encircled a large body of water. The orange light from the setting sun bounced off the dark, glassy surface, creating over a dozen rays that resembled individual portals, reaching to the heavens.

Extraordinary.

The hairs on my arms stood, and something inside my chest shifted, as if somebody pushed a sliding door aside, allowing whatever resided in there to creep out. A shot of adrenaline caused my heart to hammer.

Tree stared at the river in wonder, his eyes drinking in the beams of light. "I think I might have to eat my words," he said, giving me a sidelong glance.

Brayden looked over his shoulder at Tree. "Eat your words? Why?"

I knew exactly what Tree meant, but when I opened my mouth to respond, Nathan answered him instead. "When Paige had described the cave to Tree, he was doubtful, telling her it sounded like something straight out of a fantasy novel."

Brayden looked at me for confirmation. I smiled and nodded.

Tree laughed. "Man, did I piss Paige off."

Brayden gaffawed. "I bet." He looked at me, then glanced away.

I could see on the left bank of the river two males and a female standing near the mouth of a cave. Anwar halted, and we all stopped. He turned, his face strained, eyes almost pleading when they darted between Nathan and me and then finally resting on Nathan. Nathan's grip tightened around my hand, and I could feel his body tensing.

"Nathaniel, I am sorry for causing you any grief," Anwar said and shifted his gaze to me. "And you, too, Ms. Paige. Maybe one day you both will understand my motives and why."

"Bael or Roeick is coming this way," Tree said, causing Anwar to turn back around.

It was Bael. I knew it. His choice in vessels was so predictable that I almost wanted to say, "Really?"

We walked to the dark-haired guy who was sauntering toward us with a cockiness in his stride. "Good evening, Paige," he said, a warm smile crossing his handsome face. "I trust your trip here was a comfortable one?"

"Yes," I simply stated, staring at his glowing blue eyes, wondering if there was a way I could rid this world of him but knowing in my heart there wasn't. He was too powerful and would always be a pain in my ass. Unless maybe there was a way I could trap him, like a genie in a bottle. I made a mental note to check into the possibilities of it, along with Aosoth, once this whole mess cleared up. But in the meantime, I'd stay focus on keeping Tree safe and on the task at hand.

"Splendid," he answered. He cocked his head to the side, and his face became tense. With his eyes still fixed on mine, he continued in a low voice, "I'm aware of how inconvenient it is for you to have Aosoth and Roeick in your presence." He leaned next to my ear and whispered, "But I assure you, the results in the end will be most satisfying to you."

I jerked my head back in surprise, his face inches from mine. His gaze dropped to my lips and then back to my eyes. The muscles in his features softened. His lips parted, like he wanted to say more, but Nathan pulled me to his side. My thoughts swirled, confused. I had to remind myself he was a malevolent being who always had an agenda. What it boiled down to was this: his kind gestures veiled his self-serving ways. Plain and simple. I recalled riding in the Tahoe with him and the whole puppeteer conversation. I bristled at the memory and released myself from Nathan, throwing him a "it's okay" look when he frowned.

I stepped in Bael's space and grabbed a fistful of his maroon T-shirt, pulling his six-two frame forward. He showed no resistance and bent his head so I could whisper in his ear. "Know this. Always. I know who you are. I know hidden behind your generosity is an agenda that only serves *you*. And I don't owe you anything in return for whatever marvelous thing you do for me. Ever." He pulled back to look at me, but I jerked him forward again. "I'll never be your damn puppet." I released him and returned to Nathan's side. He was smiling and so was Brayden. They heard it and obviously approved of what I said. Tree, on the other hand, appeared confused.

"Well, then," Bael said. "Let us proceed with the task of finding Solomon's incantations, so you Paige, can satisfy your terms of our agreement and destroy them."

I made a shooing gesture with my hand. "Lead the way."

He turned, but then pivoted to address us one last time. "Aosoth and Roeick has no idea Paige is going to destroy the incantations, so mind your tongues." He strolled off, not bothering to see our reactions, and we followed, not knowing what awaited us in the cave.

Chapter Thirty-Three

Paige

Aosoth and Roeick stood outside the mouth of the cave, looking smug. I flexed my free hand, fighting the urge to punch Aosoth in the face. Nathan sensed my anger and squeezed my other hand in an attempt to bring me comfort. It didn't work. I still wanted to shatter those perfect features with the high cheek bones, full lips, and doe eyes that stood out against the fair skinned human she was possessing. She flicked her platinum locks off her shoulder and sneered when we locked gazes. I straightened my back and gave her the dirtiest glare I could muster. If looks could kill, she'd be toast. Roeick; however, kept a wary eye on Nathan. His cockiness left when he noticed the tension in Nathan's face, lips smashed into a tight line. Nathan's upper body tilted forward toward Roeick, as if he were going to charge at him. The vessel Roeick had chosen looked of Spanish descent. Handsome, of course. He raised a trembling hand to his forehead to wipe the dampness off.

Brayden stepped in front of me, blocking my view of Aosoth and Roeick. "I think you need to keep your distance from Paige," he told them. "Because if you don't, and you continue on with your bullshit"–he stepped to my side and pointed at me, Nathan, and Tree– "all four of us will throttle you both."

Bael got between us and Aosoth. "Let's play nice here, shall we?"

Twilight was upon us, the faint light of the sun quickly diffusing in the darkening sky. A cool breeze kicked up, rustling the leaves on the trees and foliage around us. The hair on my shoulders stirred, tickling my face. Tucking the locks behind my ears, I glanced over my shoulder and saw Anwar standing with his arms hanging by his side. He gave me a slight nod of acknowledgment and shifted his attention to the gap between Brayden and me, where he could see Bael.

"I think it would be best," Bael continued, "if Aosoth and Roeick remain behind me while you four and Anwar walk ahead. However, I'll stay behind Paige." He looked at me and smirked, at the same time Nathan's grip tightened around my palm.

"Okay. Whatever. Let's get on with it." After I said the last word, a pungent odor of sulfur reached my nostrils, and white light flashed around us. I looked up. Ribbons of red and blue lightning were sparking across the sky, the colors bright against the darkness.

"What's that nasty smell?" Tree asked, holding his nose, looking at me for the answer.

I shrugged, pinching my own nose. Nathan cupped a hand over his mouth and nostrils while Brayden lifted the collar of his T-shirt and held it beneath his eyes. In the distance, a rhythmic drumming began. The atmosphere was getting creepier by the second. It didn't help that Bael's smirk stretched into a grin, revealing a dimple in his left cheek.

"What?" I asked him, annoyed, still squeezing my nostrils.

"The village witch doctor knows I'm here," he said, his blue eyes dancing with amusement. "They're doing a ritual, asking the ancient spirits to eject me from their land and to protect the four of you." He laughed and so did Aosoth.

God, the sound of her laughter grated on my spine. She sounded like an over excited hyena. Her shoulders even bounced erratically.

Nathan removed his hand from his face and placed it back into mine, interlacing our fingers. He breathed in. "The smell is not bad now," he said.

Still annoyed and refusing to look at Bael and his two puppets, I pulled Nathan forward as I walked toward the cave, bumping Bael aside with my shoulder. As soon as my foot stepped inside, the shifting I felt within me earlier grew. A strange, tingling sensation surrounded my core. I paused, the prickling feeling rapidly invading my body. The cavern was pitch black, but my immortal eyesight could see the limestone pillars on either side of the cave and the fluted archways ahead. Just as I was wondering how Tree would be able to see in here, Bael slapped a flashlight in my hand.

"I don't need this," I said, giving it back to him.

He waved it away. "No, but your poor choice in friends might."

Right.

I looked around for Tree and nearly bumped into him when I turned. He had an odd expression on his face.

"Why are you staring at me like I belong in a freak show?" I asked, frowning. But then in that split second, I had déjà vu. The last time he gave me this same look, we were at Caroline's antique store. I had a vision of a cave, and when I snapped out of it, he and Carrie said I was glowing.

"You're–" he started to say.

"Glowing," I finished, looking down at my chest, seeing an orange ring of light expanding the width of a baseball across it. I watched in amazement as it covered the empty space in the middle. But it didn't end. I stuck my hand out in front of me, and it was radiating the same as my chest, all the way up my arm. I was like a living beacon. The cave came to life from the brilliance expanding from me.

"Oh, shit, Paige," Brayden said above Aosoth's gleeful squeal. "You know what this means?"

Bael took the flashlight from me and stuck it in a cargo bag he had slung over his shoulder. He slipped it off and handed it to Roeick to carry. "It means we're close," he said, grinning.

"What do you mean?" Aosoth demanded. She jerked a finger at me, her lips twisted in disgust. "What does the light inside *her*, have to do with finding the incantations?"

Nathan leaned near me so his lips were next to my ear. "Are you okay?"

"Um, yeah," I said, marveling at the radiance.

"She's had visions of this place," Bael answered indifferently. "This light is part of her psychic ability. It's letting us know her clairvoyance is correct."

Aosoth squealed again and clapped her hands. It took everything I had within me not to reach over and squeeze her scrawny neck.

"Paige," Anwar said, startling me because he suddenly appeared before me. I almost forgot he was around because, like Roeick, he hadn't said a word. "Remember what I taught you on the island."

"What? How to fight?" I said with an edge of sarcasm in my tone, knowing exactly what he meant but pretending like I didn't. I mean, really. He could have taught me more on how to hone in on my psychic abilities, but he didn't. I still had no idea what I could and couldn't do, except for a few things I'd discovered on my own. If he would have taken the time to work on it with me, I'd be more confident in finding Solomon's spells right now.

"I taught you how to focus," he simply stated. "To calculate moves of your opponent before they are made." He placed his huge hands on my shoulders, his brown, soulful eyes peering into mine. "Dat is what you must do here, Ms. Paige. Focus. Step outside yourself. Connect with the past. Feel Solomon's energy dat was bestowed upon you, like you would with your opponent."

I was trapped in his gaze, the wheels turning in my mind with thoughts and memories of our time on the island. I recalled all the quips of wisdom he threw at me while I labored over the tasks he had me do. At the time, I didn't think much about what he told me. I just did it. But now, as I pondered, his direction had a deeper meaning.

The pieces snapped into place, and though he taught me very little on how to connect with the elements or about my extrasensory capabilities, I saw the whole picture now. He wasn't only teaching me how to defend myself but to become the aggressor as well.

"I get it," I whispered.

Aosoth let out a heavy sigh. "Are you almost done? I'm bored and want the incantations before—"

I glanced at her and saw Nathan's hand clenching her throat. Roeick advanced on Nathan, then retreated a few steps when Nathan shot him a furious look. Nathan's ears were dark red. Yeah, he was pissed. Brayden and Tree moved toward Roeick, but Bael stepped between them.

"I promise you," Nathan said in a low, growling tone, "you're going to wish you never returned to this earth when I'm through with you."

Wet choking sounds gurgled from her throat. Shock filled her wide eyes, but then a layer of sheer defiance glazed over them.

"You're not helping matters, Nathan," Bael said, his voice calm but stern. "Or let me put it in another way. In elementary terms, so you can understand what I'm saying," he mocked.

Nathan whipped his head around and glared at Bael. "Fuck off."

"As I was saying," Bael continued, unperturbed, "your actions are compromising Paige's precarious situation."

Nathan released Aosoth and shoved her away from him in disgust. Her arms flailed and her back bowed as she began falling backward. But Roeick caught her before she smacked the ground.

"Bael's right," Brayden said. "We need to try and get along so Paige can find the incantations." His eyes fell on Nathan's hand slipping in mine and then on his face. "You need to learn to control your anger. Maybe go to anger management classes."

Tree made a pfft sound. "Ass kisser." He scowled at Brayden. "Nathan had every right to react the way he did considering all the horrible shit Aosoth did to Paige's family."

I closed my eyes, tuning their bickering out. I imagined being in Solomon's shoes, long ago. I envisioned what it was like to have so much power that it nearly destroyed me. I would need to hide it from the world.

A cave.

But where?

This cavern was one of the largest in the world. We were searching for a needle in a haystack.

Doubt skittered across my thoughts, dispersing them.

Focus, Paige.

Think.

Let go.

I emptied my mind and concentrated on slow breaths. In the center of my chest, I felt a slight tugging sensation. It reminded me of when I first met Ameerah. I had felt drawn to her. We figured it was because before her human bodied had died, she was psychic. Our similar energies must have had a sense of recognition, which created such a response. It made sense at the time, and now I was beginning to think we were right after all. The power of the ring inside me wanted to reconnect with its sister part—the incantations. At least, I hoped so.

I released Nathan's hand and walked deeper into the cavern. White light sparked behind me. I glanced over my shoulder. Strobes of light danced outside against the darkness. A peal of thunder cracked against the sky. Beneath the layer of sound, my hearing picked up the cacophony of the harsh drumming in the nearby village.

The chamber we stood in fell silent. No more childish bickering from the others. I say childish because though I understood and agreed with Nathan and Tree, now wasn't the time to air their grievances with the others and vice versa.

I continued moving forward, not surprised when Nathan and Tree joined me. Brayden was on the other side of Tree, and Anwar walked next to Brayden. I knew without checking, Bael ambled close behind, along with the other two. Our shadows were thrown against the rocky walls from the brilliance pouring from me, creating elongated figures bent and curled in a ghastly manner.

We walked parallel to the subterranean river and approached a block of stone full of stalactites hanging from the ceiling like icicles. On the ground were rows and rows of jagged rock jetting up. It gave one a sense of being inside the mouth of a giant beast. I noticed several passages we could take and paused. The pulling in my chest branched out like two splayed fingers. North or east?

"Which way, Paige?" Tree asked, looking about.

"I'm not sure. Hold on," I told him.

"You don't know which way?" Aosoth said incredulously, her tone pitched in irritation and spite.

I gritted my teeth and spun. "Okay, then," I glared at her and pointed east, "you and Roeick go east, and we'll take the passage to the north."

"I'm not letting you out of my sight," Aosoth shot back, sneering.

"Why?" I countered. "You have the ring. It should direct you to the incantations. In fact, why don't you lead the way?" I stepped aside and made an ushering gesture with my hands, inviting her to take my place.

She let out an indignant snort. "Maybe so, but the ring is doing nothing at the moment, and I prefer to be near Bael."

Roeick's face hardened. He stared at the ground, the muscles in his jaw twitching.

I leaned forward and jabbed the air with my finger. "Then shut your mouth." I turned my back on her, hearing the others snickering.

I took a deep breath and closed my eyes. My grandmother had said I was a skeleton key and could open the doors to the realms closest to ours. I had no idea how to do it, only that if I focused on a particular person like I'd done when I played my whistle for my father, I was able to reach him.

But Solomon's spirit was nowhere to be found, which meant it would be a fruitless attempt. I didn't have time to waste, so I concentrated on the incantations instead. I envisioned them written on a scroll, protected by some kind of spell he created, the same charm used to protect the ring my grandmother was able to find. The two items were separated, but once you possessed one, it would eventually reunite with the other. However, the circumstances had to be right–everything lined up perfectly like the stars in the sky. But it didn't end there. Obstacles had to be placed in between. A test of endurance and will. If one desired something bad enough, she wouldn't give up and would overcome the challenges placed in her path to achieve her goal.

A test.

I opened my eyes and went east. I didn't know why, but I felt a strong urge to go that way. I entered the narrow hole and walked several yards down the passage until something caught my attention on the wall. Ancient script written in a language I didn't recognize.

Damn.

"What's wrong?" Nathan's eyes followed mine, and then he looked at me, confused.

"What does this say?" I asked, thinking he might know.

"Does what say?" He still looked confused.

"This message on the wall." Surely he knew what I was talking about. It was right in front of his face. But when his eyebrows knitted, my stomach clenched.

"I see it," Tree said on the other side of Nathan, leaning in front of him, tilting his head to get a better look.

I looked at Tree, surprised he could but not Nathan. "Really?"

"Yeah," Tree answered, pointing slowly to each word like a mother would to get her child to read. Nathan stepped out of the way so Tree could have a better look. "It appears to be angelic or Theban script."

"How do you know?" I asked.

He shrugged and let out a bewildered laugh. "It's crazy, but I can tell you what it says."

A low, guttural growl sounded down the narrow passage, startling me. I glanced in that direction and saw Bael squeezing past Anwar and Brayden. His eyes were glowing. His face filled with rage. His forceful energy rolled toward me like a Mack truck. I grabbed Tree's wrist and pulled him behind me to where he was sandwiched between Nathan and me. I turned my back on him to face Bael.

"What's your problem?" I asked when he reached me.

He didn't answer right away but stared at the wall instead, his chest heaving. "He's right," Bael said, raising his blazing eyes up to where Tree stood.

"You can see it then?" I asked.

"Of course," he said in an angry, arrogant tone.

"Nathan, move down the passage a ways. I want to see if anyone else can," I said.

After a few long moments of the others checking it out, we discovered only the three of us could see what was on the wall. They moved back to their original positions so once again, Bael and I were standing in front of it.

"What does it say?" I asked him.

Tree's arm was pressed against mine. He ran his finger along the wall, beneath the sentences, and answered me before Bael could. "It's similar to a riddle."

"The boy is right," Bael seethed.

Tree bellowed a painful moan and dropped his head into his hand.

"What's wrong?" I took hold of his other hand, a riot of panic storming through my veins, quickening my heartrate.

Unable to find his voice, he squeezed my hand in short spurts.

It was only one word.

Michael.

Chapter Thirty-Four

Nathan

When Tree clutched his head, releasing a painful cry, and the color drained from Paige's face, I immediately became alarmed. Prior to it, I was bombarded by a barrage of swirling thoughts activated by Brayden mentioning I had an anger problem. It knocked me down a few pegs, though I didn't give him the satisfaction of letting him know. However, his comment forced me into some self-evaluation. Even though Tree came to my defense and Aosoth deserved my reaction, my temper didn't help matters in this perilous situation.

And then there was Paige emitting a powerful light as if she were a living bulb. With her every movement, her brilliance followed and illuminated the dark, dry cavern. I wasn't only intrigued by this phenomenon but memorized as well. It made me wonder a lot of things; thus, the endless mind chatter . . . I wondered if I were good enough for Paige and if Anwar was right about me devoting my life to tracking dark spirits instead of being with her. Realizing those thoughts were bred out of the darkest part of my soul where it gave birth to self-doubt and insecurities, I mentally shook them away. Then Paige asked Bael what the angelic script said.

Now, the intensity in the air grew with Tree's agonizing moans. I noticed Paige taking his hand. He pressed it several times, secretly transmitting Morse Code. As if she could sense my worry, she reached for my hand. She squeezed it like Tree done with her, relaying his message to me.

Michael.

My mind quickly put two and two together, and my stomach dropped out from under me.

Impossible.

Or was it?

My thoughts zipped through the history of Solomon. The legends. It paused on one about the giver of the ring. Saint Michael the Archangel.

Tree took a deep breath and lifted his head, telling Paige he was fine. The pain had subsided. Brayden handed him a water bottle he retrieved from the bag Roeick carried. Tree took it gratefully and guzzled the water while Bael read the message out loud in a thick, scathing voice. "The Ark of the Testimony filled with treasures. Infused with power which should have never been granted. Its contents dispersed throughout the land. Each one with a purpose, forged and tempered out of freewill and love for humanity. The noble man will align with divine intelligence. He will speak its language and lead his army in the direction of Jerusalem where a wrong shall make a right. The one who bears unworldly gifts will gain access if the intentions are of the purest heart."

Paige gasped. "I know what it means." She released my hand and pushed her way back in the direction we came. "We have to go north," she called, and I was hot on her heels.

Chapter Thirty-Five

Paige

Without question, I knew what the ancient message meant. Anwar was right. My premonitions were prepping me for moments like this.

I plowed my way past the others, pushing Aosoth aside extra hard. Childish? Maybe, but honestly, I'd like to do more than slam her against a rocky wall. She released a painful yelp, but I pretended not to hear, though anyone seeing the smile on my face would surely know it wasn't accidental.

In no time, I was back in the first chamber. My heart pounded in my ears, my adrenaline pumped at high speed. Tree was the noble one. Now, why didn't that surprise me? He was the best person I knew. Of course, he would be a conductor for the Divine. The last sentence spoke of me. Obviously. I found it weird to be mentioned thousands of years ago. How did the author know?

I entered another narrow hall made out of limestone. I followed its zigzag pattern for about half a mile alongside the subterranean stream and then stepped into a small chamber. The ceiling was high and eroded. A few stone pillars dotted the room. The air felt much denser and cooler in here, and I knew we were moving farther into the bowels of the earth.

The pulling sensation in the center of my chest increased. As I moved toward another passage on the far wall ahead, it became stronger. I could feel Nathan behind me, hear the rocks shift beneath hurried steps. I dashed into this tunnel and followed it to a tall, airy vault with massive columns and stalagmitic walls, which was cone-shape material poking out like horns on a dragon's back. I crossed the area through a fluted archway to another room. The cavern quickly turned into a labyrinthine due to the many pillars and huge stalagmites shooting up from the earth. Maneuvering my way around them, I continued to allow the pulling in my chest to guide me, shifting my mindset on becoming the aggressor.

At the end of the maze a few yards away stood two soaring obelisks of jagged stone, spread evenly apart about sixty feet high. They loomed like two sentinels in front of a rocky wall that had a small gap, eight feet wide in the center. I knew it was impossible for any of us to fit through, yet the powerful urge to continue consumed me. As I neared it, my ribs vibrated. It felt like I was in a vehicle with the bass of a song blasting, thumping loudly, rattling the windows. Goosebumps broke across my flesh, and the hair on the back of my neck rose. My body tingled as if every cell was wiggling.

Bael quickly moved to my side when a low humming noise erupted from me. Nathan joined my other side. I turned, looking for Tree. He was with Brayden, not far behind. I stretched my hand, and he took it.

"This is it," Bael said, his eyes glowing with excitement and something else. Something hauntingly boastful?

"I can't believe this is really happening," Tree mumbled, standing so close to me that I could feel his body heat on my back. "I'm sorry, Paige. You were right. The way things are going I wouldn't be surprised if we ran into some goblins. This place is unreal."

"Why is there a sound coming out of *her*?" Aosoth demanded.

Bael turned, his gaze moving past Brayden and Anwar to address Aosoth. "Connection. Paige is connecting with Solomon's incantations, my dear," he told her in a sickening sweet tone which made me want to gag. "Why don't you and Roeick come join us?"

I flashed him a sharp look. I didn't want her or Roeick near me.

Besides, I had no idea how we would get to the other side of this wall.

Turning his face away from the group to where only I could see it, he winked. I gave him a weird look and rolled my eyes. I didn't have time to figure out another one of his ploys and secret agendas. Right now, I was more concerned with what my next move should be.

"There's magic here," Anwar announced.

"How do you know?" Brayden and I asked in unison.

Aosoth and Roeick stood next to Bael, staring at the rocky wall dumbly. I looked at Anwar to clarify his statement. He moved closer and placed his hand on my shoulder. "What did you feel when you entered this area?"

I thought about it before answering. "My flesh chilled like when you're suddenly spooked and the hair on your nape stirs. The same effect swept over my entire body."

He nodded like a teacher would to his student who gave the correct answer. "Dat was your body's way of reacting to its energy."

Instant frustration bloomed inside me. How in the hell was I supposed to have known that? I've had those feelings before without magic involved. Nathan took my hand and turned to me. He must have felt me stiffen because when he spoke his voice was soft and inviting. A veil dropped around my surroundings, and it was only him and me. "Remember when you turned the lights off for Carrie and Tree?" I didn't answer, just stared into his deep, blue eyes. "You used magic to accomplish it," he continued. "How did you feel afterwards?"

My heart stopped when realization quickly settled in. I'd felt the same as I did, minus the goosebumps and rising hair. Those two things had nothing to do with the magic in this room. It was the odd tingling sensation I felt. My mouth dropped, and I kept staring at him as the synapse in my brain linked together forming a new pathway for this revelation.

I threw my arms around him and laughed. "I know. I know now, how to tell when magic is in my presence." I pulled back to look at him. He bent his head, and I captured his face in my hands and kissed him.

"Thank you."

"Anytime," he said with a crooked smile, causing my stomach to flip.

"The recognition will mature as you get more acquainted with dat side of yourself," Anwar said, bringing everything back into focus. "Now you need to concentrate on your objective . . . what you want. See it in your mind. Reach out to it."

"You can do it, Paige," Brayden said. "I have faith in you."

"Okay, everybody be quiet," I ordered. "I need to focus." I shook out my tense muscles to relax and closed my eyes. Slowly, I breathed in through my nose and exhaled out my mouth. I did it several times, releasing all thoughts. Surprising enough, the low humming noise aided me in this process. I envisioned a large, wooden door in front of me, snatching the memory of the ones I encountered when I dream walked to save Carrie. It made the process easier, and I could clearly see it in my mind. I imagined placing my hand on a shiny, gold lever, feeling its cool texture as I wrapped my fingers around it. I pushed it down and heard an intake of breath behind me and Aosoth's high-pitched squeal. It yanked me out of my trance.

I glared at her while she bounced on her feet, clapping with glee. "I told you to be quiet. How am I supposed to–"

"Paige," Tree said.

I sighed and glanced behind me. "What?"

He grinned. "Look in front of you."

I did and gasped.

A vein of golden, glittery light outlined an image of a round door.

I laughed. "I can't believe this."

"This is too cool," Tree said. "I almost feel like I need a sword."

"One that glows when a goblin is nearby," Brayden told him.

Tree snapped his fingers and pointed at Brayden. "Exactly!"

Bael sighed, annoyed. "Okay, children. Paige needs to finish what she's doing, so hold your tongues."

I took a deep breath to quell the bubbles of excitement within me. The tugging sensation still remained, but the familiarity had dampened my awareness of its existence. But now, as I once again stilled my mind, falling into the droning sound between my ribs, I felt the force of it grow even stronger. I threw my hands out, palms facing the door, and closed my eyes. The tips of my fingers prickled like they would if they were falling asleep. I imagined the door opening.

Nothing.

I peeked with one eye. No change, only the glittery outline of a round door like before. I closed my eye and tried again. I could hear Aosoth making impatient sounds and shuffling her feet. I ignored it, though it was almost near impossible to do so. I concentrated harder, my hands still held out in front of me.

Then something happened. My right index finger moved up and down. At first I thought it was me doing it, until I tried to jerk it down and couldn't. It was like somebody had a firm hold on my hand, forcing the finger to move up and down and in circles. I opened my eyes. Black scripted words formed on the wall in the center of the outline. The penmanship was beautiful and in Latin, something I could read.

"This is astounding," Anwar said. "Your connection with Solomon gains you passage to lock onto his own enchantments."

This message was a spell to unbolt the door. Anwar caught it right away, and now that I had full control of my hand, the text fully laid out before us, I knew. I knew he was right.

"Say it, Paige," Tree urged.

I pushed my hair off my face and stood straight, bracing myself. My heart was pounding so hard that I thought for sure they could hear it. I cleared my throat, and in a strong and powerful voice, I said the incantation in Latin and translated it in my mind:

Darkness roams this earthy realm. In spirit and flesh the heathen stands at its own helm. A gift from above granted power to a king. The potent words poisoning the ears of a demon with a flick of his ring. Controlling the diabolical with admirable intent will destroy the doer until he relents. The charms are cast and will remain unbroken. Until these words are spoken.

The wall trembled and pieces of rock fell to the ground. We stepped back as more toppled over, creating a small cloud of dust. I continued to chant the words, ignoring the murmurs around me. The low humming noise between my ribs escalated, vibrating them. A sharp crack pierced the air. The bottom outline of the door split, fracturing up and around to the other side. Slowly it opened outward, scraping against broken rock.

I stopped chanting and held my breath. Strangely enough, the humming noise quit, my ribs no longer quivering. I released the air from my lungs. Still rooted to my spot, I stared into the pitch black room.

When my eyes adjusted to the darkness, a loud whooshing sound echoed through the deep chamber. Torches along the stone wall came to life. I stepped forward, only to be knocked aside by Aosoth and Roeick. I stumbled into Nathan. His quick arms caught me, preventing me from falling.

And then I was surrounded by screams and moans. Tree was on his knees, once again clutching his head. I moved toward him, but he rose, no longer holding his head. His expression was one of wonder instead of pain, and he mouthed, "He's coming."

Whose coming? I marveled.

"Look," Nathan said, turning me back around.

I leaned forward to get a better look into the chamber. There were words written in some strange language and symbols covering the walls. Aosoth and Roeick were immobilized in the center of the room, their eyes wide with horror, and their bottom jaws grotesquely extended to their chests. Horrific shrieks issued from their mouths, their faces twisted in agony.

I looked at Bael who had a devious smile on his face. "What's going on?"

"It's a deadfall." He pointed in the direction of their feet. They were standing in a circle. Above them were strange symbols. "One of Solomon's clever tricks."

Nathan's head jerked around to where he faced Bael, but he didn't say a word. Then I remembered Nathan telling me about it. But before I could finish those thoughts, my attention pulled back on Aosoth and

Roeick. They fell on their backs, their bodies violently twitching, their painful cries echoing.

"This is insane," Brayden said behind me. "I never knew you could do this to a dark spirit."

"Only to the dimwitted ones," Bael snapped. "And the knowledge how to accomplish it is lost. Besides, only a powerful caster can execute it."

I couldn't take my eyes off Aosoth and Roeick. I searched within myself for an ounce of sympathy but there were none. Instead, I felt relief and thought maybe circling karma was true, because they were certainly getting theirs now.

The arched ceiling above them opened into a black, gaping hole. A dark funnel spun downward, enclosing Aosoth and Roeick in its whirl. Oddly enough, there was no wind or sound except for Aosoth and Roeick's cries. The mini tornado lifted from the ground with Aosoth and Roeick trapped inside. I could see them through the transparent spinning top, but I could no longer hear them. They were now standing, their hands pressing against it, palms facing us, their elongated mouths opened in silent screams. The funnel moved upward, disappearing into the night. The ceiling was once again intact to where for a brief moment I wondered if what I saw really happened.

Once the moment passed, I turned to Bael. "How did you know this would happen?"

"Destroy the incantations, and I will gladly enlighten you." He made a dramatic sweeping gesture, ushering me forward.

I lifted my foot with the intent on fulfilling my agreement with him, when I felt a strong presence enter the room, like you would if the most important person in the world stepped into your space. The chill in the air warmed—another indicator we weren't alone. A low feral growl rumbled from Bael's chest. Baffled, I turned at the same time Nathan did and saw the most beautiful person I'd ever laid eyes on.

Chapter Thirty-Six

Paige

He was tall, fair-haired, his eyes the color of blue glass. There was an inviting smile on his handsome face. I wanted to fall into it–to be a part of his essence. Not in a sexual manner but awe-inspired. I wanted to go to a place where the lion and lamb could lie peacefully beside one another. No strife, no heartache, no underhandedness—only love. And I somehow knew he'd been to such a place we only hoped to experience.

"Michael?" Tree asked, breaking the silence, gaping at this beautiful man.

Pulling the sleeves down on his black trench coat in a presentable manner, he nodded. "I apologize for causing you discomfort," he said to Tree. "Please forgive my intrusion on your person, but considering the circumstances, it was the only gateway available which would allow me to be in your company."

"No worries," Tree answered. "But why me?"

"Because you've chosen the path of a light walker," Michael answered with great reverence, "though your human consciousness bears no recollection of this arduous yet highly regarded field."

My stomach dropped. What was he talking about? Would Tree be leaving us? The very thought set my pulse racing. I slipped my hand in Nathan's for comfort. "What does that mean?" I asked, my voice cracking on the last word.

"It mean, Ms. Paige," Anwar said, "dat Jack's spirit chose the ultimate path dat very few embark upon, because the road to become a light walker is in the beginning a treacherous one. The soul goes through a continuous reincarnation process. It must experience everything to reach total and complete understanding of all things. Once he does dat, he can be a light walker and enter the realm of Nirvana whenever he so desires."

Wow. I would have never guessed this sort of answer and was rendered speechless. My thoughts even stilled, hovering in the abyss of my mind like an alphabet letter in a bowl of beef broth.

"So I chose to be a guardian angel?" Tree asked.

"Something along those lines," Michael said. The corners of his mouth turned down into a little frown. "But we don't have time to delve deeper." He placed a hand on Tree's shoulder. "I promise, though, in time you will learn more." He looked at me, his blue eyes sparkling and captivating. "Shall we see what Solomon has in store for us?"

"You have no right to be here," Bael spat.

Michael crossed the room and stopped in front of Bael. "Actually, brother, I do. You see, I made a horrible mistake, and I'm here to correct it. I've waited for thousands of years to connect with Solomon. Let's hope his spirit dwells in there." He nodded toward the chamber.

That's right. Zeruel told me nobody knew where Solomon's spirit was, and they figured he'd invoked a cloaking spell to hide his whereabouts. I wondered if Bael knew about it.

"I don't understand," Brayden said, confusion etching his features. "Why don't you stop Bael and all the other dark spirits?"

"Freewill," Michael answered. "It also would upset the balance of the universe. Besides, nobody should have such power, because eventually it will destroy the person like it nearly destroyed Solomon."

"Oh," is all Brayden said. He opened his mouth to say something else but must have thought the better of it and closed it.

Before anybody could do or say anything, I released Nathan's hand, squared my shoulders, and stepped inside Solomon's chamber.

A round pedestal table made of marble stood at the back of the room. A diamond shaped crystal sat in a slot in the center of it. The length had to be at least two feet. As soon as I entered, colorful rays shot from it, creating a wave of prisms against the walls and ceiling, similar to the aurora borealis. The words on the stones shifted, the letters rearranging themselves. I still didn't know what language it was, but it slowly began to make sense. It was then I realized these could be the incantations.

I opened my mouth to recite the words about darkness cannot hide and by the chains of power it will bind, but then I remembered my pact with Bael. I pressed my lips together and glanced about for him. My eyes darted around. Everybody was here except Bael. My gaze caught Anwar, and he moved toward me. Red, blue, green and yellow colors danced across his black face.

"Where's Bael?" I asked.

"He bolted," Brayden answered instead, stepping next to Anwar.

"Dat is true," Anwar replied. "However, through me he remains present. So do keep your word Ms. Paige. The agreement with Bael dat is."

Warm fingers intertwined with mine. I looked up to Nathan's crooked smile. I pressed my hand into his, mirroring his expression that told me this would soon be over.

A red beam of light shot across the chamber, the prism of colors gone. The crimson ray moved backward, shrinking until it reached the center of the room. A hologram of an African man appeared. He wore a brown tunic shirt and loose tan pants, his attire simple, matching the humble look on his face.

"Solomon," Michael said with a welcoming nod. "It is nice to see you after all these years."

Omigod. This guy was Solomon. King Solomon. But he looked so plain, like a peasant who might be serving him. Why wasn't he wearing a crown of jewels and a cloak made from lambskin and wool?

Solomon bowed to Michael. "Forgive me for abusing what you had so graciously gifted me to thwart evil."

"Your repentance is unnecessary, old friend," Michael said. "What you have done to make your wrongs a right is quite impressive. Besides, the only forgiveness you should seek is your own. There is no judgment but self-judgment." He touched his chest and continued. "We are our own worst critics."

"You have suffered for my indiscretions and wretched, unholy behaviors," Solomon bitterly said. "My spirit became darkened with power and would have destroyed me if I had not taken these drastic measures you see lying before you."

"I have suffered not. My will is my own. I am to see my wrong make a right," Michael told him.

Solomon's gaze shifted to me. A warm smile formed on his face. "I see the power of the ring dwells inside you, child."

I tried to swallow, but my throat became dry the moment he looked at me. All I could think about was being in the presence of two great men and how awe inspiring it was to listen to them converse. I was at a loss for words, so I nodded instead.

"This power used in conjunction with the incantations I must take from you. It wasn't mine to give," Solomon said to me. "Besides, eventually it would intoxicate and destroy you, like it almost ruined me." He reached into his front pocket and produced a small purple vial. He gestured for me to come closer. Nathan squeezed my hand before I released his. "What you see before your eyes," Solomon said to us, addressing the words on the walls with his hand, "are the incantations." He snapped his fingers, and the words disappeared.

The vial now glowed between his fingertips. He threw the tiny bottle on the ground. A sharp, shattering sound amplified around us, but the broken glass didn't scatter across the cave floor. Instead, it flew up in the air, forming the shape of a clay pot like one you would see in a Native American shop. Slowly, it spun, puffs of smoke billowing from the top. It gained speed, producing a thick, gray vapor, engulfing the entire shape. Solomon smacked his hands, startling me. He spread his arms and said, "Gone."

There was a loud "pop," and what was before us a second ago vanished.

I moved to him and was able to find my voice this time, though it sounded raspier than normal. "Why didn't you destroy them in the first place?"

"My will to do so was weak," he said, his face falling in shame. "My righteous self no longer embodied my spirit. I had abandoned morality for ego and hedonism. I lost my way, and in order to reclaim what I once was, I had to take drastic measures." He paused, and his features softened; his dark eyes filled with sadness. My heart ached when I thought how lonely and ashamed he must have been for thousands of years. "I had to outwit Bael. The queen of Shebah, who was my wife, helped me do so. She knew a white witch with flaming hair who came from a faraway land. In secret we consulted with her. This witch was also a seer and foretold her descendent would break through my magical barriers when all my sins were absolved."

Chills broke across my flesh. "She was my ancestor?" I whispered.

He nodded.

"What about the rest?" Michael asked Solomon, giving him a knowing look. Recognition entered Solomon's face.

"Rest?" Tree asked. I looked at him, and he shrugged.

"The Ark of the Testimony and Aaron's rod, among other powerful items," Michael clarified.

Was he serious? My mind shifted backward to when I used to go to Sunday mass with Carrie's family. The Ten Commandments were supposed to be in the ark. Before I could stop myself, words flew out of my mouth. "Aren't the Ten Commandments in it?"

"No," Michael said. "There are no commandments. What is right and wrong is already ingrained in your soul. But the ark holds a great power Bael would love to possess."

"I am incapable of answering your question," Solomon told Michael, addressing his question about the rest of the artifacts. "What you see before you is only a part of my spirit. Through the witch's help, I cast a spell to shed and cloak pieces of it to protect the treasures that have no business in this realm. Once each item is righteously discovered, returned to its rightful owner, and destroyed, then I shall become one and join the heavens."

"Raphael needs to lay claim to the ark," Anwar said to no one in particular.

Michael frowned, marring his perfect features, his blue eyes dimming with concern. "Yes, and unfortunately he shows no interest in confiscating it."

"Why?" Brayden asked.

"Raphael is in love with humans, and so am I," Michael admitted. "In order to become a light walker, the soul goes through cycles of reincarnation to reach complete understanding, like Anwar said earlier. A number of those cycles are in human form, which enviably creates an unshakable love for them. A handful of us went against the grain of the universal creed, exercised our freewill and for a period of time went rogue. We ignored our responsibilities and replaced it with using our divine knowledge to fashion magical tools humans can use to rid earth of demons or perhaps control them, among other things.

"I created the ring and incantations. Raphael built the ark. Despite our wisdom, knowing what we were doing would disrupt the balance in this realm, our compassion and love for humanity lured us from truth and reason. I have come to my senses, but there are others who have not, including Raphael."

I couldn't believe what I was hearing. It seemed surreal, and I found myself wishing Carrie were here to see this. A fierce sadness plowed through me. I missed her and couldn't wait to be with her, chatting her up. I could picture her face in total shock and awe when I finally got to tell her about this and everything else.

"You AWOL?" Tree asked, pulling me from my thoughts.

"Yes," Michael answered, regret scratching his lovely voice, "and until we correct our mistakes, we cannot reenter Nirvana, thus, my reason for being here." He turned to Solomon, who stood patiently waiting for Michael to finish his tale. "You destroyed the incantations. Now I'm ready to see you take the power I once bestowed upon you from Paige and return it to me."

I shuddered and glanced over my shoulder at Nathan. I threw him an uneasy look. I wasn't sure about this. I had no idea how Solomon would perform this act or if it would hurt. I could see the anxiousness in Nathan's eyes. He took a step toward me, but Solomon held his hand out, halting Nathan. "You need to remain where you are." He looked at me, and his face softened. "I give you my word; I will do no harm onto you. You will feel a slight pulling, but I assure you it will be all."

I bit my lip and nodded.

"Look into my eyes," he instructed in a soft, soothing voice.

I did as he said. They were deep brown, gentle and kind. He began to mumble something under his breath. Even with my keen sense of hearing, I couldn't make out the strange words. His pupils contracted and dilated. When his hand flicked out, I jumped, but my gaze remained locked to his. I had no desire to look away, and though we just met, I felt a profound trust toward him. His quick movement had caught me off guard, but now I was prepared for whatever he decided to do. When his hand touched my chest, I remained still. It formed into a claw, his fingers pressing against my shirt and skin. His lips continued to move, the words still too silent to discern. A twitching sensation developed inside my chest, beneath his hand. It moved around as if I had a living being inside me. I imagined this was how it felt to a pregnant women when her baby became active.

"Holy shit, Paige." Brayden's alarmed voice caused me to break eye contact with Solomon and look at Brayden. At the same time the tugging feeling Solomon told me about came in full force. Brayden's wide eyes met mine. He pointed where Solomon's hand was on me.

I looked down. A bright cone-shape of white light was being pulled from my chest. Solomon's fingers were curled around the tip. As he moved his arm back, slowly drawing it out, the radiance from me dimmed. The chamber became less bright with each backward movement of his arm. He reached with his other hand and placed it beneath the cone, cradling it in his open palm.

I broke out into a cold sweat. The room spun, and my mouth filled with salty saliva. My legs shook, then gave out, but Nathan caught me before I smacked the ground. He picked me up and held me in his arms. "Are you okay?" he asked, his voice low in my ear. He wiped the hair off my sweaty forehead, his eyes searching my face for any hint of pain.

"I-I think so," I said. "I feel weak and kind of weird, like empty inside."

Nathan turned so we were facing Solomon who was pushing down on the tip of the cone, molding it into a glowing sphere between his palms.

Michael stepped beside Nathan and placed his hand on my arm, making it tingle. "You'll be fine in a few minutes. Your body is acclimating to the changes. However, some of Solomon's gifts will remain a part of you in the company of your other extraordinary abilities." He released his hand and continued while gazing at me with intensity and warmth. I suddenly felt shy in his presence. "You have a lot to learn about the powers you possess, but in time you will. I assure you, help will be along the way to aid you in reaching your full potential."

Tree moved to the other side of Nathan, anxious energy pouring from him. "What can I do to help?"

Solomon was moving the ball of white light in his hands, spinning it. He stood, patiently waiting for Michael to answer Tree's question.

"You are one of us but an apprentice nonetheless. Bael is now aware of your true identity, as he is of Carrie's hidden talents."

Still cradled in Nathan's muscular arms, I jerked my head back and looked up at Michael. "How did you–"

"I discovered this information in Summerland," Michael said. "You, Jack, and Carrie are the Devil's third."

Nathan's arms twitched around me in surprise. "Wait a minute," he said. "I thought the Devil's third meant the executive, legislative, and judiciary."

"Yes, the dark spirits think as such and rightfully so. Bael has managed to infiltrate the government, but he's been doing it since its inception."

Michael shrugged, like it should be obvious why throughout history there had been governmental corruption. "The truth is that Bael needs Paige, Jack, and Carrie. The power of three, and he wasn't too pleased when he discovered tonight that Jack is the third party."

"Why would he need me?" Tree wanted to know.

"You chose the path of a light walker; therefore, you have it within you to reach the ones who went against the universal creed. As you now know from our earlier conversation, they are no longer in Nirvana. Bael needs you to keep them at bay. You see, he had not anticipated my arrival tonight. It is why he fled. It became clear to him that your assistance along with Paige's and Carrie's would be invaluable to him." Michael turned to Solomon and extended his hand to receive the glowing orb. Solomon gingerly handed it to Michael.

"You can put me down," I told Nathan. "I feel better now."

"Wait." Anwar said as Nathan set me on my feet, causing all of us to look at him. Desperation twisted his face. Nathan, Tree, and I backed out of Anwar's way, so he could approach Michael. I looked at Brayden who stood to the side in silent observation, deep in thought.

"I made a foolish mistake," Anwar said to Michael. "I performed a blood oath with Bael. Is there a way you can break it?"

In that instant, I remembered Bael telling me in Carrie's hospital room that he couldn't participate in a blood oath with me because I had Solomon's power inside me. Maybe there was still hope for Anwar. But then I thought about his betrayal and underhandedness. He had caused both Nathan and I a lot of grief. I wasn't sure if I should say something. A moral dilemma raged within my thoughts. But then Tree spoke, reprieving me from making a decision on the matter.

"Bael couldn't create a blood oath with Paige because of Solomon's power," he said to Michael. "So it stands to reason you can use it to break the chain between Anwar and Bael, right?"

"It is not Solomon's power," Michael corrected. "The power was created by me in a higher realm." He turned his attention to Anwar. When he moved, the red ray of light, anchored to Solomon's back, reflected off the gleaming ball Michael held between his palms. Several beams bounced from its side, then disappeared when Michael shifted his body toward Anwar, away from the holographic umbilical cord that sustained Solomon's presence here with us. "I can. However, your body does not have the components to withstand such power. Therefore, it will kill you."

Anger flashed in Anwar's eyes, rage distorting his dark features. His mouth fell open, and the sound that sprang forth was like a monstrous beast, growling and clawing its way out of captivity. Anwar fell on his hands and knees. His body quivered. He lifted his eyes to Michael. They were black as coal, and he bellowed in a dark, ghastly voice, "Nooooo!"

Chapter Thirty-Seven

Nathan

I held onto Paige the moment she hugged her arms and looked at me with horror creeping into her sad child-like eyes. We all knew it was Bael protesting against this dire arrangement.

Michael kneeled before Anwar and stared directly into his face. In a flash, Brayden stood beside us, poised to assist Anwar to his feet, but Michael shook his head, stopping him.

"If Anwar agrees, brother, through my mercy upon his soul, the binds you placed around it shall be broken," Michael said in an even, matter-of-fact tone.

Anwar's lips curled over his teeth, and his chest rumbled. A deep, fierce growl erupted when his mouth formed a circle. "Noooo. He's mine."

Anwar hung his head. With shaky arms, he attempted to push himself off the floor. Michael stood and took a few steps back. He nodded to Brayden who immediately assisted Anwar to his feet.

Anwar's hands were balled into fists. He raised them to his temples and hunched his shoulders. "Do it," he said between moans.

"Wait a minute." Brayden took hold of Anwar's arms, turning him so he had to look at Brayden. Anwar's eyes were closed. He opened them. They were clear and focused. The connection with Bael, severed. "You can't die. You're the closest I have to a father," Brayden tearfully said. "There's still so much I need to learn from you."

"I am sorry," Anwar apologized, a raw sadness in his eyes. "I made a foolish mistake, and I must fix it. You would not want my soul enslaved to Bael, would you?"

A choking sound escaped Brayden's lips. He shook his head, blinking back tears. My vision clouded, and I swallowed against the lump rising in my throat. I knew the story quite well of Brayden's father ditching him and his mom for another women. But it wasn't why I found myself in a sudden state of sorrow. The fond memories I shared with Anwar is what caught me in this web of emotions. He had known my family which–despite the turmoil he'd caused Paige and me–linked us together. Anwar was the only living person, other than myself, I could talk to about my brothers, father, and mother, and in turn he'd share something about them. He helped keep the memory of my family alive, but in my heart of hearts I knew he was doing the right thing.

I released Paige and pulled him into a hug. "Godspeed to you, and may you finally find peace on your next adventure."

"Thank you, Nathaniel," Anwar said, embracing me in return. "I had hoped Solomon could break this curse upon my soul, and I thank the stars for this opportunity Michael has given me." He dropped his arms and stepped back. "I must accept. Do you understand?"

"I do," I said, wiping the water from my eyes. "If you see my family–" I paused to take a deep breath to keep my voice from faltering.

"I will," Anwar interjected, knowing me well enough to fill in the blanks.

Paige stepped between us and threw her arms around Anwar. "Take care."

"You, too, Ms. Paige." He looked down at her and continued. "I am sure your parents are proud of you."

Paige gave him a weak smile and then stepped away, joining Tree, Brayden, and me.

"The four of you must leave now," Solomon said, looking straight at us. "When Michael locks his arms around Anwar, this room will seal and disappear along with this part of my soul."

"What will happen when he does hold Anwar?" Brayden asked.

"The power to control the dark spirits will be pushed into both of them," Solomon answered, "wheeling it to the realm of its creation. Being the rightful owner, Michael will destroy it, opening the gate to Nirvana where he will once again have access. As for Anwar, it will be up to him where he will reside."

"And you?" Paige asked.

"This part of my soul will join another part and will only become whole when the light walkers collects and returns their effects to its origin and destroy them," he told Paige.

"It will be up to you, Jack, and Carrie," Michael added, "to find these powerful items and convince my brothers to make their wrong a right."

"The Devil's third," Tree whispered to Paige, who didn't look happy about this load being placed upon her shoulders.

I knew what was going through her mind, because the same thoughts raced in mine. We had hoped, once the incantations were destroyed, we could move on with our lives. Of course, we would still protect humanity against the dark spirits and delve into what abilities Paige possessed, among other things. Knowing Bael's intentions now, having another yoke placed upon her shoulders was hard to digest.

"Take the torches to find your way out," Solomon said with a note of finality. "I trust I shall see you again," he said.

We said one last goodbye and left. As soon as we stepped outside the chamber, a bright white light flashed from it, momentarily blinding us. Red dots danced before my eyes. I rubbed them and blinked a couple times, refocusing. The doorway disappeared, the rocky wall once again solid.

"Amazing," Tree said, staring at it with an expression of awe on his face.

"Let's get out of this shithole." With the torch in hand, Brayden stomped away, not bothering to see if we were behind him.

The air became thick and heavy with his sudden mood swing. I lifted my eyebrows at Tree. He shrugged and followed Brayden out. Without saying a word, Paige and I tailed them. We walked in silence, lost in our own thoughts. As we wandered down dark narrow passages leading to different chambers, the flames from the tortures flickered, creating eerie shadows on the walls.

When we entered an airy vault with fluted archways and soaring pillars, the sound of water dripping and flapping wings above us caught my attention. I raised my gaze to the high, eroded ceiling and spotted a colony of bats flying about. Paige looked over her shoulder at me and pointed upward, making a face. I smiled and laughed. She swatted at me, and I captured her hand, falling in step beside her, parallel to the subterranean river.

Like a hound dog hot on a trail, Brayden continued leading us back the way we came. He ducked into another passageway of polished white limestone. Without question, we tagged behind in silent single file. Ahead, I could see daylight. We increased our pace and emerged into the main entrance of the cave. A collection of sighs issued from us. Even Brayden appeared relieved. He rubbed his forehead and tossed the torch in a pool of water near the wall of the entrance. We followed suit, making splashing sounds as ours made contact with the water.

Paige yawned. "Let's go home."

I slung my arm around her shoulders. "Brilliant idea."

"I think I'm going to sleep the whole way there," Tree said, stretching and yawning.

"I think I will, too," Brayden admitted. "I'm exhausted."

Together we stepped out into the sunshine and were met with applause. Dumbfounded, we stood squinting until our eyes adjusted to the natural light. A hundred or so Africans milled among the age-old trees, huge boulders, and waited along the bank of the river inside the canyon. They clapped their hands and cheered. We glanced at each other in confused bewilderment, but then something caught Tree's eye. He looked past me, his brows furrowed. I turned and saw a bald African man wearing a grass skirt and a string of bones around his neck similar to the ones hanging from black beads off his earlobes. He headed toward us. Thick white paint covered his large forehead, around his eyes and the upper part of his cheeks. The pigment broke into four lines curving around to the hollow part of his face. The village's witch doctor was my best bet.

"The one whom walks in the light," he said, his eyes fixed on Tree, disregarding the rest of us. He took hold of Tree's hands, causing him to take a step back in surprise. Then he kissed them before letting go. "My name is Baako, and my people thank you. They want to hold a feast in your honor."

Tree shifted his weight and adjusted his beanie hat. The corner of his mouth twitched into a nervous smile. "Um, I don't know what you're talking about, but thank you for the offer."

"It was because of you," Baako said, "Michael came here, causing the beast to flee our land." He lifted the necklace of bones over his head and held it up to Tree. "Please, take this as a token of our appreciation." He dangled it in Tree's face.

Tree looked at Paige as if seeking her guidance. She nodded and gestured for him to lower his head. With a wary expression, he bent his head, allowing the witch doctor to place the strand around his neck.

"Wonderful," Baako said with a grin, revealing yellowed teeth. "Oh, look. David." He turned to shake hands with David, whom I was glad to see and hoped we could be on our way.

"Hey," Tree said, his voice low and guarded, pulling my attention away from David onto him. "Do I need to give him something in exchange?"

"What?" Paige said, stepping closer to him.

"Do I need to give the African dude something for giving me this?" He pinched the necklace between his finger and thumb and shook it, rattling the bones.

"Why would you?" Brayden asked.

Paige covered her mouth and giggled.

"I don't think so," I answered.

"But you don't know for sure?" Tree asked, throwing nervous glances past me.

"I don't," I admitted.

"What are you talking about?" Brayden demanded.

"Tree is referring to some Native Americans," Paige told him. "If a gift is presented to you, you have to give one in return; otherwise, it's considered rude and insulting."

"I don't want to insult them," Tree said in a high whisper.

"David says dat he must take you back at once," Baako informed us.

"They need sleep and to return to America," David said, joining us. "We must not delay their journey home any longer."

"David's right," I said. "Our dear friend is in the hospital, and we need to get back as soon as possible."

"Please," Baako said, "let us give you food to take with you."

"Your offer is very kind," I said. "We would be honored."

"Thank you," Baako replied, smiling. "The honor is mine." He turned to lead us back to his village when Tree placed a hand on his arm, stopping him.

"I would like to give you something in return for your necklace," Tree told him.

Baako waved his hand to show it wasn't necessary, but Tree insisted. Reaching underneath his T-shirt he pulled out a silver necklace with a charm on it. I recognized it right away. Thor's hammer. Paige drew a sharp breath but didn't say anything. She watched in stunned silence as Tree took it off and placed it over Baako's head. "This is for luck and protection," Tree told the witch doctor.

Baako took Tree's hands and kissed them again. "Thank you. I will treasure it and keep it close to my heart always. And know, one who walks in the light, you are always welcomed here."

Tree's cheeks reddened, mixing with the purplish bruise, making it appear darker. We followed Baako to his village, his people smiling, animatedly talking to Tree, treating him like a celebrity. Brayden, Paige, and I stood on the sidelines watching Tree handle his newfound fame with grace, even though I could tell by his glances our way how uncomfortable he was with all this attention. I gave him an encouraging smile as the events of the past week swirled in my head like a slow moving tornado. I was beat, and my sluggish thoughts were becoming a byproduct of fatigue. Snippets of the prior affairs flashed in my mind: Paige's letter, tracking her, Ameerah, Jade, discovering Carrie was once a witch in a prior life, Paige going on a journey with her guide Moradin, Tree becoming a light walker, the Devil's third, and Anwar.

My chaotic thoughts halted. They reversed to the first day I met Anwar in 1856 when my father brought him to our farm after Anwar saved my brother from being beaten to death. And for the rest of the morning, I thought about Anwar and nothing else, until I was able to close my eyes on the way to the airport and fall into the dark chasm of sleep.

Chapter Thirty-Eight

Paige

Our return flight to Portland was uneventful. We slept most of the way and ate when we were roused from sleep. We didn't talk much until the drive back to Astoria when we were alert and rested. It was early afternoon. The sky was dark and cloudy, the cool air feeling damp with a thick smell of rain filling our nostrils. *Welcome back to Oregon.* I couldn't help but smile to be home again. I loved this state. I loved the plush greenery, the woods, the mountains, the ocean—all of it. I couldn't wait to see Carrie and was on the edge of my seat waiting to learn what Tree found out while he used Brayden's phone to call her mom. I tried to eavesdrop on his conversation, but Nathan was talking to me about making a trip to visit Pip, and I didn't want to be rude.

"Well?" I asked, turning in the front seat to look at Tree. He just finished chatting with Carrie's mom and from what I gathered half listening to his discussion, her recovery was fantastic.

"She's awake," he said, grinning. "And she's doing awesome."

"Yay. We must see her now," I said, bouncing in my seat.

"Yes," Brayden said, sighing with relief.

"What wonderful news," Nathan replied, smiling at me. "We'll go there right now."

"We can't," Tree said, frowning. "They're starting to run some test, so we're not allowed to visit until tomorrow morning at eight."

I slouched in my seat. "That sucks." I turned to face Tree, when a thought occurred to me. "Do you think she remembers she was a witch in a previous life and what was told to her when she was in the other realm?"

Tree shrugged. "I don't know, but I'm anxious to find out."

"Me, too," I said.

Brayden sat up and looked at Tree. "I can't believe you're on the path to become a light walker, and Carrie is a witch."

"Neither can I," Tree admitted. "I still can't fully wrap my head around it."

"Michael said you'd learn more about it later," I reminded him. "I wonder how though?"

"I don't know," Tree mumbled, staring out the window.

"I was surprised when you gave Baako your necklace," I told him. Tree had that charm for years. He bought it at some mystical shop when he and his family went to Germany to visit relatives, and since then he never went without it.

He fingered the bones around his neck and wrinkled his nose. "I really don't know how I feel about this, but I thought the trade was the right thing to do."

Nathan glanced at me. "I remember something I forgot to fill you in on."

The tone of his voice bordered on cautious, which made my stomach drop. Brayden sat up, his jaw clenched, eyes hard. If Nathan said the wrong thing, I knew Brayden would pounce on him. Tree placed his hand on Brayden's arm and shook his head when Brayden shifted his gaze to Tree. I tore my eyes off them to focus on Nathan.

"Jade told me to tell you," Nathan went on, "your guide Moradin will be taking you on a journey to different realms."

"What?" I wasn't sure I heard him right. My guide? And did he just say his name was— My mind went totally blank. All I could do was blink.

"Your guide is named Moradin," Nathan stated once again. "His task will be to lead you into new domains so you'll get a better understanding of yourself and how things work. You'll be going through an orientation, and she said it has already been decided by the council."

"Council?" Brayden blurted. "Who the hell are they?"

"I think I know," Tree said. "But I'm not sure." He screwed up his face and rubbed his forehead in slow circles like he was trying to loosen the information from his brain's tight grip.

"Do tell," Brayden said, crossing his arms.

Tree dropped his hands and sighed. "The council is a group of highly evolved souls. They've been associated with Paige at one point or another. And I wanna say, like all of us, before Paige incarnated, she sat with them to review her life chart."

"How do you know this?" Brayden asked.

Tree shrugged. "I don't know. It's weird. It's like since we met Michael, and he told me about me aiming to be a light walker, things are coming to me in little spurts. But then again, it could be all bullshit. However, I feel what I just told you is correct."

"When?" I asked Nathan, my nerves on the verge of fraying. I didn't know if I was ready for this. I mean, it would be cool to meet my guide and travel through Wonderland like Alice, but I had a lot on my plate as it was. How much more did these people think I could handle? I had the sudden urge to tell them to all leave me alone for a while. I wanted a halfway normal existence with Nathan. Sure I would protect humanity against the dark spirits, but in the interim I wanted to enjoy life as well. Were those things too much to ask?

"She didn't say," Nathan answered, pulling up to Tree's house and parking on the side of the road.

"Can you and Tree go inside for a few minutes while I talk to Paige, I need a minute alone with her," Brayden said.

"It's fine," I told Nathan when I saw the hesitation in his eyes. He slowly nodded and exited the Jeep with Tree. I climbed to the backseat to be closer to Brayden. "What's up? Are you okay?"

Brayden shook his head. "No, I'm not."

I placed my hand over his. "Tell me."

"I know you don't want to hear or believe it," he said, covering my hand with his. "I still feel we belong together."

"Brayden," I began, but he cut me off.

"We do, Paige. Look at the whole picture. You, Carrie, and Tree are the Devil's third, and I fit in there somewhere. There was a reason all four of us grew up together and became as close as we have. And don't you think it's weird you and I were both chosen for immortality?"

"I do," I admitted. "I'd asked Anwar when he told Nathan and me about you being marked if it was normal—two people who grew up together having the opportunity to become immortal."

"What did he say?"

"He said it happens, but it's rare."

"That's what I'm talking about."

"What?"

"It's rare, so there's a reason behind it." He rubbed his forehead and shook his head. "I don't believe in coincidence, Paige," he said, peeking from beneath his dark eyelashes. "There's no such thing."

I didn't say anything, because honestly I didn't either.

"Anwar is dead," his voice cracked, and he cleared his throat. "A few days ago he was talking crazy stuff like he willed his house in Seattle to me . . . and his Hummer. I didn't take him seriously because I knew even if he were to kill himself, he'd still be bound to the blood oath until Bael released him."

"What do you think Anwar would have done if Michael hadn't saved him?"

"I have no idea, but I'm sure he would have found a way. He has tons of journals dating back hundreds of years of his experiences and what he's learned from them. I'm sure some are packed full of ancient rituals and magic. Hopefully, they'll be in his house, because I would love to get my hands on them."

I gave him a wary look. "Brayden, it makes me uncomfortable to know you plan to be the most powerful immortal and reign over our world. Maybe you having those journals wouldn't be such a good thing."

"I disagree," he said. "I think having high aspiration and bettering yourself is admirable. Our world has no structure. Immortals can do what they want, which is fine. However, humans would have better protection with accountability and some form of rules laid out to follow and not breach, like the Constitution."

"I see your point, but what would the consequences be if one of our own decided not to abide by these new laws?"

Brayden shrugged. "I haven't thought about that part yet, but it can be done." He took my hand in his and fixed his eyes on mine. "We can do it together, Paige. We were meant for each other. There are no coincidences. I think if you were honest with yourself and not blinded by your feelings toward Nathan, you'd agree. I also believe we have a connection far deeper than yours and Nathan's. If you were to open yourself to it, you'd discover how right I am about it."

"Bray–"

He placed a finger on my lips and continued. "You're all I have, Paige. Sure, I have Tree and Carrie as well, but without you, my world is less bright. You know we make a great team, and together we can accomplish magnificent things and have a wonderful life together." Tears filled his eyes.

Sadness gripped my heart, twisting it. My love for him swelled, and I wiped the wetness off his cheeks. He was right about us on so many levels, but I knew I couldn't go there. I was in love with Nathan and only wanted to be with him. I wondered, though, if it was possible to be in love with two people at the same time. I imagined what my life would be like with Brayden and compared it with my life with Nathan. An agonizing ache hollowed out my chest at the thought of not being with Nathan, which gave me my answer. I loved Brayden, but I wasn't in love with him. My decision was final. I wanted to spend my life with Nathan and not Brayden.

I held his face in my hands and hoped my voice would be gentle, yet resolute. "I love you, Brayden. I always have and always will, but my heart belongs to Nathan."

He glanced away, the corners of his eyes brimming with emotion. I dropped my hands and sat back, waiting for his reply. Rain fell, pelting the roof of the Jeep, making a loud drumming noise above us. Water poured down the windows, blurring the world around us, giving the illusion of us sinking into the ocean in a metal coffin. I pushed the dismal thought aside and looked at Brayden.

"I'm going to go," he finally said.

"Where?"

"I don't know. But I do know this . . . I'm not giving up on us. *Never,*" he said with hard determination.

Before I could respond, he kissed me on the forehead and bolted out of the Jeep, disappearing in the watery abyss.

Chapter Thirty-Nine

Nathan

Paige told me everything Brayden said to her. His behavior didn't surprise me; he was in love with her, and I couldn't blame him for it. But what stuck in my craw was his relentlessness and utter disrespect toward her relationship with me. I also didn't like the fact he made her feel like shit whenever he poured his heart out about how he felt, using the bond they shared as a fulcrum in his favor. Paige didn't say much after she shared their conversation. She stared out the window, twining and untwining her fingers in her lap. I wanted to make her feel better and get her mind off Brayden. I thought of the perfect thing to say, right when I was pulling into her driveway.

I pulled the key out of the ignition and touched her arm when she moved to open the door. "No more Aosoth or Roeick," is all I had said.

Paige whipped around, her mouth open, eyes wide with forgotten surprise. I watched as the reality of it dawned on her. Her bright dark green eyes, now sparkled like emeralds from her sudden elation. The corners of my mouth turned up, and she laughed. "I totally forgot about Aosoth and Roeick," she said between giggles. "How could I have forgotten such a huge thing?"

"It's understandable, Paige. We've been overloaded with a lot of information. Not to mention how exhausting it all was."

"Yeah, but still . . ." She threw her arms around my neck. "Oh, it doesn't matter. What matters is they're gone, especially her."

I crushed her to my chest and whispered, "Ding, dong, the witch is dead."

She laughed again. "The wicked witch," she said, catching my cult reference. She released her arms and pulled back, the grin still on her beautiful face. "I'm so happy." She gave me a quick kiss. "I want to do something for you, but first I need to take a shower." She hopped out of the Jeep and disappeared. I followed and found her standing on the front porch holding Zeruel.

"Hi, Zeruel." I reached out and petted him, his loud purrs a welcoming sound to my ears.

"He says, hello and thank you for your assistance in this fragile matter," Paige relayed to me.

"You can still hear him." It wasn't a question, only a statement spoken out loud, more to myself.

She beamed. "I can. Solomon left the gift of speaking to animals with me. Zeruel told me so, but even if I couldn't he would still be able to communicate with me, like he had with Anwar." She bit her lip and worry clouded her face.

"What is it?"

"He's basically telling me what Michael and Solomon told us. He said Bael has retreated for now. He'll be back, though, and will try to convince Carrie, Tree, and me to join him." She kissed Zeruel's head, and he vanished from her arms. "I'm going to go take a shower," she said, back in high spirits.

We stepped inside. The lingering aroma of cinnamon and nutmeg filled my nostrils. The wonderful smell of home. I breathed in, savoring it. "What did you tell him?"

"I told him I'll do the right thing." She headed for the stairs.

"I have to go home," I told her, remembering I no longer had my stuff here. She paused, and her face fell. "After I read your letter," I explained, "I packed up my belongings and took them home as you requested."

"Oh . . . wait." Her face lit up. "There are some clothes in the dryer I didn't get around to folding." We went to the laundry room. She opened the door to the dryer, and sure enough some of my clothes were there. "Now you don't have to leave," she said, rummaging through the load and handing me a pair of boxers, socks, jeans, and a black long sleeve T-shirt.

"This will work," I told her, pleased I didn't have to leave after all.

"Great." She hopped on her toes and kissed me. "I'll be done in a minute, and while you're taking your shower I'm going to prepare myself."

"For what?" I didn't have a clue what she was talking about, and the mischievous smile on her face had me curious.

"It's a surprise. Something I've been wanting to do for you for a long time. I don't know if it's going to work, but I have to practice anyway." She shrugged and left the room before I could respond.

I stood with an armful of clothes, staring after her, wondering what she planned. Finally, after a few minutes of pondering with no conclusive results, I decided to call Ameerah to let her know we were back and fill her in on everything. I pulled the piece of paper from my pocket with her number on it and used the phone in the kitchen.

"Hello," she answered after a few rings, caution coloring her tone.

"Ameerah, it's Nathan."

"Nathan. Are you back? What happened? How's Paige?"

"Paige is great," I answered and then went on to tell her about our adventure. I decided not to tell her everything, like about the Devil's third and Tree. I also skipped over the information about the other light walkers but did tell her about Michael and Bael's falling out with him and Anwar being freed from the blood oath. I saved the best part for last–Aosoth and Roeick's demise. When I told her, she squealed so loudly, I had to pull the receiver away from my ear.

"I'm doing a happy dance right now," she said. "I wish I had the opportunity to make the bitch suffer for a while. What sort of spell did Solomon use?"

"The deadfall. I think it's the same one written in the grimoire you're holding for me," I replied.

Silence.

"Ameerah?" The sound of the blow dryer spilled down the stairs. I had to end our conversation but needed to find out why Ameerah's enthusiasm diminished in a matter of seconds. I could hear her cursing under her breath and a sickening feeling slithered into my stomach. "What's wrong?"

"Aosoth and Roeick were transported to the lower world," she said.

"And," I prompted when she fell silent again, saying another string of curses.

She blew out an irritable sigh. "There are different levels to the lower world, and there's a possibility she can find a way back here. But I don't know. It all depends on which deadfall Solomon used."

"There's more than one?" I ran a hand through my hair and groaned.

"Yes. Each one has a different purpose."

"Bael somehow knew Solomon rigged the chamber his incantations were in, because he set up both Aosoth and Roeick and did everything but push them into the room."

"Okay, I feel a little better," she said. "Maybe they are gone for good then . . . well, at least from this world. Once their spirits accept the help offered to them, they can move on, or so I've heard."

"I have to go," I said. "Why don't I pick you up tomorrow afternoon, say two o'clock? If Paige isn't ready to help you yet, I'll let you know. I need to give you back your Jeep anyway. Thanks again for allowing me to borrow it."

"No problem," she said. "I'll bring the grimoire with me, but I prefer not to go to Paige's house."

"Oh, right. Zeruel. I forgot."

"I'm no longer afraid to be trapped in his light," she piped. "I hate to admit this, but I'm ashamed to be in his presence."

"I understand. We'll go to my house instead."

"Thanks, Nathan. Tell Paige I said hi, and I'm glad she's okay."

"I will. See ya tomorrow."

I hung up after she said goodbye and took a shower downstairs, knowing Paige still had the upstairs one occupied. After I was finished, feeling much better being free of all the dirt and grime I'd collected on my skin and in my hair from going days without a solid washing, I entered the living room. I knew right away what Paige planned on doing–at least part of it. The thick smell of sandalwood, cypress, and pine resin gave it away. They were used to help increase her psychic powers. I didn't think she needed it, though, and had full confidence in her ability. But regardless, if having props made her feel at ease, I supported her one hundred percent. "Hey, you," I said.

She stood from the couch and smiled. Her dark purple sweats hung low on her hips and her button-up white long-sleeve thermal top clung to her hourglass figure exactly right. I noticed the top three buttons were undone, revealing a hint of white lace. Sexy. I had the sudden urge to take her right there but looked away instead, forcing myself to focus on the matter at hand.

Paige tilted her head to the side and walked up to me, her face inches from mine. "Why are your eyes bright?"

Damn, I had hoped they wouldn't be. So much for being discrete.

"You turn me on." My voice was low, almost a growl. Having her this close made my resolve to wait for the proper time to ravish her waver.

She took my hand, leading me to the couch. "Later. Right now, we have more important things to do, believe it or not." She pushed me down. "I want you to sit and get comfortable."

"All right, love," I said in a British accent, knowing how much she liked it, "but do tell me what you are up to. Otherwise, I might go mad."

She laughed. "You *are* mad."

"I'm mad about you," I countered.

"Well, the feeling is mutual." She kneeled in front of me and placed her hand on my knee. Excitement danced in her eyes. "If you can talk to any relative of yours, who would it be?"

Instant realization came to me on what she was about to do. A lump materialized in my throat. I swallowed against it and cleared my throat. "Are you going to . . ." My voice faltered.

She smiled. "I'm going to try. You told me back in the hotel, Ameerah believes I can and wants me to contact Nadia for her. I figured I should try with you first. Besides, I've been wanting to do this for you because I know how much you miss your family."

My throat constricted, rendering me speechless. This selfless gift she was offering to me—the possibility to talk to one of my relatives—overwhelmed me with such fierce emotion that I couldn't stop the onslaught of tears. I hung my head and covered my face in an attempt to get a grip on myself. I had always wondered what I would say if I had one last chance to converse with my father, my mother, or one of my brothers. Against Anwar's urging not to, I had told my father my immortal secret while the rest of my family mourned for me. His loyalty to me never faltered, even when my poor mother fell into a deep depression. The guilt, though. The gut-wrenching guilt I've had for almost two hundred years of putting my father in a position where he had to watch his beloved wife suffer and could have easily taken it away by revealing my secret had eaten a hole inside of me. But now. Now, there was a chance I could make it right and even the slim chance, the possibility of it, had me crying like a little girl. Not my proudest moment.

"Nathan," Paige said, her tone soft and gentle. She placed her hands over mine and peeled them off my face. My eyes were closed, but when I felt her warm hand cradling my cheek, I opened them. "Remember, I won't be able to contact your family unless one of them is residing in Summerland or a realm closest to ours."

I didn't say anything, only nodded. I remembered what Kora had said; however, even the possibility of it had my emotions reeling.

"It'll be okay," she reassured, brushing the tears off my face with her thumbs. "Do you want me to get you a cold washcloth?"

"No." I sat back and ran a hand across my face. "I'm fine." I swallowed hard and cleared my throat. "Thank you."

She rose to her feet. "Don't thank me yet. I don't know if it's going to work."

"Regardless," I said, "your willingness to try means the world to me."

"You can thank me later." She waggled her eyebrows.

I laughed. "Oh, I will. You can count on it." The heaviness in my chest lifted, and I could breathe easier. But to say I was nervous was an understatement. I was anxious as hell and clasped my hands in my lap while I watched her position herself at the edge of the room, like she had when she contacted Kora. She lifted her hands above her head, her palms positioned skyward, and in my mind I said a prayer to please make this work.

Chapter Forty

Paige

I closed my eyes, and in a strong, commanding voice, I said, "In love and pure light, I call forth Nathan's immediate family to join us in this room." Just like the last time, a tingling sensation developed on my palms and at the crown of my head, moving up my arms and through my body, leaving an energizing warmth in its wake. "In love and pure light, I call forth Nathan's immediate family to join us in this room." I repeated in the same forceful voice.

"Paige," Nathan whispered, causing me to look.

In the center of the living room, three glowing basketball sized orbs hovered in the air. Bright, beautiful colors swirled inside them: violet, pink, orange, green, blue, and so forth. It was like a living lava lamp in a white round ball.

My heart leaped in my chest.

I did it!

Nathan sat on the edge of the couch, his legs apart with his forearms on his thighs. We grinned at each other, and I continued, "Forgive me for the intrusion, but Nathan would like to have a word with you."

The orbs plummeted to the floor. When they bounced, two men and a woman appeared in the center of my living room. I could see Nathan's likeness in all of them. There was no doubt in my mind who stood before me. They had to be his dad, mom, and one of his brothers. Nathan rose to his feet and moved beside me, his mouth agape.

"Nathan, darling," the woman said, "how wonderful to see and talk to you once again."

She was pretty with dark blonde shoulder length hair, curled at the bottom and the sides held back with jeweled silver combs. She wore a simple white and blue striped dress that brushed her ankles.

"Mom," Nathan said. He breathed in and out a couple times. I was guessing to control his emotions, because I could feel them rolling off him. "I'm sorry for what I put you through." His gaze shifted on the handsome older male. "I apologize to you as well, Father. Please forgive me."

His mother moved toward us, gliding across the room. Her smile reaching her blue eyes. "You've been punishing yourself over this far too long, son. There is nothing to forgive. You chose an honorable path, and I understand now why you deceived us."

"I should have told you," Nathan said, his tone drenched in bitterness.

She shook her head. "No, son. You and your father did the right thing. I know it now and carry no ill will toward you or your father. In fact, I have a deep respect for you both."

A tear escaped Nathan's eye. "Thank you. I-I love and miss you both terribly."

His father and brother joined his mother's side. His father had dark brown hair and eyes, whereas is brother's hair was a lighter brown, his eyes a bluish gray in color. They were taller than Nathan by an inch–six feet two to be exact–and wore black knee high boots, brown trousers with buckled suspenders over a long sleeve white shirt. The only difference was Nathan's brother had on a newsboy cap and held a mischievous glint in his eyes like he was always looking for a good time.

"We've been watching you off and on throughout the years," his father replied. "We're proud of you and share the same sentiments."

Nathan opened his mouth to say something, then closed it. More tears trailed down his face. He wiped at them and sniffed a couple times.

"What's with the waterworks?" his brother asked, his tone light and full of humor.

"Give me a break, Thomas," Nathan said, half-smiling. "I didn't think I'd ever see you again. Where's Jeremiah and Samuel?"

"They moved on," his mother said in a matter-of-fact tone. "But they loved you very much."

"They wanted to be with their families," Thomas clarified.

"What about you?" I asked.

Nathan blinked, and his body jerked as if he'd been startled out of a deep sleep. "Oh, I'm sorry. How terribly rude of me." He gestured to me. "This is Paige. Paige, this is my father, Jesse, my mother, Sarah, and my brother Thomas."

"Please to finally meet you," I said, sticking my hand out to shake theirs, but then quickly dropped it, hoping nobody noticed. *How lame. They wouldn't be able to shake it. Duh, Paige.*

"The pleasure is all ours, dear," Sarah said with a warm smile, and Jesse made an agreeable sound.

Thomas touched the brim of his hat and nodded. "I can see why my little brother is smitten by you." An appreciative smile crossed his handsome face.

"Oh, well . . ." I stammered, not knowing what to say.

"To answer your question," he went on, "my family is with me, but we'll be moving on as well."

Their images flickered, signaling their time here was about to come to an end. I was surprised how short their visit was and frowned in disappointment.

"We have to go," Sarah said and turned her attention to me. "I cannot thank you enough for allowing us to reconnect with our son."

"I'm glad I was able to," I said.

"Will I see you again?" Nathan asked with a hitch in his throat. He didn't want them to go. I knew the feeling quite well. My heart squeezed when the sense of longing to be with my own family washed over me. I knew Nathan must be going through the same heartache.

"Perhaps," Jesse answered. "I'd like to think so. But your mother and I plan on leaving Summerland now that we were able to visit with you."

"I understand," Nathan said lamely.

"You've done well, little brother," Thomas said. "I'm proud of you."

"We all are," Jesse stated.

"Always remember, son," Sarah said as they faded away. "Our love for you will never perish."

"Bend an elbow for me," Thomas' disembodied voice called.

Then, they were gone.

Nathan sat on the couch and ran a hand through his hair. He tilted his head to the side and squinted at me. "Thank you."

"Are you okay?" I wasn't sure because his expression was unreadable. "I didn't think their visit would be so short." I felt bad he didn't have much time with them, like it was my fault. Maybe if I would have concentrated harder or had said something else when I was invoking their spirits–

He took my hand and pulled me onto his lap. "I'm absolutely wonderful." He hugged me to his chest, tightening his arms around me. "I cannot stress enough how heavy of a burden I had on my shoulders and the guilt I'd been harboring for all these years. Thanks to you they're gone now."

"But you didn't get to spend much time with your family."

"I would love to spend hours with them, but I understand the veil can only be lifted for so long." He patted my arm. "Don't feel bad about it."

"What does bend an elbow mean?"

Nathan laughed. "It means have a drink."

I laughed with him. "Thomas seems like he'd be fun to be around."

"He is. It didn't surprise me Jeremiah and Samuel moved on. They were always restless."

"Your family is nice. I'm glad I had the chance to meet them."

He kissed my cheek. "They liked you as well."

"Really? How do you know?" For some reason it meant a lot to me to have his family's approval, even though I'd probably never see them again.

"Oh, I could tell."

An idea came to me that had nothing to do with what we were talking about. But I felt good and up to trying it. "Since I appear to be on a roll, can you call Ameerah and have her come over?"

"I spoke to her earlier while you were in the shower," Nathan said. "She won't come because of Zeruel. I told her I'd pick her up tomorrow afternoon and we'll go to my house. She said hi, by the way."

"Oh, right. I forgot about Zeruel." I sat up, causing him to loosen his arms around me. I shifted in his lap, facing him. "Call her anyway. We can pick her up right now and go to your house."

"Okay, but first," he said, running his fingertip down my cheek, over to my lips, his dark blue eyes brightening, "I need to pay my debt to you." His hand went to the back of my head, and he pulled me toward him, kissing me. My stomach flipped and a wave of heat shot to parts of my body. Our tongues connected. I held his face in my hands, kissing him deeper, softly moaning in his mouth. Our breaths quickened, hearts beating faster. "I want you," he said, his voice low almost feral.

I took my thermal top off, leaving on my see-through, white lace camisole. My nipples were erect against the material. At the same time Nathan removed his shirt, baring his smooth, muscular chest and hard abs. Locking eyes with his, I ran my hand down his torso. He shivered and lolled his head back, breathing heavy. I pulled him on top of me, our tongues once again connecting, exploring, his skin hot against mine. The air grew thick and heady with passion as we huffed into each other's mouths. My elbows were next to my ears; my hands held fast to the arm of the couch as his mouth and tongue roamed my body. First down my neck and then through the flimsy lace until he pushed it up, making contact with my bare breasts. My moans rose, and I arched my back when his hands slid between my thighs, his mouth moving downward, leaving a trail of heat in its wake.

An hour later, I was lying in Nathan's arms on the couch. We were both happy and for the first time in a while—content. I knew I made the right decision to be with him. I was crazy in love with Nathan and wanted us to spend the rest of our lives together. I also somehow knew this bullcrap that kept coming between us to try and break us up had ended. Finally, it was just him and me and nothing else.

Now, I needed to help Ameerah reunite with her girlfriend Nadia. I said a quick, silent prayer that Nadia was still in Summerland. Otherwise, I feared Ameerah might backslide and return to her old, dark ways.

Oh, please have Ameerah find peace and happiness once and for all.

Chapter Forty-One

Nathan

Ameerah was happy to see us when we picked her up. She hopped in the backseat with a black backpack slung over her shoulder and chatted with Paige the whole way to my house. They acted like old friends catching up on lost time. One of the first things she said to Paige, though, was she had nothing to do with Volac and his group ambushing us. It seemed important to her, like Paige's opinion mattered. I found it odd for a dark spirit to care what an immortal thought, but then again Ameerah was in the process of evolving herself, stepping away from the dark planes of existence. I had to give her credit for it and did so when Paige made a point to tell her how proud she was of her for wanting to make things right. Unable to accept our compliments, Ameerah shrugged them off and quickly changed the subject, shifting the attention away from herself. "I have a picture of Nadia," she said, digging in her bag. She withdrew a photo and handed it to Paige. "It's the only one I have. Isn't she beautiful?"

"She is," Paige agreed. She turned it so I could have a quick look. It was a black and white picture of a girl around Paige's age, with long dark hair and round doe eyes. There was a tiny smile appearing shy against her delicate features. "She has a haunting, sad look," Paige noted, handing it back.

Ameerah stared at the photo for a long while before answering, "Nadia had the misfortune of being born into the wrong family."

I parked in front of my house. The lights automatically came on, illuminating the broad deck. A strained, uncomfortable silence fell between us. I didn't know how to respond to her comment and shot Paige a helpless look. She winked at me and turned to Ameerah. "C'mon," she said, sounding cheerful. "Let's go see if I can reach her."

Ameerah didn't budge. "I'm scared."

"Of what?" I asked.

"There's nothing to be afraid of," Paige told her. "Nathan and I are with you."

Ameerah lifted her eyes off the worn photo. "What if Nadia doesn't want to be with me?"

"You're being silly," Paige said, playfully rolling her eyes. "It'll be fine."

"What if I'm not forgiven?" Ameerah's voice shook, and her bottom lip trembled.

Paige took Ameerah's hand. "From what I understand . . . you only need to forgive yourself."

"And if you're wrong?" Ameerah questioned with wide, turbulent eyes.

"Then I'll help you until you are forgiven," Paige said with such a fierce conviction it left no doubt in my mind she'd keep her word.

Ameerah cast her eyes down to Paige holding her hand. "You're a good friend. Thanks."

I opened the door and stepped out into the cool night, then stuck my head back inside the Jeep. "Shall we, ladies?"

Ameerah grabbed her pack and sighed. "I guess."

"Fear not, Fallen One. All will be well," I said as they exited the Jeep.

"Fallen One?" Paige asked, wrapping her arm around mine.

Ameerah scowled. "Don't call me that name."

"Jade acknowledged Ameerah by labeling her the 'Fallen One,'" I said in a staged-whisper.

"I can hear you," Ameerah said, raising her eyebrows.

"Fallen from grace?" Paige guessed.

Ameerah made a face and kicked a rock. "Something like that." She looked at me as we climbed the steps on the deck. "Cool pad. I've always loved A-frame houses. The wood and stone complement each other beautifully."

"Thanks." I unlocked the door and turned on lights. "Make yourself at home."

Ameerah stood by the front door, breathing in through her nostrils. Her eyes fluttered closed, then opened. A pleasant smile formed on her face. "Your house smells like pine and oak. I love the earthy aroma the two create." She wandered to the living room and absently set her pack on the couch while looking around. She pointed to the wood railing bordering the loft above. "Was this made by hand? The scroll work is superb."

"I believe so," I answered. "I bought this house from a recluse who had impeccable tastes as you can see."

I remembered the man clearly. When I had followed Matt to Astoria from Seattle, I knew right away I wanted to buy a place here. I also knew since I was a tracker, I needed my privacy and had a great fondness for the forest. One afternoon I decided to drive around in the mountains and woods and came across this house with a for sale sign. It was sheer luck, but I took it as fate. It was exactly what I wanted, and I didn't hesitate to knock on the door. An older gentleman with salt and pepper hair and beard answered. We talked the whole afternoon about philosophy and how the world was in a state of disarray. He preferred to live alone. After his beloved wife passed from breast cancer, he closed himself off to the world and consumed himself in great works of literature and the mechanics of the human mind and spirit. I enjoyed his company and told him we should visit again. He said he would like to; however, he was also dying of cancer, thus selling the house, and he didn't know how much longer he had. Three weeks after I purchased his house, I heard he put a bullet in his head.

"Nathan, do you still have incense?" Paige asked, standing by the stone fireplace, looking gorgeous as ever in her gray cargo pants and a white zip up hoodie which hugged her curves just right.

"In the kitchen." I headed toward there, remembering I stuck some in a drawer beneath the window. "I'll go get them."

"Hold on," she called as I stepped into the U-shaped kitchen. "Forget it."

I wondered if she changed her mind and how Ameerah would feel about it. "Do you want to do it some other time?" I asked, retracing my steps. I entered the living room and watched Ameerah hand her the grimoire. My stomach sank. "You're not planning to use a book spell to contact Nadia are you?" I asked in a flat tone.

"There's not one. I've already checked," Ameerah said, sitting next to Paige on the couch. "I wanted to show her this. It's yours and hers now."

Paige held the grimoire in her lap and grimaced. "I can't believe it's bound in human flesh. Gross." She looked up at me with disturbed eyes. "I can feel the dark energy." She pushed it off her lap with one swipe. It fell to the floor with a dull thunk. "I don't think we should have this disgusting thing in your house."

Ameerah pulled a dark purple velvet cloth from her bag. She picked up the book and wrapped the fabric around it. "This will lock its life force. Have Nathan build a wooden box from an aspen tree and place this grimoire inside it. It will give you double protection from any negative energies that might seep out." She glanced at us in turn, a forewarning etching her features. "You need to keep this in a safe place where no one can find it, and don't breathe a word about it to anybody. Even your closest friends." She raised her eyebrows. "Do you get me?"

"We won't," Paige promised, jumping to her feet, moving to the front of the room.

Ameerah looked at me, waiting for my reply. "It will remain a secret between Paige and me," I told her and meant it. The last thing we needed was more trouble or hassle in our lives. I would make sure no one would discover it.

Ameerah sighed and nodded. "Good."

"Why didn't you want the incense?" I asked Paige and laughed because she was shaking her body as if she suddenly had the heebie jeebies. "What are you doing?"

She stopped and ran her fingers through her hair. "I wanted to make sure I had all the dark energy off me."

"You're silly, Paige," Ameerah said with a faint smile. "Dark energy can't cling to you unless you allow it by inviting it in or being in a constant negative state of mind."

"Maybe so," Paige said, shrugging, "but it made me feel better anyway." She paused and turned to me. "I'm going to cast the spell without the incense, like I did when I contacted my grandmother. My energy level is still up, so I think it'll work."

"I think it's a great idea." I gave her an encouraging look, proud of her decision, because my thoughts were this: she might have to tap into her abilities one day when supporting resources weren't available to her. It was better to practice without them, so she would gain the confidence she needed to work her magic. Of course, with some rituals she would have to use tools in order to perform them, such as dream walking or conjuring dark spirits. However, with this particular one, she was free to discharge her powers without any aids.

"I'm nervous," Ameerah announced, fidgeting with the strap on the backpack. "My stomach is in knots . . . well, this human's stomach." An empty laugh escaped her lips.

Paige gave Ameerah a thoughtful look. "What did you look like when you were human?"

"I was a few inches taller than you," Ameerah said. "I had dark curly hair that was in a cute bob style. My eyes were hazel." She paused, perhaps remembering the time. She raised her hand, dancing her fingers in front of her face. "I had a splatter of freckles across the bridge of my nose and a small chip in my front tooth."

"How did you get the nick?" I asked, sitting beside her.

"I know what you two are doing." She narrowed her eyes at us, accusingly. A beam of light swiped across them.

"Is it working?" Paige asked, flashing her an impish grin.

Ameerah pointed at Paige. "You're bad, but it worked."

"Good. Now, I'm going to get started, but I'm not promising you anything," Paige told her. "I'm still new at this."

I could hear Ameerah's heart pounding. She shifted in her seat and tugged at the bottom of her sweater. She combed her fingers through her hair before smoothing it. Instead of commenting to Paige's statement, she nodded.

I took Ameerah's hand and squeezed it. "You look fine. Stop fussing over yourself."

"You look beautiful," Paige said.

Ameerah's cheeks turned the color of a tomato. She dropped her gaze to her lap and gestured for Paige to start. Paige moved to the side of the room. Standing straight, feet apart, she threw her hands in front of herself, palms facing the empty space between the stone fireplace and where Ameerah and I sat.

"In love and pure light, I call forth Nadia to join us here," she said in a strong and commanding voice. "Ameerah would like to visit with you."

The lights flickered and dimmed.

"Ameerah, where are you? I can't find you," a faint, teary voice called in desperation.

Ameerah shot to her feet. "I'm here, sweetie." Her eyes swept the room, searching for Nadia.

"Ameerah, where are you? I can't find you." The voice repeated in the same tone.

"Nadia. Can you hear me?" Ameerah hollered. She glanced at Paige. I couldn't see her face, but I imagined it to be filled with panic. "Help me," she pleaded.

Nadia sounded lost and disoriented. A terrible ache grew in my chest as the thought of her distress took form. Then the what ifs followed: what if Nadia were unreachable? What if Ameerah never saw her again? What if? I halted those heartbreaking thoughts by telling myself they could be wrong. I had no idea how the spiritual world worked, so to get in a knot over something I had no knowledge of was foolish. The tightness in my chest eased, and I focused my attention on Paige. Her arms were hanging by her side, her lips tucked inside her mouth, eyebrows pulled together in sympathy.

She nodded at Ameerah, and threw her hands above her head, palms facing skyward, like she'd done to contact my family. "In love and pure light, I call forth Nadia. If you can hear me, Ameerah is anxious to reunite with you."

"Ameerah, where are you? I can't find you," Nadia said once again, but this time her voice was louder and echoed throughout the house.

Ameerah paced the room. Tilting her face up, she raised her voice and pleaded, "Nadia, can you hear me?"

Silence.

She paused and dropped her face into her hands. Her shoulders shook from her silent sobs. I moved toward her, but then a muffled scream came. I sat again, thinking stepping into her space wasn't such a good idea after all. She dropped her hands, rage twisting her features. I watched her closely to make sure she wasn't going to take it out on Paige. My muscles tensed in preparation to lurch forward if need be.

She raised her fists in the air and shook them. "Why? Why are you doing this to us? I'm changing my ways. I'm doing the best I can, yet you're still punishing us. Don't you have any mercy or compassion?"

"Ameerah," Paige said.

Ameerah's blazing eyes shifted to Paige. "They're a bunch of assholes," she hissed. "Now I understand why Bael went rogue."

"You don't mean what you're saying," I told her, concerned she might backslide and return to her old ways.

She whipped around, facing me, her teeth clenched. "You're damn right I mean it."

"Ameerah," Paige said again, pointing to her left a few feet away from the fireplace.

At first I didn't see anything. I narrowed my eyes and stared at the empty space Paige indicated. Both she and Ameerah moved to the couch to where I sat. It became obvious they saw something, but then I saw it as well. A tiny ripple in the air–a refraction of blue light forming rings, reminding me of a stone pitched into water, causing the liquid to ripple, expanding in circles across the surface. The center coned backwards and widened into a picturesque scene of a vast meadow surrounded by enormous mountains in a circular pattern beneath a pale lavender sky. They were covered in lush, thick emerald grass and tall trees. The waterfalls cascading from them had prisms of colors dancing along the front. I'd never seen such a beautiful landscape, and my breath caught in my throat. A tall figure appeared in the meadow–a glowing silhouette moving toward us in an easy manner, like there was no care in the world.

"Who is it?" Ameerah wondered more to herself than us.

"I don't know," Paige replied, her eyes trained on the newcomer.

I rose to my feet. "We're about to find out."

Details of his appearance came into focus as he approached. He reminded me of a younger version of Bob Dylan with the shaggy brown hair, sideburns, a long nose, and deep blue eyes. The top buttons on his white collared shirt was undone, the bottom haphazardly tucked into his blue jeans.

"You know who he looks like?" Ameerah whispered, looking at Paige and me.

"I was thinking of Bob Dylan in the early 'sixties," I commented.

Ameerah nodded. "I always thought he was adorable."

"I think he's a light walker," Paige mused.

"You're correct," he said, stepping into the room, a warm glow around his gentle face.

"Where's Nadia? Why can't she hear me?" Ameerah demanded.

"She's in the lower world," the light walker told her. "She's in the part where shell shocked souls reside."

Ameerah stared at him, speechless.

"What does that mean?" Paige asked.

"Sometimes spirits become confused when they have no recollection of their death and have a strong attachment to earth or to somebody who still dwells on this plane," he said with a note of sadness. "These souls remain there until we can snap them out of their stupor and help them crossover."

"Nadia," Ameerah croaked, horror leeching the color from her face.

"We've tried reaching her to no avail," he said. "But take comfort in knowing we never give up. One day–"

"Take comfort?" Ameerah's voice rose. "How can I take comfort in knowing my girlfriend is aimlessly wandering, trapped in a vicious cycle of confusion, repeatedly calling my name and looking for me?"

"I understand your grievances, which you have every right to," he said, unfazed by her outburst. "But these heartbreaking situations are a drop in a bucket compared to what lies ahead once the veil is lifted from them."

Ameerah's lips tightened. "How can you be so callous?"

"I'm not," the light walker answered in a matter-of-fact tone. "I understand it, and though this pains me to see, I know the end result. I've experienced it myself and can assure you this blemish on these souls will pass."

"Ameerah can help Nadia snap out of it," Paige said, sounding hopeful.

"Yes, I can. I know I can." Ameerah took a step forward but stopped when he shook his head. "What? You don't agree? Because if you don't that's a bunch of bullshit," she seethed.

He gave Ameerah a thoughtful look, the depths of his eyes pooling with so much understanding and love I was overwhelmed. I glanced away, and Tree entered my mind. One day, this is what he would be doing, filled with knowledge beyond my comprehension. I then wondered if he ever experienced what Nadia was going through. If not, in time he would, so he could gain the understanding of a heartbreaking situation and the ability to assist those lost souls.

"It has been determined," he said to Ameerah. "Yes, your presence would crack through Nadia's confused state and bring her to her senses." He paused, but when Ameerah opened her mouth, he continued, causing her to bite her tongue and glare. "However, you still have unresolved issues which need to be addressed and dealt with before you have the capability to assist her."

Ameerah blanched. "But-but I turned my back on the dark ways. Am I not forgiven?"

I didn't think he implied those things, but I knew it was a fear weighing on her for quite some time. Her question didn't surprise me, and I hoped he'd be able to take this burden off her shoulders.

"The only forgiveness you need to seek is your own," he told her, "and you're not there yet, but I'm here to guide and aid you."

Ameerah crossed her arms. "So what you're telling me is until I learn to forgive myself and overcome my *issues*"–she made air quotes–"I can't help Nadia?"

He nodded. "Correct."

She made a face. "And how do you propose I do this?"

"Rehabilitation," he simply told her.

Ameerah held her hand out. "Oh, hell, no. I went through that bullshit when I was human, because my parents double-crossed me."

"This is different. You go through a–"

Ameerah pointed past him. "Fuck that. I'll deal with it on my own, then go to Nadia myself. I'm sure Paige can help me."

I glanced at Paige at the same time she looked at me. She raised her eyebrows, surprised at Ameerah's erratic behavior.

"There is only one way to get to the lower world without being propelled there, and Paige doesn't have access to it," he said.

"Well, I'll find a way," Ameerah spat. "You're unbelievable. You people should know the hell I went through when I was human, yet you want me to relive it?"

Paige turned to her. "He doesn't. If you'll give him a chance to explain how it works, I'm sure you'll see it'll be nothing like what you went through." She took Ameerah's hand and sandwiched it between hers. "Please, he's trying to help. Please, let go of your anger and listen to him. He's not attacking you. He's on your side."

I watched as the anger in Ameerah's face melted, releasing its grip, her features turning fragile and on the verge of breaking. Next entered despair, and her bottom lip shook; a lone tear escaped the corner of her eye. "I can't do it," she whispered to Paige.

Paige turned to the light walker in desperation. "Can I go with her if she agrees to it?"

I shot Paige another look, shocked at her question. But her eyes were fixed ahead of her. If she knew I was watching her, she didn't acknowledge it.

"Unfortunately, you cannot," he said. "She needs to do this on her own."

Ameerah pulled Paige into a quick hug. "I gotta go. I'll keep in touch." A sob escaped her lips. She released Paige and looked at me. "Thank you, Nathan. You're a good friend, as well. I'll see ya around." She crossed the room in quick strides, swiped the keys to the Jeep off the table next to the front door and left.

Chapter Forty-Two

Paige

After Ameerah left, an awkward silence fell between us. I was sorry for her and Nadia, but I also felt bad for the light walker. He extended a helping hand, yet she wouldn't take his offer. It was heart crushing, really.

I stared after Ameerah, wanting to go chase her down, but I knew my effort would be fruitless. She chose to deal with her issues on her own—if she could. Silently, I prayed her desperate need to help Nadia would motivate her enough to overcome her demons instead of turning back into one.

"Eventually she'll come around," the light walker said, meeting my eyes. "She harbors a lot of hurt and bitterness. I had hoped she would've accepted my help." He sighed. "This is one of the most difficult parts of my job . . . when a soul becomes unreachable or refuses us."

Nathan ran a hand through his hair. "I imagine so."

"My best friend Tree is striving to be a light walker," I said as I thought about telling Tree this bit of information so he'd know what he'd have to deal with someday. "What's your name by the way?" I added out of curiosity.

"John," he answered with an inviting smile. "And I'm well aware of Jack."

"Really?" The tone of my voice rose in surprise. "You know about Tree?" I was shocked he knew Tree's name and about him. I wondered what else he knew.

"Yes," he said. "All light walkers know about each other. We're informed when a soul chooses this path, and we counsel the individual before a decision is reached. When Jack made his, we thought nothing of it except the usual welcoming a brother into our fold, until his case became a unique one."

"How so?" Nathan asked even though I was almost positive he knew the answer to his own question like I did. But I was glad he asked because I wanted to hear it spoken out loud.

"Thanks to Michael, Jack is now aware of the path he'd chosen," John replied. "I don't begrudge Michael for enlightening Jack on his universal purpose. He had his reasons. But no soul striving to become one of us has ever been made aware of it while in the flesh. Jack also has a girlfriend who was once a powerful witch, his best friends are immortal, one of them has extraordinary abilities still untapped, and he knows about the dark spirits." John paused and rubbed his jaw, collecting his thoughts I suppose. "What Jack does and how he handles things could be catastrophic or a blessing in disguise."

He didn't need to fill in the blanks. I knew if Tree were to decide to be Team Bael, he could help prevent the light walkers—who went against the universal laws—from intervening. However, if Tree used his newfound knowledge for good, this world would be in a better place. A silly thought occurred to me then: Tree would be like a superhero. His quirky childhood dream could actually become a reality. I giggled when the image of Tree wearing tights and a cape entered my mind. "Sorry," I said when Nathan and John looked at me with curious expressions. "I was imagining Tree being a comic book hero." I cleared my throat and shifted my full attention to John. "Tree won't disappoint you," I assured him.

"We're counting on it," he said. "I must take my leave now. It's been a pleasure." He nodded to Nathan and me.

The corner of Nathan's mouth curled into a crooked smile, causing my heart to skip. "Likewise."

"I enjoyed meeting you," I said. "Thanks for trying to help Ameerah."

"Perhaps I'll have better luck next time," he said as he turned to leave.

"Hey, John," I said, stopping him mid-step. "Why do you look like a folk singer?"

He flashed me a grin over his shoulder. "This is how I appeared in the late 1960s and early 1970s before I passed from this earth. I feel this image represents my persona, even though some people used to mistake me for Bob Dylan."

I grinned as well. "Funny you said that, because we were talking earlier how similar you look to him. You're a cutie." *Omigod. I can't believe I told him he was cute.*

He winked before stepping into the meadow. "So are you."

The edges of the scene pulled together to where it became one vertical glowing line suspended in the air, and then it disappeared.

Nathan pulled me into his arms. "I can't believe you were flirting with a light walker." He laughed softly next to my ear.

His strong arms felt wonderful around me. I relaxed in them and breathed him in, loving the woodsy smell. "I didn't mean to," I answered, feeling the heat in my cheeks. "I just think he's cute, but you're cuter," I quickly added.

"Good to know," he said. I could hear the smile in his voice. He kissed my cheek, his warm lips pressing against my skin. "What do you say we scrounge in the kitchen for something to eat? I might have a frozen pizza we can pop in the oven."

At the mention of food, my stomach growled. Without saying another word, we headed to the refrigerator in hope there would be something good to eat.

* * *

Early the next morning, Tree called to tell us he was at the hospital with Carrie, and she was doing great. He sounded elated, his voice more alive and chirpy since before Carrie's accident. I couldn't wait to see her and jumped into action. I threw on my clothes, brushed my teeth and hair and out the door I went with Nathan hot on my heels. Thankfully, while I was rushing to get ready, Nathan had the presence of mind to brew coffee and poured some in travel mugs for us. I was eternally gratefully for this thoughtful gesture and told him so when I slid onto the front seat of his pickup as he handed me the yummy java. I noticed he had sleepy eyes. They weren't quite focused and were heavy lidded. I imagined his thought patterns were as cloudy as mine. We had stayed up most of the night chatting, so it stood to reason our brains were all foggy, and we seemed to be moving in slow motion. I took a sip of my coffee, welcoming the caffeine into my bloodstream and thanking the gods for it.

When we arrived at the hospital, Tree's mom Tori just got off her nightshift. I waved at her as I passed the nurses' station where she was gathering her stuff to leave. She beamed and returned the wave. "Carrie is recovering fabulously."

"Tree told us. Thanks," I said, rushing to Carrie's door, wishing I could use my immortal speed instead of moving at a much slower pace. I did an internal sigh. But my frustration evaporated when I opened the door.

"Paige!" Carrie squealed, throwing her arms up.

I tried not to pay attention to the clear white tubes hanging from her arms, the constant beeping of the machines, or the white patch on the right side of her head. Not to mention the antiseptic, alcohol smell hanging in the air. For some reason when Tree told me Carrie was doing great, I thought all those mechanical devices and tubes would be gone. I could feel my face falling but quickly recovered by fixing my gaze on Carrie instead and bending over her silver bedrail to hug her. "I'm so glad you're okay," I said, pulling back to get a good look at her. She had some color in her face, and her brown eyes were bright and alert, which gave me comfort.

"Thanks to you," Carrie said. She waved Nathan to her and opened her arms. They hugged, and it touched me Carrie cared enough about Nathan to embrace him. "Thank you, Nathan, for being such a wonderful friend and so good to my Paige."

"It's my pleasure," he said, moving to Tree on the other side of the bed where he sat in a wood and vinyl chair. Nathan took the empty one beside him.

"I told her everything," Tree informed us.

I raised my eyebrows and turned away from Carrie, my hair draping the side of my face, shielding my profile from her. I caught Tree's eyes and said in a low voice, "You told her about you working on being—"

"A light walker," he finished in an even tone. "Yup."

Carrie looked at me wide-eyed. "Omigod, Paige. I can't believe it . . . I mean I can, but it seems so surreal."

"So you know about Michael?" I asked, knowing he was Carrie's favorite archangel.

She gasped. "Yes. I wish I could have met him."

"We met another one last night," I said, bracing myself for their reaction, knowing they would be intrigued. I was right. Carrie gaped at me and Tree leaned forward on his knees with an intense look on his face.

"Paige was trying to help Ameerah connect with her girlfriend Nadia," Nathan added.

"What happened?" Tree asked.

I frowned. "Nadia is stuck in the lower world, the part where shell-shocked spirits go."

Concern entered Carrie's face. I bit the inside of my cheek. Maybe I shouldn't have shared this information. I didn't want to upset her fragile state. She then asked me to explain it to her, so I did, thinking maybe she was up to it. I told her and Tree what happened with Ameerah and our meeting with John. After I finished, the worry in Carrie's eyes was no longer there. Tree was a little taken aback that John knew about him, but when I explained to him what John told me that all light walkers knew about each other, understanding sparked in his eyes. Of course, Tree wouldn't know now about the others, because he wasn't one of them yet. I wondered how it would all play out for him. Would he and Carrie be allowed to be together? I didn't see why not and imagined it would be much like Nathan and me. Nathan would be tracking dark spirits while Tree would be off helping other souls. But then I remembered Nirvana.

Crap.

Carrie wouldn't be able to go there. So then what? There had to be some sort of solution to a situation such as theirs. There had to be, because I knew without a doubt Tree wouldn't give up Carrie for—

"What are you thinking, Paige?" Tree asked, scrutinizing me. "You look like something is bothering you."

I could feel Carrie's eyes boring into me. I didn't want to upset her, so I lied a little. "It bothers me Carrie has all these tubes in her." I pointed to them and made a face.

Carrie playfully shoved my arm. "I'm fine. I get to leave in a few days. The doctors are amazed at how fast I'm recovering."

I eyed the small white patch on her head. "How do you feel about this?"

She touched it and groaned. "Don't even get me started. I have a bald spot on my head, and now I'm going to have to wear a hat until my hair grows back."

Tree pointed to the black beanie on his head. "I have several of these if you want to borrow one."

Anger flashed across Carrie's face. "I can't believe those assholes shaved your Mohawk."

"They got theirs in the end," Nathan said.

"Thank God," Carrie breathed and flicked her hand toward Tree. "Look what they did to his poor face."

Tree touched the yellowish bruise below his eye and on his cheekbone. "It's not so bad now."

"Aosoth and Roeick are no longer here," I said, grinning. I still couldn't believe my good fortune and refused to believe what Ameerah had told Nathan—there was a possibility she could come back.

"Yes, I know," Carrie said, sharing in my delight. "I was so happy when Tree told me."

"Do you remember?" I started to say, but stopped when she nodded, the look on her face telling me she knew exactly what I was getting at.

"I remember *everything*," she said. She paused and tears filled her eyes. "I can't thank you enough for saving me."

I squeezed her cold hand. "You already have. You told Nathan what was going on, and because of you, he found me. Besides, you're my best friend. I would go to the ends of the earth to save you."

Carrie squeezed my hand back. "Me, too."

"Do you remember Jade, Carrie?" Nathan asked.

"Yes, I do," she told him. "I really like her. I have to admit, though, my mind is still reeling about the part of me being a powerful witch in a previous life."

"Don't you think it's cool?" I asked.

"Hell, yeah, I think it's cool," she said, smiling. "I was given instructions by this beautiful woman on how to get reacquainted with that side of myself. I can't wait until I fully recover so I can start working on it."

"We can practice together," I said. "I'm basically in the same boat as you anyway."

"Ooooh, it's going to be so much fun." Carrie clapped her hands. "We can train together and test one another." She bit her lip and fell silent, the excitement draining from her face. "I'm sorry about Anwar. I know you two were angry with him, and I don't blame you." She looked at Nathan. "But you had a history with him. He was a part of your family."

Nathan blinked, surprised at her sudden shift of topics and that she was expressing her condolences to him. He ran a hand through his hair, resting it on the back of his head and squinted at her. "Thanks, Carrie. He did the right thing, though."

She nodded. "Yes, he did. I laughed when Tree told me how pissed Bael was when Michael stepped in and broke the blood oath Bael had with Anwar. I was like, 'Yay, Michael. He rocks.'"

We laughed with her, and I had to agree. Michael did rock.

"I take it you know about the Devil's third, then?" Nathan asked her.

"I do," Carrie answered. "I think it's comical the dark spirits think it has to do with the government."

"Not to defend them or anything," I said. "But from their perspective it does make sense."

Carrie shrugged. "I guess so, but I wonder if Ayperos knows the truth about it."

"I wouldn't doubt it," Nathan said.

"Has it sunk in your heads yet the Devil's third is us three?" I asked. "Because I'm still trying to wrap my head around it. I mean *us*." I pointed to myself, Carrie, and Tree. "*We* are the Devil's third, and Bael will do everything he can to sway us to his side."

"It is hard to believe," Tree admitted. "As for Bael, he can kiss our asses, because we will *never* join forces with him."

"Never." Carrie echoed.

I nodded in agreement and laughed when Carrie stuck her hand out, palm facing downward. It immediately took me back to junior high when we teamed up against another group of kids to play kickball. "The Devil's third," she said in a strong and determined voice.

Tree shot me his signature goofy grin, stood, and placed his hand on top of hers. "The Devil's third," he chimed in.

I reached over her bedrail and placed my hand on Tree's. "The Devil's third," I said, mirroring their smiles.

Carrie's eyes swept to Nathan, sitting in the chair watching us. She gestured with her other hand for him to join in. "C'mon, Nathan. You're part of this as well."

Nathan gave her a funny look, though I could tell by the softness in his eyes he was touched by her invitation. "No, I'm not," he said.

Carrie rolled her eyes. "Um, yeah you are. Bael just doesn't know it yet," she said, sounding mysterious. It made me curious about her respite in the other realm. "Trust me and get your ass over here."

Nathan laughed. "Yes, ma'am." He stepped beside Tree and added his hand on top of mine. "To the Devil's . . ." He hesitated, unsure on what to say.

"Four," Carrie said.

"To the Devil's four," we all said in unison.

Preview:

TANGLED ROOTS

Keep reading for a preview of *Tangled Roots*,
the captivating companion to the *Beyond the Eyes* trilogy. . .

Chapter One

Carrie

I had never given much thought to reincarnation, at least not until the spirit of an ancient witch named Jade made her presence known to me. Somehow, a part of my spirit had reached out to her when I was in a coma, recovering from a car accident. I remembered it as if it happened twenty minutes ago, or so it seemed.

I remembered *all* of it.

Tree had wanted me to tell him every last detail. He wasn't satisfied with the loose interpretation I gave my best friend Paige and her boyfriend Nathan. It wasn't like I didn't want to divulge my fantastical experience in another realm. I did and still planned to do so, but they had too much on their plates right now. Actually, Paige had many crosses to bear, and I would not load another one on her, at least not until she could relax a bit. Maybe take a short sabbatical with Nathan, away from all this strife concerning the dark spirits. With my incessant urging, Paige finally gave into my pleas to do just that. Of course she waited until I was out of the hospital for a few weeks, and being the most awesome best friend ever, she threw a surprise welcome home party for me.

"Don't worry," she had said, slinging her arm around my shoulders as I stood in my living room in amazement, looking at the black and red glittery WELCOME HOME banner placed on the wall above the bar that divided the kitchen from the living room. She even made a red velvet cake for me. "There are no clowns here," she finished saying, bumping my hip with hers. I laughed. She knew I hated clowns, and her little remark warmed my heart.

Now, she and Nathan were in England visiting Nathan's friend Pip, and I missed her terribly. They were going to be gone from Astoria, Oregon for the whole month of November. A whole frickin' month. We'd never been away from each other that long, and it felt like a part of me was missing.

"Describe Jade to me," Tree said, putting a filter in his brown and white 1968 International Scout. The oil he drained mingled with the dirty, gassy smells in his dad's garage. I was used to it, and oddly enough, it gave me comfort.

I picked the socket wrench off the floor. The heavy metal felt cool in my hand as I thumped it against my palm, imagining her in my mind. "She was beautiful," I said. "Her black skin made her green eyes pop. They were startling in the sense that when you gazed into them, you felt like you were standing on a plateau, looking through a lens with restrained knowledge, so eager to be released."

Tree rolled out from under the engine on the creeper. His long legs seemed to stretch forever. Rubbing his forehead with the edge of his thumb, he looked at me. "Nathan said the same thing, except his description of her paled in comparison to yours. Maybe you should consider being a writer."

"Whatever." I snorted. "Have you forgotten... the many book reports I had Paige do for me?"

He picked up a rag and threw it at me. "No, but it seems since you woke up from your coma, you can perceive and focus on things a lot clearer than before."

I snatched the cloth before it touched my chest. It was damp and grimy from oil. Gross. I tossed it in a bucket behind me and placed the wrench in the tool box against the wall. "Maybe so." I shrugged, not really knowing how to respond to his observation.

"What else do you remember about her?" he asked, prompting me to continue as he proceeded to add fresh oil to his Scout.

I handed him the bottles as I continued, "There was fluidity to her graceful movements, like a ballet dancer telling a story through animated gestures."

"Those words are what I'm talking about," Tree said, glancing over his shoulder at me.

"What?"

"Your descriptions. I'm starting to think you came back with some heightened abilities, or something along those lines."

"I don't know," I answered, waving it off because I didn't want to go there at the moment. "But let me continue. I don't want to lose my train of thought." I slapped another container in his palm and screwed the top off for him.

"Go on, then." He turned back to what he was doing.

"Okay, well, I remember her dark, purple robes billowing behind her as she approached me in the realm of rehabilitation, where I was sent by Paige's parents to recover from my accident."

"What was it like?"

"We were in a vast meadow surrounded by enormous mountains forming a barrier around us. The mountains were covered in lush, thick emerald green grass and tall trees. The waterfalls cascading from them had prisms of colors dancing along the front. I remember becoming immediately enchanted by the beauty of it all," I said. "I could hear a soft melody playing—part instrumental and part humming. It sounded like a peaceful lullaby." I closed my eyes and softly hummed the song. Of course, my rendition sucked. Regardless, though, I heard the music in my head and could easily fall under its spell.

Something that sounded like a plastic bottle hit the floor.

I opened my eyes to Tree staring at me in awe. "It's a lullaby," he said. "I've heard the tune before."

I furrowed my brows. "Where?"

"After Paige did her dream walking thing to save you, she hummed it for me."

"She must have heard the melody when I crossed over to the other realm," I mused.

"She did," Tree said.

"How do you know it's a lullaby?"

"I don't know." He touched his black knit beanie hat and rubbed the material against his forehead. "Ever since Michael told me I was on the path to becoming a light walker, pieces of knowledge from different realms have been filtering into my conscious mind. It's crazy."

I found it both interesting and disconcerting that Tree's soul was striving to become a light walker, or guardian angel in human terms. From what I understood, his spirit had to go through a shitload of lives in order to become one. Michael told him, in order to reach a deep understanding about things, Tree had to experience every aspect of it. Once he arrived at the apex of his training, he'd be able to move onto the next level in the spiritual realm where he'd be allowed access into Nirvana. I of course was exempt from it, which I totally understood, but what concerned me was what would happen to us? It depressed me to even acknowledge those cold hard facts, so rarely did I allow those thoughts take form in my mind.

"You're right. The melody is a lullaby," I confirmed, sidestepping his last comment. I wasn't ready to dip my toes into the pool of knowledge seeping through the cracks of his subconscious mind. Not yet. "The music lulls the spirit to a restful state. Most spirits who enter this realm go there to be cleansed, to sleep, then reawakened and counseled," I said. I could almost smell the pine from the thick forest there.

Tree screwed his face in concentration, his brown eyes staring past me at nothing in particular. "I think I know the answer to this question, but I'm going to ask it anyway. How does a spirit get cleansed? How does the process work?"

"They enter from the northern portal, then they go straight to the west, which represents water, death, and initiation. From there, they go through a waterfall and to the cleansing chamber."

"What's the cleansing chamber like?"

"It's like a glass coffin set into the wall of the mountain," I replied.

"What happens when the spirit enters the chamber? What does it do?"

I rubbed my nose and pushed my finger onto the side of it, closing my eyes, trying to figure out the best way to tell him. Moving my hand away from my face, I sighed and looked at him. "I'll try to explain how it works the best I can." I took a deep breath. I didn't know if I could, or if he'd grasp the whole concept.

"Go on," he said. He knew full well that I tended to stall when I was unsure or nervous about something.

"Okay." I took another deep breath. "When a spirit steps inside the chamber, it's like its essence explodes. You see, we're an energy force and each experience we have throughout our existence becomes a part of it—positive and negative. So the energy disperses, and a fine mist fills the chamber, soothing all parts of the spirit from the life it just led. After the spirit is rested, it enters another realm, within the first to converse with its guides."

"I have no recollection of such a place," Tree said. "I thought maybe I would, but I don't. Maybe I'd never been there before."

"I'm sure you have," I said, hearing the confidence in my voice.

He made a face. "Why would you think so?"

I rolled my eyes. "Duh. You've been through countless lives, both good and bad. I have no doubt that at some point, you had to be rehabilitated."

"Good point." He grabbed my wrist and pulled me into his warm embrace. "So tell me more, or should I tickle it out of you?" He wiggled his fingers against my side, causing me to squeal and squirm against him.

I giggled and pushed his hand off me. "I'll tell you. I'll tell you," I gasped. "But you need to take a shower first." I pulled away, causing him to drop his arms, and I pinched my nose to emphasize my statement. "You smell greasy and oily." My words came out all nasally.

He stood straighter and knocked his fist against his chest. "I smell manly. Ya know why?" His lips twitched, as if he were holding back a smile.

"Why?"

"Because I do manly jobs." He raised his grimy hands, palms facing me. They were huge and could totally cover my face and part of my head. "See how rough and calloused they are?"

"Yes," I answered. "I also see black goo under your fingernails."

"These hands are creating our future," he said, ignoring my last response, "in a dying vocation due to the lack of interest our generation has for it. They'd rather take desk jobs, working on computers than industrial work—the very jobs that built our nation, such as a mechanic"—he pointed to himself and grinned—"a machinist, a painter, etcetera, etcetera. The manly jobs are a dying breed. What's going to happen to our country when these trades expire with the people who once made a living building the world we live in today?"

I chewed on my bottom lip. "I've never thought about that before." What would happen to our country if we no longer had people help maintain and build its infrastructures? If Tree was right, our future looked rather bleak.

"Yup. So this wonderful aroma you're smelling off me is the scent created from the backbones of people such as myself, so society can step away from their primitive conditions to a comfortable one."

"Okay, you're right, but now I'm depressed." I frowned.

"Don't be," he said, picking the empty plastic containers off the floor. "It is what it is. If I didn't have hope for the future, I wouldn't be helping Paige and Nathan." He chucked the bottles in a large trash can. They thunked against each other, startling me. "Bael is the oldest dark spirit of them all. If he had his way, we'd be far less populated and living like we did hundreds and hundreds of years ago."

"We are the Devil's third... well, actually fourth, counting Nathan of course," I said, feeling my mood brightening. "With us against Bael, he'll never get what he's after."

"Precisely, which is why I need you to tell me everything you know, so we can figure out a way to tap into the part of your soul that was once a witch in a previous life. We need to build a strong force between the four of us, then find those artifacts when Paige and Nathan return."

I bit my lip. "I don't know how we're going to accomplish it all." I stared at my black Doc Marten boots, feeling hopeless again.

"Hey." Tree lifted my chin so I had to look at him, concern filling his brown eyes. "We will prevail. It won't be easy, but something worth having never is."

"I suppose," I mumbled, shrugging.

"C'mon." He took my hand and intertwined our fingers. "I'll go take a shower while you watch reruns of *Buffy the Vampire Slayer*, then we'll talk more about this."

"I love Buffy," I said as we walked toward the garage door, stepping over the puddles of grease. "She reminds me of Paige."

"So then you would be Willow, right?" Tree pushed the button on the wall. The garage door clunked and rattled as it slowly lifted.

I smiled. "Yeah, and you would be Spike because he's cool and dresses like a punk rocker."

Tree laughed and wrinkled his nose. "But Spike was in love with Buffy, and Paige is like a sister to me. I've never had those types of feelings for her, it would be like incest." He shook his head as if he were trying to dislodge a horrible image from his mind. "I don't even want to think about it."

We stepped out into the cool night. The skeletal oaks in Tree's yard looked black and haunting against the bright moon. He went back inside the garage to push the button again. While I waited, someone riding a bicycle in our direction caught my attention. I absently wondered if it was a neighborhood kid going home for the night. Tree darted out of the garage as the door descended with a weird groaning noise.

"Lucky for me you only have feelings for yours truly." I hooked my arm through his and hugged his bicep.

"I've always loved you," he said. He made a move like he was going to kiss me, but something caught his eye—the bicycle rider. "Who is that?"

"I don't know." I could see now it was a boy around the age of twelve. If he were my child, he wouldn't be out here at night by himself. What was wrong with his parents? "I thought maybe he was one of your neighbors."

"I've never seen him before."

The boy turned off the street in front of Tree's house, onto his driveway. "Excuse me," he said, pedaling to us. His brown hair was disheveled, and I quickly made the assessment he styled it that way on purpose. He had a BMX bike, Vans skater shoes, and a vintage Suicidal Tendencies T-shirt over a long sleeve thermal shirt. If anything this kid had good taste, and I found myself at ease around him. "Are you Carrie Jacobson?" he asked.

"Yes, I am. Why?" *How in the hell does he know me?*

He reached into his pocket and pulled out a folded piece of paper. "I'm supposed to give this to you." He handed it to me.

"Who is it from?" Tree asked.

"My great grandmother," he replied. "My name is Rex."

"Why would your grandmother give me a note?" I asked, eager to open it, but something inside me told me to wait.

"You're a witch aren'tcha?" Rex asked.

I shoved the letter in my cargo pants pocket. "Maybe... I don't know. Why?"

He smiled, the splatter of freckles bunching on his round face. "Read it, and I'll see ya soon." He turned his bike around and left the way he came. We watched in stunned silence as he turned the corner at the end of the street and disappeared from our sight.

What readers are saying about *Tangled Roots*:

Rebekkah Ford grew up with the paranormal in her own tangled roots and it shows in the way she creates the psychological motivations within her characters. She has mysteries in her head and it shows vividly, dramatically, on the page.

In this, a stand-alone adjunct to the *Beyond the Eyes* trilogy, Carrie Jacobson's soul stirs as mystical powers arise in her with supernatural force. She is 18 and has confusing, jigsaw-puzzle flashbacks to Europe in the 1600s when she was a witch named Isadora.

Long ago, she cast a spell she now understands must be broken. As her old powers mature and Carrie set out to reconnect the past with the future, her boyfriend, Tree, at first shocked, even afraid, of the changes he sees in Carrie, realises he is the only way who can save her from herself.

Rebekkah Ford weaves delicious erotic imagery through her universe of ghosts, magic and the supernatural. Read one of her books and you will be an instant fan.

~ Reader's ★★★★★ review

You can tell when a writer loves to write. It shows in their story, characters and background. Rebekkah Ford is one of those people. In *Tangled Roots*, she took characters that we've grown to love through her *Beyond the Eyes* trilogy and developed a whole new prose.

What I love the most about her style of writing is you don't have to have read the first three novels to understand *Tangled Roots*. As always, she manages to pull the rug out from under your feet when you least expect it. She did her homework on this one and I think it's my favorite novel she's ever written.

~ Reader's ★★★★★ review

Even though this is a companion novel to her *Beyond the Eyes* series, Rebekkah Ford wrote this in a way that it can be a stand-alone novel. Having not read the series, it is now on my TBR list, I still understood the plot and followed the characters.

Tree and Carrie are great leading characters and really come across as strong. As they battle to save Carrie's life from a dark witch, who is Carrie in a previous life, they learn that in darkness there is a little light. Even evil has some good in it.

Over all it's a great read and I highly recommend it for anyone who likes paranormal.

~ Reader's ★★★★★ review

About the Author

Rebekkah Ford grew up in a family that dealt with the paranormal. Her parents Charles and Geri Wilhelm were the directors of the UFO Investigator's League in Fairfield, Ohio. They also investigated ghost hauntings and Bigfoot sightings in addition to extraterrestrial cases. Growing up in this type of environment and having the passion for writing is what drove Rebekkah at an early age to write stories dealing with the paranormal. Her fascination with the unknown is what led her to write the *Beyond the Eyes* trilogy and its companion, *Tangled Roots*.

Rebekkah resides in rural North Dakota, in a farming community of about 1,800 people and loves where she lives. She has an irreverent sense of humor, loves coffee, and yummy food makes her happy. She also loves books, history, antiques, animals, connecting with her fans and other authors, as well as watching her favorite TV shows.

Other Books by Rebekkah Ford

Beyond the Eyes trilogy
Beyond the Eyes
Dark Spirits
Tangled Roots: (a companion to the trilogy)

By Moonlight (Paranormal boxset):
15 novels and novellas from your favorite or
soon-to-be favorite paranormal authors

Where To Connect With Rebekkah Ford

Author Rebekkah Ford: rebekkahford.com
Wandering Thoughts of A Writer:
themusingwriter.blogspot.com
Author Rebekkah Ford's Facebook Page:
www.facebook.com/rebekkahford2012
Twitter: twitter.com/RebekkahFord
Goodreads: www.goodreads.com/author/show/6180865.Rebekkah Ford
Pinterest: www.pinterest.com/rebekkahford/
Google Plus: plus.google.com/102242636096208798568/posts

Sign-up for Rebekkah's monthly newsletter. Get updates on Rebekkah's books, such as new releases, excerpts, giveaways, top secret information and much more! Your information is kept private. Rebekkah doesn't share, sell, or spam newsletter subscribers. http://rebekkahford.us7.list-manage. com/subscribe?u=06bbb5773fe9e17e6ba0e860e&id=51f0af6e94

Thank you for taking the time to read *The Devil's Third*. If you enjoyed it, please consider telling your friends or posting a short review. Word of mouth is an author's best friend. I appreciate your support.

www.ingramcontent.com/pod-product-compliance
Lightning Source LLC
Chambersburg PA
CBHW020822180626

46814CB00001B/77